99
PERCENT
MINE

Also by Sally Thorne

The Hating Game

99 PERCENT MINE

SALLY THORNE

wm

WILLIAM MORROW

An Imprint of HarperCollins*Publishers*

P.S.™ is a trademark of HarperCollins Publishers.

HarperCollins books may be purchased for educational, business, or sales promotional use. For information, please email the Special Markets Department at SPsales@harpercollins.com.

FIRST EDITION

Designed by Diahann Sturge

Library of Congress Cataloging-in-Publication Data has been applied for.

ISBN 978-0-06-243961-1 (paperback)
ISBN 978-0-06-288428-2 (library edition)

19 20 21 22 23 LSC 10 9 8 7 6 5 4 3 2 1

For Roland, the Flamethrowers,
and me

Chapter 1

Nobody taught me this when I first started as a bartender, but luckily, I was a quick learner: When a group of men are walking in, you should work out which one is the alpha.

If you can handle him, you might get a bit of respect from the rest. Tonight, I can pick him straightaway. He's the tallest and best-looking, with a *you're welcome* gleam in his eye. How predictable.

He and his friends have spilled out of a local frat party, bored and wanting adventure. They're all wearing pastel polo shirts. Well, buckle up, buttercups. If you play your cards right, things could get downright exhilarating. Devil's End Bar is not for the faint of heart. I see some of the bikers exchange amused looks over the pool tables. By the door, our security guy is sitting up straighter. Weird how we have the most trouble when this type of boy walks in.

2 • Sally Thorne

I don't smile at the alpha. "Are you lost, kids?"

"Hey there, mister," he responds—a jab at my short haircut—and his friends laugh and intone, *Ohhhh shit.*

My name is Darcy and he's unknowingly made a Jane Austen joke. I doubt he'd get it. The laugh fades out of him a little as I narrow my eyes and stare harder. Alpha Boy remembers I have full control of the alcohol. "But seriously, it looks hot on you."

My colleague Holly is backing away. She's too new at this, and she's feeling their eyes. "I'm just going to get more . . . register rolls." She vanishes out back in a puff of gardenia body spray.

I'm still holding my hard stare with the alpha and I get a ping of triumph in my gut when he looks away first. I'm the alpha now. "We must go to the same barber, because you're looking real pretty, too. Now, order something or get out."

The boss boy is not used to this from a woman and to his surprise he likes it. He chews gum in an openmouthed way, his avid eyes on my face. "What time do you get off work?"

I imagine a Ken doll left out in the sun too long, and I step on that soft tan head like it's a cigarette. "Not for a million years."

He's visibly miffed. After all, being good-looking is his life's backstage pass. Shouldn't it work on me? Am I broken? The light hits his face in a shadowless beige pan of color, and he's nothing that could interest me. I'm a face snob. It's all about the shadows.

"What do you want?" I'm already gathering shot glasses.

"Sambuca shots," one guy shouts. Naturally. The elixir of morons.

I pour a row and take payments, and the tip jar gets fuller. They love being treated like dirt. These boys want the full biker-bar safari experience, and I am their tour guide. Their leader continues to flirt with me, determined to wear me down, but I walk away midsentence.

It's Sunday night, but the people in here aren't worried about being rested for work tomorrow.

My grandmother Loretta said once that if you know how to pour a drink into a glass, you can get a job anywhere. She was a bartender in her twenties, too. It was good advice; I've poured drinks into glasses all over the world, and I've dealt with every possible variant of alpha male.

I wonder what Loretta would say if she could see me now, pouring this beer with an insult preloaded on my tongue. She'd laugh and clap and say, *We could have been twins, Darcy Barrett,* because she was always saying that. There was a slideshow of photographs at her funeral, and I could feel the sideways glances at me.

Twins. No kidding. Now I'm sleeping in her bedroom and finishing off her canned goods. If I start carrying crystals in my purse and reading tarot cards, I will officially be her reincarnation.

Holly must be picking up those register rolls from the factory. One of the leather-jacket bikers has been waiting too long, and he's looking sideways at the Pastels. I nod to him and hold up my finger—*One minute.* He grizzles and huffs but decides against causing grievous bodily harm.

"Are those leather pants?" A Pastel boy leans over the bar, looking at my lower half. "You're like Bad Sandy from *Grease.*" His eyes focus on the fake name tag I've pinned above my boob. "Joan." His skeptical eyes slide lower. I guess I don't look like a Joan.

"I'm obviously Rizzo, you idiot. And if you don't quit leaning over like that looking at my tits, Keith is gonna come over. That's him, by the door. He's six foot ten and he's bored."

I twinkle my fingers in a wave to Keith and he copies the wave back from his stool.

"He's bored, I'm bored, and the Leather Jackets are very, very bored." I move along the bar, handing out glasses, taking payment, bumping the till drawer closed with my hip over and over.

"Joan's right. We're very bored," one of the younger bikers says in a droll tone. He's been leaning against the bar, watching the exchange with interest. The Pastels all flinch and stare at their phones. The biker and I grin at each other and I slide over a beer on the house.

I'm sick of their huddling. "Sambuca will shrink your nuts. Oh wait, too late. Now, go fuck off." They do.

Holly's big eyes peep around the door when the dust has settled. There is nothing in her hands. She's all legs and elbows, and she was hired by our boss, Anthony, without being asked a single interview question. Faces like hers are very hireable. She can't count change, pour drinks, or deal with men.

"I'm always so relieved when I see we're rostered on together." Holly sits on the bench and exhales long and loud, like she's been working hard. Her name tag says "HOLLY" and she added a pink glitter heart sticker. "I feel safer whenever I'm with you. I bet you're even looking out for Keith."

"That's true, I am." I catch Keith's eye and he tips his chin up in acknowledgment, leaning back against the wall on his stool. Another bartender tip? Make friends with security. I get these guys drunk, and Keith keeps the lid on this place. It occurs to me that I should be giving Holly these pearls of wisdom. But I don't want her sticking with this job longer than necessary. "When I quit, you're going to have to get tougher."

Holly purses her lips. "How much longer are you here?"

"The renovation on my grandma's place starts in two months, unless it gets pushed back again. And then I am outta here." Holly's glitter sticker stresses me out. "I'd never put my real name on my chest in this place."

She tips her head to the side. She'd be a great bridal model, in a full white cupcake gown and tiara. "I never thought of making a fake one. Who could I be?"

If my old pal the label maker has any clear sticky roll left inside it, it'll be a stone-cold miracle. Anthony's care factor about employee turnover is summed up by this bulk pack of name tags. There are about a hundred more to go before he needs to give it any thought.

"You'd be a great Doris."

Holly's nose wrinkles. "That's so old-lady."

"You want a sexy fake name? Come on, Hol." I crank out a label and assemble the tag. When I give it to her, she's silent for a while.

"You think I'm a Bertha?"

"Definitely." I serve a few more customers.

"I'm more of a Gwendolyn. Or a Violet?" Dutifully, she pins it on anyway.

I make her hand over her old tag and I throw it in the trash. Maybe I can relax a fraction on my shifts if she continues this trajectory.

"One day you'll be Dr. Bertha Sinclair, counseling depressed parrots, and tucked up in bed every single night at nine P.M." I sound like an overprotective sister so I tack on, "Or you might be a vet in the South American jungle, helping the macaws learn to love again."

She tucks her hands in her tight pockets and grins. "We honestly do more than parrots at vet school. I keep telling you."

"Hey, babe," a guy says to Holly. Bad boys love good girls.

"If you say so," I say to her. To him, I say, "Fuck off."

She keeps playing our game. "I bet that when I'm performing a diagnostic laparoscopy on an old tabby, you'll be in the South American jungle, with your big backpack on, hacking through the vines." She makes a chopping motion.

"I've actually done that in the Andes," I admit, trying to not sound like I'm boasting. Nothing worse than a smug world traveler. "Boy, I could use a bush machete right about now." I look across the room at our clientele.

"I looked through your Instagram a bit. I lost count of how many countries you've been to."

"I misplaced my passport, otherwise I could count the stamps for you." I begin gathering up dirty glasses. I mentally scan the floor plan of the cottage again. Loretta's ghost is possibly messing with me. Either that, or my brother, Jamie, hid it.

Just the thought of Holly's pretty eyes looking at my old life is giving me the privacy prickles. Imagine my exes scrolling through it. Curious one-night stands. Old photography clients. Or worse, Jamie. I need to make that account private. Or delete it.

"And there were photos of you and your brother. I can't believe how much you guys look alike. He's so good-looking. He could be a model." Those last bits were said in an involuntary blurt. I've heard it many times before.

"He tried it once. He didn't like being told what to do. Anyway, thanks. That's a compliment for me, too," I say, but she doesn't get it.

Jamie and I look alike because we're twins. There's a twin ranking, and we're at the bottom. A boy and a girl. We can't even dress the same and swap places. Fraternal, what a yawn.

But if we reveal our twin status, we are fascinating to some people. They always ask, who was born first? Can we hear each other's thoughts? Feel each other's pain? I pinch myself hard on the leg. I hope he's yelping in a fancy downtown bar, spilling his drink.

If he's handsome, I should be good-looking in theory too, but I've been called *Jamie in a wig* in school too many times to believe it. If you lined us up side by side, with my face washed clean, I'd be mistaken for his little brother. I know this because it's happened.

"Where will you go to first?" Holly is definitely the kind of girl who would wear a beret on a cobblestone street. A baguette in her bicycle's basket.

"I'm going to bury all of my name tags in a Japanese death forest called Aokigahara. Only then will my soul be free of Devil's End Bar."

"So, not Paris," she says, toeing a mark on the floor with her white sneaker, and I nearly laugh at how right I was. I lean a mop against her leg but she just holds it in both hands, resting the pole against her cheek, like someone in a musical about to break into song. "Why do you travel so much?"

"I've been told I have impulse control problems." I pull a face.

She's still thinking about what she's snooped. "You were a wedding photographer. How?" She looks me up and down.

"It's pretty easy. You find the lady wearing a white dress and go like this." I hold up an invisible camera and press my finger down.

"No, I mean, weren't you always traveling?"

"I worked the wedding season and lived here with my grandma. I traveled the rest of the year." *Shoestring budget* would be an understatement, but I maintained this arrangement for six years. "I work in bars when I need cash. I do some travel photography, but it doesn't sell too well."

"Well, no offense—"

"This is usually the part where someone says something offensive," I cut in, and am saved by one of the old biker guys, blue tattoos bruising his forearms and a brown stain in his beard. He's the physical embodiment of repugnant, but he says nothing as I pour his drink, so I smile at him as a reward. He looks disturbed.

When he's gone I go to the bathroom and politely smile at myself in the mirror. I look like I haven't tried that in a while. My reflection looks like Shark Week.

Holly is good at pressing pause on her thoughts. I mess around with my hair, put on more eyeliner, wash my hands for ages, and still when I return she continues seamlessly, "But you don't seem to fit into the wedding scene."

"Why ever not, Bertha?" I've gotten this comment from countless drunk dudes at wedding receptions, jostling around by my elbow while I'm trying to get the first-dance shots.

Holly says, "Weddings are romantic. And you aren't romantic."

"I don't have to be romantic, I just have to know what the client thinks is romantic." I shouldn't be offended, but I kick a cardboard box straight under the counter and glare out at the unwashed masses.

There's a couple making out right now on the back wall

by the bathrooms. The humping swivel of his hips makes me want to barf. But every now and then, when they come up for air and their lips break apart? His hand is in her hair and they look at each other. That's when I'd click. I could make even those assholes look beautiful.

Then I'd turn on the fire hose and spray them out of here.

"So, no romance with that guy Vince?" Holly asks like she already knows the answer. When she first saw him slinking in here, she said, *He's not a nice boy, Darcy.* I replied, *He has a tongue stud, so part of him is pretty nice.* She was open-mouth speechless.

I review the stock levels in the fridge closest to me. "I've got a sonnet in my back pocket. When I see him next, I'll read it to him."

"But you're not in love."

I laugh in response to that. I've given up on feeling anything with a man.

"He's a way to kill time. I've been here a lot longer than I was planning to." Please don't ask the follow-up question, *Have you ever been in love?* "Hmm, okay, I guess I'm unromantic."

"Why'd you quit weddings?"

That word *quit* is a sore point, and Holly sees it in my eyes. She looks down and fiddles with her Bertha tag. "Sorry. Your website said you're closed for bookings indefinitely. And you do product photography now. What's that?"

"Why don't you google it, Bertha?" I try to make it a joke but I'm angry. Why does she constantly try to be friends like this? Doesn't she get I'm leaving?

I am deleting that entire website.

"You never tell me anything properly," she protests in a weak voice. "You're never serious." Her beautiful face is all pink and smushed up with concern. I go to the far end of the bar and turn my back on her. I take down the beer glass containing my name tags. I'm sick of being Joan. I decide to be Lorraine for the rest of the shift.

I'm sick of being Darcy.

"I'm sorry," Holly says again in a small voice.

I shrug and drag around bottles of vodka in the end fridge. "It's okay. I'm just . . ." *Trapped, without a passport or a booked plane ticket. Living my nightmare.* "A bitch. Don't mind me."

Out of the corner of my eye I see the light catching in a bottle of whiskey, giving it a gold glint. I feel a twinge low down in my stomach and I exhale until I have nothing left inside. I've had a chronic case of the heavy sad sighs lately, especially when I think about weddings. Which I refuse to do.

I ran my own business for years, and I feel like I have X-ray vision for things that are going to become a major problem. Holly still hasn't been given any payroll forms. Stock levels are alarmingly low. Maybe alcohol is not Anthony's main source of income. I go to the back office and write on a Post-it: *Anthony—do you want me to do a stock order? —D*

For a tough bitch, I've got embarrassingly girly handwriting. I sure don't see the guys on the daytime shift writing conscientious notes for the boss. I scrunch it up.

When I come back out and begin to count cash in the till, Holly tries again, rewinding to the part before she blew it. "I don't think Vince is the guy for you, anyway. I think you need one of them." She means the Leather Jackets.

I keep counting cash. Five hundred, five fifty. That's interesting, coming from her. She's petrified of them. If a glass breaks, it's me trudging out with a dustpan and broom. "Why do you think that?"

Holly shrugs. "You need someone even tougher than you. What about him? He looks at you all the time, and he always makes sure you serve him."

I can't be bothered even looking up from the register to see which one she means. Six hundred, six fifty. "I'd rather die alone than end up with one of these assholes."

The same young Leather Jacket who helped me scare the college boys is weaving back to us. Free beer obviously goes down easy.

"Thirsty boy tonight," I say, and pour his usual whiskey this time.

"Very," he says in a way that sounds sexual, but when I look at his face, he's serene. "Bored and thirsty, that is."

"Well, that's why you're here. Now, if you're gonna beat up those kids later, do it in the parking lot, please."

His crystal-blue eyes flick to my name tag. "No problem. See you around, Lorraine." He pays, tips me, and walks away.

"That's the one that loves you," Holly says, far too loud.

Chapter 2

His boot misses a step and a splat of whiskey hits the ground. Gamely, he recovers and walks off, looking rattled. I hiss at her, "*Shuddup.*" I've never even registered his existence properly, but he reveals himself to be tall, handsome, tattooed. Muscles, butt, boots. Tick, tick, tick. Decent bone structure, too.

I picture myself trying to talk to him. Touch him. Know him. Then I think of him trying to do the same to me.

Maybe he could drive me to the airport.

"Pass." I give her a mind-your-own-business look and she receives it, loud and clear. We avoid each other politely for probably close to an hour; she serves drinks, each transaction like a novelty for her, blinking at the register in earnest. I dread to think whether the final tally will balance.

I lug a new keg out of the storeroom and a familiar chest-rattle begins. I should know better, but every time is a surprise, because I'm a moron. You'd think that a lifelong heart arrythmia would be something I am used to, but every time: Gosh, that thing again. It's the tripwire that I forget about the instant I'm past it, and despite my being an otherwise healthy twenty-six-year-old, I have to sit in Anthony's chair, my vision pixelating and my heart palpitating.

"You okay?" Holly calls, her face peeping around the corner. "Girls aren't supposed to get the kegs."

"Twinged it a little," I lie outright, indicating my back. "Go out front."

"Shoulda gotten Keith," she says mutinously, and I point my finger until she leaves.

Meanwhile, my heart is running up a skyscraper's fire stairs, and it's got a little wooden leg. Step-pause—*hop-scramble*. Up and up, no handrail, don't panic, don't fall backward into black. I've just got to endure the blip until it passes. But this time, I'm breathing like I'm taking the stairs, too. I can almost feel Jamie's angry alarm fogging around me in these moments; he'd be using his strength of will to make my heart beat right.

Jamie caused my heart condition. He unplugged my umbilical cord to take a leisurely swig, smirking, watching me turn blue before giving it back. My cardiologist told me that was impossible, but I'm still convinced. That's very on-brand for Jamie.

Apparently, I was lined up to be the firstborn, but at the last second, Jamison George Barrett swooped around and beat me to it. He belted out of Mom first, rosy and strapping, screaming *Touchdown!* He was in the upper percentile for everything.

I came out jaundiced and was kept in one of those newborn pressure cookers for a week with a heart monitor. Jamie's been outpacing me ever since, scoring endless touchdowns in classes and offices and bars, mirrored surfaces, and probably beds. Ugh, gross.

Maybe the reason I can deal with the guys in the bar is because I was dealing with an alpha male in the womb.

It was raining today in Jamie's new city. I can picture him walking down the pavement to his dream job as an associate at an investment bank. I don't know what he does except I imagine it involves swimming in a vault of gold coins. He'd be in his Burberry trench coat, black umbrella in one hand and phone in the other, *Blah, blah, blah. Money, money, money.*

What would he say right now, if he were speaking to me again?

Breathe, you're going gray.

Distracting myself with thoughts of Jamie always seems to work. I can focus my irritation on him rather than my faulty engine. My tormentor is also my anchor.

Darce, you gotta do something about this heart.

I pay exorbitant health insurance premiums, on account of my dud heart, and my earnings from this place only just cover it each month. When I think about it, it adds an extra layer of depressing to this job.

My heartbeat is now back to its sad version of normal, but until Jamie speaks to me again after my epic fuckup, I'm attempting the impossible: being twinless. I contemplate sending him a casually abusive text, but then I remember I can't, even if I want to. I'm attempting a second impossible thing in this day and age: being phoneless.

I was out with Vince two weekends ago at Sully's Bar and I dropped my phone in the toilet. As it sank to the bottom, the screen lit up with an incoming call and a picture of my brother's smug face. How typical; the first time he'd tried to contact me in months, and he was forty fathoms deep in pee water. The phone went black, and I washed my hands and walked out.

My parents would kill me if they knew I had no phone. They would kill me if they knew I don't wear a bathrobe around the cottage on cold nights. *Your heart! Smother, smother!* I have a worse feeling that no one will even notice I'm uncontactable. Ever since I fucked things up and Jamie left, my phone had stopped ringing. He's the bright sparkling one everyone gravitates to.

I hear a smash out front and a few guys echo *oooh*. Men are electrified by breaking glass. I hear the fortifying inward breath I take. I've done this on and off for years, but still, I wouldn't describe this part as getting any easier.

"What's up?" I clomp out in my boots and a row of guys are smirking. Holly is trying to stack pieces of broken glass and her face is red. There's beer everywhere and the front hem of her T-shirt is soaked. I've never seen a girl more in need of rescuing.

"Dumb bitch can't even pour a beer." The alpha of this group is a mean-lipped construction type. "Lucky she's hot. Unlike this one." He means me. I shrug.

"It's okay," I tell Holly. She nods without a word and disappears out back. Is this the shift that's going to break her?

This guy won't just pay and leave. He's looking for stimulation. I argue on autopilot and the details are boring. I'd be better-looking if I didn't have such short hair. I'd be so good-looking if I tried harder. I kinda look like a guy wearing makeup. Okay, that one stung a little. I'm a real tough bitch, aren't I? Every comment or insult is something I can easily bat away, and I'm counting out five double whiskeys when he goes too far.

"Who do you think you are, anyway? Someone special?" His voice cuts through the fog and I jerk my eyes back to his face. There's a sensation inside me: a big split, like I've just been axed in half like a dry log. I cannot come up with any response to this. He sees he's hit the mark and smiles.

I've been abused so much worse than that, in so many languages, but tonight it feels like the worst thing anyone's ever said to me.

Actually, it is. It's the same thing my brother said to me before he left.

"This one," I tell Keith, like I'm choosing a goldfish, and he muscles him out by the scruff. The rest of the group mutter and curse. Anger is a blowtorch-bright inside me. "All you have to do is order, pay, and tip. Don't talk. Just do those three things and get out of my face."

Holly returns and gets down on her knees beside me, scraping glass into a dustpan. "Ouch!" Now she has a thin line of blood running down her shin, into her white sock and shoe.

"Show it to me," I manage to say without sighing. As I dig through the first-aid kit, I think of where I can rehome her.

"Can you do any basic sewing? My friend Truly might need an assistant soon. You could probably do it from home."

"I made the quilt on my bed. It's just straight lines though, it wasn't hard. I could do it if it was simple." She wipes away her melted mascara and looks around herself like she's realizing what I've known all along: This place is a mistake for her.

I patch her up, split our tips, and send her home early. "If you don't want to come back, just text Anthony." She tearfully nods.

She is the nicest girl, but for her sake I hope she quits. She might end up like me.

It's almost ten P.M. The bar doesn't close until four A.M., so the real bad bitches who do the graveyard shift arrive. They're what I'll become. I put my tips in my purse and we spend a few minutes talking over which douchebags in here to keep an eye on.

"Bye," I tell Keith as I walk past his stool near the door, but he's already hauling himself to his feet.

"You know the rules."

"The rules here are bullshit."

"That's life," he replies with a shrug.

"Who walks you to your car?" I watch him mull that over.

"You probably would." He smiles at that realization. "If you ever want extra cash, I could probably hook you up with some security work. You'd be a natural."

"I probably would be, but no." I push through the front door, resigned to the fact that he'll be behind me. I step out into a haze of cigarettes and exhaust fumes. "Seriously, you don't know how much I hate you babying me."

"I've got a fair idea," Keith responds dryly. When I look back, he's scanning the parking lot with practiced eyes. Something happened a long time back to a girl who worked here, long before my time, and the side alley feels tainted with an awful, shivery wrongness.

I give up and start walking. "Come on, guard dog, time for your walkies."

Keith's insanely long legs easily keep up with my irritated marching through the little groups of guys standing around near their bikes. Someone says, "Wait around a minute, babe."

"I can't tonight," Keith replies in a girly voice, causing them all to crack up. "Are you okay, Darcy? You seem a little fragile."

I shouldn't underestimate how perceptive he can be. He watches people for a living.

"Ha, me? I'm fine. Thanks for before. Must be the best part of your job, watching them bounce across the concrete." I dig in my bag. I don't need a key clenched in my fist with a shadow this big.

"Not quite." Keith leans an elbow on the roof of my car. He's Sasquatch in size, on the handsome side of plain, and he has a gold ring. "By the way, I still owe you that twenty bucks from the other night. I wanted to say that I appreciated it . . . and thanks for listening."

I feel bad now, because I wasn't listening at all.

I checked the roster like a compulsive brownnoser, circling the fuckups and gaps, while Keith sat on a bar stool telling a story about his wife, mother-in-law, and a misplaced wallet. Something about sickness and working all the time. Some sighs and a drink coaster torn into tiny shreds. As doleful and sweet as he is, twenty bucks was a bargain price to end that conversation.

"Don't worry about it." I always get a proud swell in my chest when I'm generous. I wait, but Keith just keeps leaning. "Seriously, I don't care about twenty bucks. You can buy me a drink to celebrate when I finally get out of this place. I'd better go. Wine doesn't drink itself."

"Could drink it in there," he points out. "It's a bar, you know."

I make a face. "Like I'm going to breathe the same air as those dudes for longer than necessary."

"I'll get you a stool next to me," he offers, but I shake my head.

"I do my best drinking at home on the couch. With no pants. And the Smiths getting me all nice and depressed." That was a bit too honest.

I put my hand on my car door, but he just blows out a deep breath. He's stalling for some reason. I'm beginning to think he's working his way up to a bigger loan. "God, what is it? Spit it out."

He squints up at the stars. "So, some night, huh?"

I put my hand on my hip. "Keith, you're being really weird. Please stop crushing my car."

"You feel it, right?" He looks down at me in a strange way. Sort of like he needs to sneeze.

"A stampede of dinosaurs?" I don't make him smile. He

just keeps looking at me and he won't let me leave. "What? What am I supposed to be feeling?"

"Me and you. This." He points between us.

Shock plus surprise equals anger. "Keith, what the hell."

"You look at me a lot."

"Because you're the bulletproof vest we keep on the stool by the door. No, don't even try." I snatch my arm back when he reaches for it. "I bet your wife would be real impressed with you." Unfaithfulness is the most abhorrent thing I can think of, because it's the opposite of weddings—and that's what I've marinated myself in for years. Someone promises to love you forever, and then you go staring at girls at work? "Fuck you, Keith, seriously."

He slumps, hand on the back of his neck, the picture of misery. "She's barely got any time for me since her mom got sick. I feel like you and I have a connection, you know?"

"Because we were friends. Were." I wrench open my car door and feel a spike of fear when his hand wraps my wrist, holding me in place. I pull and he gets tighter. I get angrier and pull harder. My wrist is burning worse than when Jamie twisted it on purpose when we were kids. But I want it to hurt. Better than standing still.

"If you would just listen—" Keith tries, but my skin is too soft for him to retain any purchase on, and I slip out of his grip like a silk scarf. The parking lot is now inexplicably deserted. My heart rate perks up, like a guy looking over the top of his newspaper: *What's going on here?* If it craps out on me now I am going to be furious.

I point my finger at Keith's face. "I thought you were one of the good ones. Wrong as usual."

I get my butt in my seat. I slam the door and hear a faint woof of pain. I'm out of here, doors locked. This is my personal specialty: slipping out of a too-tight grip and getting the hell out. My former friend just a cheating cardboard cutout in my rearview mirror. "Wrong as usual, because there are no good ones."

When I hear my voice say it out loud, I know it isn't true. There's still one solid-gold good man left out there. He's the high-tide mark in a world of inch-deep puddles. Quick, I'm having a winemergency. Drink tonight and go to sleep and forget.

I drive a meandering route to the convenience store near my house, checking my rearview mirror. I put my heart back in its box and I endure a ten-minute argument with my base female self. Was I too friendly with Keith? Too casual, too naughty and rude and loose with my smiles? No, fuck him.

I rework different conversations that I've had with him, cringing at how easy and enjoyably platonic I found them. Maybe I even used him as a substitute for my brother. Did I pay Keith twenty bucks to be my friend?

Oh God, I'm pathetic.

I wonder how many Keiths are in wedding portraits I've done over the years. I prod my stinging wrist. It's a good reminder that no matter how careful I am, it'll never be enough. I am going to need a lot of wine tonight.

I pull my car up at the curb. This used to be a piece of

parkland, stitched into the seams between my childhood home and Loretta's cottage. Progress was unavoidable, but a neon-bright 7-Eleven store just feels insulting. I still can't drive past my old house. It's been painted mauve. Still, I could probably stand to look at that purple palace before I could make myself turn and look at the run-down white house across the street.

Feelings again. Wine. Wine.

"Not again," the cashier, Marco, says when I walk in. "Not. Again."

"I'm too tired for your shit so don't even start." This place is as convenient as the neon sign out front says. Otherwise, I wouldn't endure this. Marco read a book about sugar and it changed his life.

"Sugar is white poison." He starts telling me a fake-sounding story about sugar-addicted lab rats. I choose a cheap bottle of sweet white wine and a can of fish guts for Diana, and then go into my favorite aisle in the entire world.

"They chose the sugar over food and eventually died of malnutrition." Marco sells a pack of cigarettes to someone without comment.

I put my head up over the aisle. "That's what I plan on doing. Please stop talking to me." I hate that I've been stuck here long enough that a store clerk even knows who I am. I will not let him ruin this. This moment is special.

It's incredible the forms that sugar can take. It's art. It's science. It's cosmic. It's the closest thing to religion that I have.

I am in love with these cartoon colors. Acid gummies

crumbed in granulated cane sugar. Patent leather licorice twists, happy bags of Skittles. Pink and white marshmallows, softer than rose petals. It's all here, this rainbow spectrum of sugar, and it's waiting for me.

"Diabetes . . . cancer . . ." Marco is a radio being tuned in and out.

My friend Truly—my only friend from school who still lives here—thinks that women should buy themselves an indulgent weekly consolation prize. You know, for putting up with the world's shit. She buys herself flowers. As my treat, I jack up my insulin and blood alcohol levels.

Sunday night is my personal weekly Halloween.

I walk along slowly and drag my fingertips along the bars of chocolate. Goddamn, you sexy little squares. Dark, milk, white, I do not discriminate. I eat it all. Those fluorescent sour candies that only obnoxious little boys like. I suck candy apples clean. If an envelope seal is sweet, I'll lick it twice. Growing up, I was that kid who would easily get lured into a van with the promise of a lollipop.

Sometimes, I let the retail seduction last for twenty minutes, ignoring Marco and feeling up the merchandise, but I'm so tired of male voices.

"Five bags of marshmallows," Marco says in a resigned tone. "Wine. And a can of cat food."

"Cat food is low carb."

He makes no move to scan anything, so I scan each item myself and unroll a few notes from my tips. "Your job involves selling things. Sell them. Change, please."

"I just don't know why you do this to yourself." Marco looks at the register with a moral dilemma in his eyes. "Every week you come and do this."

He hesitates and looks over his shoulder where his sugar book sits under a layer of dust. He knows not to try to slip it into my bag with my purchases.

"I don't know why you care, dude. Just serve me. I don't need your help." He's not entirely wrong about my being an addict. I would lick a line of icing sugar off this counter right now if no one were around. I would walk into a cane plantation and bite right in.

I've been working on this jet-black disguise for many years now, and it's bulletproof. But some people can tell that I'm a weakling, and they try to baby and help me. It must be a survival-of-the-fittest thing. But they're all wrong. I'm not a lame gazelle; I'll be the one chasing the lion.

"Give me my change or I swear to God . . ." I squeeze my eyes shut and try to tamp down my temper. "Just treat me like any other customer."

He gives me a few coins' change and bags my sweet, spongy drugs. "You just remind me of how I used to be. So addicted. When you're ready to quit, borrow the book from me. I haven't had sugar in nearly eight months. I just sweeten my coffee with some powdered agave . . ."

I'm already walking out. No sugar? Why is life just about giving things up? What have I even got left that I enjoy? The heavy-sigh feeling inside me gets worse. Sadder. I pause at the door.

"I'm writing to your head office to complain about your service." I'm a hypocrite, pulling the customer service card, but hey. "You just lost yourself a customer, *sugar*."

"Don't be like that," Marco roars as the doors slide closed behind me. I settle back into my car, lock the doors, idle the engine, and crank the music even louder. I know he can see me, because he's banging on the window of his little murder-proof cube trying to get my attention. Men in a Perspex nutshell.

I open a pack on my lap and cram four jumbo pink marshmallows into my mouth, resulting in chipmunk cheeks. Then I give him the finger and his eyes pop out of his head. It is one of the best moments of my life lately, and I laugh for probably five minutes as I drive, sugar dust in my lungs.

Thank God I'm laughing, otherwise I think I might be crying. Who do I think I am, anyway?

"Hey, Loretta," I say out loud to my grandmother. She's hopefully up there on a cloud right above me as I stop at a red light and put my hand inside the cellophane bag, pillowy softness on my fingertips. If anyone is going to be my guardian angel, it's her; she'd insist on it.

"Please, please, give me something better than sugar. I really need it." Just saying it aloud chokes me up. I need a hug. I need someone's warm skin on mine. I ache with loneliness, and I still would, even if Vince came and went.

Who do I think I am? I'm unloved, untethered. And I'm twinless.

The light turns green like it's given me an answer, but I

have a few more marshmallows before I bother accelerating. The world has gone to bed, and I'm completely alone.

Except maybe I'm not.

I pull into Marlin Street and see a strange car parked in front of my house. I turn down the music and slow down. It's a big black utility truck, just like that construction redneck would drive. It looks brand new and shiny, with out-of-state plates. He's found where I live? The hairs on my arms are standing on end.

I turn my head as I roll past slowly. There's no one sitting in it. It can't possibly be Jamie—he'd never accept a truck from a rental place, and he'd park in the drive, not in the street. I drive around the block with my heart trying to beat itself to death. I briefly wish for Keith before I remember.

Then I get mad.

I pull into the drive with an aggressive engine-rev and put my headlights on high beam. Rolling my window down a few inches, I say over the deafening throb of my heart, "Who's there?"

I hear a yap and a stiff-legged old Chihuahua canters out of the shadows, dressed in a striped sweater. A man emerges too, and I'm okay now. Even without the dog, I'd know his huge shape anywhere. I'm not about to be murdered. I'm now the safest girl on the planet.

"Thanks, Loretta," I say to the cloud above me. There's only one thing sweeter than sugar. "That was quick."

Chapter 3

Tom Valeska has an animal inside him, and I've felt it every time he's looked at me.

Jamie found him locked out of his house across the road. Jamie called it *that house for poor people* because sad families moved in and out with alarming regularity. Mom would scold him for that. *Just because we have a lot, it doesn't mean you can be nasty, Prince.* She made Jamie mow that lawn for free. Every six months or so, we'd make a welcome basket for our new neighbors—usually scared women, peeping around their new door frames, shadows under their eyes.

But summer had been hot. Mom had a lot of singing students, Dad was busy at his architectural firm, and Mrs. Valeska had been notoriously difficult to pin down. The welcome basket was already wrapped in cellophane and tied with a ribbon, but Mrs. Valeska was off at dawn in her rusty car, always carrying buckets and baskets of cleaning gear.

Her son, eight years old like us, strayed around, chipping at a log on his front lawn with an axe to pass the time. I knew because I saw him days before Jamie found him. If I'd been allowed outside past the doormat, I would have gone over and bossed him. *Hey, aren't you hot? Thirsty? Sit in the shade.*

Jamie, allowed to roam the street as long as he could see the house, found Tom locked out late and brought him home. He dragged him into the kitchen by the sleeve. Tom looked like he could use a flea bath. We fed him chicken nuggets.

"I was going to sleep on the porch swing. I don't have a key yet," Tom explained to my parents in a shy husky whisper. They were so used to Jamie's bellow, they could barely hear him. He was so calm about the prospect of no dinner and no bed. I was in awe. Dazzled, like I was in the presence of celebrity. Every time he took one-second glances at me with his orange-brown eyes, I felt a zipper in my stomach.

He looked like he knew me, from A to Z.

That night was a game changer at the Barrett dining table.

Tom was virtually mute with shyness, so he weathered the onslaught of Jamie's talking. His one-word replies had a growly edge that I liked. No longer required to referee the twins, our parents could smooch and murmur cozily to each other. And I was forgotten and invisible for the first time in my life.

I liked it. No nuggets were stolen from my plate. Nobody thought about my heart or my medication. I could play with the old Pentax camera on my lap in between bites and sneak glances at the interesting creature sitting opposite Jamie. Everyone had accepted at face value that he was human, but I wasn't so sure. My grandmother Loretta had told me enough fairy stories about animals and humans' swapping bodies to make me suspicious. What else could give that edge to his stare, and make my insides zap?

The welcome basket was delivered to his exhausted mother late that night. She cried, sitting with my parents for a long time on the front porch with a glass of wine. We decided to keep Tom for the summer while she was at work. He was the buffer our family never knew it needed. My parents literally begged to take him to Disney with us. Mrs. Valeska was proud and tried to say no, but they said, *It's really for our benefit. That boy is worth his weight in gold. We'll have to wait until Darcy's medication level is worked out, and then we'll all be free to travel a lot more. Unless we leave her with her grandmother. Maybe that would be best.*

And after that first dinner, I admit I did something very weird. I went to my room and I drew a sled dog in the middle of a notebook I kept hidden in the heating vent.

I didn't know what else to do with this sensation that filled me. On the sled dog's name tag, too tiny to be read, was: *Valeska.* I imagined a creature that would sleep at the foot of my bed. He'd take food from my hand but could tear out the throat of anything that opened my door.

I knew it was weird. Jamie would crucify me for creating a fictional animal based on the new boy across the street—not that he'd have proof. But that's exactly what I did, and to this day, when I'm alone in a foreign bar and want to look busy, my hand will still draw the outline of Valeska on a coaster, with his eyes like a wolf, or an enchanted prince.

I'm an excellent judge of character.

When one of the spoiled blond Barrett twins fell into a crevasse, our faithful Valeska would appear. His pretty, spooky eyes would assess the situation, then you'd feel his teeth on your collar. Next, his strength and the humiliating drag to safety. You're useless, and he's competent. Barbie convertible broken? *It's just the axle. Click it.* Actual car broken down? *Put the hood up. Try it now. There you go.*

It wasn't just me as the female twin. Tom has tugged Jamie by the collar out of fistfights, bars, and beds. And in every city I've ever traveled to, when I've turned the corner into a dark scary alley by mistake, I've mentally summoned Valeska to walk the rest of the way with me.

And that's weird, I guess. But it's the truth.

So, to recap, my life sucks, and Tom Valeska is on my porch. He's lit by streetlight, moonlight, and starlight. I've got a zipper in my stomach and I've been in a crevasse so long I can't feel my legs.

I get out of the car. "Patty!" Thank fuck for small animals and the way they cut the awkwardness. Tom sets her down and Peppermint Patty taps stiffly up the drive to me. I've got one eye focused on the black porch behind Tom. When no elegant brunettes step out into the light, I get down on my knees and say a silent prayer.

Patty is a shiny shorthaired black and tan Chihuahua, with a big apple dome head. She's got a judgmental narrowing to her eyes. I don't take it personally anymore, but sheesh, this dog looks at you like you're a steaming turd. It's just her face. She remembers me. What an honor to be stamped permanently in her tiny walnut brain. I pick her up and kiss her cheeks.

"What are you doing here so late, Tom Valeska, world's most perfect man?" Sometimes it's a relief to hide your most honest thoughts right out in plain view.

"I'm not the perfect man," he replies in kind. "And I'm here because I'm starting on your house tomorrow. You didn't get my voicemails?"

"My phone is in a bar toilet. Right where it always belonged."

He wrinkles his nose, probably glad he wasn't summoned to retrieve it.

"Well, everyone knows you don't answer your phone anyway. Approvals came through already, so we're starting . . . well, now."

"Aldo kept pushing us back for the most bullshit reasons. And now it's two months early? That's . . . unexpected." Nerves light up inside me. Things aren't ready. More specifically, me. "If I knew you were coming, I would have stocked up on Kwench."

"They discontinued Kwench." He smiles and my stomach zips, silver strong, all the way up to my heart. In a confiding tone, he adds, "Don't worry. I've got a wine cellar full of it."

"Ugh, that stuff is just black plastic water." I feel my face go weird; I put my hand on my cheek and I'm smiling. If I'd known he was coming I would have perfectly folded a bath towel and stocked the fridge with cheese and lettuce. I would have stood at the front window to watch for his car.

If I'd known he was coming, I would have gotten my shit together a little.

I walk along the edge of the path, feeling the bricks wobble. "You should only drink it on special occasions. You could have a glass of Kwench with your cheese-and-lettuce sandwiches on your eightieth birthday. That's still your lunch, right?"

"It is." He looks away, defensive and embarrassed. "I guess I haven't changed. What's your lunch?"

"Depends what country I'm in. And I drink something a little stronger than off-brand cola."

"Well, then you haven't changed either." He still never gives me more than a one-second look before blinking away. But that's okay. One second always feels like a long time when I'm with him.

I talk to Patty. "You got my Christmas present, little girl." I mean her sweater.

"Thank you, it fits her great. Mine does, too." The vintage St. Patty's Day T-shirt he's wearing, probably out of politeness, is stretched wafer thin, trying to cope. If it were a person, it would be an exhausted wraith, gasping, *Please, help me*. It fits like a dream.

The kind of dream you wake up from, all sweaty and ashamed.

"I knew you wouldn't be too cool to wear a Patty T-shirt." I found that T-shirt in a thrift store in Belfast, and in that moment, I'd found Tom again.

I hadn't talked to him in a couple of years, probably, but I felt lit up on the inside. It was the perfect gift for him. I sent an airmail parcel containing the two garments addressed to "Thomas and Patricia Valeska," laughed for ages, then realized his girlfriend would probably sign for it. I'd completely forgotten about Megan. I didn't even slip a key ring in the package for her.

I check his left hand—still bare. Thank fuck. But I've got to start remembering Megan's existence. Right after I say this next thing.

"So, good T-shirts can die and go to heaven." I grin at his expression: dismayed, surprised, and flattered. All erased in one blink. I'm addicted.

"You're still a teenage dirtbag." Prim with disapproval, he looks at his watch.

"And you're still a hot grandpa." I press that old button and his eyes glow in irritation. "Had any fun lately?"

"I'd ask you to define *fun,* but I don't think I can handle the answer." He lets out a grumbly sigh and taps his boot on the dilapidated stairs. "Want me to fix this or not, smart-ass?"

"Yes please. While Daddy stays serious, we'll have fun, won't we, Patty?" I bounce her gently like a baby. Her eyes have a milky blue tinge. "I can't believe how much she's aged."

"Time passing generally does have that effect," Tom says dryly, but he softens when I look up. "She's thirteen now.

Seems like only yesterday that you named her for me." He
folds down to sit on the top step, his eyes on the street.
"Why'd you drive past just now?"

I've still got one eye on the dark space behind him. Surely
Megan's about to step out. This is the longest uninterrupted
conversation Tom and I have ever had. I need Jamie to slap
through the front gate.

I can never decide if Tom's hair is the color of caramel
fudge or chocolate. Either way, yum. The texture is like a
romance novel that's fallen into the bath, then dried: vaguely
sexual crinkle waves with the occasional curled edge and
dog-ear. I want to jam my hand in it and make a gentle fist.

Those *muscles*. I think I'm starting to sweat.

"You scared the shit out of me. I thought you were—"
I shut my mouth and dance Patty on my folded knee.
"Honestly, she's so cute."

"Who'd you think I was?" His husky voice gets more
bass to it and a scared-twist feeling in my gut tightens. Big
men are so casually brutal. Look at the size of those boots.
Those fists. He could kill. But then I overlay the memory of
an eight-year-old boy over the top of his adult shape, and I
remember Valeska, and I exhale.

"Just some dude I threw out of the bar. Seriously, Tom, you
nearly gave me a heart—" Goddamn it. His eyes snap to my
chest. "Don't," I order firmly, and he slouches, picking at the
side of his boot. He knows the rules. Fussing is forbidden.

"I can worry if I want, Princess," he grumbles to the
ground. "You can't stop me."

"No one calls me Princess anymore. Do I look like a princess?" I put Patty on the grass. He gives me a one-second glance, top to bottom, and looks away, the answer locked in his head and a lift to the corner of his mouth.

Oh man, the urge to get that answer out of him is intense. It'd probably require putting my hands on him and squeezing.

I get to my feet slowly to avoid a heart scramble, then look back at the decal on the side of the black truck. The penny drops. I spin around to him. "Valeska Building Services. Holy shit. You're free."

"Yeah," he says like he's admitting something, one eye narrowed as he looks up at my face.

"You did it." I can't stop the smile spreading across my face. "You got away from Aldo. Tom, I am so fucking proud of you."

"Don't get too proud," he warns, ducking his head so I can't see that he's pleased. "I haven't done anything yet."

When Aldo came through town to assess the cottage, he suggested a place where we could hire a bulldozer. That's his level of tact, discussing our deceased grandmother's estate. Jamie laughed at the joke, so there's his tact level, too.

I reminded them that it was literally in Loretta's last will and testament that the cottage be restored, and she'd stipulated a budget be set aside for it. The laughing stopped. Aldo heaved a sigh and filled out the council approval paperwork, saying several times that his pen didn't work. I slapped another one in his hand, and he narrowed his bloodshot eyes at me.

This will be a labor of love, Aldo said. *A huge expensive risky mistake.*

I told him, *No shit, Sherlock. Keep writing.* Why did Loretta make the final condition that Jamie and I sell? Did she never stop to consider that I might want to live here forever, wallowing in my loneliness? With twins, everything has to be split and fair.

"I guess Aldo taught you the most important lesson of your career." I wait a beat as Tom mulls it over. "What not to do."

"True," Tom says with a faint smile, his eyes on the decal on his truck. "When in doubt, I'll ask myself, what would Aldo do?"

"And you'll just do the exact opposite. You know he grabbed my butt? Like, when Jamie and I visited you on your very first job site? What a piece of shit. I was barely eighteen. Just a kid."

"I didn't know that." Tom's mouth flattens. "Did you break his hand?"

"You're lucky I didn't call you to bury a body for me. You would, right?" I can't help it; I want to know if I can still summon Valeska, as much as I shouldn't. He belongs to Megan now.

"I've got a shovel in the back," he says, nodding at the truck. It's a disturbing thrill to know he's not kidding. If I needed him to, he'd dig a hole with his bare hands. "I know he was an unprofessional asshole, but he gave me my first chance. I didn't have a lot of options, put it that way. Not like you and Jamie." He sits himself up straight and puts his boots together like a good boy. "There will be no ass-grabbing on my site."

"Depends on who's doing the grabbing," I say in a thoughtful tone, but crack up when Tom's eyes get scary. "I know, I know. No one is more professional than you. My butt is safe."

"I'm going to do everything perfectly." Tom won coloring-in competitions as a kid. This house is going to be his big-boy equivalent.

"I know you will." I look down at Tom's shoulders. His T-shirt is trying its hardest. He's gotten so big since I saw him last. He's always been tall and muscly, but this is next level. He's been working himself into the ground. "Well, what are you waiting for? I bet you have a key. Let the renovations commence."

"I might start in the morning, if you don't mind." He laughs, groans, and stretches in one movement. Like he's flat in a bed instead of on some rickety old stairs. "I do have a key. But I know how you feel about . . . privacy."

He says it like *privacy* is only one of the options he could have gone with. He always does this; he gives me one tidbit on what he thinks I'm like, then he clams up until Megan jingles her car keys and he's gone for another six months.

The tidbit leaves me ravenous, and I'm wiring my own jaw shut to not press and ask for more. I'm sweating so much my tank is stuck to my back.

We watch Patty as she paddles through the leaves on the lawn, nose to the ground. She half squats and changes her mind. Tom sighs wearily. "Now it's time to pee? She's had nearly an hour to do this."

"Well, I'm more determined than ever to find my passport now. It's definitely in the house, but Loretta's hidden it." I click my fingers for Patty. Come back, li'l buffer. I haul myself down to sit on the step beside him.

"Might have to order a new one," Tom says with a tone of reluctance.

"The old one has all my stamps in it. It's like my scrap-book. I'll find it tomorrow when I pack." Looking up to the sky, I tell Loretta, "I need to get out of here. Give it back."

"Maybe she wants you to stick around for once." He took a risk there, tacking on *for once*.

"I'll ignore that," I warn him, and he just looks up at the starry sky and smiles. I'm predictable, apparently. So is my stomach. It fills with sparkles.

His is the kind of bone structure that makes me blurt stupid things. So I do. "Every single time I see you, I can't believe you're not a kid anymore. Look at you."

"All grown up."

His torso looks like a pack of chocolate, with the squares visible through the wrapper. You know how chocolate has that matte-glossy texture? That's his skin. I want to scrape across him with my fingernails. I want to start my weekly Halloween binge.

Megan, Megan, diamond rings. The incantation doesn't completely work.

He has the kind of density that makes me constantly

guess to myself how much he'd weigh. Does muscle weigh more than fat? He's a ton. He's six-six, and I watched him get this tall, but it's a surprise every time I see him. It's the body you see on first responders. Think big-ass firemen kicking in doors, ready to save you.

"How do you cope with a skeleton that big?" I ask, and he looks down at himself, mystified. "I mean, how do you coordinate all four limbs and actually ambulate around the place?" My eyes are back on his shoulders, following the round lines down, the flat sections, the dips and shadowed lines, the creases on the cotton.

I can see his belt, which doesn't know how lucky it is to be strapped around that, and a lush half inch of black underwear waistband, and my cheeks are burning and I can hear my heart and—

"Eyes up, DB." He's busted me. Not that I was very subtle. "Me and my skeleton get around just fine. Now, what's going on with this rickety porch?"

I try to think of how I can explain it. What did happen to the house? I think I messed up and neglected it. That loose board, for example? I should have found a hammer and whacked it flat.

"My theory is that Loretta's magic held the entire house together." I rub my palms briskly on my thighs to banish the crying feeling I know is going to well up inside me.

He always knows when I need him to change the subject. "And what happened to your hair? Your mom broke the news."

"I think she called everyone she knows. Hysterical, over a

freakin' haircut. *Oh, Princess, why?*" I mock, trying to keep my movements casual as I pass my fingers through it. It feels like a boy's head now. I cross my legs and my tight leather pants squeak. I smooth them with a black-nailed hand. I have never been less of a princess.

If Mom knew I have a nipple piercing now, she'd give me the lecture about how my body's a temple. Sorry, Mom, I hammered a picture hook into myself.

"She rang me, crying. I was up on a roof. I thought that you . . . anyway." Tom's forehead creases at the memory. "Imagine my relief that Darcy Barrett had just cut her plait off. You went to a barbershop?"

"Yeah, I got an old barber to do it. What? I wasn't going to a women's hairdresser. They'd give me a pixie cut or something nauseating like that. I specifically wanted a World War Two pilot's haircut."

"Okay," Tom says, amused. "So, did he know how to cut it?"

I slap at a mosquito. "Yeah. But he changed his mind and didn't want to do it."

Tom looks at where my hair used to be. "It was kind of special."

I didn't know he thought that. Goddamn it. "He'd forgotten lady hair was soft. He begged but I made him. The sound of the scissors going through it . . ." I still get goose bumps. "It sounded like he was hacking through sinew. He prayed in Italian. It was like being exorcised."

Tom is wry. "Making scared men pray. You really, really haven't changed."

"Amen." I stretch my arms up to the sky and my humid clothes barely move with me. Sitting around with Tom Valeska has given me one hell of a lust-sweat.

The urge to take it too far always overwhelms me. It has since we both hit puberty.

"I love it when they pray in Italian," I whisper, sexy-hushed, and he won't meet my eye. "Please, please, Signora Darcy, don't make me."

"*Signora* means you're married, doesn't it? You're not married." His voice is faint and when I study him sideways, the hairs on his forearms are raised. How interesting.

"Yeah, who'd marry me." It's now my turn to slouch down, pick at my boot, and change the subject. I do it clumsily. "Hey, does everyone assume one day they're going to get a call that I've dropped dead?"

He doesn't know how to answer that, so I guess it's a yes.

"Mom's good at dramatic phone calls and forwarding photos. I got a Mom Special about you." I refuse to look at him now. I wrap my arms around my knees and growl. "Goddamn it, Tom. What the hell."

He knows exactly what I mean. "I'm really sorry."

Tom's engaged! Finally, it's been so long! His mother is fit to burst! Two carats, can you believe? Darcy, say something, isn't it fantastic?

If I'd been up on a roof, I would have ended up in traction. Instead, I went out and drank twenty toasts to the beautiful couple. It was a bender eight years in the making.

I woke up to a photo of a sugar-lump diamond on a perfectly manicured hand and puked. I was late to the wedding I was shooting. One of the main courses at the reception was sea bass and the room stank like a wharf. After the bride articulated her opinions about my lack of professionalism, I threw up in an umbrella stand by the door.

And meanwhile, Loretta was going out into the garden to hide her coughing fits from me, and Jamie was applying for fancy jobs in the city and spending less time with me. That entire year was one massive vomit, and the taste is still in my mouth.

"I don't accept your apology. You never called me yourself, you jerk. Do we just use my mom as a communication method these days? Aren't we pals?" I kick his boot with my smaller one, more gently than I want to. "Am I gonna be blinded by this ring when I see it?"

It's as close to *Congratulations* as I can manage. Or, *When's she getting here?* Hey, I sent them a card. They probably laughed their asses off picturing Darcy Barrett in the Hallmark section.

Tom opens his mouth to answer but is distracted by a car that grumbles past the cottage at a walking pace. It's a muscle car, heavy and low to the ground. Its engine thrums as it rolls up to the curb.

I have a bad feeling I know who this is, and Tom doesn't like him.

Chapter 4

Tom begins to stand, and the car accelerates and squeals off. Oh, to have such a big scary silhouette. Life would be so easy.

"Who was that?" Tom sinks back down.

It was Vince, coming around here like a tomcat. "No idea."

I put a marshmallow in my mouth so I can't talk anymore. Tom knows I'm lying, and when he begins to argue, I stuff a marshmallow in his mouth, too. He's annoyed and amused. I felt his lips on my palm. This night isn't all bad.

As his eye fixes onto my boot, the streetlight creates a black blade under his cheekbone. I'd click my camera right now. Now, as he looks at my legs and his lashes create a dark crescent shadow. Now, when those eyes cut to mine and there's a spark of light in them, and another thought about me in his head. Then he looks away.

One second is all it takes to get my heartbeat flipping like a fish in a net.

I blurt, "Can I take your photo yet?"

"No," he replies, soft and patient, like he has every time before. He doesn't understand his own face. He has to be dragged into the Christmas picture, posed behind Megan with an unconvincing smile that looks more like concern.

Oh, that's right. I'm a prime candidate to be taking pictures of him in a suit at the altar.

"That's okay. Human faces aren't really my bread and butter these days." I link my fingers together and try to dredge up some self-control.

Get it together, Darcy. It's not his fault he was born with your favorite kind of bones. He's a sweet shy solid-gold human. Someone's fiancé. You're a teenage dirtbag. Leave him alone.

He's clammed up completely. We're running out of topics. Work is a safe zone. "So you're finally your own boss. How did Aldo take it?"

Tom huffs a relieved laugh. "How do you think he took it?"

"He's going to have to do some actual work himself. Yeah, I'd say it went badly." I feel myself inflating with overprotectiveness. Bigger. Darker. "Do I need to go and make him apologize to you?"

Tom laughs at whatever I look like. "Don't get growly."

"I can't help it. People take advantage of you. Even us." *Us* means the twins.

You guys don't take advantage of me." He's braced back now with his palms flat on the porch, endless legs splayed out. I lean back too, just to feel how our bodies compare.

My hand is positively Chihuahua-sized next to his Valeska paw. My boot is halfway down his shin. I turn my head. My shoulder? It's an upturned mug sitting beside a basketball.

I'm not a particularly petite woman, but he makes me feel like I'm soft. Little and light. A princess. I frown, sit up, and force myself back into a geometric shape.

"Aldo wanted to bump your house for a bigger, easier job. I said it couldn't wait any longer. If you guys have changed your mind about renovating, I'm kinda screwed," he says, barely joking. "I took most of the crew with me."

"Don't worry, we're all good. Make the place beautiful and get me out of here." He took the crew? I cannot imagine him making that kind of power move. I look at his brute frame in my peripheral vision, and maybe I can. "Take it from me, it's weird not being on a payroll." I nudge his shoulder with mine, resisting the urge to rest against him. "Thanks for choosing us over him."

"Well, thank you. For, ah, employing me."

"Oh, I'm your boss now?" Just as a dopamine surge fills me and I think of so many sleazy, funny responses that I could go with, the image of Megan's face makes me bite my lip shut. Teasing him is my Olympic sport, and I can only compete once every four years. But he's going to be her husband soon. "Think of us as business partners."

He gives me a strange look. "Are you okay?"

"Sure, I'm fine."

He gets to his feet. "I was bracing myself for a classic Darcy zinger. How did you manage to resist?" He holds a hand down and pulls me up so easily I momentarily leave the ground.

I sigh. Another of life's pleasures is over. "I officially retire. For obvious reasons."

I climb a couple of steps to be closer to his eye level. Patty is still tootling around in the garden. "Hurry it up," I tell her, hugging my arms around my waist. "I'm getting cold."

"What's that?" Tom's noticed the reddened mark on my wrist. He can always sniff out danger.

"Just a reaction to my new perfume."

Tom reaches for my arm but stops when an inch separates our skin. He opens his hand over the mark and measures it. He's pissed. Outraged. Mouth open from the sheer audacity. I'm surprised the sky doesn't unfurl into black thunderclouds, crackling with lightning. "Who did it?"

"Don't fuss." I wrap my forearm behind my back and put more marshmallows into my mouth. Through the white sugar foam I say, "Looks worse than it is." What a horrible sentence.

"Who did it?" He repeats it, his eyes supernatural orange. He looks back at the street. He's going to hunt that black car down. He's going to tear out Vince's throat.

How does no one else ever notice this beast inside him?

"No, not that guy. Another fucking idiot at work. He knows to not do it again."

I've already got my follow-up retort locked and loaded: *I can take care of myself.* He knows it. We stare like we hate each other.

I can feel the energy in him shimmering. He's got thoughts and opinions, but he's swallowing them, and they taste awful. He's probably thinking about what he'd do to anyone who put a mark on Megan. He'd lick up blood.

"If he needs reminding, let me know," he manages at last. He's twisting away from me now, putting distance between us. This is something he doesn't like about me. My dark, messy lifestyle scares the shit out of him.

I'm struggling with my temper too, for a different reason. I wouldn't mind betting Megan's too simple to realize what she has. She's at home embalming herself, bleaching her cuticles and lubricating her follicles or whatever it is that well-groomed women do. She's an aesthetician after all, and no one can trust a slovenly beauty therapist. I bet she's staring at her own face in the mirror.

Meanwhile, her fiancé is like an apple pie on a windowsill, and this world is full of sugar addicts like me. It's her goddamn carelessness that has always gotten me.

If he were mine . . . I can't let myself think it.

My jaw aches from not blurting everything out. "Let's go in."

Valeska shakes the snow from his fur. I shake the snow from mine. He holds up an ancient key ring. "Check it out."

"Well, that's a blast from the past."

It's a key ring given to Tom by Loretta when we were kids; it's Garfield, wearing earphones, with Odie next to him, mouth open in a bark. Printed is: *SILENCE IS GOLDEN!*

That was Loretta's nickname for Tom: Golden. I was Sweetness, and Jamie was Salty.

Nicknames were everywhere, growing up. Prince, Princess. My dad's special name for Tom that made him go red and pleased: Tiger. Maybe Dad did know what we brought in that night.

"I love that you have a key," I say without thought, like a creep. "This would be a collector's item, probably." I use his Garfield key to unlock the door, and he scrapes his thumbnail into the empty screw holes where my BARRETT WEDDING PHOTOGRAPHY brass plaque used to be. He's probably thinking about how I'll never shoot his wedding. "Yeah, yeah, I'm sorry." But also, I'm not.

I push the door open with my knee. He's looking now at the remaining plaque that reads MAISON DE DESTIN, hung by Loretta to set the mood for her tarot clients. *Ooh. Something about destiny. Fancy.* He's wistful as he uses his thumb to check if it's screwed tight.

"I miss her so much," he tells me, and we are sad and silent until Patty does her jackhammer run through our legs, sneezing and huffing. Thank you, little animal.

I click on the nearest lamp, and the first thing we see is my underwear. Above the fireplace, there's a row of fancy black bras hanging up to dry on the old nails that once held our Christmas stockings.

"Well," Tom says after a beat. "That would give Santa a stroke."

I laugh and throw my keys onto the coffee table. "I wasn't expecting company." The echo of Vince's car reverberates through the room like another lie. Patty sets off with single-minded determination down the hall.

"If you pee inside, you are getting in trouble," Tom says to her departing form.

I unhook the bras and toss them on the armchair. "Christ, what a night. I'm glad you're here." I pull out the wine bottle and use the hem of my top to work on the screw-top lid.

He holds out a hand. It would be easy-peasy for him. "Here, I'll do it."

"I'm perfectly capable." I step around him into the dark kitchen. If I'm not firm with him, he slips and starts trying to do everything for me. Princess Mode. "Do you want some? Or do good boys like you need to get into bed?"

Eyebrows down. "Good boys like me get up at five A.M."

"Bad girls like me go to bed at six A.M." I grin at his despairing head shake. He reaches for the light switch on the wall, but I stop him. "You'll get a zap."

"Seriously? Have you been zapped?" Aghast, he looks at my chest. It contains the one thing he cannot fix.

"No, because I learned from Jamie's mistake." I can't help grinning. *Holy fuck! Ow! Darce, stop laughing! That hurt!*

"Smiling at the thought of your brother being electrocuted." Tom doesn't want to be amused but he can't help it. "Such a bad girl."

"I'm the worst." I use a wooden spoon to flip the switch. "Okay, so it's looking bad in here."

I watch him scan the room from top to bottom: the water-stained ceiling, the bubbling wallpaper, the floorboards that bounce under his feet. I've been used to it, but now I see the full extent of the room's shabbiness.

"Can you tell me what your fight with Jamie was about? I've heard his side. But I want to hear yours." He turns away, his eyes following the line of a crack in the wall. Behind his back, I drink my entire glass of wine soundlessly. When he turns around, I'm holding a second full glass. The perfect crime.

"What can I say? My temper got the better of me." I sip daintily.

"Okay," Tom half laughs as he turns on the kitchen tap. It splutters and sprays him, and when he turns it off, we hear a loud dripping. He finds the sink bucket in the cabinet underneath. "Aw, jeez."

His phone chimes, and he looks at the screen, a smile on the edge of his mouth. He texts back, probably something like, *It's okay, I arrived safe. Miss you, Megs.*

A hot feeling grabs me by the throat. I want to take his phone and flush it all the way to the sewage plant. I drink a mouthful of wine and it helps a bit.

"So, the day I made Jamie very mad. Where do I start? We had been driving each other insane. Living in bedrooms next door to each other was easy when we were kids and we had you in a bunk bed to mediate."

But with no buffer, we were agitating and arguing. Jamie wanted us to move to the city. I wanted to stay. I couldn't buy him out. It was a tug-of-war argument that I couldn't win, because like Mom said, Loretta wanted us to tart up the cottage and split the money. *Think of it as a little nest egg,* Mom said, patting my heart.

I told her that I didn't want a nest egg. The way I'd earned it was too much for me to bear. Mom was gentle. *I'm sorry, Princess. I know what she meant to you. This is her way of showing what you meant to her.*

"So there was a knock on the door one Saturday morning. Jamie was out jogging. It was early and I was very . . . tired."

His eyes move to my glass.

"Okay, it was like eleven A.M., and I was hungover as hell. On the doorstep was some good-looking hotshot giving me his business card. I thought I was having a sex dream."

"So far this is matching Jamie's version exactly." Tom unlatches the kitchen window, lifts it a fraction, then jiggles it all the way open. Only someone who practically grew up in this house would know that little trick. "I always meant to fix that for her." Sad eyes now. He never met his own grandparents. I'm glad he could share ours.

"Loretta would have told you that window isn't broken." The wine is warm satin in my veins. I'm somehow pouring my third glass. Tom thinks it's my second. Heh.

"So you were possibly having a sex dream . . . ," Tom prompts, and I realize I'm standing in the refrigerator light, staring at nothing. What am I going to give him for breakfast? A body like that needs protein. A Viking banquet table, mugs of ale, a crackling fire. An animal skin draped low on his hips.

Me, lying boneless and spent in the crook of his elbow, still asking for more.

I fill my mouth with wine and shut the fridge.

"A sex dream," Tom prompts again.

I spray the mouthful of wine onto the fridge door. My overdue phone bill is now a watercolor.

"Yeah, so he's got me out on the front path. He's telling me how sorry he is about Loretta, blah blah. He was talking like he knew her. Even though he was flirty, I knew it wasn't a sex dream, because his clothes were still on. He was bumming me out about how bad the cottage looked. Then I realized. He was a developer."

"Douglas Franzo from Shapley Group, right?"

"Yeah." Jamie's probably ranted this to Tom a hundred times before. *Douglas fucking Franzo! The son of the CEO! Important! Rich! Powerful!* "I asked him to leave."

"According to your brother," Tom says on a grunt as he pulls the stiff window back down, "you went ballistic and he tore up the written offer. Then you chased his car down to the corner of Simons Street, barefoot, wearing nothing but a robe."

"So that's a detail you remember, huh?" I try my alpha-dog eye-contact stare but he doesn't look away this time. One second ticks into two. Three. I look down into my wineglass. "You know I hate when you compare our stories. Why even ask me if you already know how it went? Jamie came jogging around the corner in his sweatbands bellowing, *What the fuck,* and the rest is history."

I hope my twin didn't finish telling it. World War III happened in this very kitchen. After he left, unable to trust himself to not kill me, I knelt on the floor and picked up the pieces of the Royal Albert dinner set we'd smashed. We'd thrown it at each other, plate after plate.

Another beautiful thing the Barrett twins could not deserve. *Who do you think you are, anyway?*

Tom gives me a *don't get grouchy* look as he toes his boot around the skirting boards, wiggling and loosening everything he touches. "I don't believe all the things your brother tells me about you. They always sound made up."

"Then you find out it's true, and your illusions are shattered, yet again."

"I don't know about illusions, exactly. I've known you a long time."

My third glass of wine goes down the hatch. "Jamie crawled around the front path finding the torn-up pieces of the offer. He taped it together. Can you believe that?"

"Yes. There would have been a dollar sign motivating him."

"He set up a meeting with the guy, tried everything. He literally sent him a fruit basket. But I'd fucked it up."

"Knowing you, you don't regret it," Tom says. I watch his expression settle into thoughtful, and I lean on the broken oven and watch him move around the room. What's he looking for? The one thing that is salvageable?

"What's your next big adventure, then?"

"I'll help pack up this place. Then I'm going to get on the

first plane I come across." I shrug when he looks dubious. "I mean it. I'll probably just get a good deal on somewhere warm that doesn't need a visa. And what's your next big destination?" I can't say *honeymoon* because it will come out like a burp. I picture Tom and Megan lying on a beach. Then I crop Megan out of the image.

"I'll find something cheap and flip it. That's what I'm always doing next."

"Enough work! Make sure your hotel has a fabulous pool," I suggest through my teeth. Teenage Darcy used to sit on the edge and count his laps. I'd lose count, hypnotized by his rhythmic gasps of air. It took me a few years to realize they gave me the stomach shivers because they were hopelessly erotic. "You're still swimming, right?"

He rolls his shoulders reflexively. "I haven't had time. Not in probably two years. Where are you moving after this? Getting a rental?" His nose wrinkles. "Do me a favor, get a nice place."

"I don't know. I've only just gotten used to having a mailing address. I'll put my stuff in storage and I'll stay at the beach house when I'm back." I hope that didn't sound like, *I'm traveling like a big spoiled baby forever, and when I'm not, I'll be in Mommy and Daddy's house eating breakfast in bed.*

"I rebuilt their back deck. It was too small for them." Typical Tom, sweating for the Barretts whenever required. "I'm sure they're out on it right now, kissing under the moonlight."

"Ugh, gross. Probably." Mom and Dad have chemistry. I

will leave it at that. "You didn't even swim in the ocean while you were there?"

"I didn't even think of it," he says, looking a little surprised. "Whoops."

"You belong in water. Next time, swim." I go back into the living room and throw myself onto the couch. Patty hammers in from nowhere, louder than a *T. rex,* a pencil clenched between her teeth. I've got to ask the hard questions, to get them out of the way.

"Where are you going for your honeymoon?" No answer. I'll try again. "I've been everywhere. I can give you guys help with your itinerary." He avoids my eyes and I slump down into the cushions. Maybe if I don't agree to be his photographer, I'll be lucky to even get an invite. I can imagine Mom explaining it to me now. *Small. Intimate. Only their closest family and friends.*

Holy shit. That's it. I'm not invited and he's trying to work out how to tell me.

Tom moves to the dining room and risks turning the light on. It's my little photography studio now. Boxes of merchandise sit against the wall. "This is what you do these days?"

"Yep." I dig in my bag of marshmallows. Time to plug this aching void inside. I hit shuffle on Loretta's retro stereo and the Cure comes on. The void gapes wider in a delicious way.

"Mugs." He says it doubtfully. "You take photos of mugs so they can be sold on websites? I definitely thought Jamie had made that up."

"It's true." I pack my mouth with sweet white foam and sip some wine to dissolve it all. "Not just mugs. Don't look in that one," I warn Tom when he goes to look in the boxes.

"What is it?" He flips open the box lid. "Okay then."

"It's surprisingly hard to get the lighting right on a ten-inch purple dildo."

"I'm sure it's impossible." He is scandalized to the core. It is adorable. He looks back down, unable to resist.

"Don't go digging in that dirty box, Tom, you'll need brain bleach." I have the strongest feeling he wants to.

I'd give my left ventricle to know what he thought about all that silicone. Disgusting? Interesting? On par with what's in his navy cargo pants? It's so hard to tell when he looks up. He rearranges his expression into prim disapproval.

God, such a good boy. I grin like a shark. "They let me keep stuff sometimes." I watch as he skitters around the room off walls and furniture like a big pinball. Then I relieve him. "I've got so many mugs."

"Mugs," he says again like it's the cause of all that is wrong in this world. "I don't think this is very . . . you. You're an award-winning portrait photographer."

"Au contraire. Wistful portraits of sex toys are very much me these days." I shrug at his expression. "Hey, I just shoot what they send me. I've personally taken every single product shot on the entire Internet."

My voice blurs drunkenly at the edges and I know he

hears it. "No one thinks about who takes the photos. They just click and add that dildo to their cart."

I arch my back, unclip my bra, and sag back down with a groan. Out the armhole and I toss the bra onto the pile. Tom averts his eyes through the whole thing.

Except somehow, I feel like he watched me do it.

Chapter 5

I can't stop myself from pressing my little wound again. I don't feel like Tom's scolded me for it. I deserve a lecture.

"Jamie said even Loretta would have said I was crazy to pass up that developer's offer. Maybe I would have reacted differently if I knew I'd basically lose my brother over it."

Wow. I sounded completely normal saying that out loud.

Tom says in such a kind voice that I want to cry, "You haven't lost him, DB. You've just pissed him off."

"I've witnessed him ice out so many people over the years. I never thought it would be me. Remember that guy he worked with, Glenn? He made him repay a loan when his wife was in the maternity ward."

"Yeah. Because Glenn got the promotion he wanted. He's so good to the people in his circle—"

I huff. "And it's a tiny circle."

"But if he's crossed, or slighted, or he thinks he's been 'betrayed,' he just turns into . . ."

"Ice. He's ice. Just like I'm ice."

"You're fire," Tom says back without thought. "You're opposites."

There's another tidbit. Another surprise view on me. Any man who saw me at work tonight would have said I was cold to the bone. "I want to be ice."

"Take it from me, ice is the worst. Please stay fiery." He pauses and sighs. He's sad about something. "Anyway, I don't think you did the wrong thing. You'd be okay with an apartment complex here? And going against her final wishes?"

"Of course not. Well, it's never happening anyway now. I pissed that guy off so bad he just picked another street. Let's just say I can't go next door for a cup of sugar anymore." I drink from my wineglass. "As a twin, the bigger issue was that I made a decision on my own. No consultation: the cardinal sin."

"You yanked his chain, big-time." Tom knows my brother's buttons just as well as me. There are three big ones, labeled MONEY, LOYALTY, DECISIONS.

The wispy remnants of my heart medication, from whenever I last remembered to take it, are mixing with the wine in an interesting way. I've worked hard to build up a tolerance.

I toe off my boots. "I'm still kind of drunk on the power of actually being fifty-fifty owners with Jamie in something. I don't think it's ever happened."

He moves to the wall and begins to press at the bubbles in the wallpaper. "Sure it has."

"Come on, relax." I point at the armchair. He moves the bra pile and sits. He can be so lusciously obedient. "Jamie has never let me actually have half of anything. Even if Mom gave us a piece of cake as kids and told us to share . . ."

Tom finishes my sentence. "Jamie would cut it sixty-forty."

"He said it was because he was bigger. He deserved more." I eye Tom now, sitting there in that chair, looking like a piece of cake, or another beautiful photograph I'll never get to take. The lamplight loves that face of his. I'm getting drunk but I can't stop myself. "I never got to share you."

I watch him mull this over. He can't deny it. Our entire childhood was spent at opposite ends of the dining table, my bossy blond brother always talking, laughing, dominating. Functioning as the line between us. *Leave Tom alone* was a common refrain. *Ignore her.* Sitting here with him alone is a novelty.

We're all shareholders in Tom Valeska: Jamie, Megan, and me. His mom and my parents. Loretta and Patty. Everyone who's ever met him wants a piece of him, because he's the best person there is. I quickly count up all of those people. I include his dentist and doctor. Maybe he's only 1 percent mine. That has to be enough. I have to share.

The wine is washing through my veins in a warm cuddly wave. "Why'd he have to be born first? I swear, if I was his big sister, everything might be different."

"Your dad always joked that Jamie was the prototype." Tom's sparkling with humor. "That means you're the final product."

"Pretty crappy final product, complete with defects." I clap my chest and my breast jiggles shamefully.

"I was meaning to ask," Tom says carefully, avoiding eye contact like he's edging close to a silverback, "how's your spool?"

That's what he calls my heart, since we were kids. It's been too long for me to remember why. To him, inside my chest is a spool of cotton thread. This guy has so many methods to manage the Barrett twins, it's truly impressive. His cute euphemism always untwists my knickers.

"My spool is just fine and dandy. I'm going to live forever. I'm going to pour Kwench on your grave. Ugh. No way I'm going to explain that to elderly Megan. I've changed my mind. I'll die first."

"I worry about you."

"I worry about big hot dorks who ask too many questions, who are stuck in a house late at night with me." I stretch my legs and my tank slips off my bare shoulder. I wonder if my nipple piercing is doing what it does best, through my clothes: punctuating the obvious. Judging from the way he's looking at me, the bras, and the darkness outside, he's just realized that our eighteen-year friendship has finally hit a belated milestone.

We're alone.

I look into his eyes and I feel that crackle in him again. Everyone else sees a mild-mannered sweetheart. What I feel, between us? It's never quite human. "You know why this feels so weird, don't you?"

A door creaks open and we both jump. If anyone had a secret passageway behind a bookcase into this house, it would be Jamie.

Loretta's cat Diana walks in, huffy and annoyed, her green eyes trained on Patty. She's another one of our inheritances. I dislike her on a personal level, but again I have to appreciate how animals can break tension like magic.

I snap my fingers at her and she gives me a look like, *You're fucking kidding, right?* "I hate to be cynical, but do you think Loretta had this cat to add to her mystical tarot-reader persona?"

Tom shakes his head. "She wasn't a scammer. She really believed in it."

He's pretty much tried everything on Loretta's menu. She was fascinated by his palm. Predictably, he has one hell of a heart line. *Like a blade has cut right through you,* she told him with a slicing motion. *One big one.* His little-kid face pinched in surprise as he looked at his hand like he was searching for blood.

Loretta's specialty was tarot, but she offered everything: tea leaves, I Ching, numerology, astrology, feng shui. Palms, dreams, and pendulums. Past lives. Power animals. Auras. Once when I came over as a teenager, I was halted by a *Séance in Progress* Post-it note on the door.

I gesture around us. "I know. And I think she was the real deal. But holy shit, she backed herself up with a lot of ambiance."

The wallpaper is blood-red hyperreal hydrangeas. The curtains are fringed with jet-black beads that glitter in the light.

The low coffee table transforms easily enough when a thick, sparkling cloth is put over it, even more so with the crystal ball.

It's like sitting inside a genie's bottle. When the fire crackles in the hearth and the ruby lamps are on, you could believe anything in this beautiful room. The air is still heavy with Loretta's signature incense: sage, cedarwood, sandalwood, and the faintest incriminating whiff of pot. In this room, I miss her the least.

"That fireplace is in my top five favorite things in this world." I tip my face toward it. "I can't wait until it gets cold and I can light it again." I mentally count forward the pages on the calendar. "Oh. Well, shit."

Tom links his fingers together and leans forward. "We can light it again before . . ."

I nod and try to swallow the sad. "Just one more time would be great. I guess I haven't completely thought about what I'm going to have to say goodbye to."

With a dismissive nose-wrinkle, Diana jumps up on the arm of Tom's chair and Patty vibrates with outrage. These dear, sweet buffers.

"I begged Jamie to take her." I open a new bag of marshmallows, because the void is getting bigger. "Every evil overlord needs a fluffy cat to stroke."

Tom offers his hand to her and she roughly rubs her white cheek along his knuckles, before looking at me with smug acid-green eyes. Fair enough. I'd love to do the same to him. He yawns and slumps a little, unaware that my screws are getting looser by the second. I remember something.

"So, Jamie's room is an issue."

He seizes the chance to leave the room, so I guess my stare is getting to him. I call after him, "It's not my fault. I didn't know you were coming."

"It's up to the ceiling," he says from the hall. "Darcy, seriously."

"I don't have any storage space, and Jamie just won't come and get his stuff. So I just . . . stacked it to the ceiling." I am sloshing wine into my glass again when he appears. He confiscates the bottle, towering over me, holding it up to the light to look at the level.

"That's enough for tonight." He tousles my hair with his fingers to soften the scolding. "I can't get used to it. It really is so short."

He still hasn't said that it looks good. I won't ask, because he can't lie. Megan has a beautiful glossy dark mane. Even I want to touch her hair.

"I look like I'm in a Korean boy band, but I don't care. I can feel the air on the back of my neck." I stretch as his fingertips depart, and hopefully he doesn't notice. I need physical touch more than sunlight, and it's embarrassing. A hologram of Vince appears and I blink it away.

"I personally didn't know you had a neck. What happened to your plait after it was cut? Not the bin." The thought horrifies him.

"I donated it. Someone out there is walking around with a big white wig. So, do I look like Jamie now?"

He laughs and the room gets brighter. I'm not saying that

to be cute; it's true. The lamps all blaze up. Shot electrical wiring—or Loretta spying on us? I know which I'd put my money on. "What did your brother say when your mom sent him the photo?"

"That I look like a wannabe Goth Joan of Arc and that I chopped off my only redeeming feature. I don't care. I love it."

He puts the bottle and glass out of reach, then takes the bag of marshmallows that I've been cradling and puts them on the mantel. "You look nothing alike."

"I look like Ms. Pac-Man with a bow on my head. I'm like the scale version of him."

"You're really not."

"Is that a compliment or an insult? My brother is beautiful, as you know."

He shakes his head in amusement but still says nothing. I've been fishing on this same pier for many years. He steps closer, and feather-soft, he reaches down and nudges the mark on my arm.

"This is not okay. And I'll . . ." He bites down on the rest of that sentence and the tendons of his jaw flex. The hands by his sides curl and squeeze. I know what he'll do. He doesn't have to say it. I feel it.

I've just decided to reach up to uncurl his fingers when he decides to retreat entirely to the only place I cannot follow.

"I'm going to take a shower," he says, going outside before reappearing with a huge suitcase.

"What's that? Are you flying internationally somewhere?"

"Ha, ha," he replies dryly. He's not an easy flier. The image of him crammed into a tiny plane seat, nervously clutching the armrests, is weird. And cute. And makes me sad. Wine kind of does that to a person. The Cure also assists.

I lie back and cross my legs at the knees. "Now, that shower has gotten a bit temperamental. Should I come in and show you?" I keep my tone straightforward, but I can see a rose-gold blush on his cheekbones as he unzips his bag.

"No, thanks." He pulls out some pajamas and a black zipped bag.

"Oh wait." I get to my feet and run down the hallway, Patty at my heels. "I'd better check . . ."

"Darce, relax," he says behind me as I scoop up puddles of underwear from the floor. "We practically shared a bathroom when we were growing up." And it goes unsaid but he lives with a woman. He's seen everything.

The room shrinks by half. I don't leave.

"You'll have to go out now." His hand cups the hem of the T-shirt. Then he grips it. Everything twists tighter. There's an inch of stomach, and it's tanned like caramel fudge. I plead with myself. *Eyes up, DB.*

His knuckles start going white. "Go on. Out."

I don't know if he's talking to me or Patty. I pray for St. Megan to give me strength. He herds me out. "Towels in the usual spot?"

"Yeah," I say, hating the fact that he's audibly turned the lock. How embarrassing. How prudent. "I'm sorry I'm weird to you."

"That's okay." On the other side of the door, Tom is getting naked. *Come on, Maison de Destin. Collapse your walls.* "You forget, I've known you a long time."

"And I've been weird to you the entire time."

"Yeah." There's a banging noise, then a blast, and he yelps. "These pipes." I can hear the shower curtain flutter. I slide down the wall and Patty looks like she has a twin sister. I'll keep one when he leaves.

"What a fucking lucky drain." The wine has knocked my legs out and maybe I should be worried. I didn't have much. Am I dying? My heart feels steady, ticking away valiantly. I look at the two little faces next to me. "Patties, that shower doesn't know how good life is right now."

Let's review how this night has turned out.

Tom Valeska is putting his flawless face under the spray of my shower, suds sliding down, rinsing his gold skin. Muscles dripping. I have seen him climb out of pools roughly ten billion times by now, so I think I know what he looks like. Almost.

I pull up the bottom of my top and blot the sheen from my face and neck.

He's got legs for days and a beefy butt. Straddle-worthy hips. Those shoulders? Streaming with water now. The shower's off, and now one of Loretta's towels is probably around his waist. Those towels barely wrap around me.

I am having mental images that need to be taped shut inside that box of dildos, like it's a cursed sarcophagus.

I don't think this can be happening. I've fallen asleep on

the couch and am having a delirious, dehydrated sex dream. But if this were a dream, the door would be ajar, steam curling out to me. If he asked me to come in right now, I would pull the pins out of the hinges with my teeth, spitting them on the floor.

I can say this with absolute certainty: No man has ever made me want to lick a foggy bathroom tile before. "Megan, Megan," I whisper to myself, icy-white diamonds behind my eyelids as I drag myself to my feet.

In my room, I scrub my eyes with makeup wipes and change into leggings and an old band T-shirt. I'll let my teeth decay tonight. When Tom appears in the doorway, wearing another tight T-shirt and sweatpants, I'm starting to doubt reality again.

"You're forgetting something." He points a thumb next door. "That room." His jaw tenses and he swallows a yawn. My hospitality leaves a lot to be desired. "Where do you want me?"

"In my bed. Not with me! I'm on the couch tonight." I eye my bedside drawer. "Wait, let me burn the room down real quick."

He laughs like he's got my number. "I'll take the couch."

"You can't fit on it. Here." I pull the blankets back, take him by the wrists, and toss him down. It's weirdly easy. Shouldn't he be difficult to manhandle and throw down? Maybe I'm super strong. Maybe he's light as a feather.

Or, most realistically, he's exhausted. But still, he gives me a look that makes my inner thighs quiver. And when he pulls up the comforter, it's low on his hips. He looks like a beautiful big Viking, even under candy stripes.

"I shouldn't." He leans back against the headboard and contemplates my nightstand with sideways eyes. I don't feel too worried. This here is a cast-iron moral compass. Mine, on the other hand? Not so much. I need to get out of this room. Out of this country.

"Jamie would kill me if I let you sleep on the couch or the floor. Consider me the hostess with the mostess."

I sound incredibly drunk. How strange; I'm starting to feel very sober indeed. I dig around in the big wooden chest at the foot of the bed, searching for a quilt. I hear an uneasy mattress squeak. The sound seems to come from his soul.

I tsk at him. "What? Sleeping in my bed isn't cheating on Megan. And they're fresh sheets, before your mind goes there." In my peripheral vision, he regards the empty space where Vincent would go with slack-jawed horror.

I avoid looking in his direction as I snatch up a pillow. I don't have to look to know that Tom fits my king-sized bed like a dream. One of those dreams you defile yourself after.

"Okay, good night." I retreat backward down the hall, knocking my elbows on everything, and fall onto the couch.

I cocoon myself, knowing it'll be icy in this room by morning, and then I decide to set myself an impossible little target.

It's nothing too aspirational. It doesn't involve my finding the courage to loosen my fingernails from the edge of this couch and walk back down the hall. Skin-on-skin-on-sweat physical contact isn't in the realm of possibility.

Not now, not ever, not Tom.

I thought that having just 1 percent of Tom Valeska's heart feels like hitting the jackpot, but I think I was wrong. It's now not enough.

I'm going to make him 2 percent mine.

Chapter 6

I didn't sleep much last night, because I kept thinking about that time a long time ago when Tom told me exactly how he felt, and I didn't understand. That time when I was possibly at 100 percent and didn't know it.

I was eighteen, putting black platforms on over my fishnets to go hang out with a bad crowd, and Tom had leaned on my door frame and asked me not to go out. It had been no secret that he didn't approve of all the black-clad guys and how I stayed out all night. I thought it was typical Valeska-in-the-snowdrifts stuff. Tug, tug, away from danger.

In my careless way, I'd snapped at him. *Why not? Why shouldn't I go?*

Tom told me in a steady, reasonable voice: *Because I love you.* And I'd replied without thought or gravitas, *I know,* because I'd always felt it. How could I not? How many times had he saved me? I'd have to have been a moron to not know it. To this day I know he loves me, in that old, stitched-into-my-family way.

Turns out, *I know* wasn't the right reply.

He'd rusted over with embarrassment and left. He wouldn't turn around as he walked down the front stairs, through our front gate. He wouldn't stop even as I chased him across the street and he shut the door in my face.

That was the very first time I tore up a once-in-a-lifetime offer.

I bailed on my friends and I went to Loretta's house instead. When I told her what had happened, she said, *I saw that coming.* What else would I expect from a fortune-teller? She shook her head. That's not what she meant.

That boy would take a bullet for you.

We sat outside and shared a joint, and it was a thrill. *Don't tell your father! How'd I birth such a prude? It grows in the earth, for God's sake.* She told me about her first husband, way before she met Grandpa. I never knew she had been married twice, so I was gobsmacked.

I was just a kid, she mused, eyes narrowed on her inhale. *Maybe if I'd met him ten years later . . . it was a terrible mistake. I hurt him badly, because I was too young and immature to love him right. I still regret it. Let yourself grow up and live your life. You're a wild one, just like me.*

I'd laughed and said there was no risk of me getting married. This was just me and Tom kissing, if it didn't feel weird.

Loretta hadn't been remotely amused. *He loves you more than that. I can see you don't take this seriously.*

Like it was an emergency, she bought me my first plane ticket and gave me some cash. A few days later, under the cover of darkness, she drove me to the airport. It was a transformative moment. I was suddenly completely responsible for myself and not part of a set of twins. It was like all the turmoil I'd caused was released out of a pressure valve, and I knew it was the right thing to do.

Loretta handled the fallout from my parents and brother, and I threw my first coin into the Trevi Fountain in Rome, completely addicted to this new reckless anonymity. Nobody saw a girl with a heart condition and a more electric brother. They saw me for the first time, and even better, I could walk away from anything I didn't like.

My wish, when I threw that coin into the fountain? That Tom wasn't too bruised by my carelessness.

I drift off now, on the couch with the quilt over my face, imagining myself walking down the carpeted jet bridge from the gate into an airplane. That's my favorite part: walking out of real life so that everyone I love can exhale.

Except that first time I did it, I walked out a little too long. When I returned, ready to look into Tom's eyes and be guided by what I felt, I was pulled up short by the sleek, composed girl at his side who would one day wear his beautiful ring.

And here's the real kicker: Jamie introduced them.

* * *

"ALIVE?" THERE'S A voice above me. I wake with a snort, flip the quilt away, and open my eyes. "Ouch." Tom has sympathy in his voice, so I must look pretty bad. He puts a takeout cup on the coffee table. Next, a takeout box.

I attempt to speak with my dead mouth. "Have I mentioned that you are the world's best person?"

"A few times. Waffles. That's still right, isn't it?" Just like his cheese-lettuce lunch, my hangover food hasn't changed. I nod and pull myself up onto my elbows. I'm glad he doesn't know about my trip down memory lane.

"What time is it?" The coffee is the most perfect temperature and sweetness and I drink it in a series of gulps. I'm a hummingbird. "Oh my God." I tip the last drops into my mouth. I lick the inner rim. "How was that so good?"

Does everything taste this good when delivered by his hands? Megan, you lucky bitch. He could make a cold toast crust succulent, I swear. He takes the lid off his own coffee, pours in a bunch of sugar sachets, and gives it to me. Such charity. Such goodness.

And I tore it up. I tore it all up.

"Don't cry, they're just waffles," he says, smiling. "It's heading toward lunchtime. I've got stuff to show you before we call Jamie." His phone begins ringing. "Speak of the devil."

I take the ringing phone and hit speakerphone. Even with tears in my eyes and a regret-thickened throat, I can still say: "Hello, you've reached the micro-penis counseling service."

There's silence on the other end, then a deep sigh that I'd know anywhere. I heard it before I was born, probably. Tom grins, teeth white, and it's probably a better feeling than a stadium of people laughing. He's 2 percent mine. It's official.

Jamie speaks. "Hilarious. She's just hilarious."

"I thought so," Tom replies.

I stay in character. "How small is your penis, sir?"

"Don't encourage her," Jamie orders as Tom breaks and begins laughing. "Darcy, where's your phone?"

"Women's bathroom at Sully's. Second stall from the end."

"Well, get a new one, dimwit."

"I've got an old one in my car you can have." Tom's all about solutions, especially when his boss Jamie is within earshot.

"No, I think I like things better this way," I tell him. Coffee, waffles, Tom, Patty leaning against my shin, and my brother is calling me dimwit again? Tom's fixed everything.

Jamie says, "So, let me guess. She's so hungover she's a ghost."

"Ah, well . . . ," Tom says, because he doesn't have a lie mode.

I've got lie mode on autopilot. "I've just gotten back from a walk."

My brother just laughs in response, for a little too long. "Sure. Are you going to stay out of Tom's way while he gets started on the house?"

"I'm sure I'll be gone before he even opens his toolbox, don't worry."

"That'd be right," Jamie says, sarcasm dripping. "Skip out before anything hard. Poor Tom's going to have to do everything himself."

"Poor Tom is here to do a job and get paid," Tom reminds Jamie.

I open the box lid and there are two perfect waffles. "Hey, I have to pack the house. That's plenty hard." I drown them in syrup and begin breaking them apart with my hands. I feed Patty a tiny piece and myself a huge piece.

"You'll flirt Tom into doing it."

"I will not," I snap, mouth full, licking my fingers. Above me, Tom's face is partway between pained and amused.

"You will. You're going to be worse than ever now." Jamie scoffs. "No doubt your sympathy was completely unconvincing."

"I'll be worse why? What does he mean?" I look up at Tom. He shrugs and interrupts our petty flow.

"We've got a lot to do between now and next Monday when the crew arrives. Darce needs to pack, and I want you both to agree on the style we're doing."

"Modern," Jamie says at the exact same moment as I say, "Vintage."

Tom groans and plops down heavily on the end of the couch. I move my legs just in time. He pinches his hand across his eyes. "Goodbye, cruel world."

"It's going to be fine," I assure him through my bite of waffle. "Don't you worry." I tear off a chunk and feed it into his mouth.

"Easy for you to say," Jamie says. "You're going to be walking around in a random country licking an ice-cream cone while Tom and I do all the hard work. What's next on your personal reinvention journey, by the way? You've done the piercing and the tough haircut. It's gotta be a tattoo next."

I step over that, because Tom's looking for the piercing. Nose? Ear? Eyebrow? Nope. Now he's averting his eyes, and his mind is running through the remaining possibilities.

I give the phone a glare. "So your hard work will consist of sitting on your ass in your office and occasionally answering Tom's calls and emails? You'll pick out a faucet or some tiles online? That's hard work?"

"It's more than you'll do," Jamie hisses back. Something inside me lights up; I want to retort, like old times, *Challenge accepted!* But my hungover brain scratches around and comes up empty. Could I pack the house super-fast?

"It goes without saying that I'm doing the hard work, and you're paying me to do it," Tom interjects, ever the calm referee. "Does five percent of the sale price work for you, Darce?"

"Math isn't her strong point," Jamie says cruelly, at the same time as I say, "Sure."

"You don't even know how much that will be," Tom prompts, unwillingly agreeing with Jamie. "Do you know what the current market is in this area?"

He holds the phone away a little and lowers his voice. "Make sure you know what you're saying yes to. This is your inheritance, Darce. I've got contracts that you both need to sign. Even though we're all friends, everything is going to be done right. You're both clients as soon as you sign."

"Business is business," Jamie's voice says faintly from the phone. "I taught you well."

I'd have said yes to ten. Twenty. Five percent of his heart. Anything.

"What's the big deal? I trust you. I'm sure it's fair. As long as the house is restored, that's all I care about."

"You've got to start caring about money more." Tom doesn't look like he's glad that I've got blind faith in him. He looks like he's feeling sick.

"Hear that, Tom? You're the only person on earth Darcy Barrett trusts!" Jamie says, a little too exaggerated, a lot jealous. I narrow my eyes at the phone.

"He's the perfect man," I say, just to jab at Jamie.

"You've got to stop saying things like that," Tom says in a pained way. To himself, he says, "No pressure."

"You've been telling her the truth about everything, have you?" Jamie says, and there's a long silence. Endless. The cotton threads on Tom's body squeak. "Ah, I see," Jamie says, speculation in his tone. "Yes, I think I know why you're playing it this way. Smart."

For the first time, I feel a sliver of doubt. Tom won't look at me now. "What the hell are you two cooking up?"

"Nothing," Tom tells me with a heavy sigh. "All right, this is going nowhere. I've got a guy coming to look at the foundation. I really need you two to agree on the style before Wednesday. I've got to order stuff."

"Just make it look exactly the same, but new." I nod. Case closed.

"Make it look like my apartment," Jamie orders him. "Just deal with her until she leaves and do your standard modern renovation. Like that place you did last year, with the fancy gray feature wall. Do what sells."

"Gray feature wall? Loretta is laughing until she's crying right now." I look around at the beautiful wallpaper. I thought I could trust Tom to take care of this place. "You know that an old cottage like this would look ridiculous done modern."

"We'll need to have a weekly budget meeting," Tom says, persevering, "and any changes once we've set the baseline will have to be agreed on by both of you. I'm having this job come in early and under budget."

"I know you will," Jamie says, his voice nothing but confidence. I've never heard him sound like that. "I'm going to a meeting. Tom, make it modern." Jamie hangs up. Tom tosses the phone onto the coffee table and leans back. Under the blanket, my feet are pinned by his thigh.

"Modern vintage," Tom says to himself. "Barrett versus Barrett. I'm not sure how I'm going to pull this one off. You know I can't make you both happy, right?"

"You just have to decide who you want to make more happy. Hint: It's me." I smile at him. As doubt pinches his features, I smile wider, cuter, a nose-wrinkle, putting every bit of *spoiled baby sister* that I can into it.

"I do like making you happy," he admits grudgingly, and I'm bumped up. Three percent. I feel like a store's millionth shopper.

"Why was Jamie hinting about a secret? You can tell me, you know."

He takes the empty takeout container from me, and I

swipe the syrup container and drink the rest. Judging from his expression, that was gross.

"You're going to get diabetes," he says faintly. "Or rot your perfect teeth right out of your head."

Perfect? "Worth it."

"There are no secrets when it comes to this renovation. I'll be up front with you both."

His eyes catch on my mouth. I lick and everything's sweet. Everything's heavy. He's still sitting on my foot and I didn't know that was a fetish, but hey, what did I know two minutes ago? I sit up with an ab-muscle tremble and it was a mistake, because now we're closer.

"Do you still live on-site when you renovate?"

"Yeah, I've got my camping gear." One second is up, and he's passing his palms over his knees like he's wiping away sweat. "Did Jamie say you pierced yourself somewhere?"

"Yep. And it hurt like a bitch."

He won't ask me where it is. He refuses to. "Thought you've had enough needles in your life."

"I needed one more." I was so cavalier about it, imagining my next heart review and how tough it'd look. It hurt like my entire body and soul had been pierced and I loved it, because in that all-consuming agony, I couldn't think about diamond rings and my brother's fury.

Plus, it looks *hot*. Silver and pink is one hell of a combination.

He's thinking about where it could possibly be, I just know it. Time to get Megan back in the room with us.

"What does Megan think of you being away from home so much? She hates it," I conclude without pause.

"She doesn't care," Tom says with no bitterness. "She's used to it."

"If you were mine," I say, and the words seem to run down his spine because he sits up straight, "I wouldn't like it. You know what I'm like, though."

"What are you like? I have no idea," he adds when I cast him a *come on* look.

"With most guys? I couldn't care less if they lived or died. You, though . . ." I look at the two empty coffee cups and feel the weight of his goodness and I want to tell him the truth in return.

The thought of how a million people must abuse his kindness—myself included—makes me crazy.

I want to walk two steps in front of him, wherever he goes, bulldozing the world a little flatter for him. If he were sleeping on a building site, and he were mine, I'd be in that tent, too. All night, every night, as the wind whistled and the rain beat down. I'd never let another woman sit as close as I am right now. Megan seriously lets *this* walk around on earth, completely unattended?

If I were Megan, I would fuck me *up* for sitting close enough to smell the scent on his skin. He smells like birthday-candle wishes. I've never in my life felt even a passing possessiveness for another man, but Tom Valeska? It's something I have to keep lashed down inside me, hard and tight, because I have no right to it.

Maybe he's not the only wolfy sled dog around these parts.

Some of this is in my eyes because he blinks and swallows. He's trying to ignore the undercurrent between us. It's because he's a good guy. My brain doesn't want him to be any different. But my body wants him to pick me up and put me against the wall. Windowsill. Floor. Bed.

I have to salvage this situation.

"Oh, come on. You know what I'm like better than anyone. Now, are you going to tell me this secret?"

"It wouldn't be a good idea, trust me," he says carefully, but his pupils give him away. They're black drugged eyes, and I know he wants to tell me. Why else would he leave a little gap for me to squeeze through? He didn't just say no.

It's on the tip of his tongue. I need to bite it off. I wonder if I can make myself persuasive. "Is it about the house?"

He shakes his head like he's hypnotized. His brown eyes? They're my favorite. In this morning light, they're a treasure trove. Gold, sands, tombs, coins, riches. Egyptian pyramids, eternal life. Gilded sarcophagi. Cleopatra's dinnerware.

"Is it about Jamie?" He shakes his head no again. I put everything I have into it. "You can tell me."

He seems to give himself a little mental slap, and his brow creases downward. "You can stop it now."

"Stop what?"

"What Jamie said. Stop trying to flirt things out of me." He's disgusted. "You really should get into Loretta's line of work."

If I can occasionally hypnotize him, Jamie can make him walk over hot coals. This house is a sitting duck in the hands of my tyrannical genetic copy and someone who has never had any creative license in his entire career.

"And you should stop hiding something from me. I'm going to work on the house."

As I say it out loud, something clicks down into position inside me.

It's the perfect retort I should have said to Jamie. The usual feeling of chickenshit guilt dissipates like squeezing a zit. I'm going to work on fulfilling Loretta's wish for this place and protect it from anyone who can't appreciate Maison de Destin's inherent magic.

"I feel like if there's any chance to get back into Jamie's good graces, it's going to take blood, sweat, and tears. I'm going to redeem myself."

"Not too much of your blood, or tears. Or sweat," Tom says, thinking. "Just be around when I need to call Jamie to get a quick decision made. Can you move out and stay with Truly?"

"No way. I'm working and I'm staying here in a tent, just like you. I'm on your crew."

He grins at the thought, but it fades off. "Sorry, no."

"Any particular reason? Don't you need free labor?"

"I can't focus when you're around," he says with complete honesty, and a little starburst thrill pops inside my stomach. His eye contact is uncomplicated so I don't think there's anything more to the statement. "But it's your house, so I can't stop you. You could help on the occasional small project. Maybe painting the new front fence."

"No. I'm not doing the girly stuff. I'm using tools."

"No heavy lifting, no manual labor, no ladders, no electrical—" Tom stops himself. He's imagining me with my finger in a socket, I bet. He's got a big brow crease. "I don't think my insurance would cover this. You're a liability."

My mouth drops open, the void opens up like a canyon inside my chest, and everything's whooshing. A liability.

"I didn't mean it like that." He is obviously horrified at what he just said. "Darce, that came out completely wrong."

"Fine, it's fine. It's true. Do whatever you want to the cottage. Like I care. It's being sold to some rich Jamie clone, anyway. What does it matter?" It's a miracle I can still speak. I struggle up and nearly trip over the coffee table.

"You do care," he protests, hot on my heels as I make a beeline for the bathroom. I slip in, shut the door, and lock it. "You care so much it's crazy. I'm not going to do a job that you're going to be unhappy with."

"I don't care. I'm going to be about ten million miles away by the time you crack open a can of paint. Just do whatever Jamie wants, liability free." Time to get these feelings together like loose sheets of paper. Tap them into a stack. Stick them into a shredder.

"I'm so sorry."

Time to leave before I do something I can't undo.

"Open up, please," Tom says, knocking again. Does he have no self-preservation? "I really didn't mean it how it sounded. Of course you aren't a liability."

"You never lie."

"I do lie. Every day."

I look at myself in the old speckled mirror. I look terrible. Under each eye is a purple mark. Each cheek has a vaudeville spot of color. I've studied Megan at every Christmas party I've been home for. I'm telling you, she is *poreless*.

"Go away," I say because I can feel he's still there. He can't follow me here. I pull my clothes off and look down at my weird body, with its too-big joints and waffle-belly fatness. The piercing on my nipple now looks like it's part of a costume.

"I could unscrew the hinges," he says in a friendly voice. I think of myself last night, lying on the floor outside like a hound.

"If you do that you'll be scarred for life. I'm taking a shower."

"Don't go back into your shell. It's okay that you care about this house. And I want to hear how you picture the finished product." Through the door, he says in a new tone, "DB, please get dressed so I can hug you and tell you I'm sorry."

"You heard your boss. Make it modern." My voice sounds even harder when it bounces off the tiles. I crank the shower and it spits and steams. Then I stand in the water and when I cry, the tears wash away. The perfect crime.

I'm standing in the exact same place that Tom Valeska stood naked.

I'm not going to think about things like that anymore.

Chapter 7

An electrician arrives after lunch, walks in, and flips the switch beside the front door. There's a *pop* sound, the lights blink, and the electrician curses, snatching his hand back. The house is a viper today. It wants to hurt somebody.

This mug says *#1 ASSHOLE* on the side. It would be the perfect birthday gift for Jamie. If we're on speaking terms by then.

I click the camera, turn the mug slightly on the little white turntable, take another shot, and then record a three-hundred-sixty-degree rotation. Then I transfer the digital files and label them with serial numbers. I tick the checklist. If I lose track of which mug is which I will lose my mind. It's slow, boring, meticulous work.

If I think about the fact that I won the Rosburgh Portrait Prize when I was twenty, I get a shake in my hand and have to redo the set. Why did Tom have to remind me of that?

I'd nearly left the memory under Jamie's bed, along with the canvas print.

"Number one asshole. Maybe I need this one," I tell Patty, who is asleep on a cushion. "I'm pretty sure it's my mug."

I pick it up and spy out the window at Tom, who is currently looking professional and competent, all slid into his clothes in the right way, pointing up at the roofline with a saggy tradesman nodding by his side.

I have lost my goddamn mind in a short period of time. If I had my phone, I'd look at the photo of Megan's engagement ring again to recalibrate myself. I close my eyes and I can picture it: cushion cut and colder than ice. Like she could press a button on the side and a white lightsaber would come out.

I wouldn't want something like that. I'd want something like Loretta's ring: a black sapphire. I should clarify: I want Loretta's ring, full stop. The fact she left it to Jamie in her will is inexplicable to me. She knew I loved it. She let me borrow it for weeks at a time and said to me, *Oh, sweetness, doesn't it suit you.* Was it her way of punishing me for something?

I offered in the solicitor's parking lot to buy it from him, which was a tactical error. His gray eyes shifted into blue. "No," he replied with relish.

Now that he knows how badly I want it, that ring is worth more than the Mona Lisa. Luckily for me, no one would be insane enough to marry Jamie either.

It's sunset when I decide I should grow up and get things

back to normal. I find Tom in the backyard alone, writing in a notebook. The tip of his tongue is caught between his teeth.

"Look at you, being all meticulous."

"Sure am." He takes a photo of the back stairs with his phone. I've never really noticed them before, but they are beautifully rustic. I clomp down them, feeling them bounce.

"I'm so sorry—" he begins what is probably a rehearsed statement. I wave him silent.

"It's fine." I take his phone and look at his last shot. "You could probably win an award with that shot. How annoying, I should have been the one to see that. Is there anything you can't do?" I'm not really joking.

"Plenty. Why don't you get your camera and do it? Or maybe you could start taking photos of people again." This might be the closest he's going to get to asking me to shoot his wedding. He hesitates, and I know it's about to come. The request that I won't be able to say no to. "If taking a photo of me—"

A big wave of *don't fucking ask me* almost knocks me over. I interrupt him instantly.

"I'm taking more photos than ever, and I'm never going back to people again. Mugs don't complain. They don't have little mental breakdowns and ruin their mascara. They don't write reviews online."

"Did someone do that?" Googling me would never occur to him.

"Scathing" is all I can say. Apparently, I very much deserve those empty screw holes by the front door.

Unprofessional. Late. Hungover—possibly still drunk? Distracted. Poorly presented. Surly and rude to guests. Blurry. Badly framed. Ruined my memories. Contacting my lawyer.

Tom wisely tucks the impending request back in his pocket. He shouldn't risk getting his memories ruined, too. "Maybe if I'd gotten the studio done, you'd still be doing portraits."

He is now looking at the long, narrow building beyond the fishpond, against the fence line, that has had a lot of plans attached to it. It was once Grandpa William's carpentry hideout, and it still smells like cyprus pine. Loretta used to sit in there on a folding chair, drinking coffee and thinking about him. It was going to be my photography studio, and before that, Loretta's tarot room. One summer, Tom got as far as cladding the inside walls and putting down carpet before Aldo sent him on to his next job—then the next, and the next. An unfinished project would weigh heavily on Tom.

"Don't feel bad," I warn him, but I think I'm too late. "You've been busy. You are not the cause of my career change." I mean, technically yes, but he doesn't need to know that. I was already on a long downhill slide.

"If you'd called me, I would have come," he says with the barest hint of accusation. "You know I would."

"Don't worry about that. You're here right when I need you most. Like always."

Patty is standing on the edge of the slime-filled fishpond. One foreleg lifts. I pick her up and kiss her little dome head.

From the laundry window, Diana's aghast face is like the feline version of *The Scream*.

I tilt her up to me. "Patty, you've gotta stop flirting with danger."

"Says the girl living in a house with fire-hazard wiring." Tom gives me his notebook and begins unfolding a ladder. "I can't believe Loretta lived in this place. Why didn't she get me to renovate years ago?" He's getting mad. "She shouldn't have lived with these issues."

I have to laugh.

"She couldn't be bothered packing. She said, and I quote, *You can deal with it.*" I flip through the last few pages of his notes. I almost forgot his handwriting: square blocks, flat lines, and intriguing shorthand. Arrows up and down, measurements, estimates of cost. Page after page of bad news. "And she thought the issues were quirks. Which they are."

"You are so similar to your grandmother that it's scary." Tom hooks the ladder on the side of the house. "Please, just promise me you won't touch any of the outlets. Or tell my fortune."

"I know how to manage this house. I've lived in this house part-time for most of my life, remember? Every single ski season." My parents are obsessed with sliding down snowy hills in matching padded onesies. I wonder what it's like.

"Did you used to hate me?" He took my place on those ski trips. I stayed with Loretta, took photos until I lost the light, and read books by the fire, my hand in a candy bowl. Lovely, but it was no black-diamond run.

I shake my head. "No, I was glad you went."

I'm glad you all got to live a little, unencumbered by my shortcomings.

"Glad for me because I was poor," Tom says in a wry voice. He looks up the ladder and puts a foot on the bottom rung. "Glad that your parents are incredibly generous and took me everywhere."

"No, glad for you because staying behind sucked, and I wouldn't wish it on you."

I remember Loretta saying to me, *Wave goodbye for God's sake, they might all have a plane crash. You'll regret it if you don't.* That kind of statement is even more startling when said by a fortune-teller. *Smile and let them enjoy themselves.*

The only translation I could possibly make from that was: Who could relax around me, the ticking time bomb?

"I'm glad you all got a vacation from stressing out about me."

"We weren't vacationing from you," Tom says, surprised. He begins climbing up the ladder. "Loretta let you believe some things that weren't true."

For one sharp moment I feel like he knows that I confided in Loretta and she got me the hell out of town. But there's no way he could. I've never told a soul. His eyes are mild and have no bad memories in them when he looks down at me.

"If you need anything switched on or off inside, ask me. I hid your hair dryer."

"That just means you put it up somewhere high, out of my

eye line? Your hiding skills are terrible." I watch his butt as he climbs higher. "What are you doing up there, anyway?"

"Just looking at the gutters back here."

"Me too." I grin breezily up at him as he glowers back down at me. "What? I'm interested in the state of my house."

There's a loose rattling noise. Tom shakes the entire gutter about a foot away from the roofline. Slimy leaves splatter down onto me. Patty and I both yap like seals.

"You asshole."

"You deserved that, you deviant." He rattles the gutter again.

"Get your mind out of the gutter."

"Do you want to climb up this ladder while I stand down there looking at your butt? See how it feels?" Busted again. If he registers every time my eyes are on him, I'm doomed.

"I've got nothing on you, babe."

"You sure did hide in the shower a long time. Didn't know the water heater could handle that." Tom's hand goes to his back pocket and he pulls out a screwdriver.

"That water heater is a tin can. It was freezing by the end." I just let it go cold, numbing me down to the bones, cooling the strange restless energy inside me to manageable levels. I've never actually taken a cold shower over a guy before.

He looks across at the neighbor's roof, and in his profile, I see him swallow. In his mind, he thinks, *Ew, gross.* Darcy Barrett, a shivering drowned rat, boy hair flattened to her skull.

He hoists himself a little higher onto the edge of the roof.

There's a tile-scraping sound and the ladder trembles. I leap on the base of the ladder and wrap my entire body around it. "Fuck! Be careful." Another wet leaf plops down on my face.

"It's fine," he says, treading down the rungs. He doesn't turn, but instead spends a lot of time pulling the ladder down, folding and refolding it. I'm glad. I can hide my sudden heart jolt.

"I thought I was going to have to catch you then." I move to the fishpond, my back to him. My heart has jumped up into my throat. I swallow again and again, but it won't budge. Blood begins sliding the wrong way in my veins.

My heart says, *Oh hey, did you just have a little fright? Cool, I'm going to make a big deal out of it.* And now we're pumpin'. Palpitations, pixelation, it's all cranking into gear.

Quick, think about something else.

Aside from my heart situation, a worse pattern keeps repeating. I tease him like always, he calls me on it, and I remember Megan. I crush myself down inside like an empty beer can. Then I look at him and that joyful feeling expands, and the cycle happens again.

I know what the solution to this problem is, and it involves a cab to the airport.

"I bet you would catch me. You'd just . . ." He holds his arms up to the sky. "Get squashed flat. Hey." He's noticed my stillness. "What's happening?"

"Nothing," I say on a slow exhale. My heart is climbing up out of my body, fluttering and struggling in the base of my neck.

Tom's hands are on my body. "Your little spool of thread,"

he says with deep empathy. "Aw, it's rattling around in there, isn't it?"

"Stop it. Don't fuss." I tug away but he steps with me. "It will stop if I can just take my mind off it. Your hands are making it worse."

He drops them like he's been scalded.

He smells like he always has: a blown-out birthday candle, sharp and smoky. It's that smell in your nostrils when closing your eyes and making an impossible wish, and your mouth is watering for something sweet.

"Breathe," he says, encouraging me just like Jamie would. When I give myself one glance up at his beautiful face, the stark look in his eyes reminds me of why I stayed behind at the airport as a child. I am stress. Fear. Uncertainty.

I am a liability.

I make myself fake a big breath out. "Don't worry. It's nothing a little time on a beach somewhere can't fix."

He eases away and the chilling air fills the space between us. I step completely out of his reach and then put the fishpond between us. I pat my chest like I'm burping a baby. If I do it firmly enough, I can't feel the individual off-kilter beats.

Tom is a little wretched. "I'm sorry about what I said before. You know that, right? You're not a liability. This is your house, and you have every right to work on it." He turns back to his notes, but he's looking at them without seeing. "But I don't think you should travel. You're clearly not okay."

"I've been like this for years. Don't," I warn, and he sighs heavily.

"So, my ladder wobbles and you can throw yourself on it like it's a grenade, but you turn into a wax statue and I'm supposed to, what? Just ignore it?" You know he's getting close to the end of his tether when his hand is on his hip. "You've got a set of rules that I can't agree to."

"I've had a lifetime of fussing." I put my hand up to grip my plait and my hand finds nothing but air. It's a good reminder. I'm a new person now. "Just worry about this house."

"I'm worried about you," he says in a *cut the shit* voice. "Tell me what's really going on with you. I have never seen so many empty wine bottles in my life." He jerks a thumb at the recycling bin at the side of the house. "You are not doing well."

"Don't start," I begin, but he silences me.

"You're drinking when I know you shouldn't. Your medication's so old it's expired, did you realize that? You're working somewhere where guys grab you. Bruise you. Drive past all night."

"It's not like that—"

"Your fridge is empty. You're not taking real photos," he says in a tone like it's a tragedy. "And you're trying to keep me at arm's length, as usual, by doing that thing you do."

"What do I do?"

"You know exactly what you do. You mess around with me."

"Well, what is it like being messed with by me?" I can't stop looking at how his short, neat fingernails are pressing into the cotton at his hip. I'm sweating now. I need to press my sleeve to my brow, but he'll see.

"Being messed with by Darcy Barrett?" He considers the question. "It sounds like she's joking with me, but it feels like she's telling the truth. And I never know which is right."

Whoa. He really has my number. "You're a smart guy, you'll work it out."

He puts a hand into his hair. That bicep. Those lines. He's art. "See, you're doing it again. It's your technique to put me off track, so you won't have to actually answer me."

He turns back to the house like he's looking for its moral support. Patty obliges, running to him and standing up on his shin. He looks down at her. "I'm just a chew toy, Patty. Aunt Darcy likes hearing me squeak."

"If I were Megan, I'd punch me in the face." I ball up my fist and give myself a soft uppercut. "I'm really sorry. I don't know what comes over me. If it's any consolation, I don't do it to anyone else. You're . . . special."

"Really?" His eyes have a new light in them when he looks back at me. It gives me a bad little flashback to Keith. Tom's heart is the Rock of Gibraltar, but I shouldn't risk it.

"You shouldn't like hearing that," I remind him. "Face-punching, remember?"

"She wouldn't care." It's the same phrase he used before, when I asked about his tent. He's trying to tell me something about her, and I don't know if I want to hear it. She's clearly as cool as her ice-white diamond. She's secure in herself, and she has the most trustworthy man alive.

He confirms it. "We're not like that."

"No jury on earth would convict her." I seem to be using

my messing-with-you voice. Sounds like joking but I'm serious. "If I bagged and tagged a beauty like you, I'd turn vicious. I bet she's the same."

He laughs and it's not a happy sound. "I guess it's redundant to point out that you're already pretty vicious." A pause, then he says awkwardly, "She's not like you at all."

"That much is obvious." I run a hand up and down my inferior face and body, and he's confused. "Well, I won't push my luck with her. Like I said, I'm going to find someone new to torment. You're off the hook. Pity my doomed future husband."

I think about Loretta's ring again and hold up my left hand to study my bare fingers.

He snorts in disbelief. "You'd never get married."

"I would." I hide the little paper cut his incredulous tone gives me. "Why the hell wouldn't I? Am I too much to take on?" I drag both hands through my hair so it's up and pointy. I hope it's horns.

"I just never pictured it." He sighs and the shape of his body droops as he looks up at the house, like a switch has been flipped off inside him. I take a few cautious steps toward him. He's sad?

I can't imagine what kind of bad news he's heard today. "What did the electrician and plumber say?"

"What do you think they said?" He's desolate. "They would be the most expensive jobs of their careers. It's a tear-down. Most of the pipes need replacing. New waterproofing. Then new tiles. Then new wiring. New everything. I cannot name one thing so far that doesn't need replacing."

"Will Loretta's budget cover it?"

He stalls. That means, *Probably not.* "I'm going to put every-thing into a spreadsheet for you guys."

"Unspeakably expensive then. So expensive that formulas and cells are involved. And it'll all be spent on chrome and gray paint. Jamie will get his way. You know he will. You're his."

Tom gives me a wry look. "He's way out of my league."

"One hundred percent his." I tap his pinky fingernail. "Jamie would maybe let me have that much of you."

He shrugs. "He's not here now. I hereby gift you this." He holds out his other hand and I realize he means his other pinky fingernail. I now have two. I'm absurdly pleased.

"I'll treasure them always." We go inside together, collect-ing Patty along the way.

"What do I get in return?"

"You know, heart, soul. The usual."

"Oh, Darce." He sighs like I've learned nothing. "You're messing with me again."

Chapter 8

I inexplicably wish for Jamie. He'd walk in and fill this expanding awkward silence with talking, jokes, and insults. I feel like I'm fast-tracking a total implosion of my relationship with Tom. When it happens, I'll have lost another person.

Loretta, my parents, Jamie, Tom, Truly. How many more special people do I have left? I itch to walk out. No one can leave me if I've left first. This disturbing thought knocks a little air out of my lungs. Loretta died when I was suspended over an ocean in an aisle seat. Maybe my strategy sucks.

Maybe I should be holding on to people I love with white-knuckled intensity.

Tom checks his phone. "Are you going to be here tomorrow afternoon? The power's going to be off for a bit."

"Not sure." I consult the calendar on the fridge. It's been refreshing to go analog. "I'm helping Truly do some sewing late in the afternoon."

"So you're sewing tomorrow? Not losing your temper and hightailing it to the airport?" Tom sounds so hopeful that it puts a little crack in my hard old heart.

"Am I that impulsive?"

"You are the most impulsive person I know."

What did he say before? He likes making me happy. Let me try it.

"No, I still can't find my passport." It doesn't ease that tension in him. I try again. "I'll stay a little longer." It was the right thing to say. I can't handle it when he looks at me like this. Right now, in this moment, the rest of the world fades away. We're suspended in a golden, fragile bubble. Pleasure is glowing in his eyes, candle-bright.

He clears his throat and now I'm his client again. "I really think I need you to stay until we've all agreed on how this place should look."

I nod. "I'll start packing the house tomorrow morning. Maybe I can get some of the guys at work to help move the furniture."

Now I've altered the ions in the air. He looks at my bruised wrist and says in a bass snarl, "Are you kidding me?"

"Most of them are fine."

"Would you dig a grave for me?" He repeats my earlier joke without humor.

"You know I would." I go into my bedroom and tap a few of my chalky pills onto my palm. They have indeed expired. I'm sure it's better than nothing. "I'll dig it real slow so I don't aggravate my crappy old heart."

Behind me, Tom is still vibrating. "I'm moving the furniture."

"Well, you clearly feel very passionate about it, so go ahead."

He's in the doorway now, leaning on the door frame, watching me sort through my wardrobe. "Where are you going?"

"Up the ladder. I'm going to go sit on the roof for a bit." I pull a short dress out and shake the wrinkles out of it. My little smart-ass quip has him relaxing a little.

"It'll be cold up there."

"Of course that's your first thought." I circle my finger.

He twirls on the ball of his foot to face away. He knows this drill by now. "You were never very good at closing your bedroom door," he says, voice heavy with resignation. "Who's this guy, then?"

"What guy?" I quickly pull the dress on, tug on my boots, and treat myself to a few dots of the perfume oil Loretta made me. She didn't use recipes, so it's irreplaceable. A label on the base of the bottle, in her handwriting, reads: LIQUID DYNAMITE.

"Who's the guy you're putting perfume on for?" He rotates to face me again. He hasn't fully shape-shifted back into human form yet.

"I'm putting it on for myself, not wasting it on male nostrils. He's no one," I say more forcefully when I see the frustration on his face.

"I'm trying to make conversation with you, about what's

going on in your life. Who are you dating?" He sounds like he's reading from a script. At gunpoint. Did Jamie tell him to report back?

"Someone you wouldn't like, and I wouldn't call it dating," I reply flatly, and duck out of the room under his arm. "You can sleep in my bed again tonight. I'll take the couch when I get home. There's a Thai place that delivers, the menu's on the fridge. Say hi to Megan for me."

Behind me, his boots are following.

I grab my keys, bag, and jacket in fluid swings of my arms and keep on walking. There's no way I want to stay and marinate in this awkward tension. I'll flag down a cab from the main road near the convenience store. Out the door, up the path, he's behind me.

"You look like you're running away from home, Darce. Worried you're actually going to have to think about the wine bottles and your heart?"

If he keeps pressing me, I'm going to tell him what the problem is: Primarily, that I want to unzip his pants. Second problem, I'm the worst fucking person to be having these thoughts about an almost-married man.

Third: I'm so jealous of Megan I'm going to rev the engine of a combine harvester and convert her into a bag of bloody grain.

But these have always been my problems.

"I think you should stop following me." I turn and walk backward. "Unless you want to come out. That might be too much fun. That might actually classify as living life."

Valeska badly wants me back behind the picket fence where nothing bad can happen to me. I can see it in him— the strain of his body, the hands folded at his sides. Guard and drag, that's what he wants to do.

"I have to start early. Darce, please stay in tonight."

No way am I going to indulge myself in his overprotective Princess Mode. It's too succulent, too lovely. I can't be under the same roof as him alone. "Nope."

"I promised everyone I'd look after you," he tries again, before realizing what he's done. Saying that will only make me walk faster.

"I can't," I call back to him. "I don't trust myself anymore."

I turn as his jaw drops, and now it's just the sound of my boots. I don't have to look back to know he watches until I'm out of sight.

It's what he does.

* * *

Tom is writing *JAMIE SPORTS* onto a box of my brother's sports gear. We are attempting the impossible: emptying his room. "So, how was your night? You must have come in pretty late."

"Barely midnight. I guess that's pretty late for an early bird like you."

"Did you have a good time?" He's quite formal.

"Sure." Not even for a second did I have a good time. I didn't see Vince, or anyone I knew. I travel alone overseas, so I'm used to my own company. But something has changed.

I was desperate to get back home. I wanted to lie on the couch with a movie on, listening to Patty's claws clicking and Tom padding around. His fingers tousling my hair and the clink of a teaspoon in a mug. To quash this weird domestic fantasy, I sat in McDonald's and ate hot-fudge sundaes, then I got a cab home when I felt confident he was asleep. I'm a McCoward.

I need a new place to sleep tonight, Tom said as I was brushing my teeth this morning, and I'm glad my mouth was full of toothpaste. I might have reflexively replied, *No you don't.*

He has charitably erased that weird moment last night. He's good like that.

I try to do the same. "Jamie's sitting at his desk, poking away at a calculator. Witness me, officially working harder than him. He sure does like books about dudes being framed by the government." I'm stacking them into a box.

"Books with short chapters and briefcases of cash," Tom says, dragging crap out from under the bed. He's read plenty of Jamie's discarded books in his time.

"Women with glossy red lips. Speedboats in Monte Carlo." I pick up one with a revolver on the cover, and it flips open a little too easily to a dirty bit. I read it, leaning against the bed frame.

Tom looks up from stacking some dumbbells together. "Your hard work didn't last long."

I hold my finger up. There's a foaming, grunting climax and I wrinkle my nose. "And now Jamie and I have read the same sex scene. It's in both of our brains." I have a full-body shiver. "Why can't I stop disturbing myself?"

"No idea," Tom laughs. He takes the book, and to my surprise he reads the entire scene too, flipping over the page with a crease on his brow like he's studying for an exam.

I watch his eyes move side to side, sweaty words in his head.

My heart wrings itself out, gives me a new flush of blood, and I think I have pink cheeks. If I'm this scandalized just watching Tom read a sex scene, I'd better not let my brain take the logical next step.

Too late. Look at those big hands. Knuckles like walnuts and nice clean nails. They're the kind of hands that you want all over. And now I'm picturing the huge upward push of his body, locking himself into me, 100 percent deep—

He snaps the book shut and snaps me out of my reverie.

"Well, that was remarkably straightforward." He tosses the book in the box, his eyes giving me no clues. Is that scene a reasonable proposition to him?

"The guys in these books are drilling for iron ore."

Tom laughs. "And the ones written in the seventies always mention a *brassiere*. I was at least seventeen when I realized that was just a bra."

"You were quite a naïve boy. There are always puckered peaks and nests of curls," I grunt, lifting a second half-empty box up. "And the women all orgasm after eight hard thrusts. *Oh, Richard!* Give me a break." I write on the box: *JAMIE'S FUCK BOOKS.*

Tom takes the marker and crosses out the middle word. "I seem to recall that Loretta liked her books on the spicy side."

I snort. "While you guys were off being wholesome and skiing, I was here, warping my brain on her soft-core porn novels. Explains a lot, huh. I'm the person most likely to have a thousand dollars' worth of sex toys in her dining room."

"I peeked in her books occasionally," Tom confesses, the corner of his mouth curling.

"You didn't." I laugh in delight. "Well, good for you, Tom Valeska, you dirty kid."

"When Jamie was in the bathroom or Loretta was making sandwiches, I'd just read a paragraph. I got my sex education right in this house." He's stacking junk into a new box. "A bit disjointed, but I eventually pieced it all together. It did give me some . . . unrealistic expectations."

I want to know what he means very badly, but I just say, "You and me both, buddy."

I write a lot of checks that my body cannot cash. A heart like mine doesn't let me get too vigorous, and the guys I choose have no idea. I write on the second box of books: *JAMIE'S TWISTED FANTASIES*. I hoist the box onto my hip and the edge of the box snags my nipple piercing. I grab my boob and howl.

"Are you okay?" Oh dear, he thinks I'm having a heart attack.

"It's the piercing. No matter how much time passes, it likes to remind me that it's there. I'm pretty sure it's hot-wired straight to my brain." I watch Tom process this information.

I can't tell if he's repulsed. "It's a pain you feel in the roots of your teeth."

Faint, he says, "Why get it?"

"It's pretty."

Tom plucks the box out of my grip with uncharacteristic violence. He walks out to the garage with me trailing him. "There's no point in wrecking yourself. You've packed most of these. Not even Jamie could accuse you of not putting in effort today."

I walk back into the house for the other box.

"I'm taking it. I'm-taking-it." I do a quick systems check. Heart's rock-solid. Everything's fine. Except Tom's parked his muscles in the doorway. "Move it."

He takes the box. "Yeah, yeah. I'd rather you be mad than unconscious." Off he goes.

In defeat, I fill a box with Jamie's shoes. "Maybe I can handle a box of fucking shoes," I say to Diana, who has jumped up on the windowsill. I bet she has big plans to sleep on Tom's bed. "Live the dream, girl."

I don't bother packing these carefully; Jamie would have a whole new wardrobe of shoes by now. When he left, it was with one suitcase. That's how fast he had to leave before he committed homicide.

Tom returns. "Thanks for letting me use your room. I don't think I've slept so well in years. Your mattress is . . ." He can't even think of a word. I know what he means.

"If I marry anyone, it will be that bed. It's why I sleep so much." I'm getting more wiped out by life. When I travel,

I have to lie down in the afternoons. Together, we flip the generic mattress on Jamie's old bed, and we make the bed with fresh flowered sheets. "When I travel, I miss my bed more than most people I know."

"You must love traveling to leave a bed like that."

"As hard as it is for you to believe, yeah. I do. I swear, if Jamie took my passport I am never going to forgive him."

"Sure you would," Tom says tentatively. He's got a rawness in his expression. "You're exaggerating, aren't you?"

"Anyone who knows me, knows that that would be the worst thing to do to me. I hate being forced to stay." I wish my brother would stop intruding on my limited time with Tom. "Are you even going to fit on this little bed?" Jamie didn't get a lot of action when living here; hence the books.

"I'm sure I will. Don't forget, I'll be out in my tent when the renovation starts," Tom says after a beat. "Hey, what's this?" He's pulling out a large canvas from under the bed, and we lean it against the wall. It's my Rosburgh Portrait Prize–winning portrait. Of who else but my brother.

"He really worked the room like a celebrity that night," I say as we stare at Jamie. He stares back at us.

Objectively, it's a phenomenal image. I clicked the camera, but I didn't do it alone. That's just the way Jamie's face interacts with light. That night of the award, he was drunk on his own beauty and cleverness. And champagne, naturally. I felt like he'd won the prize, not me. I had to give short interviews as the youngest award winner and watch Tom fading into the sidelines, Megan hooked onto his arm.

"He slept with two different cocktail waitresses that night. Two." Tom is dumbfounded, like it is scientifically impossible. It occurs to me that Megan is his one and only. The combine harvester keys are in my hand, so I begin to babble.

"Well, if you insist on carrying the boxes, you could move those five, and the room's basically done. Jamie won't believe I helped, probably. Maybe I should soak a handkerchief in sweat and he can get it verified by a lab."

"You're obsessed with proving you can work harder than him. It's just a permanent battle with no ending." Tom regards the portrait with an expression I cannot read. "You two are so tough on each other. Why don't you try being friends? When you are, it's amazing." He grins at a memory.

"I have to prove myself. Every time I call someone out of the blue, they've got this tremor in their voice. *Hello?* Like they're imagining me making an emergency call with my blue half-dead hand. That's why I like guys like Vince. They don't treat me like an invalid."

"Vince," Tom says, seizing on a name at last. He turns it over in his mind like one of Loretta's tarot cards. "Vince. Not Vince Haberfield from high school."

"Yeah, Vince Haberfield. He either doesn't know about my heart, or he forgot, so when we hang it's not this huge deal." I don't really care for Tom's expression so I go into the kitchen and unearth a takeout menu. "Should I order a pizza for you before I go over to Truly's? Silly question. Of course I should."

He's now sitting on his new bed. "You're with Vince Haberfield? How'd that little piece of shit turn out?"

"He's still a piece of shit. And I'm not with him." I hold out my hand until he realizes what I want; he gives me his phone. I order a pizza I know he'll like and hand the phone back. "Say something."

He's just sitting there. I don't know what he's processing, but it seems like a lot. I pat him on the shoulder. "I can see you're not exactly overjoyed. Bad news to report to Jamie, huh?"

"I'm not reporting anything." He says that with a tight jaw. But he's still himself. I don't get that hint of wolf that I thought I might when we look into each other's eyes.

"Hey, don't judge. Dating is an absolute nightmare. Be glad you don't have to worry about it."

"I thought you weren't dating him." He's got me there. "Well, I have to worry about it now." He rubs his hand on his face.

"You are not looking after me," I tell him in my most firm voice. "No matter how much you want to, I'm not yours to look after."

I watch as something like a wordless protest twists up out of him, and he's groaning and putting his face in his hands. He's miserable. I'm breaking his brain just being in this house.

Time for me to get out of here. One wrong move and he'll be jamming his stuff back into his suitcase like Jamie did.

"I'm going to Truly's now for a while. Save me some pizza."

I don't need to change my dusty clothes. Keys, wallet, shoes, I'm out the door. I am the queen of the instant exit. I'm practically jumping out a dog door. "Bye."

"Wait," Tom calls from back in the house, surprise in his tone.

Patty slips out behind me. "Hey, come back!" I chase her up to the pavement and scoop her up. "Naughty."

There's a car approaching, and it's not a pizza delivery car. That'd be one instant miracle pizza. It's a noisy, black car. I know this car. I set a sprint record running back to the front door, my blood whooshing in my ears, and stuff Patty into Tom's open hands. "Bye."

The black car stops at the top of the drive, blocking my car in, and the ignition is turned off. The driver's door opens.

Vince has either perfect timing, or the worst timing of all time.

Chapter 9

Moments like these make me certain that Loretta is lying facedown on a cloud, stuffing popcorn into her mouth, nudging Vince's car a little faster down Marlin Street. Two minutes later, I'd be gone, and Vince would be just cruising past.

Vince rounds the hood of the car, sees me and Tom, and stumbles a little in surprise before recovering. He sits on the hood of his car. Speak of the devil.

"You still have no phone." That's Vince's way of saying: *I haven't seen you for a while, I wanted to see you, and this is tough on my ego.*

I've got new eyes now, looking at him. Tom's straightforward gorgeousness has spoiled me for my usual type. Vince is whipcord lean, pale and dark haired, dressed in head-to-toe black. Tattoos galore. Dark circles and an air of tortured artist. He cups his hands around a cigarette, there's a flick, and now he's exhaling plumes of gray.

"Thought I'd drop by." Vince clearly hates these sorts of moments where he's got to justify his actions or give a shit. I've never required it from him. Another drag, and his blue eyes look anywhere but at me. "But you've still got company. Tom Valeska, right? Haven't seen you for years, man. How's it going? Cute dog."

"Just great," Tom says on a half laugh, Patty straddling his forearm. She's got a toadlike expression. Cigarettes make her sneeze. "I'm fantastic."

"And I'm fine," I aim sarcastically at Vince. He just grins at me, looking at my body in my clothes.

"No argument here." Vince narrows his eyes at Tom's face, assessing him. "Are you here to start on the house?"

"Yep," Tom says.

"About time. What a dump. And you're staying here?" Vince is looking at the truck, and thinking about what opportunities may be impacted by this.

Tom would cross his arms if he weren't holding a Chihuahua. "I'll be here. Every day for the next three months. She's working on it with me."

Vince mulls this over. "Heard you were out looking for me last night. Lenny sent me a text, said he saw you at Sully's." He jingles his key ring at me. "Let's go out."

"I wasn't looking for you. I've got other plans tonight. Beat it, shithead." I point at the road.

"Wow. Way to make me feel used and abused." Vince adds with a sly smile to Tom, "She only wants me for one thing." He's technically correct. Tom raises his eyes to the sky like he's praying for strength. At this rate, I'm going to have to dig a small, thin grave.

For the last few years, Vince and I have used each other repeatedly in the little gaps of time when I arrive back in town. I don't even bother telling him when I leave, because who cares? Not him.

Sex with Vince is like going to the gym; I feel slightly better after having done it as the sweat cools on my body, but I make a lot of excuses to myself as to why I shouldn't go.

Tom's dealt with enough of my boys to know that the best response is to be infuriatingly polite. "Where are you working these days, Vince?" You'd never guess he called him a little piece of shit two minutes ago. Butter wouldn't melt in that perfect mouth.

Vince looks sideways at the decal on Tom's truck. "I'm between gigs at the moment. I'm trying to get Darcy to hook me up with a job at the bar, but she's holding out on me. I could get into construction, though." A lingering, job-offer-sized pause is left here.

I shake my head. "Like I'm going to babysit your ass at the bar. You can work there when I leave."

Tom stares at Vince. "And what do you think of the fact she's come home with a bruise from working there? From a guy?"

Vince looks me all over but can't see anything amiss. "She handles herself. I bet she fucked him up." He falters under Tom's eyes and adds awkwardly, "Are you okay though, Darce?"

"Fine. And you're correct. I can handle myself." I like how

Vince sees me. Unquestionably tough and with no need of saving.

"Who did it?" Vince is more curious than outraged.

I huff. "Keith. The big dumb dipshit."

"Shiiiit." Vince whistles. "He's got a thing for you, you know. Pretty obvious. The boys all laugh about it."

"Well, you could have given me a heads-up. Did a barrel of Viagra roll into the water supply? Because last time I checked, I wasn't irresistible."

I scuff my boot around in the gravel. I'm still embarrassed every time I think about how I'd joke around with no thought of keeping my guard up.

"He was trying to tell me something I didn't want to hear. He grabbed my arm to make me listen. That's all it was. It wasn't some violent thing. It was an annoying thing." I'm telling all of this to Tom.

"It was a grabbing-someone-at-work thing. A bruise thing. Absolutely not okay." Tom's eyes are Valeska orange. In my black and white world, it's the only color. For one deep throbbing instant, I want to be in his arms, those big hands cradling my head. No one could put a bruise on me.

"You don't want to take him on, man," Vince advises Tom. "That guy is huge." He's noticed Tom's expression and looks away with a grin, half obscured by smoke. "Well, you might do all right. You've been hitting the gym."

"Nope."

"This here is a hard-work body," I tell Vince. I'm starting

to get annoyed at him and his light, snarky, sexy banter. A conversation with Vince is like trying to thread a live worm onto a hook.

Then I realize something, and it's enough to stop my heart. Vince is the same as me. How does Tom even deal with me? Oh shit. I've got a type all right: It's me. His tongue stud winks in the dusk light. My variation winks back from the dark cup of my bra. We're so similar we could be twins.

"I'm serious, I've got to leave." I unlock my car. "You're blocking me in."

"She sure is good at leaving, huh?" Tom says to Vince in an unexpected moment of kinship.

"She's a pro. So what else is up, man? I heard you're marrying that hot brunette. Congrats."

Vince heard about it during one of my drunk sad Sully's booze fests. I didn't think he was properly listening. Who knows what I said.

I'm starting to get a hot, embarrassed face. My key ring is being an asshole, every key twisted and caught on the next. I'm shaking them in fury and I cannot bear to hear even one piece of wedding news.

Tom's voice cuts through everything. "No, we broke up."

I turn on the point of my boot and frown at them both. He never lies. Why would he feel the need to?

"Oh. Sorry." This seems like bad news to Vince. He looks between me and Tom, sizing things up, and then decides something. He detaches his butt from his car, treads on his cigarette butt, and saunters over in boots that are very similar to mine.

He puts a hand around my waist. In a nauseating nicotine exhalation he whispers, "You're a bit irresistible. Come over later. I'm gonna fuck you so good." His bottom lip brushes my earlobe.

I hope Tom doesn't have good hearing.

Vince has told me far worse, and with much more detail, but I recoil and push him away. "Pass."

A pizza delivery car pulls up against the curb. "I'll get it," Tom says shortly, digging in his pocket for his wallet, Patty deposited into the violets.

"Aw, come on. Let me convince you." Vince likes when I'm a challenge. He's just another one of those bar guys, being treated like dirt and loving it. If I went all soft and mushy with Vince, I guarantee I'd never see him again.

"See you later, Darce," Tom says, walking inside with his pizza. Patty follows him, her nose turned up like a snob. I brace for the door slam, but he closes it quietly.

"Don't come driving around here," I say to Vince with a threat in my voice. "It pisses him off."

Vince nods and puts a piece of gum in his mouth. "I remember him from high school, and what he was like around you. Got a little pushy with me once." Vince seems to have surprised himself. He looks at me with a new expression. "Hey, we've known each other a long time."

"No, you've got it wrong. Jamie was the pushy type."

"Nope, definitely Tom. Watch out he doesn't fall back in love with you," Vince says in a voice that sounds like he's joking. Words that sound serious. "You'd wreck a guy like that when you leave. See ya."

Before I say anything, he's getting into the car and revving the engine unnecessarily. He reverses without checking his mirror, swings back in a showy loop, and screams off. I stand there for a long moment, trying to settle myself.

How did I not notice that I have been casually screwing my male doppelgänger? Does the whole thing count as a weird kind of masturbation?

Something about the soft sound of the front door closing bothers me. I bet he thought I'd cave in, forget Truly, and get in Vince's car. I've gotten into countless black cars. He stays home. It's what we do. If leaving were a sport, I'd be a Hall of Famer.

Back in love.

Back in love with you. Was I blind? Even dumbass Vince knew it?

My key slides into the front door like Loretta's hand is steadying mine. I walk through the house with no thought in my head except that I need to find Tom and tell him that I'm going to do better. Be better. I'm cutting the shit.

This house feels like a tuning fork. There's no sound, but there's vibration in here now, a deep bass line that I feel in my stomach. Tom is standing in the kitchen with his back to me, a hand on each side of the old, deep sink. My personal life is clearly sickening.

"Sorry about that," I say, and he jumps in surprise, hitting his head on the cupboard above him with a crack. He howls in pain.

"Shit. Sorry, sorry." I run to him and pull his head down. I rub my hand on the top of his head. "Oh, poor Tom. I'm sorry, I'm sorry. I didn't mean it, I was careless." The words run together and I'm not talking about his head now. It's a relief to be able to say it.

"Normally I can hear you walking a mile away." Tom rolls his shoulders, agony in his voice, and when he straightens back up to his full height my hand slips to his shoulder. "Don't sneak up like that."

He's leaning back on the sink now, and I'm leaning on him. He doesn't seem to notice, lost in his private world of pain, his hand on his head. I try to push free, but his other hand tightens on my waist.

From this new perspective, I'm looking up at the curve of his throat and the heavy slab of his bicep. White perfect teeth biting into his bottom lip. Pain looks so much like pleasure. How can he be elegant despite his brute bulk? Michelangelo would be hollering for a fresh block of marble.

Me? I want my camera. And that's something I haven't wanted in a long, long time.

If this were my regular view, and I could stand between his knees whenever I wanted, I'd be a permanent fixture. What the fuck is wrong with Megan? A big throb of frustration goes through me. She's making the same mistake I did. She doesn't know what kind of heart she has. I wonder if I should try to explain it to her, somehow. And how would I do that without seeming like a psycho?

I feel the exact moment that his pain recedes and he realizes that our bodies are together. He'd step back, but he's got nowhere to go. I'd step back, but his hand curls into a squeeze.

I've sat shoulder to shoulder with this kid on car trips, but we've never been this close face-to-face. I can see everything now, the candy-crystal facets in his eyes and the brown-sugar stubble on his jaw. He's so delicious my throat aches.

The look he gives me makes me wonder if I'm in trouble. "I thought you were going out."

"I wanted to come back and say I'm sorry," I tell him, and I put my arms around his waist and hug. "You shut the door in a way that made me sad, and I wanted to tell you that I'm going to do better."

"Do better at what? How'd I shut the door?" His other arm wraps around my shoulders. He crosses his feet behind my heels, and now his entire body is hugging me. Warm, soft, hard. I thought my mattress was heaven, but that's before I laid myself on this person. How am I going to ever peel myself off?

I inhale his birthday-candle pheromones. I want to know what his goddamn bones smell like. Let me start down in his DNA structure and work my way back out.

I speak into his muscles. "You shut the door like you've just accepted that I don't come back. I'm going to start being like you. Completely, one hundred percent honest." I hover on the precipice and decide to try. "This is the best hug of my life."

His heart below my cheekbone is diligent and regular, and I need it to beat forever.

"Yeah, it's pretty good," he agrees, amused, and I can't see how I'm pulling my weight in this. He's the one doing all the work. I tighten my arms and press closer. That gold-bubble feeling expands around us again. I've never felt this with another man. I know what this is: joy. The weight of his arms is the only thing stopping me floating off the floor. I have to tip my face back to see if he feels it, too.

He smiles at the wonder he sees in my expression.

"Complete honesty from Darcy Barrett? I can't handle that. And I'm not as honest as you think I am." Some of his pleasure fades.

I pull back a fraction. "Why are you always trying to convince me that you're not perfect? To me, you are. Completely perfect. Believe me, I've undertaken a worldwide census. No one else measures up."

His hand slides up my back. "How could I possibly deserve Darcy Barrett's total honesty, as well as her blind faith? I'm not perfect. I don't know what I'll do when you realize that." He swallows and tries desperately to change the subject. "Oh hey, your new neck. I still can't get used to your hair."

On my nape, that warm hand clasps down, and I light up.

Hands on my skin are how I recharge. It's always been this way for me. Is it a twin thing? Is it because I slept in an incubator for a week? I don't know. It's a Darcy thing. To feel another human resting against me just clears out the crazy inside me, and Tom's leathery big palms are next level.

I know my eyes probably go black and crazy, but I press back into his palm and exhale a weird purr. His reaction is instant. I'm bumped away and my skin goes cold. He looks shocked, like I've just coughed up a furball.

"Sorry, sorry." I put my hand where his was and rub it vigorously. "That's my thing."

"Necks?" He says it faintly.

"I've got hungry skin. All I ever want is someone touching me." Do I have a phantom bruise against my stomach? Did his body give mine a low-down, hard press? Surely not. Look what I'm doing. Ruining a beautiful moment. "I'd better go to Truly's place now."

I flip open the pizza box and take out a slice. Pizza is an excellent recalibration tool. I bite, chew, and he says nothing. He's completely frozen.

"Say something," I say on a swallow. "Tell me I'm a freak and get it out of the way."

"Is that why you need Vince?" He tries to clear his throat but it's just a growl. "Your skin is hungry? What does that mean?"

I bite my pizza, holding his eyes. "He's better than nothing."

"How'd you get from Loretta's romance novels to 'better than nothing'?"

"While you've been with one person, living your best life, I've been getting disappointed a lot. And probably disappointing others, if I'm being truthful." It does help my ego that he looks like he doesn't believe me. "Vince isn't that bad."

Tom chooses his words carefully. "You want my opinion on your fuck buddy? I've got a sledgehammer in the truck. I'd be glad to show him how it works."

A spiky thrill unfurls inside me. "See. You always tell the truth. I'm going to do the same. How the fuck isn't Megan just hugging you permanently? You're one hell of a hugger." Her name aloud brings me back to the scene on the footpath. "Why'd you bother lying to Vince before?"

He knows exactly what I mean. "I didn't lie."

"Of course not. You never lie. Except . . . Megan. You haven't broken up." I pull apart the pizza crust with my fingers. "He's hardly going to feel threatened, or care, if you live here with me."

"We did. We broke up."

"Hilarious. Really funny. Quit fucking with me." I offer a corner of crust to Patty and dust my hands on my pants. I wait, and he doesn't say anything. He just stares at me. "But you're going to force me to be your wedding photographer. You'll ask, and I'll say yes. You'll both be sickeningly photogenic." I put a hand on my hip. I glare at him but he doesn't crack. Is he serious? "Exactly how long has my phone been in the toilet?"

"We broke up about four months ago. I told your family that I'd tell you in person."

"But it's just a break. You'll get her back."

"No," he says gently. "I won't."

"But you want her back. I'll help you." He just shakes his head. And I briefly lose my mind.

I dodge sideways toward the back door—I need air. I need sky and stars and cold; I need to sit on the rings of Saturn dangling my boots into the black universe to be alone, but he steps easily around me, and now I'm the one leaning on the sink.

"Stay here."

"Are you okay?" I want to grab him by the shoulders and check for physical damage. I'll crack open his chest to check how bad his heart looks.

"Me?" He thinks for a second. "Everyone just asks if she's okay."

"Yeah, because she's just lost *you*. Are you okay? Do I need to go and beat the shit out of her?"

I notice one of the cabinets above me is ajar. For something to do, I put a hand up to close it. When my fingers hook into the tiny handle, the web-thin hinge breaks. Now I'm standing here with a broken door in my hand. I lean it against my leg and try to look cool, but I'm practically auditioning for *SmackDown*.

Unwillingly, he laughs.

I am going to beat Megan with this door until she realizes what a fuckup she's made. He knows exactly what I'm thinking.

"You're always so vicious, DB." A smile quirks at the edge of his mouth as he looks at the damage I just inflicted. My viciousness thrills him. "How do you know it's not me that deserves the beating?" He takes the cupboard door from me. More to himself, he says, "This is going roughly how I thought it would."

"Is your heart broken?" I reach up and yank off the next cupboard door along with a satisfying crack. I hand it to him.

"It's . . . sore. Not broken." He looks up at the next cupboard door along. Something like *fuck it* crosses his mind, and he breaks off a door himself.

"Who ended it?" *Crack.* Another door gone.

"Well . . . I've been trying to work it out. After eight years, it was kind of a joint decision, like most things. I'm sorry. I know you really liked her. Actually, no. I never could tell if you liked her."

I pull off one of the lower cabinet doors and try to break it in half over my knee. I can't do anything else with this energy. He's single. The first time in eight years. And I need carpet burn on my knees and a wall against my back, and to lick the shower spray off him and feed him cold pizza in the middle of the night so he keeps up his strength.

Megan is a red stain behind my combine harvester, and that's the extent of my pity for her.

He tries to ease me with a hand on my shoulder. "Why are you doing this?"

"If I don't do this, I'll do something else." Something so deeply irreversible we won't be able to make eye contact when we pass each other in the nursing home hall. Fuck it. That complete honesty I pledged? Here it comes. Up my throat and out loud. One big terrifying blurt.

"Are you going to put your hands on me, or what?"

Chapter 10

Tom looks at his own hands, holding a cabinet door. He tries to compose a sentence for a long time. Finally, he manages, "Excuse me?"

"'Cause I swear, I need your hands more than I've ever needed anything."

I wipe my hand over the back of my mouth. Fuck it. He's a big boy, he can handle pizza breath. My body is taking over. Everything is boiling up out of me—years of stolen looks and tight T-shirts and that bone-deep certainty that the animal in him wants me, too.

How else could he always make me feel this way? Brighter, darker, hungrier? No one else has me standing in a cold shower or breaking down a kitchen with my bare hands. I want him crying with pleasure. I want to be the only one he can think of.

"Take your shirt off. Shoes off. I'll do the rest." Lust has broken my voice box; I'm raspy. I point at my bedroom door.

"Bed. Get in it." I'm looking at the solid square of his belt buckle.

"Are you out of your mind?" He's stunned.

When I reach for him like a creepy sex zombie, he steps away, almost cowering against the fridge—a huge man terrified of my outstretched fingertips. He reaches up and pulls down the broken retractable blind from the window and throws it on the floor between us, as if it could possibly keep me back.

"Darcy, are you joking?"

"Do I look like I'm joking?" I watch him swallow and his jaw tenses, the tendons like ribbons. I think I look like I'm a predator. "I'm not joking. I just told you, I'm telling the truth from now on. I want you, bad. I feel how much you want me. So show me what you got." My breath is puffing out of me, light and fast.

"DB, you have lost it. Quit messing with me."

Holly's right. I'm not romantic. I'll fix it later. "Tom Valeska, get in me."

He lets out a shaky breath and there's a light of fear in his eyes. I'm a scary bitch. He's a bashful sweetheart with pink cheeks. Valeska is nowhere in sight. The first moment of doubt hits me, and I narrow my eyes at his face. Seriously? I thought I'd have teeth on me by now. "Well?"

He pushes at his belt buckle like it's uncomfortable. "I'm sorry you've had a shock. I should have told you as soon as I arrived."

He turns his waist away and I'm certain. He's got an iron

erection, and it's for me. I'm having it, pressing in an inch at a time until I can't even blink. This house can go to hell.

The look in my eyes makes his breath crack in his lungs. I don't need a mirror to know I must look fucking intense.

I'll give him a second to compose himself. "Why didn't you? Jesus, Tom. I've been making a complete ass of myself. How many times did I bring her up, and you said nothing?" I go to the pantry door. The big fucker. It's all I can do.

Crack. Tom catches it before I'm flattened underneath.

"A lot of times." His face is pained as he puts it on our growing pile of debris. "You're a lot harder to lie to than I thought." He looks at my bedroom door again and shakes his head slightly, like he has water in his ear. "Did you just tell me to—" He can't finish.

"You tell the truth to Vince, but not me?"

"I lost my temper," he says without humor. Out there, he was his usual perfect self. I'd dismiss him as cold, but when he looks back to me, he's glittering darker now. Hungrier. There's a magnet dragging us together. Finally.

"Says the guy with a sledgehammer in his car." I shake my head and pull all the knobs off the broken oven and toss them at his feet. "You are my one straightforward person, you know that? You are the one person who tells the truth. And you've been lying to me since you arrived. Why?"

"I thought it would be better this way. If I told you after the renovation." He says it like it's reasonable.

"And why's that?" A little voice inside my head whispers, *Oh no.*

"Because of this." He gestures around the room, his eyes catching on my mouth. I lick my lip and think about the syrup I drank. He's not walking out of here alive.

Then he brings me back to reality, in the sweetest, kindest Tom way possible.

"I thought it would be safer if I didn't tell you until the house was done. I thought this might happen." As if he can't help himself, he reflexively looks at my bedroom door. "And it won't happen." His chest rises and falls.

His eyes are profoundly disturbed. He won't be getting in my bed, because he doesn't think about me like that. At all. And I've just showed my entire poker hand to him. This is like my asking to buy Loretta's ring from Jamie in the parking lot, one minute after he inherited it. Why don't I ever try to strategize? Everything just erupts out of my volcano mouth.

He says, "I thought it would be safer to lie."

Hot red blood is filling my body, rising up my torso, my neck, to the roots of my hair. Humiliation is dissolving my skeleton. "Safer." My voice sounds very far away to me. "Safer?"

My parents would probably understand the reason for his sweet white lie; Jamie definitely does.

"I need to focus on the house," he says, very reasonably. "I've never run a business before single-handed." He's got a sweat sheen on his skin and he's still struggling to catch his breath. "I've known you since you were melting Barbies with a lighter. You're Jamie's sister. I promised your parents that I'd look after you."

And just like that, I understand. Life's all about finding buffers.

Megan was a buffer because it's been clear for years that the moment she was gone, I'd pounce. Christ, I didn't last one minute. I have no game. For a habitual liar, I seem to slip up at the crucial moments.

He has his first job for his own company and doesn't want me smooching around like Pepé Le Pew. I'm the client. I'm his best friend's sister. I'm Mr. and Mrs. Barrett's weak-hearted daughter. I'm the liability he swore to take care of.

I'm a kitchen-trashing psychopath who is going to tear his clothes off his body and kiss him down to his bones. And I need to get a grip.

I make myself laugh and nod. "Okay. Fair enough. That's probably smart, actually."

I somehow walk to the front door on my trembling legs and the cool evening air floods in. I will find the nearest ocean and walk in, all the way down to Atlantis, and inquire about real estate. "Next time I see you, you can't make me feel shitty about this. Pretend it didn't happen. But you know what? I thought you had more guts."

* * *

I GO TO a liquor store, buy something cheapy sticky sweet, and then go to Truly's house. She opens the door and blinks owlishly out into the night.

"I need to lie on your couch for a bit," I tell her, toeing off my boots. "I just did something unforgivable."

"Okay," she says without hesitation, like the excellent friend she is. We've been lying on each other's couches since high school. I will lie on her couch until the day I die.

Except lying on her couch is not an option, as it turns out. It's stacked with underwear. Truly seems to have hardly registered my arrival; she goes back to her sewing machine, illuminated by a bright overhead lamp, and the whirring resumes.

Truly Nicholson is the queen of a cult indie underwear label called Underswears, and no, her name is not a nickname. Well, it was initially. She was called Truly in utero when she finally made her appearance on an ultrasound screen. That little baby was *truly a miracle.*

I assess her bent-over back. "Finish up now. I think you've done enough." I doubt she's eaten anything in hours—possibly days—worrying about grease on her fingers. Crumbs, stains, and drips are her mortal enemies. "Truly, I need to tell you about a totally insane thing I just did."

Wheeeee. The sewing machine rolls about two inches of tiny stitches. There's clicking, and then, *wheeee.*

Robotically, Truly lifts the machine foot, repositions, depresses the foot, and then, *wheee.* Her eyes are completely blank. I'm pretty sure she's already forgotten I'm here. When I see she's finished sewing the current pair, I turn the lamp off from above her.

The terrible enchantment is broken. She slumps down onto her forearms while I find some chocolate-flavored milk that hasn't expired. I pull piles of laundry off a little-used armchair, deposit her on it, and hold the straw up to her mouth.

"A little dramatic," she whispers, hoarse, and her pale green eyes roll over to focus on me as she drains the entire glass. Her hands are useless to her by now.

Her strawberry-blond hair seems to have dulled out to the color of straw, and her dimpled cheeks are pale. She calls herself plush-sized. She has a spectacular bust line and a bottom like a heart. Her every line connected to a joint is curved, like she's been drawn with a pinkish calligraphy pen. I wish things were different, so I could marry her. I will hate whoever she chooses.

Except no one would marry me. I'm insane.

I look at the completed underwear. Ten in a stack. I begin counting. There have to be three hundred pairs done, easy. Probably more. "How long have you been doing this?"

"What time is it? And what day is it?" She's not even kidding.

"Tuesday night."

I put the glass aside and take her cold hand in mine. She closes her eyes as I gently try to straighten her fingers. The tendons resist me like wires. I begin to rub. I don't think she can feel anything by now. "You are destroying yourself."

"My website glitched and double-sold. Two . . . hundred . . . and . . . fifty . . . *pairs.* I cried for over an hour." She's detached. "Five hundred pairs total."

The Jamie part of my brain works out what kind of money that would look like. Math isn't my forte, but it's a lot. "You should have just reversed the transactions."

"I just . . . couldn't. People would have been disappointed." She takes her hand from mine and holds out the other one. The fingers are curled and this time, when I flatten them out gently, she whimpers in pain. "Ow, ow, ow."

"You don't owe anyone *anything*. The money isn't going to be worth it if your hands turn into lobster claws. Carpal tunnel is no joke."

The urge to ask her if she has been to the doctor is almost overpowering me, but I hate it when people ask me. I bite the tip of my tongue and go into the kitchen again. Her fridge is about on par with mine. I find bread in the freezer and put some slices in the toaster.

"If I can just clear these orders . . . ," she says from the other room, her voice drowsy. "I'll get this lot done and sent, and then . . ."

"Then you'll think of another great swear word or insult, and this entire process starts again."

Underswears are high-waisted, organic cotton underwear with thick, seamless trims and sturdy bulletproof gussets. Your butt cannot eat these undies. They all have an insult or offensive phrase printed on the butt. I'm wearing a pair right now that say FUCKER in graffiti script.

While I wait for the toast, I look at the new release. They are red with a blue sailor stripe, with the words HUMAN

FLOTSAM. I photographed the prototype a few weeks back. "Human garbage, nautical style," I say to myself. "I need a pair of these. Are they missing something?"

Truly groans. "Li'l anchors. Why did I decide to add the anchors?"

"Whimsy. You're all about whimsy."

"Well, my whimsy means five hundred miniature anchors. That's your job, please." She gestures to a tiny parcel.

"Sure." I'm no stranger to sewing on tiny fixings, ironing, and packing. I lug crates of underwear down to the post office. The sheer number of anchors momentarily overwhelms me, but I squash it down. Truly must feel so much worse. Besides, I need to take my mind off what I've just done.

I just pushed down the Looney Tunes red ignition handle and imploded my fragile friendship with a person who really didn't deserve that.

The manual task is exactly what I need: something to focus my entire being on. Anything less than perfection risks being deemed a second. I check the cotton color, measure the exact center of the waistband, thread a needle, and stitch the anchor on, using five not-overly-tight stitches. Tiny neat knot, clip, next. Only 499 to go. I show it to her, and she nods without saying anything. Her phone is lighting up with rapid-fire text messages.

"Who's that?"

"My secret fake lover," she drawls, tucking the phone in her back pocket. She could have a real lover if she wanted one. I watch her expression and realize that she's got a secret; it's caught in the upturned corner of her lip and the spark in her eyes. Someone's been thrilling my Truly.

"I'll let you keep this secret a little longer. Then you're gonna spill it."

"I'm sure I will. You're hard to lie to." She's the second person who's said that to me tonight. I stitch and try to not notice how my bottle of wine has a sexy cold bloom on the glass.

"I'm going to give your number to a girl I work with, Holly. I think she'd be good at this. I think it's time you got yourself a more reliable drone than me." I begin again. Stitch five times, knot, clip. "And I'll get a new phone. Come and get me next time."

"Sorry. I just freaked out and started sewing." Truly's voice is drowsy.

"If you ever double-sell again, I'll draft the email and cancel the orders. I'll be your faceless management asshole. They can deal with their disappointment."

"I kind of need the cash," Truly says, which is very unlike her. "If I want to scale up, I need to get a loan. This looks good in my account."

We sit together for a long time in silence, Truly's eyes closed. I begin a new anchor. "Tom's in town. The renovation is starting."

Truly's mouth tips downward. "That means you're leaving, doesn't it."

"No, I'm going to stay for the renovation. I'm going

to work on the house." I sigh in a big grandiose way so she doesn't know I'm about to be serious. "My stupid way of trying to apologize to Jamie for breaking his financial heart. And I want to make sure the house turns out how I want it."

I think about money for a bit. I don't like to. But how can I get more for Truly? Jamie works in a bank. "Maybe Jamie's got a contact who could help with your loan. Or"—I perk up—"once the house is sold, I could—"

"No." Truly shakes her head, eyes closed. "No connections. No Barrett savior. I'm doing it on my own."

"Jamie would hardly be a savior if he gave your name to a colleague."

"I meant you."

"Me." I laugh and reach over to the wine bottle. The dewy glass wets my hand and it makes me recoil. I can't risk getting even a single cotton thread damp and screwing this up for Truly. I wipe my hand on my leg.

"You were my start-up capital, back in the day."

"You paid me back for that." I have a twinge of embarrassment in my stomach.

"You do all the photography and don't charge. You sew on five hundred miniature anchors—"

"I've only done five."

She won't hear my protests. "You get my groceries and unbend my fingers. You're the best."

"I'm human flotsam."

"You're the best," she repeats until I smile and I don't need that wine bottle anymore. "So how's Tom? Still a hot dork beefcake?"

"I have to put a muzzle on myself every time he walks past me."

"Just like high school." Truly sighs. "Your brother's big shadow has always gotten you like that."

"I thought I wasn't that obvious. Well, here's news. The wedding is off." I count my stitches carefully. I wait for her exclamation of shock.

"I'm not completely surprised."

"I was so surprised I pulled the cabinet doors off their hinges in my kitchen. They're just in a big pile on the floor. Then I told him to get in my bed."

"Ha," Truly barks with her eyes shut.

"It's not a joke. I told him to . . ." I trail off and swallow the big lump in my throat. "I told him to *get in me.*"

She's shaking with laughter. Spluttering, she says, "Megan never seemed that into him. It was weird, because they're both gorgeous. They were more like brother and sister. I bet she's never once ordered him to"—she opens her eyes in a vivid green flash—"get in her."

"She better not have," I snarl.

"I bet she put it in her bullet journal. Saturday, six P.M. A special gold star sticker indicating sexual intercourse completed." Truly drifts half-asleep again, emitting the occasional cackle.

In my diary, written in the little gaps of time where I let Tom sleep, I'd be writing, *Sex, fucking, sucking, nearly dying, need sustenance*—with smudged ink and a weak hand. Me and my romantic heart.

I will always defend him. "You can't know what things are like for a couple when they're alone." I stretch and groan in misery. "I bet he's absolutely spectacular in bed. He's so . . . competent. She would have had zero complaints."

"Did you ever, ever see them kiss? Even once? I thought it was weird. I would have liked to see them kiss." Truly's slurring. Milk and toast are obviously strong opiates.

"Maybe she didn't want to when I was there."

Because I'd probably plunder and stab and burn. I'd watch from a hillside as her village burned to the ground, the flames crackling in my Viking eyes. I mess up my current anchor, have to clip all the threads out and start again.

Truly's a mind reader. "I'm so glad you're on my team. You'd be a terrifying adversary."

"You're mixing me up with my brother."

"He's not that bad."

"He's like the boss you fight in the last level of a computer game. Anyway, I never did anything to break up Tom and Megan. I was so polite to her."

"With your giant gray eyes staring at her during every Christmas dinner like she was flattened onto a microscope slide."

"She's so beautiful," I groan, my needle sliding in and out on autopilot. "I think I was half in love with her myself. Her skin and hair are just . . . beautiful." There's no other word I can use for her.

"So are yours."

"Hair?" I wave a hand at my bare neck. "What is this hair you speak of?"

"Darce," Truly says like I am a pitiful dweeb, "you are one tough cookie, but gosh, what a pretty cookie. Anyway, what does it matter? He doesn't care about looks."

I pause, knot, and clip. "Tom is the best person. The ultimate human man. I was used to her having him. But now . . ." I drop the needle into the carpet and curse, scratching around for it. "He's single and I think I need to shoot myself out of a cannon into space. I was sexually threatening to him just now." I prick my finger and swear. "He was afraid of me."

"Oh really." She starts giggling, delirious. She walks to the bathroom, which is very close by in her tiny apartment. She audibly pees for ages.

"He lied and didn't tell me. He was planning on telling me after the renovation was finished. He said it was safer." The word just makes me cringe. "Safer. What am I going to do, maul him?" I think back to the kitchen. "Okay, fair point."

Truly spits toothpaste into the sink. "Maybe he doesn't trust himself."

"That's really not it." I think back to the kitchen. I was so sure I'd felt one firm press on my stomach from the truthful part of Tom Valeska's anatomy. "He wants to get the renovation done without me hanging around, trying to smell him. I'm just going to have to keep a lid on myself and get through these next couple of months. Can I stay here with you?"

She smiles sweetly. "No. You stay with him." I drag her into her bedroom and turn on a lamp. I pull off her cherry-print Keds and she crawls into bed, still dressed. She starts to cry.

"What's wrong?"

"I'm so tired," she says in between little sobs. "Lying down hurts."

I smooth her hair neater on the pillow. "I know, but you're going to pass out any second. I'm going to be here when you wake up and help with the packaging."

"I bet Vince's never made you wreck a kitchen," Truly says, eyes closing, tears running down her cheeks and into her hair.

"No. He really hasn't."

"Interesting. Better not tell Jamie." For a dizzy second, I misunderstand and think she is talking to herself. She's my one person I've kept ruthlessly quarantined from him.

She's mine, 100 percent.

"No shit. He'd be on the next available flight. Business class, window seat. Snobby blond snob, drinking wine in a suit, frowning down at the world below, swooping in to save Tom from my clutches."

"That's sorta hot," she slurs as she fades off, her head rolling to one side.

Good Lord. Several barrels of Chemical X must have rolled into the reservoir. Echoes of Holly's breathy *He's so good-looking* reverberate around the room. I wonder if Jamie has buried himself into Truly's primordial lizard brain, like a tick.

If he has, I'll tweezer him out.

In the living room, I sit back down with my needle and thread. I miss my hideous handsome brother. It's moments like this, in the dark, with no music or anyone to talk to. The absence of him is the void inside me, and I don't know what more I can stuff into it. And on top of it all, I've just fucked up, big-time. I think of Tom's abject terror. I was too honest. And I was stone-cold sober.

The cheap wine bottle is just sitting there on the rug like a penguin.

"What?" I say to it. "Leave me alone for a minute." I sew, keeping my eyes on the needle.

It won't stop staring at me.

I relent after a few more anchors and unscrew the cap to smell it. I take a small sip from the bottle, then deepen my swallows. About a glass burns down the hatch. I think about Tom looking in my recycling bin. I think about the task Truly has trusted me to do.

"I've got to concentrate," I say sternly to the bottle, and put it in Truly's fridge. Getting up and down a couple of times gives me some ghostly chest flutters. I've forgotten my medication at home.

For the first time in forever, I feel concerned for myself. This is worse than when I let my Furby die under my bed, mewling and crying. How do I correct this monumental neglect? I pat my chest. "Hang in there." I really should go have a review and an ECG, but Jamie always comes with me to those appointments. I'm a baby. I'm just Princess, playing at being a grown-up, and failing.

I'm going to sew every single anchor before Truly wakes up. I'm like the elves helping the shoemaker. I will sew and sew. Maybe it will take my mind off Tom's walking around in the world, single and resplendent.

Maybe I could convince him, my brain suggests optimistically, and my needle goes into my finger.

How could I risk hurting and losing him, just to have his body? I'd have to be the worst person. The most reckless, careless person. A rebound kind of girl. Oh wait. I am.

"Human flotsam," I say to myself, and I stitch on, and on, and on.

Chapter 11

I haven't seen the colors of sunrise in a long, long time.

In my old life, I'd be loading my car with photography gear even earlier than this and heading off to a shoot, a slave to this buttercream light. Everyone looks beautiful in this glow. It airbrushes in a way that my software package never could. It puts a flush in everything it touches.

But, all that said: Kill. Me. Now. It's. Early. I lie in bed and stare at the exposed rafters above me.

I'd nearly bought a tent, but Tom had shaken his head and moved me into the backyard studio. *Just store yourself in here with your furniture, DB.* When he tossed my mattress down onto the bedframe with a sexual grunt, we never made eye contact. Not even Patty's cheerful sneezes could break the tension. Sorry little buffer, Aunt Darcy did a big, bad thing.

I tore up the kitchen and I tore up my oldest friendship.

My voice is ringing in every silence: *Tom Valeska, get in me.* It echoes louder and louder, until we're wincing and walking away from each other. He's usually so good at erasing my weird moments, but this was too much. But I feel those gold lamplight eyes are always watching me. Something deep inside me—optimism, perhaps—tells me that he's turning over my offer and inspecting it from all angles. Measuring it and testing it for faults. *Show me what you got.*

It's our first day on site; the day that Tom has been obsessively preparing for. He's been working so hard, and it's why I'm up this early, to prove that I'm as committed to this as he is. What do building crews wear? I'm not entirely sure. I go with a tank, black jeans, and Underswears that say VILLAGE IDIOT across the rump. Girl panda makeup. Elvis hair. I tie my boots tight. I am no-nonsense.

I slide open the studio door and step out into the beautiful light. I feel like I should be dragging a suitcase to the airport. I check the time on my brand-new phone. Five thirty A.M.

Time to be a grown up again.

Tom lives outside my bedroom window, down on the grass, just like the Valeska I pictured as a child. No one would make it past that tent to my studio's glass door. Right now, his tent is zipped shut. He's being very quiet in there.

I walk up to the front and scratch my fingers lightly on the flap. Patty scratches back. "Tom? Is the water turned off inside? I'm busting."

Every time I go to use a basic amenity, it's off. Or on, but can't be used. It's infuriating.

There's no sound and no reply. I unzip a corner just big enough for Patty to squeeze through. She stampedes to the nearest clump of grass and pees endlessly. I'm almost ready to join her. "Tom? Are you in there?"

"What?" His voice is blurry from sleep. There's a pause. "Oh fuck." There's a rustling sound, some struggling grunts, and Tom forces his way out of the tent like he's being born. "Fuck. What time is it?" He looks me up and down; hair and makeup and black.

"Five thirty." Anyone could hear how proud I am.

"My phone died. I slept in. Fuck." He rubs both of his hands over his face and his T-shirt slides up higher than his belly button. His phone isn't the only one who is now dead. That's the kind of flat, hard stomach you'd be able to sign an important document against, with a ballpoint pen.

Safer, I remind myself reflexively as my body responds, warming and pinching. *Safer.* Just the word gives me the strength to refocus my eyes somewhere that isn't his body or face.

"Thank God you woke up." He sighs like I have saved his life.

"No biggie."

"You . . . haven't just gotten home, have you?" He looks down from my makeup to my clothes. There's a little spark of vulnerability in that one-second glance. Does he imagine I've been with a man?

"I worked late at the bar, and I set my alarm like a grown-up. I've been right here. I'm always going to be right here."

It makes him blow out a breath. He drops his arms and the visible slice of stomach disappears. I blow out a breath, too.

"You once told me that bad girls go to bed at six A.M."

I'm not touching that one. "Is the water turned on in the house or not?"

"Yes, the water's still on." He disappears into his tent in a fluster. "Damn it. My guys will be here any second." There's the sound of clothes stretching. They make tents way too sturdy these days.

I go into my bedroom and get the new powerpack I bought at the same time as my phone. Another one of my pitiful efforts at responsibility.

"Plug your phone into this."

"This is off to a fucking great start," he is muttering to himself. A hand reaches out for the powerpack. "Please don't tell Jamie that I slept in. He won't let me forget it."

"Don't worry. I know what he's like. He'll tell the story for years. But your travel time is approximately thirty yards this morning, so you're not late. You're going to be fine." It's sad how hard he is on himself. "Even if you slept in until nine A.M., everything would be okay."

"No, it wouldn't," he responds from his tent with a bit of temper in his tone. "I am doing everything perfectly." The word sounds like a burden. I was the one that placed it on him. We all have.

I use the bathroom and brush my teeth, then walk around the empty house as the magical morning light begins to shine in sideways. I feel like everything's happening too fast; in the flurry of packing and avoiding Tom, I forgot that this is all about to be in my past. I'm not ready to say goodbye to this.

I go to the wall and smooth my hands over it, feeling the old wallpaper crackle. How can I keep this forever?

"I love you," I whisper to the house. "Thank you. I'm sorry." I go to the fireplace. I'll make sure they cover it up with some sheets so it doesn't get damaged. Each nail hammered in by Loretta is precious. I wonder how many little connections to her I'm about to lose as this house is stripped to its bones. I turn on the spot and I ache to ask Tom to cancel everything.

If I looked him in the eye and pleaded with him, he'd do it.

There's a knock on the front door. I open it to find three men standing there in pristine polo shirts, embroidered with *Valeska Building Services*. I am speechless with pride. I can't believe I almost considered asking Tom to ruin his life. He's worth more than old wallpaper. That's what I need to focus on: This is Tom's big chance.

Bartender 101? Find the alpha. "Girl Scouts again? Fuck off."

The bald one looks back at the street, checking he has the right house. The young guy grins. The old one purses his lips. There he is.

"I'm just fucking with you. I'm Darcy. Tom's nude right now, but he'll be right with you."

"I'm not nude," Tom snaps in irritation, striding into the room. He looks like he's been very recently nude; his hair is a mess, and he's got a shadow of stubble and a pillow crease on his cheek. How luscious. "Darcy, please behave yourself."

I hold my hands up. "I cannot be responsible for what I say before six A.M. And before coffee. Now, pay attention. I want this fireplace cared for like it is a human child." I pat my hand on the mantelpiece and go into the kitchen.

"Sleep in, boss?" the young one says. He doesn't wait for a reply but follows along behind me. He's a muscly little nugget, full of youth and mischief. I would definitely card him at the bar. Maybe he's an apprentice—the next-generation Tom. *Fetch. Pull. Carry.* He leans on the counter. "Did you say coffee?"

"Sure did. Who wants one?"

"We need to get some equipment unpacked," Tom says.

"A coffee won't take a second," I reply, pulling down a few mugs from the empty shelf. If I know anything in this life, it's that people feel better once they've drunk some liquid. "I think Tom needs two coffees." I grin over my shoulder at him. If I can just make things feel fun, he won't feel that perfect pressure so much.

"Unpack the equipment," Tom says in a bass tone I've never heard in my life. It's the kind of voice that should be saying, *On your knees.* My joints loosen and my body replies, *Okay.*

They all turn and walk out. Tom casts me a dark look over his shoulder as he departs. My exhalation in the empty room is like a wheeze. Imagine being bossed around by Tom Valeska. I think he's the only man I'd trust to do it right with me.

I've got to stop having these thoughts.

"Well, I don't know how, but I've fucked up somehow," I say to Patty. I've never seen Tom so deeply annoyed with me. I spoon out some breakfast into her bowl and find Diana sitting on the windowsill in the old laundry room. "We screwed up your house, didn't we, lady?"

Diana won't turn to look at me as she stares out the cracked window, her fur fluffed up and her tail wrapped around her toes. I didn't even make sure she had somewhere to sleep last night. Just because she doesn't need me, or like me, doesn't mean I shouldn't keep trying. I pick up her stiff, unwilling body and carry her under my arm down to my new bedroom. I leave her with a bowl of her favorite fish brains and an apology.

I wonder if Truly would like a cat.

Besides Diana, the main thing I need to sort out is my passport. I packed the entire house with my own two hands, but it still didn't turn up. It makes no sense. I checked every pocket, every bag, every shoebox. It's becoming a very real possibility that Jamie took it with him. I've texted him twice about it. Zero replies.

I make my coffee in my #1 Asshole mug, just to establish myself, and with Patty at my heels I go in search of the guys. They are all in the drive, unloading piles of gear. "Are you going to introduce me to everyone?" I sip my coffee and try to look nonchalant.

Tom is dragging ladders out of the back of a truck. "Yes, when we get this stuff out and the others turn up." He's got a schedule planned out in his head.

"Here, I'll take something."

He regards my outstretched hand with faint disbelief on his brow. "You're the client." Then he turns his back on me, and hoists two ladders on one forearm, and picks up a toolbox with the other. I can't even begin to wonder how much all that weighs.

"Out of the way, please," he says and walks down the side of the house. Patty has way more experience than me, standing at the side of the path. This time she's absolutely judging me.

"Excuse us," the bald guy says, because I'm in their way, too. The old one just eyeballs me, and my mug. Then he thinks to himself, *That's about right,* and sniffs. It's been a long time since I've felt this useless. Have I committed myself to several months of being in everyone's way?

"You could take this," the young guy says, and I am absurdly grateful to be treated like a human being. He gives me a heavy plastic case. Dignity somewhat restored, I follow them down the side of the house. Patty brings up the rear.

I say to the young guy, "Where are you staying?"

"The motel over on Fairfax. I'm Alex, by the way," he says as we round the corner. Tom looks at my coffee, the Chihuahua at my heels, and the case in my hand.

"I just said, she's the client," Tom reprimands Alex in a patient adult voice.

"I'm the worker," I argue back. "Listen up. I'm part of this team now." I level a stare at Tom, but he won't look back. How is my mere presence altering his usual deep calm? Am I embarrassing him or something? I remember he said he can't focus with me here. I guess he was telling the truth.

"Let's start again everyone. I'm Darcy Barrett. What's your name?"

The old guy clears his throat. "Colin."

"Ben," the bald guy says hastily, like this is school roll call. Bald Ben, I can remember that.

I point at the kid. "I've met Alex. And I know who this grumpy asshole is. His name's on your shirts. Where do you want Patty?"

"I'll put her in your bedroom," Tom says shortly. Grumpy doesn't suit him. "More guys will start arriving. Are those boots steel-caps?"

"Actually, yes."

"Why am I not surprised?" Tom's phone, revived and plugged into my powerpack, begins to ring. Judging from the despair in his eyes he's off to a bad start this morning.

"Hey. Eyes to yourself," Tom warns Alex before answering his phone. Alex looks like a smacked puppy. As he talks on the phone about a delivery time, Tom crosses to me and fussily tucks the strap of my bra under my tank. I feel it everywhere. It's the first deliberate physical contact he's made with me since that cringeworthy moment he touched my neck and I made a sound like a mountain lion. It's amazing how the mortification just never seems to fade.

"Don't." I shrug him off.

There's a familiar shape to Tom's shoulders now as he paces off. His beast is showing.

I sip slowly from my coffee and hold eye contact with the

old guy, Colin. He puts up a valiant effort, but after thirty seconds—I count them—he looks away.

Meet your new alpha, bitch.

"I want to talk to you three," I say as they begin to shuffle after their master. Time for some abuse of power. "As the client, I'm the boss, right?"

"Tom's the boss," Alex blurts, scared and wanting his daddy, despite his scolding.

"I'm his boss." They all look like they feel this is bad news. "Hey, I'm cool. But I'm not into being babied, or ignored, or stepped around. You're all going to treat me like one of the team. Especially you," I say to Colin, the sour old bastard. "I have no experience doing this, but I have two hands and a heartbeat. This is my grandmother's house."

This seems to be the missing piece of information. They all drop into more relaxed stances. Now the forceful on-site client makes sense.

"Are you going to explain all this to Tom?" Alex says, his eyes on Tom's profile. "Because he's in a bad mood. And he's never in a bad mood."

"He knows me well enough to know that this is how it's going to be." I toss my remaining coffee into the garden and put my mug on the railing. "Now let's get our asses to work."

We clomp past Tom as a team now, and I ignore his beady stare when I walk back down with a crate of electrical cords. My heart feels fine. I've set a reminder in my phone that says, *MEDICATE YOURSELF, DIPSHIT,* and my alcohol intake has been slashed.

Keep going, little heart, because I need you.

We continue to unpack. Tom hangs up from a call. He looks like he's got a caution or a scold on the tip of his tongue, but his phone begins ringing again. With a frustrated huff he answers it. "Jamie, I can't talk. We're unpacking. Yes. She's fine. I'll call at lunch."

"It would be killing him to not be here," I say to Tom as I walk past with more gear. "If we're not careful he's going to get on the next flight."

Tom winces so hard I bet he's bruised himself internally. "That is my nightmare scenario. Can you please just—" He comes to take my load from me, but the phone rings again. "Tom Valeska," he says on a sigh.

". . . Is totally frazzled," I finish his sentence to myself as I hoist gear onto the back porch. "Seriously, what is up with him?" Alex and I give each other *yeesh* looks.

More cars begin to slot along the curbs. I'm reading polo shirts: electrician, foundation, roofing, scaffolding, plumbing. There are cigarettes, takeout coffee cups, and male voices everywhere.

"He's not enjoying this," Ben comments in a hushed tone as we look at Tom, pacing around now, the phone at his ear. "Aldo was always the one on the phone. Tom's used to being the muscle."

"And what a set of muscles they are," I say out loud in reflex.

Colin doesn't look sympathetic. "He's got a few things to learn. He wanted this, and he got it." He has an air of *I told you so.* "He's on his own now."

The tinge of mutiny in his tone has my hackles up. "He's not on his own. He's got us. And anyone who isn't on his side can go that way"—I point up the side of the house—"and keep walking."

"Darcy," Tom says behind me, sharp and frustrated. Fuck, I'm in trouble. "Everyone into the kitchen, please."

I grab my mug and we file in. There are possibly the first glimmers of respect in Colin's eyes when he looks at me. I privately breathe out. I'm lucky he didn't take up my offer to walk. I'd be dead meat.

"Can you get me one of those polo shirts?" I ask Alex. I would love a Valeska shirt. The reverse imprint of those stitches on my skin would feel better than lingerie.

"Sure, I've got a spare."

I look down at my own tank top. Nothing is remotely amiss, apart from lacy bra straps poking out.

We are all assembled in the kitchen. I pour myself a second mug of coffee, and at least eight sets of eyes watch me do it. The room is warm and spicy from so many men and their hideous deodorants, so I go to open the kitchen window. Of course, it's stuck. The lift-and-jiggle technique doesn't work. I struggle and yank, right at center stage. Everyone goes silent.

"Come on, you miserable fucker," I whisper, and someone laughs.

"Morning," Tom says, and there's the boot-scraping sound of everyone straightening up and paying attention. "Thanks for coming on short notice."

He pulls up the window for me with two fingers. Lift, jiggle, the lovely flex of a bicep.

This house can be such a jerk to me.

"My usual crew is here—Colin, Ben, and Alex." He points at the three that I threatened within ten minutes of their arrival. "Dan and Fitz are plumbing. Alan is roofing. Chris is our electrician, but he doesn't get here until nine. Anyway, we've got a lot to do, and a pretty blank canvas."

Tom's bigger than any guy in here, from muscles to height, and they all look like stubbled, bloodshot messes next to him. I'm beginning to think he always has this flawless sunrise glow on his skin.

"Who's this?" one guy says at the back. He means me.

"Darcy Barrett. She's the homeowner."

"I'm the demolition squad. Here's one I prepared earlier." I gesture to the exposed kitchen cabinets. Tom keeps looking at me like I'm supposed to make a speech. A rally-the-troops battle call? I have no idea. I wish I had a bar counter between me and all these dicks.

"This cottage belonged to my grandmother Loretta. She left it to me and my brother, Jamie. I'm not sentimental about much, but this house is special to me. I know it's a total dump, but if you could just refrain from saying it over and over in my vicinity, that would be great."

Ben takes pity. "It's a great little place."

Tom nods. "What she's saying is, it's not just any old house to us. Darcy and I are staying on-site in the backyard. Anything beyond the fishpond is off-limits."

He takes my mug from my hand and takes a slow sip. Every guy watches him do it. They understand what their boss is telling them. Speculation is now in expressions and I wire my jaw shut to stop it from dropping open.

"Is there an induction checklist for us to sign off?" Colin prompts.

"What's that for?" I reply.

"Tom wants to do things right," Colin says, his tone a little dry. "He said he wanted to do a first day induction checklist for the crew to sign. So we make sure all workers have been shown where the first aid kit is. How to report an accident. What the procedures are if there's a fire. Things like that."

"Oh. Like a worker's safety thing. Okay." I look up at Tom.

"Ah," Tom says, and I can see the spike of panic in his eyes. He puts the mug back in my hand and reaches for his leather folder, jammed full of crinkled quotations and a big sample square of carpet. I dimly recall his asking me if I have a printer. It has no ink, like all home printers. This would be killing him, especially after the long nights he's sat up with his spreadsheets.

"You'll get it from me by lunchtime," I say, covering for him.

"We don't get a lunchtime," a guy replies with a pinch of sarcasm.

I give him my shark smile. "I was referring to my lunch break. I look forward to learning your schedule real good, buddy." He scuffles his boots around, eyes down.

"And what about contracts for the subbies? Tax forms?" Colin is genuinely trying to either help or undermine. At this stage, I can't work it out. Tom's jaw tightens. He's been so absorbed in ordering the right number of nuts and bolts, he's forgotten that he's a boss now.

I give Colin a glare and to my satisfaction he withers underneath it.

"I've never met someone so obsessed with paperwork. What did I just say? Lunchtime." I look to Tom. "We do a full site induction when the electrician's arrived, right?" He doesn't need to know that I've got a *House Renovations for Dummies* book on my nightstand.

Tom nods, his expression tight. "Water and power will be off for most of the morning. Porta-Potties are being delivered in the next hour or so, so hold on. One men's and one ladies'."

"He spoils you, Darcy," Alex booms. "Just wait until an hour after lunch and you see the queue." There's grossed-out laughter.

Tom's wrapping it up. "I'll come and give each of you your jobs for today. Start unpacking but stay out of the house until seven. Darcy's taking some photos for me. Then we'll do induction."

The guys begin trooping out of the house, hands all over it. Toes nudging skirting boards and hands testing door frames.

I rinse my mug. "What do you want photos for?"

There's so much energy shimmering in Tom right now as he stares down at me. His phone rings, and he rejects the call. Maybe he's about to say, *Thank you so much*. Maybe I'm an idiot optimist.

"Do you want to tell me what the hell that was?"

Chapter 12

I dry the mug. "I saved your ass. You're welcome."

He's incredulous. "I didn't need you to save me."

"Looked like it to me. You'd still be tucked up asleep if it wasn't for good old DB." Alex was right. Tom's never in a mood like this. "You need to shut that old guy Colin down. He's trying to undermine you."

Tom's hand is on his hip now. "You want to tell me about undermining. Right. What the hell do you think you just did?"

"You started to drown a little. I just pulled you up." I walk down to my studio, a grouchy shadow at my heels. "I just see where you need help."

"Did I actually hear you threaten to fire Colin?"

I step over Patty's welcome dance and pick up my camera. "He needed to be reminded whose name is on his shirt. Trust me on that." Doesn't he know that I am always Team Valeska?

"Colin's done this forever. I really need him on-site." His

phone rings again. He answers it. "Can I call you back? One minute. Thanks."

"You're being such a jerk. Please don't let this change us." I mean the renovation, but my voice breaks a little. I've been a wreck over what I did. My overly honest *get in me* has turned into *get away from me.* "I'm sorry. I'm really sorry."

"I think it's too late. It's changed." He puts a hand into his hair. "I'm being a jerk because I'm stressed, and I've got you walking around in the middle of everything."

"Ignore me."

"You're real hard to ignore." He looks sideways at the house, eyebrows pulling down. "Okay, here's where we're at. I'm attempting the first day of what should be the rest of my career, and I can't focus on it."

"Because you want to put me against a wall and kiss me." I'm taunting that thing inside him that always responds to me. It protects me and hunts me. "And you'd do it in front of everyone here. You like having keys in your pocket. It's what your whole life is about. You want to be the only one with a key to me." I count his breaths. "Am I right?"

"I am not going to answer that." His body answers anyway; a shrugging of his entire body, like something is dropping down onto him. He looks so desperate that regret fills me. What have I done to him? I love his inner animal so much that I'm stopping him from turning back into the calm, controlled version he needs to be.

I think I do an identical shudder-shrug. Get yourself back on your leash, DB. "What am I photographing?"

"Everything," Tom says, raspy. "I want you to photograph everything." He propels me up the back stairs with a hand on my waistband.

"For what purpose?"

"Two purposes. To keep Jamie in the loop, because if we don't, he's coming down here." He positions me at the doorway of the hall. "And I need content for my website. A before-and-after section. Lucky for me, I've got a professional photographer right on hand."

I don't really care for how he put a little sarcasm on *professional*. I really screwed up just now in front of his crew.

"How many times in my life have you rescued me? I can't even count. I will always do the same for you. I will not stand there and say nothing when I could step in and help. It's what we do for each other."

He blinks, trying to understand. "No one does that for me."

"I do it."

"How can I explain this in a way you'll understand?" Tom steps against my back and reaches around me. His fingers slide between mine and he raises my hands up until the camera is roughly in line with my eyes.

"Can you do your job like this?" When I line up the viewfinder on the hall, he moves our hands. I snap a shot that is, of course, garbage.

I try to shrug him off; he steps closer, dropping his mouth to the side of my neck. That mouth that sipped from my mug, telling every male in the room that I'm off-limits and untouchable. He's still too far into the dark forest place we play in. He breathes me in. I feel the briefest scrape of his stubble on the curve of my shoulder and the most intriguing hard press on my butt. I feel like an animal about to be bitten, soft and slow, by its mate. Maybe he'd do it hard enough to leave a mark. When he finally releases the breath he's been holding, his heavenly warm air goes down the neck of my top.

He says, "There's so many things I'd do, if I could."

"Well, seems pointless to tell me about them." I bump him off.

Tom Valeska is a fucking liar. He does want me. He just doesn't have the guts. In my pulse points, I'm nothing but Morse code: *bed, bed, bed.* And I'm disappointed in his lack of faith in me. No one could possibly succeed with messy Darcy Barrett around. That's what I've been my whole life, right? A complication.

He puts another wobble into the camera as I try to take a shot. "This is how hard it is for me to do anything with you here." Above my ear, his voice drops to a growl. "This house? This renovation? It's what I do. Don't step in again like that."

"Get away from me. Safer, remember?" I sound bitter.

"Oh, you're still on that?" Tom's phone rings again. I'm ready to toss that thing into an active volcano. "I don't think you fully got what I meant."

"Of course I did, I'm not stupid," I snap, and force my entire focus through the viewfinder.

"I was just . . ." There's a pause so long I think he's left. I take a few shots. "Surprised. I didn't know that's what you thought of me."

"You weren't surprised, you were traumatized. I heard you, loud and clear. From this point on, we're going to ignore this thing between us. We'll get ourselves a sold sign and we will see each other at Christmas. Maybe. There's a festival in Korea around that time that's always interested me."

"Could you tell me why you did it?" I hear the floorboards under his feet creak. "Were you lonely? Mad? Trying to get back at me for something?" He hasn't reached the conclusion that I want his body and his pleasure, more than I want water and food.

"I'm not telling you a damn thing," I reply, because I know that's what will annoy him the most. "I'll tell you one day, when we're eighty years old."

I click the camera and look at the display. It's hard to argue with reality, and here it is. This room—and this potential relationship with Tom—is not the flower-wallpapered version I've been carrying around in my head. This house is no longer beautiful, and Tom has receded out of reach. I'm down to zero.

His phone begins ringing again. "I've got to get this." He starts to walk, but I stop him.

"What you did before, in the kitchen?" I snap a couple more frames. "With my coffee? Don't do that shit again."

"What did I do?" He looks up from the ringing phone, his thumb hovering. His brow is creased. He seriously doesn't remember.

"You took a big slurp from my mug. Now your boys are looking at us like we're . . ." I can't finish.

Tom has the good grace to look embarrassed. "I guess not all sledgehammers are created equal." He answers the phone. "Tom Valeska."

I should get out of here and do my job. I should be taking advantage of the strawberry-sundae light.

I go down to the fishpond and hold the camera up to my eye. I haven't taken an outdoor photo in probably a year, and it doesn't help that my hands are shaking. What the hell just happened?

"I don't know what to shoot," I say to no one in particular. A tight feeling is in my chest now that I'm alone. Taking photos of this house? It's too real. These are photographs of something I'm going to lose.

I want my white lightbox and mugs.

"Shoot everything," a guy near me says, unfolding a metal table. He lifts a circular saw onto it with a grunt. "Because everything's going to change."

I walk around the outside of the house. "Just try to take one," I whisper to myself. The first click is the hardest, and I barely look through the lens.

I take real estate shots, coaching myself through it, but before long, I've loosened up enough that I can pick out the little details. Just for me, so I can have them forever. I lean against the fence and shoot up at the crooked weathervane, topped with a galloping horse, that hasn't spun in years.

This isn't what Tom had in mind, but I shoot the moss and ivy clinging on the side of the wall, and the way the honeysuckle hangs low, dusting everything with yellow powder. I'm photographing this house like it's a bride. As much as I ache to have it stand in the frozen fairy-tale clasp of roses forever, I know it's time to let it go. The only way that I can is because it's now in Tom's care.

Inside, time is running out, so I click and reposition, zooming in on individual hydrangeas in the wallpaper. I probably look insane, but I take a shot of the tile Loretta replaced in the bathroom—one salmon-pink square in a sea of cracked buttermilk relics.

I'm chasing the clock, and guys are stepping out of my way, falling respectfully silent as I step back and take a portrait of the fireplace. I will not let so much as a sheet of sandpaper touch this mantelpiece.

Why didn't I do this earlier? Why didn't I take days, recording and archiving these memories I have? I truly forgot that this was a skill of mine, something that could be used for a purpose other than a paycheck.

A banging sound begins, like the outside world is trying to break in.

I think I take more than twenty minutes and I'm a little drained. I really want to load these into my computer. I look at the time. I was immersed up to my neck in a state of creative flow for an hour. I took over two hundred photos. How did that happen?

I look up in astonishment and make eye contact with Tom. I wonder if he even has a website.

He doesn't smile, but I can tell he's pleased with me. Maybe all is not lost.

"Good work, Darce. Now get gloves on and get to work."

* * *

I'M WILTED WITH tiredness and it's only Wednesday. Three more months of this? Stepping out of the way, tripping over power cords, and being covered in dust? I had a bar shift thrown in last night for good measure, and just finished a photoshoot for Truly. I think I need to go to bed at six P.M. tonight.

I'm sorting through photos of butts in underwear when Jamie calls. For once, it's me answering the phone with my heart in my throat. Is he dead-dying-drowning? Surely it'd take an emergency for him to call after this long.

"What's up?" How cool I sound.

"Voicemail Darcy is picking up her phone for once in her life. That's what's up."

Even when my phone isn't in urine, I'm not a great phone answerer. Most people love their phone like a baby, but I would have left mine on the church stairs.

"There's a first time for everything."

Jamie decides how to proceed for a second. "I know something."

"That must feel extraordinary," I reply, and continue scrolling through the photos I've just taken. "You'd better let your employer know. They'll be so glad they took a chance on you." I grin as his sigh partially deafens me.

"How's the progress on site?"

I'm not his employee. "I bet you feel like I once did. Those summers I watched you and Tom mowing all the neighbors lawns, raking in the cash."

"We sweated for that. We worked like mules. Be glad you sat inside in the air-conditioning."

"I wanted to do what you guys did, but I had to watch from the window. Just like you're doing, right now." I don't hold much hope that he'll understand what I'm telling him, or why it feels so important that I see this through. "The renovation is fine. Tom and I are making sure of it."

"I know that you know. About Tom and Megan."

"Oh, that. Sure." I click and drop a file. "We're buds. He tells me stuff."

That's a bit of a stretch. I'm permanently screwing things up around here.

"Sure," Jamie says, dripping sarcasm. "But here's the thing. You're leaving him alone."

"What do you—"

"Cut the shit. When he's in the same room you're a drooling mess. Like, for years, and it's painfully obvious. That's why he tried to not tell you." Jamie confirms what I had just started to hope was a pathetic misunderstanding on my part. "He's embarrassed to be around you. He's never going to reciprocate."

Only Jamie could make a word like *reciprocate* sound like he's holding a turd with a pair of salad tongs.

"'Drooling mess' is a bit of an exaggeration. But yeah, he's gorgeous. My eyes like gorgeous things. I'm a photographer."

I hate hearing my own voice being so flippant. Diminishing Tom down to a face and body feels wrong. "Don't you go for beautiful women?"

"I go for women in my league," Jamie says forcefully, "and I don't go for childhood friends." He laughs a little. "I can't believe we actually have to have this conversation. You and him? Never happening." A pause. "So you've decided you're a photographer again?"

I'm not touching that one. "He told me it was completely over with her. He seems surprisingly okay about it."

"He's devastated. Did you know that?"

My stomach twists up. I didn't exactly try to listen before I began tearing the world apart with my bare hands.

Jamie continues. "He's been trying to find a time to meet up with her to talk it through and get back together. But you wouldn't know that, 'cause he's not your *bud*, and you never stop thinking about yourself."

"You are weirdly possessive over your childhood friend. Something you need to tell me?" The thought has crossed my mind once or twice.

Jamie doesn't take the bait. "That guy has had my back probably a thousand times by now. Now it's my turn. I want to make sure he gets the future he deserves."

"You should be a motivational speaker, Jamie. I'm inspired. He's already got his business. His dream. He got it."

"That's only phase one. Tom wants the real deal. A house, a picket fence, a wedding. Taking triplets to Disney or some shit like that. Haven't you ever noticed his obsession with taking care of things and fixing them? We're not getting younger. Darce, he's a husband and a dad."

Goddamn it, I hate when my brother is right. I don't say anything.

Jamie senses I've understood what he's saying, and his next harsh sentence is spoken with unbearable kindness. "That's what he wants. To be the dad he never had. He wants a wife and to make sure his mom is sorted out. Not a one-night stand with the queen of one-nights."

"Maybe I want . . ." I trail off. I never thought about it before. Those sorts of things are for Megan-type girls.

"Not with him you don't. Megan hasn't given the ring back. He doesn't want it back. Connect the dots, Darcy."

I feel like throwing up. "Okay, I get it."

"If you make him get all wrapped up in your drama and get a little crush on you, only for you to leave? Just like when we were eighteen? I will never speak to you again."

I shouldn't be surprised that Jamie knows about this. But I am anyway. "That was complicated."

"That was something that should have been a no-brainer and you blew it. Just like the developer's offer on the house." Jamie says "One minute" to someone in his office, then says to me, "I've got someone on-site keeping an eye on you."

"Colin." His name is out of my mouth like a curse.

"Maybe. Maybe not."

"Prove it."

"You dropped a nail gun yesterday and broke it. I've got

to go now. Funny. You're usually the one saying that." He hangs up, and I put my head in my hands.

Of course he's going back to Megan. Why wouldn't he? He's got an entire life built, painstakingly, over eight years. He just needs to walk back to it and flick on the lights and screw the house number on the letterbox.

After a minute, my door slides open and I hear the *tink* of Patty's name tag. For the first time in my life, I wish Tom would turn around and walk away.

"Oh, great, what have I done this time?" I know what I did. I blew it.

Tom sits heavily down on the computer chair behind me with a tired groan. "What makes you think you've done something wrong?"

"You only talk to me when I have." I smooth my hands over my face. I shouldn't be a jerk. He's got no animosity in him as he slumps. He's so tired I feel sad. Beside me, my white backdrop is still up and there are robes and Underswears samples all over my bed. Maybe we can start over for the tenth time. Let's try.

"Just spoke with my brother dearest."

"What did he want?"

"Just to threaten me about behaving myself and to remind me of my failures." That's the top-level truth.

"He's so hard on you." Tom is far more empathetic than I deserve. "Well, keep sending him the progress photos and we won't get a surprise visit." Tom swivels his chair gently, side to side. "The ones you took on the first day were insanely good. You know that, right? Glad to see that again." He nods at the white backdrop, set up against the free section of wall by the door.

"Everyone has a camera in their pocket these days. I'm obsolete." I haven't had enough time to pack down the emotions Jamie has just stirred up. Tom's walked in here with a white flag. I should make the most of it. But it's hard, coping with these two extremes between us. I make myself be grateful for the quiet and the civil, but I know what I want.

I crave his lust like a drug.

Let's find a really civil topic. "How's your mom doing?"

Tom groan-sighs. "She's stressing me out. No. Her land-lord is stressing me out. There's someone you can go beat up for me."

Tom's mom, Fiona, is a sweet, spacey lady who always seems to be amid some kind of low-level crisis. She's a pot permanently simmering, and if Tom takes his eye off her too long the smoke detector goes off. I'd like to say this was a recent thing, but he's been trying to take care of her his whole life. I sometimes wonder what Tom's dad must have been like. I've never met him, and I don't think Tom has either. He must be big and handsome. And a total piece of shit, obviously.

"Can't she move out?" I ask.

"She found a pregnant cat last year and couldn't bear to rehome the kittens. They're all black and white. I have no idea how she tells them apart." He rubs the heel of his palm on his eyes. "Her landlord told me she could have one cat. She hasn't filled him in yet that one has become six. Her hot water is playing up, and he's not returning my calls."

"Buy six cats, get the seventh cat free?" I point up at Diana's bed.

"Don't even think about it. The next place I carry her boxes into is gonna be the last house she ever has to live in. I can't move her again. I don't have it in me. A picket fence is what I promised her." Tom looks ten years older in an instant.

At this rate, a picket fence paling will be my tombstone. "Is that what you're saving for?"

He speaks like he hasn't heard me in the crystal-quiet room. "The guys keep asking where you are. Well, Alex mainly. Your puppy dog doesn't know what to do with himself." His eyes sharpen on mine, watching for my reaction.

Every atom in my body knows that Tom wants to see indifference. I look back at my computer and shrug. "Little turd has gotten lonely without me kicking his ass, huh?"

"He told me things are fun with you around. He's going to get the wrong idea if you keep leaning on him. He doesn't know what you're like."

"I don't lean," I retort, then I remember my shoulder pressing on something warm. Me and Alex leaning together watching an excavator being unloaded out front. "Oh, I did lean a bit."

"He worships you." Tom has affection in his voice as he glances up at the house. "He reminds me so much of myself at that age."

"Worshipping me?" I accidentally defy Jamie's direct order and immediately gloss over it. "Well, that's cute. The one I really want to worship me is that old bastard Colin. I want him to kiss my boots by the end of this."

"Should I be jealous?" Tom answers his phone. "Hi. Yes, drop them around. Before four." He hangs up. This is what our conversations are like lately. Everything is interrupted by that goddamn phone. I don't know how he's keeping it together.

"Jealous or not, it has nothing to do with me."

"I forgot, I did come in here to yell at you. Who were they?" Tom means the girls who left twenty minutes ago. "You can't just let people walk through a building site."

"They were models." I click through the images. "I just did a shoot for Truly. Funny, Tom. Last time we had a proper exchange, I got the impression that you needed me to stay out of your hair. And yet, here you are."

"This is my site and you're doing a photo shoot in the middle of it." Tom leans sideways to look at the computer. He's lip-pursed Mr. Perfect. "You should have told me. There's safety issues with people on-site who aren't inducted. If they hurt themselves—"

"Okay, I screwed up again. Don't get grouchy, or I might not give you your present."

"A present?" Behind me, the computer chair squeaks.

"Do you deserve one?" I'm stalling, because I don't know how he'll receive this tiny olive branch. It's been made abundantly clear that he doesn't need or want my help.

"I had to get a dead rat out of the wall cavity in the kitchen. I do deserve a present."

"Dead rats are Alex's job. You're a boss now." I click through my photo files, trying to feign nonchalance. "You're sitting on your present. I made you a desk. I noticed it's getting harder for you to work inside."

This is my way of apologizing for putting a coffee ring on a fairly important report for the county. "And that apple crate down there is for Patty."

Tom swivels and looks at the desk again. It's just the old kitchen table, a lamp, and a jar of pens, but he runs his hands on the tabletop in a lustful way. "I was just about to start working out of my car." He flips the lamp on. "Thanks, Darce."

"I'm not trying to lure you in here for any nefarious purpose." Ugh, why did I say that? I swivel around on my stool in a way that probably looks ominous.

Tom ignores my blunder. "Oh, I'm lured all right." He gets up and leaves, appearing again with his laptop and a bulging folder. Business cards flutter mothlike in his wake. "There is no way I'm passing up a desk."

He leaves a second time, returning with an armful of samples: tiles, carpets, laminates. Patty hops into her new bed and watches Tom, her big bug eyes lit with their usual worship.

I'm right there with you, Patty. I think I could sit here and watch him for hours, stacking bathroom tiles with that serious tilt to his head. He always was like this: a tidy boy with a straight spine and a neat desk.

Scratch that. Fast-forward things.

I could sit here and watch this gorgeous man forever, the glints in his hair and those big careful hands. The lamp-light pools in those brown eyes and turns them to honey. He breathes, even and easy, under the lead-gray weight of my stare, and makes three piles of paperwork.

He finds the old trash can under his desk with the toe of his shoe and smiles to himself.

"You thought of everything, Darcy Barrett," he says to me without looking over, and I realize he has always been aware of my staring, dazzled by the light shining through him. He's probably felt this stare for most of his life. I am intensely grateful for how he's erasing that one moment of insanity in the kitchen.

I'm not going to lose him. If I just stay laser-focused and careful, we can walk out of these three months as friends and part with a handshake.

If I can keep my mouth shut and not say things like, *Get in me*.

"This is really going to help. I can get organized." Right on cue, his phone rings, and he grabs at a pen.

As he writes himself a note and looks up at the house, biting his lip, thoughtful and lovely, I think about how much he needs to get in me. And not just into my body. I want more than that. I want him to get in my head. I think that's what I meant.

Unzip me, climb into me, don't come out.

When he hangs up and looks over at me, I pretend I was just looking up at the house.

"It's getting hard to think in there during the day."

"Twelve weeks is a crazy time frame," he says with apology in his voice. He looks back around at my room and smiles. "I feel better about you being in here now. Very cozy." He looks down the long narrow space. It only takes up a quarter of the floor space, but the room feels like it is brimming full of bed.

I turn back to my laptop.

"I'm snug as a bug. Sorry, but Truly's got a meeting with a brand consultant and she has to have a lookbook to show them. She's going to be turning up any second, saying, *Hi, are they done?* So, off you go."

"I haven't seen her for years. How is she?"

"Fucking adorable as usual." I scroll and try to squash down the panic when I look at the clock. "She thinks I have way more graphic design skills than I do."

"That's a big-deal meeting for her, isn't it? So these are Underswears." He ambles over to my workbench and laughs. "Who wears the word *dipshit* around on their butt?"

I prickle up defensively. "I do, every day of the year. Best underwear on earth."

"I'm going to be intrigued about what yours say, every day of the year."

"You couldn't handle what's written on my underwear." It's hard to ignore him when he's leaning against the bench, probably looking down at the back of my neck. I can feel the warmth of his body, and out of the corner of my eye I see that his T-shirt is layered across his abdomen like fondant icing.

He makes it harder when he lifts a hand and touches my skin.

Chapter 13

"D o you do all this for free?" He touches my shoulder and pulls my tank strap back into position. It immediately slips back off and his defeated sigh gusts across my skin. "Just stay there," he says to my tank in irritation.

"I get paid in underwear and candy. In this economic climate, alternate currencies are required. Jamie would lecture me about charging what I'm worth. But who cares. If this is how I can help her, then I'm doing it."

"You're a good friend," Tom says with such admiration in his voice that I look up, startled. "You're so generous, Darce."

"Oh, sure." I look back at my screen. This is getting too hard. He pulls me close with fang-and-claw intensity, then expects me to sit here like a sister. I'm a kitchen-trashing psycho, but at least I know it, and I'm consistent.

The problem with Tom is that he doesn't know what he

is. Not really. The question, *who do you think you are* would be really interesting to ask him, because I know he'd get the answer wrong.

"I want you to know, when I was going to renovate the house under Aldo's business, I was planning on doing it for free." I see his big fingers twist together out of the corner of my eye. "I feel real bad about taking the five percent."

"You're worth every penny," I tell him, just like my mom used to. "Don't sweat it, Tiger." I tack on Dad's nickname for good measure. Still, the reminder of my parents doesn't work. He doesn't recoil away from me like I thought he might. "Do you need to get back to work?"

He confides, a little playful, "I don't want to go back out there. Alex is right. Things are always more interesting where you are."

"I'm sure," I say, because my screen has a backside on it. But when I look up, he's looking at me, and he has softness in his eyes.

"I've been really hard on you lately. I'm sorry." He rejects an incoming call with a practiced motion. "I'm sorry for everything. Can we be okay now?" His phone rings again. He needs me. I know it.

"All you have to do is ask me." I can see he doesn't know what I mean. Instead, his eyes drop to my mouth. My pulse bumps and I rush to clarify. "Ask me to help you."

"How could you help me?" Now he's looking into my eyes, and there's that warm buzz sensation. The room gets smaller. We're shrink-wrapped together by walls and air, and I cannot stop myself. I put my hand on his forearm, just to feel his skin.

"I will help you however I can." I squeeze, and I feel his muscles squeeze back. Above my eye line, I see him swallow. "I will break my goddamn back for you."

He takes my hands in his. This is an important thing he wants to say. "Yeah, I know. But it's really important to me that I do this on my own."

Colin's words echo back to me, and again I flare up inside. "You're never going to be on your own. I'm here. I'm with you."

He looks at my growly little face with a new realization in his eyes. "Yeah. You are." He looks sideways at my bench and notices something among the mess. The one thing I was hoping he wouldn't. "Passport application?" He releases my hands.

"I concede defeat. Jamie must have taken it. But it makes no sense. I know I had it after he left. I checked the expiration date for something. I wonder if Vince sold it on the black market." I laugh, *ha ha,* so he knows that was a joke.

He doesn't find that funny. "You're going to get a lot of money when the house sells. You'll never come back."

Truly slides open the door. "Hi, are they done? An old man at the house just yelled at me." She notices how close we're standing and falters.

"Hi." Tom smiles, and it's lovely enough to make me want to shred that passport application and flush. "Colin's right. You can't walk through here anymore."

Truly looks him up and down with frank appreciation and I cannot blame her.

He's glorious, from the top of his head to the soles of his boots. He's a big, glowing, muscled miracle, and as the silence stretches on, his brow creases in puzzlement. He hasn't looked in a mirror in a while.

Truly reboots her brain. "Wowee, look at you! So muscly! Have you buried the hatchet with Darce?"

"I was just in the process of doing that," Tom replies. His phone buzzes on and on. He looks at it with a weary expression. I know from personal experience that once the voicemails begin building up, checking them feels like shoveling in a snowstorm.

He jams it back in his pocket and focuses on Truly. "How are you?" They embrace tentatively, Truly's face making an exaggerated eyebrow-raised *oh* of pleasure at me over the curve of his bicep.

"That's made the trip worthwhile, I bet," I say, sounding extremely bitter. "Not that I'm jealous, but hugs are few and far between around these parts." I hunch over the laptop like a gargoyle and begin to edit. Since Tom's full-body hug in the kitchen, I've been brittle and cold.

"Aw," Truly croons, and comes to me, wrapping her arms around my shoulders from behind. Her hugs are heaven. I wish they'd both hug me at once. "Tom, you know what our Darce is like. She's like a Tamagotchi."

"I'm a digital pet. Sounds about right." I lean back against her and close my eyes. We rest our temples together, and just in this moment, I'm crystal clear on the inside.

Tom resumes his bench leaning. "I know exactly what she's like."

"She needs cuddles more than she will ever admit," Truly says, hugging me tighter, "and she dies without them." She releases me with a kiss on my cheek. "Oh, and candy, obviously. She runs on all different colors of sugar." She begins unpacking bags of candy next to me.

"I almost feel like you're buttering me up for something." I grab the nearest bag and tear it open with my teeth.

Tom grins at Truly. "She's an animal, isn't she?"

Truly holds up a pack at him. "You can have these, if you tell me that you've made her feel better, because I know she tries her poor little heart out for you."

That's a nice way of saying, *Darcy complains to me constantly about every blister and fuckup.*

My stool is turned, I'm pulled to my feet, and Tom slowly, deliberately squeezes me against his body. "I am throwing myself at her feet. Every minute of every day. She just doesn't notice."

His hand cups the back of my head and my entire world is his muscles and the smell of his T-shirt. The wax-sweet smell of birthday candles and wishes and ugh, it's going to hurt when he lets me go. Take what you can get, DB. You're lucky he even wants to speak to you again.

I'm squeezed until I've got no air, then deposited back on my stool. I need that again, even longer and slower. Maybe a month of it. I should say something but I can't. Truly hands over his confectionary payment without comment, her eyes amused as she glances at my face.

He uses a pair of scissors from his new desk. No wild gnawing. So civilized. "How's business? Is there good money in underwear?"

He tips a few into his palm; succulent, delicious, and pink, and I want them. I'm drooling for the flavor in his mouth. A guy from the crew calls his name outside, the bleat of a lamb with no shepherd.

"Yes, weirdly. I'm loaded." Truly rummages in her purse. "I actually brought a present for Darce. Take a look."

She hands Tom a pair of Underswears—the striped nautical ones from her last release. He must have big hands because when he pinches the waistband on each side, the underpants look tiny. I know full well that when I pull those up, I'll have no belly button and a three-foot-high backside.

Truly grins. "I know that's technically a compliment, and against my company charter, but . . ."

"Let's see. Oh, that's cute." He's found the little anchor charm. My underwear in his hands. He turns them, and we both see she's screen-printed "Really Not" above HUMAN FLOTSAM.

I finally find my voice again. "I really am. Thank you. Another one-of-a-kind pair." I tuck them in my top drawer, along with all my other wearable paychecks.

Tom chews and considers the array of bad words on the screen as I scroll through again. "I really would have thought you'd make a more . . . uplifting collection than this."

Truly knows what he means. "Oh, you mean like skimpy lilac underpants with *goddess* spelled out in sequins? But then I'd completely miss my target market. Snarky girls, like Darce, who don't want a wedgie."

Her phone chimes and she glances at it for a long moment. I sense conflict and frustration in her as she pockets it. "Why does everyone say I should make nice underpants?"

"Probably because you're a sweetheart," Tom says, matter-of-factly, and Truly blushes hot pink down to her skeleton. My bones turn neon green. That's one thing I'll never be: a sweetheart. How is it so easy for these two?

"I don't deserve candy," he says, pouring the rest of the bag into his mouth. "I've been such an asshole lately. I deserve a bad word on my butt."

Truly blinks. "Are you psychic? That's what I've come to butter up Darcy about. The brand consultant wants a men's sample included in the lookbook."

"Dudes don't wear funny underwear," I scoff.

"I just said I'd wear some." Tom folds his empty candy packet.

Truly nods, glad of his support. "I think there might be a market, too. I've been working on a pair for a while now, so I had a pattern. This is the first-ever men's pair. You know what I'm going to need now, Darcy."

She sidles up to me, opening another bag of candy. I open my mouth like a baby bird and she stuffs some chewy pineapples into my beak.

"Don't make me." I make crying noises through the sugar. "Don't."

"What's the issue?" Tom walks up to the door. "Yeah,

give me one minute," he calls up to the house. There are a million things up at the house he needs to do, but he's getting tangled up.

"Quit being nosy." There's no point in wasting time with me. "Go back to work."

"Casting male models is her worst nightmare," Truly tells him. "Whenever she's put calls out for male models in the past, she's gotten photos of dicks in response."

"It's true. Just dick after dick." I look at my computer, my watch, and then her face. I ignore Tom's crossed arms. "Do I get any more time?"

"No," she says regretfully.

"Can I do a flatlay?" Even as I say it, I shake my head. "No, they'll look crap beside the model shots. Okay, leave it with me. I'll sort it out."

"Are you sure you're not tiring yourself out?" Again, Tom's fingers are on my shoulder. Again my tank disobeys and slips off. "I think you're on less sleep than me at the moment."

"If only you had someone on-site here who could do it," Truly says to me, slowly and speculatively. She turns and looks at Tom. "Someone really close by. Someone in good shape, who wears an XL." She narrows her eyes at his waist.

Tom is never going to buy into this nonsense. I save him the embarrassment of saying no. "He's too busy for this."

"Tom . . . ," Truly starts in a sweetheart voice.

He doesn't know what to say. He's coloring up. "My butt is very flattered to be considered for this, Truly. I'm not sure it's up to your standards."

"You've got to be fucking kidding me," I say in disbelief. Seriously. Has the man never reached back and felt what he has there? "We'll let you get back to work. I'll just trigger the dick tsunami."

Truly rushes to reassure him. "I hope you don't mind me saying so, but you're really the best man for this job. Please, just let Darcy take one photo of your butt and I'll buy you a steak dinner."

"Hmmm," Tom says. "Steak." I think he's trying to not laugh. I probably look like I'm about to start screaming. "What do I have to do?"

"It's easy," Truly jumps in. "Just stand there. Don't even suck your stomach in. My site is only real bodies. The models we use aren't tiny sample sizes. And Darce only uses minimal Photoshop. Real bodies," she repeats emphatically, looking at his groin.

"I don't think this classifies as a real body." My voice sounds very faint. Tom smiles like he is utterly charmed. I know my face is blood red, because he's biting his lip to stop laughing. "Hey, are you messing with me?"

"A little. I like it." He hears another bleat outside.

Truly decides to betray me. "Darcy was the butt for a few of the collections last year when we couldn't get models at a reasonable rate."

Tom's little Valeska ears prick up. "Darcy's an underwear model?" He's positively sparkling with humor and fun now. I'm flushing red, my heart erupting in my chest and sending liquid lava through my veins.

"I forbid you to look."

"She's got a great backside for underwear. You two could be the Underswears power couple, if you'd just put them on, Tom. What do you say? Steak dinner?"

"I never got a steak dinner," I complain.

"Okay," Tom says, laughing like he can't believe himself. Then he adds his usual disclaimer. "But only if no one tells Jamie."

He looks at his phone, then back at the house. "And it's a really big steak. I've really got to go. Nice to see you, Truly. Please sign a form later so I feel better about you walking through a building site." He looks at his new desk. In a chocolate-cake voice he says, "I can get that printer working."

"No, it needs to be done now. Here." Truly hands him a pair of underwear and he unfolds them. On the butt, it says, IRRATIONAL ASSHOLE. He bursts out laughing.

"Well these are very appropriate." He stares at her and realizes she's serious. "I can't do it now. That's crazy."

"It's either you, or I go talent scouting," Truly says, matter-of-factly. "That young guy up at the house would do it, I bet anything." She knows she's successfully pressed one of Tom's buttons and suppresses a grin as he turns to me and scowls.

"It's true, he would," my mouth says, because oh Lord, I want to see some skin.

Truly steps out and holds the door handle. "I'll stand out here and guard the door. Pull the drapes. This could take two minutes. Take your pants off, put these on, Darcy goes clicky-clicky, and we're done." To someone up at the house, Truly shouts, "He'll be three minutes."

The door slides shut.

"She makes it sound so easy." His hand is on the button of his pants. "Why am I considering it?"

"Because Truly has some sort of weird force field around her. You can't help but say yes. But if you do this, I will not let you treat me like shit afterward. You wanted to be distracted. You came in here. You're one big boy, and I can't keep you in here if you don't want to be. Nod so I know you admit it."

He nods. "If it isn't me, it's going to be someone else."

"Let's just get it over with. Pretend they're your swim trunks."

I tug the drapes shut and switch on the lights. I wheel over my stool. "You stand there." I point at the white void. I change settings, then blow dust out of the lens. There's a seemingly endless period of belt-jangling, stretching fabric, and movement behind me, and then Tom takes his position. I haven't seen his legs since his days on the swim team. I missed them so bad.

The poor thing looks terrified. He's gone from worksite boss to buff male model in the span of twenty seconds. He's suffering from the whiplash. He's not the only one. Those stretchy boxer-briefs look like they were made for him.

"Do you need a cigarette? Any final words? Seriously, you look like you're about to be riddled with bullets." Sometimes I love my smart mouth.

He looks so sweetly vulnerable, his T-shirt twisted low around his waist with his hands. He's a good boy in a bad-boy body. It's an underwear body.

Lord, it is too warm in this room.

Loretta was adamant he was a Viking in a past life—and she's right. He's just rowed across the Baltic Sea and now he's standing here, chest rising and falling under my stare.

"Okay." I try to not look at the skin and the legs and the hair. And is he kidding with that stomach? I see big slices every time he twists and readjusts his T-shirt. My mouth is so dry I'd drink from Patty's bowl. I've shot models and I've never seen anything like this.

"Are you okay?" he asks.

"You look fine," I say in an encouraging soccer-mom voice. I tap the ground with my boot. I will spare him the shame of making him take off his T-shirt altogether. He needs some dignity. "Turn your back to me. Pull your top up high. Higher. Yep."

I can't say it. I will explode if I don't say it. "You've got the best butt on the planet." I put the camera on high speed and begin to paparazzi his ass.

"Is Tom there?" Colin's voice is terrifyingly close. Jamie's mole, for sure, and he's about to bust us goofing off in the weirdest possible way. Tom and I freeze.

"He's just having a . . . talk, with Darcy."

"Tell him to come out front. They're unloading the timber, but he hasn't hired a forklift so we can't move it." Colin says that in a loud voice, so that Tom can hear.

"Shit," Tom says. "One second. I will be one second. Hurry, Darcy."

"It's okay, he's gone." Truly opens the door a fraction and the drapes twitch. "Oh, they look good on you, Tom."

I love her, but I get up and fix the curtain, banishing her. The rabid female timber wolf inside me doesn't want anyone else seeing this body. The worksite noise recedes.

"No one but me gets to see," I grumble to myself. "I can't believe you were brave enough to do this. Especially after . . . what I did." *In the kitchen, when I tried to maul you.*

"I couldn't stay away from you anymore. I thought having you around was bad for my concentration. But not having you where I can see you is actually worse."

"I assure you, I'm not fucking up anything in here."

"I missed you." His head shakes. "What do you call . . . what you did? In the kitchen?"

"From memory, I told you to get in me." I try to keep my tone light and amused. "I think you got a scary look at what happens when DB nearly loses control."

"That was you with some control left?" He's incredulous.

I flash back to the breaking wood, the pointing at the bedroom door, the crude honesty. But the truth is, it could have been worse.

"Well, yeah." I lower the camera. I'm breathing heavily enough to fog the display. At this rate, I'll destroy the lens. "If I lost all control, I would have—" I click the camera, just to make noise. "I probably would have—" I cover my mouth like I'm trying to hold in a burp. I can't say it. I cannot.

"Tell me," he says over his shoulder in that bass voice from the first morning on the worksite, when he said *Unpack the equipment* and the guys tucked tail and ran. It's a voice that you can't say no to.

Fuck it. If he wants honesty, I'll give it to him. "I would have undone your belt and got down on my knees, and made you pray to God."

"Jesus," he says with no air.

"Yep, you'd have been calling his name, all right." I cross one leg over the other so I can stifle the telltale heaviness I'm feeling. A sick little rush is spiking my shame. I could say almost anything to him and he'd have to stand there with his back to me and hear it. "Lucky for you, I've got a little control left. Just a little."

His massive shoulders roll and he sighs in misery.

"Come on, turn around and we'll finish up. You can go back to your flock." I swivel, side to side, and it doesn't help my aroused situation. It would serve me right if I accidentally orgasm on a stool from Kmart.

"I don't get it though," he says after a moment. "Why?"

"What do you mean 'why'?" I hear the disbelief in my voice. "You're phenomenal. You know that." When he glances over his shoulder at me, his eyes are raw and unsure. "You do know that, right? I can't even tell you how hot you are. I'd have to show you."

He shuffles foot to foot but doesn't turn to face me.

"Just the front now, and we're done. Thirty seconds. Come on, Tom, whip around." He does nothing. "Tom. Earth to Tom."

He says on a faint sigh, "I am having a personal issue."

"Yeah, you and me both. I've got a pack of double-A batteries with my name on it." My jeans feel like they've shrunk ten sizes, and the seam is nearly cutting me in half. "Let's just get through this."

"Just give me a second," he says in anguish.

"Turn around," I order him, desperate to end this. With reluctance heavy in his face, he obeys, twisting the T-shirt up. His stomach is quilted into six beautiful blocks. "Hoooooly shit." My mouth drops open and I can barely lift my camera.

"You see what I mean," he says through a clenched jaw. His underwear looks different from how it should in the front. All bent out of shape. Uncontainable. An angle that should be ending, but it just . . . doesn't. My insides clench up; *yes please.*

"No wonder you weren't impressed by my dirty box of merchandise," I blurt out even as I steady my hands and zoom. "I don't think I could get the lighting right on you."

"That's hilarious," he says in fury, reaching down and grabbing at his pants. "You just have to keep talking, don't you."

"No, wait, I need one shot for Truly." I lower my camera. "Just don't worry about it. This has actually happened before. I once did a boudoir shoot for a couple's anniversary, and—"

His hand is pressed over his eyes. "Just stop talking for

one goddamn second." Horror lights up inside me. Jamie never stops talking. Ever. Then he adds, "Your voice is so hot, I can't bear it. Obviously."

"Oh." I swivel around on the stool and put my back to him. "I didn't know that." The room rings silent.

"Of course you know that," he replies with temper. "I have never heard a woman talk the way you do." There's an audible swallowing sound. "You've got to be more careful with what you say to guys."

"I have never in my life said anything like this to another guy, and I resent the insinuation." I peek over my shoulder. Can this excruciating moment end now? One more tiny micro freeze frame and my brain's got it forever. It's now in the vault. It's a really big vault.

"This is humiliating." He tuts and huffs. "Are you this filthy with any half-decent-looking guy that catches your eye?"

"I'm this filthy with you. Only you. And you're not just 'half-decent.' I've seen Michelangelo's *David* in Florence. You make him look like a pin-dicked garden gnome."

"Done, guys?" Truly calls out.

I wave my hand in panic. "Nearly! Let's talk about something really neutral. Like, the house renovation. How's that going? Tell me all about it."

"Okay," he says, sounding encouraged.

"Talk about the guttering or the vents. That big water stain on the kitchen ceiling, how's that coming along? Or the . . ." I dig deep. "The trellis. The pipes. The architraves and the finials and the—"

He cuts in, despairing. "I think you saying vaguely architectural terms is making it worse."

"You weirdo." I hear myself a little differently now. Is it really a sexy voice? I'm pretty sure the most response I've ever elicited from Tom has been dilated pupils. Now I'm in a room that contains his hard dick.

Safer. Keep him safer.

Another minute ticks by. "Okay," he says, strained. "Do it."

I take about ten shots and before I even tell him we're done, he's bending over, jamming his legs into his pants, still wearing the Underswears. He explodes out of the room, almost knocking over Truly.

"You owe me more than a steak dinner," Tom says to her as he departs at speed. "You owe me a steak dinner on a cruise ship."

Truly comes back inside. "What did you do to him?"

"I'm really not sure," I say, patting sweat off my brow. "But I don't think we're getting those underpants back."

Chapter 14

Status update: So tired I'm possibly dying. And it's only Thursday.

I stand in the bathroom with my hands on my hips and look at the wall. I've never intentionally demolished a room before. "Ben, can you give me an outline on what I'm supposed to do?"

The strangest words trigger me back to the Underswears photo shoot. Like *outline*.

Ben's the one I can trust to give me advice that won't result in my fucking something up. Alex only knows how to carry heavy things and laugh at jokes. Colin's still on my shit list and I am almost certain he's Jamie's mole. I've been feeding him bogus information in an attempt to flush him out.

"Getting the tiles off the walls would be a good start. Use . . . this." I try not to look at Ben's shiny dome while he rummages in a box of tools. He gives me a short crowbar.

"Carefully, now. It's easy to put a hole in the wall if you just start smashing."

He toes an empty cardboard box over to me. "They'll be sharp. Wear goggles, too. There's a bin outside, but Alex will do the lifting. Then after that, take up the floor tiles."

"Fine. Thanks." Having a clearly defined task is like heaven. I knot my baggy tank at my hip and pull my jeans up a little. Gloves on. I put the goggles on the top of my head.

Tom passes the door and halts. We make eye contact, then he looks at the crowbar in my hand. His eyelids flutter and his body misses a step, like he's just seen something he can't bear. Do I look ridiculous? Is he imagining me hurting myself?

Actually, I remember what he got like when I talked to him about architraves. I swing the crowbar. "Is this a look that works for you?"

He swallows and nods. "Ah, yeah."

From up his ladder, Colin shakes his head at us wearily. We never learn.

By now, this same little loop is becoming ingrained: Tom walks past and gets distracted by me, and something in another part of the house fucks up. I am a human curse.

I jerk my thumb. "Keep walking." He does, looking flustered.

Colin says, "I don't think he expects you to actually demo."

"I think I've explained several times that I am part of the crew, right?" I wipe sweat from my brow with my forearm.

I've had to accept that I am forever glistening. "Did you get your tax details to Tom?"

Colin sulks. "Not yet."

"Oh really, Mr. Paperwork?" It's on the tip of my tongue to order him to get them in by five. But I won't. I'll stay behind the line that Tom drew for me.

I can't help but notice that Colin looks kind of cool, standing up there against the white wall background. I pick up my camera and take a quick shot. I frown at the screen. I can do better than that.

I adjust the settings, reframe, and the second shot is a lot better. Like, a lot. "How'd you like to be my muse?" I ask Colin. He doesn't bother acknowledging my existence.

I put the camera aside. Two pictures of a human face among the shots of electrical outlets and cracked skirting boards. Tom might be proud of me for that. How weird that it's awful old Colin that's inspired me.

I press my palm against the first tile in the row. It feels completely sacrilegious, but I put the edge of the crowbar on the top of the tile and it just . . . pops off. I'm too slow to catch it and it shatters at my feet.

Tom's head almost instantly appears at the doorjamb.

"Be careful." He's regretting this big-time. "Yeah, wait," he says to someone else. It's an impressive juggling act: supervising an entire worksite, and personally supervising my every move.

"I'm fine." I pop off more tiles into my palm and drop them into a cardboard box. "I'm one of the guys now, right?"

I say to Colin, who laughs without humor and says *sure.* "Bye, Tom. See you later."

He gets my unsubtle hint and walks off again.

The impromptu Underswears shoot ruined the little candy-hug truce we'd just achieved. When I walked Truly out to her car, there were crews of guys hand-carrying wood down the side of the house, Colin had his arms crossed, and Tom was furious. He'd admitted his participation was voluntary, and had promised to not blame me for it, but it feels an awful lot like another strike against me.

I tried to help carry timber too, but the moment I bent down, he was bumping me back like I'd strayed too close to a cliff.

He's starting to be more Valeska than man.

It's got to be the stress that's turning him into an animal. If I talk to one of the delivery guys? He's coming up the front path with a snarl on his lip. If I make a spare sandwich for bozo Alex, who's so far forgotten lunch every single day? Tom's leaning on the bench, jealous eyes on my profile until I pull out the cheese and lettuce.

The guys on the crew are starting to walk sideways around me. I'm starting to feel like a land mine. If Tom touches me again I'm probably just going to explode on him. Hence my permanent fever sweat.

To the bathroom crew, I say, "I've known Tom since we were eight. But some days I wonder if he'll ever speak to me again after this."

"Renovations are very stressful," Ben says diplomatically. "And so is starting your own business. Aldo has been making things difficult for Tom, especially getting staff."

"He didn't tell me that." I wonder what else he's lying awake over.

"Payroll. Insurance. Workers' safety. Subcontractors. Contracts," Colin drones from up on his perch. He snaps his fingers at me, and I know that means to hand up his cordless drill. I'm only slightly above Alex in the pecking order.

"I don't respond to that." I click my fingers back at him. "Use your words."

"Site security. Suppliers. Rental equipment. Invoicing. Budget." Colin gives me a very meaningful look and finishes with, "Client management. Pass me that drill."

I hand it up. "You've made your point. He's got it all handled."

"I don't think so. He's very distracted," Colin says in between annoying drill buzzes. He hands down a vent to me, getting gray dust in my hair. "Trash."

Feeling mildly persecuted, I toss the vent in Alex's box. "I want to argue with you that he's got everything handled, but I've recently been advised that it's none of my business." I return to my tiles, unsettled. Tom sat on the back step last night with his head in his hands. As soon as he heard my approaching footfalls, he'd smoothed everything back into that competent façade.

Is it the renovation, or Megan, that is tormenting him?

I find my rhythm again. Pop, smash. Pop, smash. I'm getting handy with my crowbar. I should give Alex a break on the trash task.

I bend down and lift the box, and my heart decides to shit its pants.

It feels like a rush of palpitations that seem to bubble upward, into my throat, graying my vision. I lean my shoulder on the wall. Okay, that does it. I think I need to go in for a quick review of the old heart situation, but Jamie always comes with me. I'm still little-kid Darcy, too scared to go to one big-girl appointment on her own.

It's weird. I haven't gotten used to Loretta's absence in my life, because she feels so close I half expect to look out the window and see her bossing someone around.

Sometimes it feels like Jamie's the one who died, because the void just keeps getting bigger. And my heart beats more lopsidedly than ever.

"Alex does the lifting. Are you okay?" Ben is at my side. "Should we get Tom? He told us to let him know if you weren't feeling good."

"Did he now." I straighten up and my hand is on my hip in an instant. Through my teeth and the pricking tears in my eyes, I rattle out, "I'm just taking a break. Ignore him."

"Ignore him?" Alex echoes from the doorway. "You don't ignore the boss." He crowds in, too.

"Just breathe nice and deep," Colin says, frowning at Alex in a *shut up* sort of way. He's concerned enough that he climbs down his ladder, every movement evidently pain-ful and arthritic. I must look like I'm dying. "Should you sit down?"

I shake my head. "There's nothing wrong with me." I'll be damned if I bond with this old codger over our mutual ailments. He shuffles off like a bloodhound, his nose on the ground, sniffing out the boss. Or worse, finding a quiet spot to call my brother with the latest intel.

"Head spin? I get those." Alex can always be counted on to blithely gloss over whatever's going on. I like that about him. "Especially if I'm hungover," he adds with a little bit of a brag in his voice.

I sympathize with this young kid. He's already complained to me about how boring his nights are, stuck in his cheap motel room in between Oldy and Baldy.

I think of the boost I got when Tom said the crew missed me. Things are fun with me here. Alex is the youth demo-graphic I need to align myself with.

"Hey, tomorrow night, get everyone to come down to the bar I work at. We'll have a little first-week celebration. I'll give you all cheap drinks. You'll have to show me your ID."

Alex brightens. "That sounds awesome. We haven't done anything like that in ages. Tom works us pretty hard."

I can see it now, morale lifting and the entire team bonding. Clinking glasses, *cheers!* "Well, I want you guys to enjoy this project." Everything steadies up and the moment has passed. I push away from the wall. "But this doesn't mean I'm in love with you. Everyone's invited."

"I know that," Alex gasps after a second, turning red. "I know that."

Ben decides to risk his life. "Fairly obvious who she's in love with." I pretend to beat him with my crowbar, he pretends to be injured, and now we're all grinning. I put the radio on and we all fall into rhythms matching the music. I don't know what's wrong with me, but I could do this forever.

They tell me about their last job, a big vacation house on top of a cliff. Tom worked all night to re-sand some floors that weren't up to his standard. They tell me what I already know: Tom is a tireless perfectionist. I think they're warning me. I work harder, neater, determined to do this perfectly. I will be faultless.

"You might be able to answer this one," Alex starts. "What's with the Chihuahua? We've never worked it out." He goes for my next full box of tiles.

"What do you mean?"

"A guy like that should have a big dog," Alex says on a grunt as he hoists. "We kind of thought she was Megan's."

"A guy like that? Tom was thirteen when he got her, and he didn't care that he'd get teased for it forever. He picked the rescue dog that loved him best. And I named her myself, years before Tom even met Megan."

The brag is clear in my voice, but I can't help it. Wait. That wasn't bragging. That sounded like ownership.

"Hey." I take Alex by the sleeve as he steps past me. I glance at Ben and Colin; they're both preoccupied. In a soft tone, I say, "I've met a lot of men, all over the world, and Tom's the best. Without a doubt, he is the best man. Try to be like him." Alex nods, absorbing Grandma Darcy's wisdom.

"A guy like that," I repeat to myself as I resume work. I want to call Alex back to give him a full sermon on all the reasons that Tom is the example he should aspire to.

Tom did a task briefing with some guys yesterday with Patty sitting between his boots. A guy like that is strong in a way that's deeper than muscle and bones, because he wears his softness on the outside. I think I met my ideal man when I was eight, and no one else has ever measured up.

"A guy like that." This time when I lean on the tiles, it's because I'm thinking about Tom in a way that makes me stop breathing altogether. If he walks past right now and puts his head around the door, I don't think I'll be able to keep my expression neutral.

I've never felt this way before in my life. I don't know what to do.

I turn back to my task, my face warm. The single pink tile is next in line. I'll take this one off carefully and keep it as a coaster. Pop. I turn it over, and it has a tarot card beneath the layer of glue.

"What!" I laugh out loud. "Guys, look. My grandma left me something." Ben and Alex crowd around me like I've struck gold.

"What even is it?" Alex is adorably naïve about most things.

"My grandma was a fortune-teller. This is the Strength tarot card." A woman dressed in white holds open the jaws of a lion. It could be a violent image, but instead it's nothing but patience and steadiness. It looks like me and Valeska.

"What does it mean?"

I try to remember. She tried to teach me how to read cards, but I was always too busy. Too tired. Too hungover. Too overseas. "I think it means perseverance and courage. But I'll have to look it up."

Ben says, "Maybe there are more cards hidden around the house. It's a sign. Tell everyone to keep an eye out," he adds to Alex, and the fact that he hasn't just dismissed it as girly nonsense has me beaming.

I finish the wall tiles by midmorning, and while I do have a few more heart-skip moments, I hold up well. Colin has been watching me like a buzzard waiting for a carcass. I forget to eat my lunch or drink and have no idea what time it is when I pull up the final section of floor tiles and blot my sweaty face into the hem of my tank.

"Wow," Tom says from the doorway. "Okay." He looks around the room like he's never seen it before.

I'm a shaky mess. "I don't know how long this should have taken me, so I can't tell if you're actually impressed." I'm nervous as his perfect eyes trace over the walls, floors, up my legs, and to my face.

"You did this by yourself?" He's shocked.

"She's a machine." Ben gives me a crooked grin and turns back to his own task.

Tom steps close and assesses me. "You didn't push it too hard?"

He takes me by the wrist, feeling for my pulse. His other hand scrapes my hair back from my face. I shouldn't like his brand of fussing. I should step out of his hands. But maybe I should try to wear a little softness on the outside. I lean into his touch.

"I was completely fine." I see Colin's lips purse. At least he didn't snitch. "Tom, look. Loretta left us something." I show him the tarot tile.

He laughs, and the afternoon sunlight turns the floating dust particles into glitter around us. It turns his eyes to whiskey, and they get me drunk. A guy like this? He's the only one who's ever made my stomach flip.

"She always liked to make things interesting." His arms wrap around me. He squeezes me tight and says above my head, "You did good. I'm so impressed."

I put my arms around his waist and I breathe in lungfuls of him, my cheek on the pad of his chest and the stud in my nipple pinching in the most pleasurable way. Any second I will screw this up. Better enjoy it while it lasts.

"Where's my hug, boss?" Alex says as he reappears. Ben and Colin both laugh. Oh my God, what is wrong with me? I'm getting high off this part-of-the-team feeling.

Tom says, "This one gets special privileges. You know that." When I lean back, I can see Tom's smiling, too. He releases me and toes at the ancient adhesive marks on the floor. "We're ahead of schedule in here. Good work, every-one."

I am so elated I'm surprised I'm not two feet off the

ground. Making Tom proud? It's like snorting a rainbow. It cannot last. "Okay, you'd better leave now."

"She's pretty good at this." Alex picks up my last box of broken tiles. "And she works at a bar. Friday night is going to be lit." He clomps off.

"What does he mean, Friday?" Tom focuses sharply on my face. "What's happening then?" Ben and Colin clear out, saying *bathroom* and *water,* respectively.

And just like that, my feet are back on the ground, and I've fucked up again.

Chapter 15

I just said I'd do cheap drinks on Friday night at the bar." I turn away to pick at a chipped piece of tile still on the wall, but Tom puts his hand on my elbow.

"Who'd you ask?"

"I just told Alex to ask everybody who was interested." I take a drink from my water bottle. "I'm sorry, but you can't come. You're the boss. No one will be able to relax."

He bangs the door shut behind him with his boot. "You just can't help yourself."

Everything inside me leaps in fright. I refuse to put my hand over my startled heart. Playing the cardio card is cheating. "Oh, great. What have I done now?"

He's angry eyes and crossed arms. "I have to push everyone hard to finish this place. When it's done, then they drink. For now, they work."

"But what they do in their free time—"

"I don't want them getting caught up in the Darcy Barrett

whirlwind. Believe me, once you're in it, you can't get out." His phone buzzes and he rejects the call hard enough to crack the glass. "This is week one, Darce. You should have asked me first."

"All I did was suggest that—"

"You invited the entire site crew out to a bar, where the *hot* homeowner"—here, he indicates quotation marks with his fingers in a way that feels insulting—"is going to lay on cheap drinks. Cancel it. Half of them have to work Saturday morning."

"Looks like I've pissed off my *hot* builder." I give him the same quotation fingers back. "You can't decide what they do in their free time. They're big boys. And I was told that I make things fun around here."

Surely he knew I'd take the bait on that?

"This entire thing? It's my thing." He makes a hand motion that apparently encompasses the entire house and everything in it. "I'm everyone's boss. Even yours. Ask me before you do stupid shit like this again." He puts his head out the door. "Friday's canceled."

"That sucks," I hear Alex say as the door is shut again.

"You're being an asshole. It really doesn't suit you." It knocks a little of his momentum out of him, but he rallies after a beat and lowers his voice.

"If I don't keep it together, this entire project will turn to shit. I have to be the hard-ass boss to these guys. And now to you, apparently."

"Well, if this is the complete reaming a new employee gets

when they make an innocent mistake, then you're not a very good boss." I aim a low blow. "Just because you have no life doesn't mean the rest of us should just stay home."

He's incredulous. "I have no life because I'm trying to sell your house."

"You've had no life for a long time now. When was the last time you went out? Had a drink, dinner, a date? When was the last time you went swimming?"

"I've got no time."

"You're always saying that. The Tom I knew couldn't live without chlorine."

"Well, the Darcy I knew took photos of real shit and of her own volition. Don't be pretending to me like your life is so fulfilling." He puts a hand in his hair. "I cannot think straight with you in here."

He leaves a big pause, and there's that familiar look in his eyes. I've seen it so many times, right before he chooses Jamie's side. "I think this whole idea of having you work was a mistake."

"Don't you fucking dare try to cut me out of this. You're overreacting like crazy."

"You just get me so . . ." Tom closes his eyes. There's that shoulder roll. Like he's climbing back into his body a little. "Just look at it from my perspective. These guys on-site, they know I'm the boss. You're the homeowner. We're a team now. I thought I got that across to you."

"Yes, but that doesn't mean we can't be nice to these guys."

He leans on the wall, coating his shoulder in dust. "Early on, I was everyone's friend, but I got walked over. I suppose that's not news to you." There's vulnerability there before he blinks it away. "I'm supposed to be in control of everything."

Colin's list of burdensome responsibilities is still running on a loop in the background, and I nearly open my mouth to ask if everything is going okay. But I can't. He'll just growl at me.

My glowing sense of pride is completely gone now. "I was really enjoying myself just now. I was looking forward to you seeing what I did. And you come in and tell me I shouldn't even be here? Real nice." I pull on the window for air. Of course, the little asshole doesn't budge.

"Leave it. I'll do it." For him, the fucking thing will probably slide up like silk. I go for the crowbar on the floor but Tom puts his boot on it. "I said demo the room, not level it to the ground."

"Another thing, Tom. Don't tell people to keep an eye on me. That's really insulting. Do they all know about my . . . ?" I tap my chest.

"Just these three know. I doubt my insurance covers you doing this. That's the risk I'm taking for you. And now I have to go and find a new roofing contractor." His eyes narrow.

"Why is that my fault?"

"I fired him." Tom might as well have a sledgehammer in his fist now.

Well, at least I know who called me hot-in-quotation-marks. "You've been marinating in too much testosterone. I was doing a job in here."

His eyes flash bright. "And that's why I have zero patience for guys who talk like that about women on a job site. I'd fire him for saying that about anyone, not just you."

Every time Tom steps up to the plate and shows me who he is, it's a relief. Aldo would have roared laughing. I look out the window. "What exactly did he say?"

"I'll spare you the details."

I put my hand on my hip. "Well, am I digging a grave or not?"

He laughs without much humor. "Make it a real deep one. He was one of my last options, too. One of the last that Aldo hasn't gotten to. Your house may have no new roof at this rate."

I gesture upward. "I'm sure the one up there is fine."

"Oh, Darce. If you knew the things I knew, you wouldn't sleep. Not even in a bed like yours."

My mattress made quite an impression. He's thinking about it right now. His pupils are dialing out. I stab around for some way to toss some cold water on the rising heat in this room.

"Megan must have loved it when you got like this."

"She's never stepped foot on one of my sites. Never picked up a crowbar, much less broken a sweat." His white teeth bite into his bottom lip. "I've never been like this. Whatever this is."

The beast I had imagined as a child and that has followed me around the globe every step I took? The one that would sleep at the foot of my bed and tear out throats? He's here in this room, but I'm not scared. If I stepped toe-to-toe with him and put my hand up, he would press his cheek into my palm. But now is not the time to explain the concept of Valeska.

"You've always been like this. Trust me."

"Only around you. Never Megan." His eyes hold steady on

mine until whatever internal guilt-pinch he just experienced eases off. "I can see you like hearing that."

I've probably got wolf eyes myself. "Of course I do. I'm a jealous bitch. She never came to visit? Not even once in a dress with a picnic basket?" He shakes his head. "Damn. If you were—" I cut myself off short.

His dark eyebrow arches. "If I were yours, what?"

I huff a disbelieving laugh. He's getting bold. The way he's looking at me right now? He's going to lick me, just to know my taste.

I chicken out. "You don't want to know what I mean."

"The problem is," he says with slow deliberation, "that I do want to know."

"Use your imagination." I have nothing. I'm outclassed here, and he knows it. There's amusement in his eyes and the sharp point of his canine tooth showing as he steps back toward the door.

"I have been. That's why I'm a goddamn wreck." He opens the door like that's going to keep us safe. A tiny bit of tension evaporates out of the room in a pink steam cloud, but it's not enough. We could still leap on each other and give the guys in the hall a show.

He advances closer again, and with one finger he slides the strap of my tank back onto my shoulder.

In a voice so quiet I almost miss it, he says, "You're driving me insane with your skin and your sweat." When he sees me recoil, he clarifies and my stomach bottoms out. "You seriously don't know you're sexy, do you?"

"No," I manage to say. "I mean, I've been told—"

His eyes turn nuclear.

"But not by you. Never by you."

"You're wrong," he argues. "I've told you in every way I could. Even when I shouldn't have. Must have been fun for you, being able to tease and mess with me whenever we had thirty seconds alone."

The eight long Megan years stretch behind us like a desert road. He thinks that was nice or enjoyable for me? Standing on the side of a bonfire, while he sat with Megan perched on his knee? Drinking until the knife point inside me dulled?

"Must have been nice for you, getting engaged and not having to give a shit about me or my skin. Look, I'm going to take the afternoon off."

I grab the pink tarot tile and duck out from under his arm and blow down the hall, stepping over cords and men's boots; out into the backyard; and into the studio. Patty's claws click around on the floor but I'm too dispirited to look at her happy sunflower face.

He's followed me of course. "I need you to keep working."

"You don't need me. I'm a novelty. No one takes me seriously. Every time I pick up a tool, I feel like everyone's thinking, *Aw, so cute!* I'm a freakin' Patty."

"You know that's not true. You worked your ass off."

I put the tarot card on my bench. "I do nothing but stress you out. I'm a liability. You said it yourself. I'm going to do you a favor and clear out for a bit."

Tom leans on the door frame of my bedroom but he won't

step an inch inside. It's probably to keep himself safe. "Jamie bet me a hundred bucks you'd quit in the first week, but I said you wouldn't. Are you going to give this win to him?"

"I'm not quitting, I'm just . . . leaving." I gesture up at the house, where an audience is building. "They're all waiting for the big boss."

He gives up on me. "Must be nice to just leave when things get hard. Some of us don't have that luxury." He walks back to the house, where he's surrounded by guys, all needing things done, answered, signed, sorted.

I rewind my memory. *Cheap drinks. Bar. Enjoy this project.* Is that really enough to derail an entire house renovation? I thought I was doing something good, but now shame is burning inside me, hot and sick.

It overrides everything; even the flush of pleasure in knowing I'm affecting him is tainted. It's not something that he wants. The worst part about all of this? Jamie was right. I'm disrupting Tom so much he can't do his job or enjoy his new challenge as boss. He's completely tormented.

I pick up the envelope with my passport application in it. I'll go mail this, then take my moldy old heart out for some day drinking. Who was I kidding? I'm not physically capable of the labor, or mentally fit to be a boss.

I have five names in my new phone's contact list: Mom, Dad, Tom, Jamie, Truly. The only five who matter, and at this rate I might lose Tom altogether. My idiot thumb still thinks it is a twin, because it chooses Jamie first. I scroll again and dial Truly. She picks up on the first ring.

"Could you come pick me up? My car is blocked in by about a hundred trucks." I look in the mirror. I am a hot mess. A gleaming, pink-faced mess, with smudgy eyes. Sexy? Tom's been marooned on this desert island a little too long.

When Truly speaks, I know she's got some sewing pins in her mouth. "Sure, I can be there soon. What's happening?"

"The usual. My heart nearly blew up, I died of malnutrition, I invited the crew out to drinks, and then Tom's head exploded." I don't hide my heart stuff from Truly, because she doesn't lecture me about it.

I hear the sound of a sewing machine on the other end. "Drinks? Already? Aren't they there for months?"

"Yes, but I was trying to bring a little fun into this."

The whirring stops and starts. "You'd be making them all think this whole project is going to be easy and fun, when it's not. They wouldn't take it as seriously."

"I want to create a team vibe."

"You can probably think of ways for everyone to feel happy to be on this project without plying them with drinks. That's kind of your default setting."

"I'm a bartender." This is not going how I thought it would.

"You don't need to be on twenty-four/seven bartender mode when you're not on shift. Just . . . be yourself for once. The real you. You know what I do when I make a mistake when sewing?"

"You have a complete mental and emotional breakdown.

No wait, that's me." I sit on the edge of my bed and heave a sigh. "Jamie would love it if I quit."

"When I make a mistake, I unpick it and I keep on sewing. And hey, Darce? You're not a bartender. You're a photographer. I wish you'd believe it again."

I dolefully look up at the flash mob forming around Tom. "I keep trying to help, but it always ends badly. I'm beginning to think the best way might be to just stay off-site as much as I can."

Truly sighs. "I'm on your side. Always and forever. But this job is about you actually staying for something big and finishing it. I love you, but that's not what you're generally known for."

I'm stung. "I did weddings for how many years? I always showed up for them."

"But you need to start looking at the bigger picture. Where's your business now? You pressed the button and imploded that, just because you screwed up one time and that bride trashed you online." More sewing noises. "You broke your own heart on that, and you need to forgive yourself for it."

I chew my thumbnail and stubbornly say nothing.

"Just go and unpick your mistake and keep on sewing. He is not coping, Darce, that much is painfully obvious. Find out what you can do for him and do it."

I pull open the sliding door and the sound causes half of the crew to look around. Fuck it. Let's see if I can unpick this.

"Hey, guys, a quick word." I try to not notice how Tom's

arms have crossed, his face taking on a careful, neutral expression. He's expecting a blaze of glory right now.

"So I jumped the gun earlier. Apparently, you have the end-of-job party at the *end* of the job." There's laughter. "My bad. I'll order pizza for everyone tomorrow. Eating it here with no alcohol whatsoever. Then we all resume working our asses off. That's my best offer."

There's no grumbling. In fact, they cheer, a big *a-heeeeey!*

That's because pizza is a precious natural resource. It can heal tiredness, bad mood, falling morale, and a fading will to live. Pizza realigns the heart chakras. It can make Tom's arms loosen and drop to his sides. It can make his eyes spark with humor. He smiles and shakes his head.

It makes him look at me like he loves me again, and that's why pizza is the greatest.

"Okay. Pizza party on Friday. Now get your asses back to work. That means you too, Darcy."

Late in the afternoon, Tom approaches me. He's tired, with paperwork in his hands. His phone has been crying like a baby all afternoon. "I'm going down to the gym to take a shower."

I want to thank him for the mental image. "The gym has a pool, doesn't it?"

"I don't have time."

"Get in the water. Even ten minutes. It's what you need." He needs time. How can I give him more time? Come on, Loretta. Give me a sign. What can I do? How can I instill a bit of calm in his life?

His phone begins ringing, and it becomes so obvious I want to slap myself. I put my arms around his waist and pull his phone from his back pocket.

"Valeska Building Services. Darcy speaking. Yep, I can get back to you on that." I pull a piece of paper from my back pocket and write, *Tile color?* "Yep. In the morning. Bye."

He stares at me. I have no idea if I'm about to be screamed at.

The phone rings again. "I'd better buy a notepad. Valeska Building Services. Darcy speaking. What? Alex. I'm answering Tom's phone from now on. If you left your phone here, it stays here until the morning. I don't know! Watch TV. Yep. Bye." I hang up. "No message required."

"You're not a secretary, you're my client." Tom grabs at it when it rings again. I hold up my finger and answer it again.

"Sure, but it'll have to be the morning." I write down, *Rental equipment confirmation.* "He's finished for the day. Bye."

I put his phone in my back pocket, and it feels like it belongs there.

"Go. If you don't come back with chlorine on you, I'm going to be pissed off. I'll clear your voicemail and write a list of questions for you. I'll call them back. It's going to be okay."

"Darce." His voice is wretched with gratitude and his body droops with exhaustion. He looks like he wants to get down on his knees and kiss the toe of my boot.

"Don't cry." I pat his shoulder. "It's just a few messages."

Chapter 16

I t's a late Friday night after my bar shift when I find Tom, still hard at work at his desk. Just the sight of him, sitting in the same room as my bed, crackles through my synapses and obliterates my exhaustion.

He looks up at me and his eyes don't change. He's exhausted.

"Hi. Did you call Terry back, by any chance?" He clenches his jaw to repress his yawn. I'm pretty sure I completely hallucinated that moment when he told me I was sexy.

"Yeah. That guy's a jerk." I unhook my earrings and toss my jacket on my bed. My feet ache. Scratch that: everything aches. I wonder if we have any pizza left over from our second Friday worksite pizza party. I'm a legend around these parts. I think if I don't buy pizza again this week, I'll break hearts.

He turns in his chair, expression apologetic. "I know. That's why I hate calling him."

"Luckily, he's met his match and I out-jerked him." I consult my notebook. "He said he's giving us a discount. I thought we'd finished demolition."

"There's some specialist stuff that we can't do ourselves. Yeah," he says as he sees me turn, nostrils flared. "I swam again. I don't know how you can always smell it." He smells his own forearm. "I do shower after, honest."

"So that's why you're halfway back to yourself. I swear, your natural state is dripping wet. To think, you couldn't swim when we first met you. Lucky Jamie taught you."

He's remembering. "I saw your pool and decided I'd better learn quick. Jamie only teased me about it for like, five solid years, but anyway." His mouth lifts in a smile. "You taught me, actually."

"No, Jamie did."

"While he was busy showing off how great his dives were, you were the one actually showing me what to do. Under the water, so he couldn't see, you'd pull me along by my hand." He blows out a breath. "Shit, Darce, I have known you for so long."

The past scrolls out. There's so much to lose. That's why I've gotta keep treading water carefully.

He knows I need a subject change. "Speaking of getting back to yourself, I looked through your camera."

"Oh. Okay." I don't like the guilty look in his eyes. "It's fine that you did. It's just progress shots for Jamie."

"That's not all that's on there. You've been taking photos of people. That one of Colin looking through the hole in the wall? You're so good." He glows.

I take a deep breath. "Thank you. I mean, they were just for fun. It's weird, but I think Colin is my muse. He's so craggy."

"He's the last person I would have picked to be your muse. I thought for sure it would've been Alex." My friendship with Alex grates on Tom.

"Alex's face has no bones." I watch Tom think about that. "No bones, no shadows, Darcy is not inspired."

"But you have been inspired. That's good."

"You swim for me. I decided to try something for you." I open a folder on my computer to show Tom my new project. "How's this for taking photos of real shit, and of my own volition?"

In my half-hour break at the bar, I shot an interesting reel of biker beards, tattoos, and grizzled stares. It was astonishing how quickly these dangerous-looking men submitted to my request for a portrait. "I realized how much better it is, taking photos of faces that have seen some hard times. I won't be hounding you anymore. You're too gorgeous."

He laughs like he's flattered and his T-shirt touches my back as he looks at the portraits. I scroll through slowly. "I'm quitting there soon, but I'm glad I realized I should do this before I do. This one told me that no one's ever wanted a photo of him before."

I tip my head up and watch Tom as he considers the frightening face on the screen. This is the part of my life he hates. The messy, dirty, scary place. The protector in him is desperate to pull me away, but he forces himself to exhale.

"I'm sure he's had a few mugshots," Tom replies, scratching his jaw. "He's looking at the camera like he's never had such a beautiful girl ask to take his photo."

My heart skips two beats. Possibly three. "I'm going to get some sunset shots of the guys fucking around in the parking lot. Did you know that their patches mean different things, like codes? I want to shoot them. I don't know why. I just feel like . . . collecting them."

"Be careful, DB. I know you handle yourself, but just—" He stops himself. "I don't have to tell you that. What could you use these photos for?"

"I guess an exhibition." I hear the reluctance in my own voice. Winning the Rosburgh prize and watching Jamie work the crowd has ruined that room-full-of-people prospect for me. It's astonishing how vivid it still feels, even after all these years. My accomplishment—arguably the peak of my career—was the result of my brother existing. Something about watching him pose beneath his own portrait had cracked something inside me.

"I just realized that winning that prize was the worst thing that ever happened to me. It made me believe I can't do anything without Jamie."

Tom leans over and snags one of Truly's Underswears lookbooks. It turned out really well from the printers. He puts it on my keyboard. "Well, we know that's not true. What about an art book?"

I consider it. Tom's so smart. "I could start posting some on social media, get a following, then try to get a book deal. I could photograph different clubs from all over the world."

His forearm wraps around my collarbone in a hug. It feels like an involuntary move. Like he has to. "Or you could focus on this club and be back in bed where you belong."

"Don't worry, I still don't have a passport." I touch my fingers on the sealed envelope. "I haven't got a stamp." I let myself lean back on him. Just a little. I feel the pleasure purr out of him, into me, and it's incredible what we can create together when we stop trying. I put my hand on his forearm and close my eyes.

"You know this is the longest I've lived in one place since I was eighteen?"

"I did know that. How does living in the one place feel?"

"It feels nice. But I don't want to admit it." I open my eyes. "You don't live in the one place either."

"No. Probably won't for a long time." His arm slides off me, and I'm cold.

He changes the subject abruptly. "You're not working tomorrow night, right? It was brought to my attention recently that I have no life."

"I don't have a life either. Don't be taking advice from someone who can't walk up two flights of stairs or eat fresh greens before they rot." I can admit the truth in this half-light. I stand up and try to escape this awkward confession, maybe take a dip in the fish pond to cool my embarrassed flush, but he just presses me to his body in a delicious squeeze.

"I'm worried sick about you." He whispers it above my head.

"I'm okay," I say to his flawless heart, beating so strong beneath my cheek.

"All I want is to take care of you, but you make it so hard."

"I know I do. But if it's going to feel this good, maybe I should let you fuss over me. Just a little, sometimes, when no one's watching."

"You better not be messing with me." He's tucking me closer, threading his forearm up my back, cupping my head. "I know a one-chance offer when I see one." He always has been smarter than me.

I whisper it. "It's only you that can fuss, though. No one else."

"It'll be hard for me to fuss over you when you're in a different hemisphere."

I think of the airport departure lounge and it doesn't give me the same tingle. Bus, train, and plane routes branch out in my imagination from every international airport I've arrived in. All I feel is tired. "Don't you want to go places?"

"I'm not brave like you, Darce. When I take a vacation, I'll start small." He smiles like he feels foolish. "The beach in front of your parents' house was as close as I've come to a vacation in years. And I didn't even get in the water. Sad, I guess, to someone like you." He eases back from me. "Maybe we can get a life together sometime, before you leave."

I didn't expect that. "What do you want to do?"

"I don't know. I haven't done this in a long time. But

you're the best person I know to teach me. Let's just go get a drink to celebrate. Two weeks into the renovation. I need to talk to you about something important."

I stiffen in terror. "Oh fuck. Just tell me now."

He shakes his head. "Trust me."

* * *

It's OUR FAKE date night. Tom wants to talk to me about something, and I think it's something important, and related to the sexual fog we're blundering around in. I have never been this nervous waiting for a man.

He's talking to some guys at the side of the house. They are all looking up at the roof. It's hard to get used to the fact that my house is now a group project. One of them says something that makes Tom's head turn toward me.

"Yeah, this is not a girl you keep waiting," I hear him reply. "Call me if you have any problems."

"Don't make me drag you," I call out to him.

"She would," he says with a laugh. There's some hand shaking and now he's walking up the driveway to me in his clean get-a-life clothes and I think about how being an adult suits him.

As a teenager, he was sweet and straightforward, with zero idea of his own appeal as he hauled himself out of swimming pools while every girl—and some of the boys—in the bleachers paused their music and leaned forward. Looking back on it, I was insane for him.

Now he's got this huge shape that I can't get used to, all

stacked smoothly into his clothes. His stomach is flat under the waist of his nice jeans and with each step the denim goes tight across the thighs. There are so many steps up the drive. By the time he reaches me, I need a defibrillator.

"You okay?"

"Yeah. I'm fine. What are they doing?" I watch as some ladders are unfolded against the side of the house. "They're here on a Saturday? That's weird."

He herds me up the drive. "They're just doing some more assessing. We don't need to be here."

"Well thank goodness for that, because I'm taking you out to get a life."

It's funny, I almost feel like Loretta is here in this moment. If I turn my head just right, she's at the front door, watching us. A throb of anger surprises me. She told me I should let him go. She bought me a plane ticket. What was so bad about me that I had to be removed? Before I hurt this good, pure person?

"Let's take a cab. I don't think I've ever seen you remotely drunk." I try to picture what he might be like with a little less self-control. Can he dance? Can he kiss?

"I've got an early start," he says, like he does every night of his life. His hands are on my waist, I'm given a lift and a boost into the passenger seat, and by the time I've caught my breath from the contact we're driving down Marlin Street.

He glances to me. "Please don't say we're going to your bar. I'd like to remain alive tonight."

I point and he follows my direction. "We'll go to Sully's.

Let's have a drink, and we can practice flirting with a few strangers. And then you can bail me out of jail." He laughs at that and I change the radio over and over. Every song is about hearts. "Have you heard from my brother today?"

Tom sighs. "Of course I have. Many times. Your photos are the only thing keeping him from getting on a plane."

"What will you do if he shows up?" I turn in my seat, just to watch his profile.

We're at an intersection, and I watch him as he waits, one hand on the shifter. What a luxury to be able to close my eyes and feel the careful turn of the car; no squealing tire or digging my nails into the side of my seat.

"If he shows up?" Tom considers the question. "I'll do what I've always done. I'll deal with him."

"That's something I've never gotten. I mean, I know he's fun when he's in the right mood. But how is anything worth the stress he puts you through? How have you stayed his friend all these years?"

I don't expect an answer and he doesn't give me one.

His fingers touch my back as we walk through the crowd and find two stools at the bar. There's a live band doing covers of old eighties songs, and the bartenders don't have to abuse anyone. The Devil's End is an ashtray in comparison to this place.

I try to keep my focus on the task at hand: showing Tom how to enjoy himself. It's hard, because I'm nervous and he's just staring at me.

"Okay. Getting a life, step one: Get a drink."

"I think I know how to do that part," he says, and orders himself a beer, and a glass of wine for me. The female bartender blinks fast when she registers his glory and gives me a congratulatory look.

"I'll pay." I scramble, but he hands over payment.

"I bet you pay for people a lot. But it's my turn. Let me spoil Darcy Barrett a little." He takes his change. "Let me get a taste of that feeling."

I relent and take my glass. I feel it, glowing out of him: exceptional, golden happiness. He looks at his phone, texts, and puts it on silent. Then he focuses on me.

"Look at me, living my actual life after work." He smiles at me and the room recedes. "I can't believe I have no one to call back. Are you all right? You seem nervous."

He's gorgeous. I want him. It's hard to carry on a polite conversation when those are the only two thoughts in your brain. But he's noticing my dumb silence and I need to make an effort. "I'm nervous as hell. You want to talk to me about something. I don't do well in these mystery situations."

I'm feeling weirdly young and out of my depth. Weak, woozy adrenaline is in my blood. He decides to proceed like this is something we do together all the time.

"Jamie forwarded me the selfie your mom took, after your haircut." He scrolls back through approximately a million texts from Jamie. It's Mom, with a tear rolling down her cheek. I laugh and the knot of tension leaves.

"I wish she'd never learned how to take selfies. Imagine her, trying to hold perfectly still with the tear in position while she fumbled around with her phone." I shake my head. "She sent one this morning, showing me her makeup, but look at Dad in the background. I am scarred for life."

There's Mom's impressive eyeliner artistry in the white cavernous bathroom. In the background of the shot, my dad is on the toilet with his pants around his ankles, his face pure grievance.

"Your dad on the throne." Tom laughs. "I don't know how I ever found my way into such a royal family."

I stretch happily on my stool and dangle my boots back and forth. I have never been this happy. Could this be life for the next three months? It's so supremely livable.

"Tigers are very noble animals," I remind him. His nickname from Dad has always been something that makes him a mix of embarrassed and pleased, eyes narrowing to focus on something, his face turning away.

"I'm lucky" is all he can say, touching his fingers on the engraved watch he wears. I know he needs me to change the subject very badly.

"Can we do this every night for the entire renovation?" I smile at his withering sideways glare. "Yeah, yeah. It was worth a try."

I feel the shoulder of my tank slip for the tenth time and don't bother fixing it anymore. This bra strap is pretty enough for the real world.

He takes my phone and looks at the picture of my parents again. "They made me realize things weren't right with Megan."

"What did they say?" I am incensed.

"They didn't say anything. You know what they're like," he says, an eye narrowed in affection.

I do know what they're like. Growing up, the unofficial Sunday-morning motto was *Door locked? Ears blocked.* "It was when I was finishing their deck. Your mom was making me a sandwich, and your dad comes up behind her and kinda . . . smells her neck." He's embarrassed. "Forget it."

"No, keep going," I say with reluctance.

"She obviously smells so good to him. Things hadn't been right with me and Megs for a long time. I mean, the diamond ring did help for a while. But I decided that next time I was home, I'd walk up behind her and smell her neck. See what would happen. Maybe it would rekindle the spark."

How very Valeska, prowling and sniffing. "And? No, wait. I'm not sure I wanna hear."

"She smelled wrong to me. Not bad, but just . . . wrong. She pushed me off and told me I was sweaty. I realized then it wasn't going to work anymore. We were never going to be like your parents, retired, still in love. I've never just . . . electrified Megs, and she deserves that." He's clearly been holding in that confession. "She and I talked all night and agreed. She's been sadder about the ring, actually."

"Did she give it back?" Jamie said she hasn't. Tom nods yes. Now I don't know who to believe. Ordinarily it would be no contest, but right now, he's carefully looking away over my shoulder at the crowd, not meeting my stare.

"You must miss her so much. I know what it's like to lose someone who's been a part of you for so long. I mean, it's obviously not the exact same thing." I cringe a little. I really haven't given him much support. "Are you doing okay, since breaking up with her? You can talk to me, you know. As a friend, anytime."

"You haven't lost your brother. And yeah. I miss her a lot. But just in a habitual way." He deliberates for a minute. "She's dating someone else already."

"What?" I say it too loud and outraged. My mind fills with angry hornets. There's no one else but him worth having. But I have to moderate myself. "Okay. How do you feel about that?"

"I feel . . . fine. I know I should feel something when I think of her with him, but I just don't."

I remember his inhale at my shoulder on that first morning of the renovation and the way he held it. The warm exhalation blowing down my tank. Did I smell right? I decide to forge on ahead with our evening.

"I said we'd practice flirting with strangers tonight, but what's going on? No one wants us. You're so gorgeous, Tom." I wonder if I have the stomach to watch him talk to another woman. "And I really might have made a mistake with this haircut."

I notice Tom's sneaker is planted on the bottom rung of my stool, his leg forming an obvious barrier.

"Weird," he says, deadpan. As his amusement fades, a new worry filters across his face. "Flirting with strangers. How am I supposed to remember how to do this?"

"Just wing it. Be your usual perfect self." I nudge his foot away. I've got to try this. I've got to give him a chance to see what life after Megan is like.

We swivel away from each other until the crowd blends again, fresh faces move forward, and a girl looks over. She's a petite little darling. She smiles at him, and he tentatively smiles back.

No. I don't have the stomach for it. I make eye contact with the smiler and mouth, *Fuck off.* She does.

"Put your foot back," I instruct, and he laughs in response, a flash in his expression like he's thrilled, down to the gut.

In my ear he says, "You little animal." And not like it's a bad thing.

I pour wine into my mouth. "Just practice flirting on me, so I don't end up on death row."

Tom spots something or someone. There's a frown on his brow, then he turns back to me with an idea in his eyes. He puts a hand between my legs and drags my stool closer until I'm in the frame of his spread denim thighs. It's the best seat in the goddamn house.

The warmth of his skin engulfs me and the noise from the room recedes. His hand cups my jaw; my face is tilted and he speaks into my ear.

"Don't look now."

Chapter 17

The room could be filled with red smoke and clowns for all I care. My jaw is in his palm and I'm not moving it. "Don't look at what?"

"Vince is here. With someone else. Blond, early twenties. He's seen us." After trailing his fingers down my throat, he hands me my wineglass. It's the smooth move of a consummate womanizer. That's how I know it's fake.

"Oh," I say after a beat. My heart is sinking because I know what Tom is doing. He's a good friend, putting a little protective padding on my ego. A set of muscles to flirt with. A kitty-cat's scratching post. "Yeah, this is his local. He's here almost every night."

"Is that why you brought me here?"

"Relax, baby," I tell him, and link my fingers into his and squeeze. "You're not part of a revenge plot. You're the beautiful, irreplaceable Tom Valeska and I am the luckiest woman alive to be sitting between your thighs." I get a ping of triumph when his worry is replaced by amusement and he looks down at our legs. "Consider me electrified."

I put my hand on his bicep and squeeze. If I'm not careful, I'll slide it. Okay, whoops, it's sliding. Too late to do anything about it. I watch myself feel up to his shoulder, dig the black nails in, and then make the glide to his collarbone.

"Why the fuck would he want to be with someone else?" He takes another sideways glance. "I mean, I'm sure she's a nice person but . . ." He looks back at me with a hot gaze and I know the end of that sentence. She's got nothing on me.

I show the indifference I know he craves. "He can do what he wants with his time. He isn't mine."

"Has anyone ever been yours?" His fingers are on my shoulder and my brain empties out. "Don't answer that."

"Of course not." I have a full-body shiver. "Once someone's mine, they're gonna stay mine. One hundred percent, forever. You know what I'm like."

He leans down and tips his face into the curve of my neck to speak over the music. He's just keeping up the façade for our audience. "If you had someone, you wouldn't be sitting here with some random guy all over you."

"You're not some random guy." I almost say, *You're the guy*. But thankfully I've still got a little of the *safer* humiliation left in my bloodstream. "I'd be sitting here with my guy and I'd be all over him."

He pulls back and our noses graze; we're agonizingly close to a kiss. His eyebrow quirks at whatever my expression is. "What if he doesn't want to be consumed, body and soul?"

My confidence sizzles out. "I guess . . . I guess I'd just have to hope . . ." Everything pulls back into focus. We're talking about a man who will not be Tom. I try to turn back to the bar but his knees press tight.

"Hey," he says, and strokes my cheekbone with his thumb. "I'm sorry. He'll love it. He'll only want your hands." He hesitates, then plunges. "Being the full focus of Darcy Barrett is something else, let me tell you. It's intense."

"Yeah, I know. Kitchen-smashing intense." I reach for my wine. "Hopefully whoever ends up mine will know beforehand exactly what he's gotten himself into."

Gotten into? It sounds too close to *get in me.* I need to make this conversation be a little more rhetorical. "What kind of guy would you approve of for me?"

This should be the perfect thing to say. It's light, it's neutral, and it covers up everything that has been scribbling so confusingly inside me. But I've said the wrong thing. His entire body flexes. The big knees squeeze, the fingers on his hand close, and his jaw barely lets the words out. "No one."

Even if he's jealous, it's pointless. I look across the room. There's Vince with a blond girl. Her face is lit up blue from her phone screen. I give him a nod, and he nods back, glum.

"Ha ha, he's having the worst night." There's not even a blip of emotion inside me.

As soon as I'm looking back at Tom, no one else exists. I'm beginning to think that it's going to be the case for life. It's why I really should make an effort to find my silver medal. "Please, tell me. What kind of guy?"

Tom responds like I'm testing his patience. "There's no one in the world I'd choose for you. He's still looking, then?" He weaves my bra strap between his fingers. "You wear some fancy stuff around my building site."

The lace stretches tight and I feel it everywhere. "Only up top. Down below, it's nothing but sturdy, abusive cotton."

"What do they say? Right now?"

"Oh yeah. They say . . ." I lean up to his ear. "None of your business."

"Your jeans are tight enough that I can almost make it out." His fingers are on my hips now, sliding into my belt loops. The tiny tug he gives me rocks me another half inch into him. I'm turned on. In public, on another goddamn stool.

"Hey, you're blushing. That's a pretty pink." He presses a kiss on my cheekbone, sits back, and smirks in Vince's direction.

With each second, the light is changing on the planes of Tom's face and he's looking more like a stranger. I couldn't care less if Vince is watching. "I swear, if you're just messing with me . . ."

His eyes spark in memory, and he uses my own words. "What is it like, being messed with by me?"

"You're so good at it, I'm starting to sweat." I blow out a breath. "Seriously, don't try this on anyone else tonight. I'll break her face."

"If I was really good at this, I'd tell you what I'd do when I got you home." He visibly checks himself, sitting straighter, reaching for his beer. He sips it and his eyes look at his watch.

Meanwhile, my body is absorbing what he just said, and it needs an answer. "Come back. Don't stop."

He puts his hand on my bare shoulder and there's a slow, warm squeeze. My nipples pinch. He sees everything, through the lace and the silk. I know he does, because his orange-stripe eyes are going black. "I've been wondering. What does hungry skin feel like?"

"I just start feeling hollow, and lonely." My throat is so dry I have to pick up my wineglass and tip it all into my mouth. His touch brings me relief, but also a restlessness. There are too many people in this room. They're all a bunch of laughing, drinking jerks who don't know that they need to get out. This is my room and my person.

He's watching his own hand as he touches me. It's unbearably sexy. "I don't like the thought of you being all hungry."

Someone jostles me and Tom's eye line cuts above my head. He transmits a male warning: *Don't touch her.* The air behind me quickly cools, his denim knees clasp gently, and he refocuses on me. It's intoxicating, being tucked so safe inside this gold bubble.

I really need to keep up with this conversation. "I just get crabby and irritated. Big surprise, I know I'm always like that. But I just need to feel someone else . . . It eases off the sharpness inside. It really is an actual thing. Skin hunger. I read a study about it."

"I think it's because you're a twin," Tom says, and his hand lifts away from me, leaving me cold. "You were squashed up together in the womb for so long." A tiny hologram of Jamie is hovering somewhere, Princess Leia–like, in our vicinity.

"No, no, come back." I press his hand back down onto my skin and although his mouth has a hint of disapproval, he strokes me in a way that feels like praise.

"Like a rose petal, DB." The fingertips trail, gentler than I thought possible; he's thinking about my softness and it's making me crazy. He's getting shy, then glances casually to one side at Vince. When he looks back he's got an edge to his stare.

"If you were mine, I'd be careful with you. I bet that's something you haven't had much of."

My stomach falls down an elevator shaft. Those words, spoken aloud in his voice, crackle through my synapses, and right now, I've never been more alive. I am heartbeat and full lungs. *If you were mine.* What a glorious thought to cross his mind; I never imagined it would.

"What else would you do?" I've got that husky voice he likes.

The animal in him is honest with me. "Everything. If you were mine, I'd do everything." Our gold bubble locks shut, and a little universe fills it. The possibilities are infinite.

"I have a big imagination. Could you be more specific?" I put my hand on the side of his neck and stroke down to the hard bar of his collarbone. His skin is hot satin. His pulse nudges me.

Mine, mine, mine. One thousand percent mine until the end of time. He looks like he agrees.

"Everything you wanted or needed, I'd do it." Amazing how he can keep it clean, but it feels so dirty. That's the thing about good boys.

"I want and need a lot."

A big white smile now. "No kidding. Well, I'm a hard worker."

I need to get to the reason we're here tonight. It's so obvious. We're about to lay some ground rules before we go home and demolish each other.

"So, are we having our talk?" When he says nothing, I gesture with my fingertips. "The bubble is officially in place."

He looks to one side, like it's something he'd be able to see. He's always gone along with my imaginary scenarios. When we make eye contact again, he sees the affection in me. But what I've said has tripped him up and he can't find his words.

I try to lead him into it. "It's pretty clear what we need to talk about."

He sits up straight and lets out a breath. There's a worried pinch to his brow and an awkwardness in his hands as he straightens his drink coaster. "I wanted to talk to you about taking the wall down between the kitchen and the living room."

I'm good at automatically laughing when I'm disappointed, and I do it now. He probably knows that little tic. I pick up my glass and it's empty. "Okay, we didn't need to go out to talk about that. The answer's no."

The charade slipped into real, and I felt like we were on

a date. That maybe I could be his. Thank goodness he's not looking at me anymore; I'm hot and embarrassed. He's got a pen and he's drawing on the back of his coaster. It's a floor plan of the cottage.

"Buyers want open-plan living. These older cottages were always built as small individual rooms, so they could be heated. But the walls block the flow and light. I think this wall needs to go." He scribbles across a line to show me.

"That's the fireplace. Where will the new owner hang up their bras?"

"The clothesline. This wall isn't a supporting wall. If we just take it out, the light comes in from three sides. When buyers walk in, they'll see all the way to the back door, and they'll think it's a big, bright place." Tom the professional is talking now. "The flooring will all match, front door to back, and there'll be a sense of flow."

"I know what you're saying, but no. That fireplace is a selling point." I'm sitting in a business meeting. What on earth did I expect? "I can't believe you'd even ask me this."

"Even if a buyer did want a fireplace, that one has got serious issues. The bricks are collapsing inward. I got the quote from the chimney guy. It'll cost a fortune to restore. We'd have to demolish it and rebuild it."

"You could do that, I bet. It's just bricks. You just said you'd do everything. That's what I want."

"Then I'd have to redo the roofing, replaster, paint. I take it out, it solves so many problems." He looks like he's beginning to panic. I can't be reasoned with.

"What does Jamie say?"

"He says he trusts my judgment." He assesses my face. "Have I . . . hurt your feelings?"

Either I'm terribly transparent, or he's perceptive. I think I know the answer from a lifetime together. He can practically feel this little tight lump in the base of my throat.

"No." I frown at him until he's partly convinced. "I'm just surprised that we're two-thirds of our way toward a wall being knocked down, and you're trying to flirt me into agreeing."

"Flirt you," he protests, a guilty flush on his cheekbones. "I'm not. I'm just recommending the best option for your sale." He thinks for a moment on how to sell it to me.

"Try to imagine you're waking on the couch in the living room after a nap. It's late Sunday afternoon and I'm in the kitchen cutting up potatoes on the marble countertop. Darce is grouchy after sleep and needs feeding."

"Talking about floor plans is not high on my list of kinks." I look up at the ceiling. "Actually . . . Keep talking."

His eyes crinkle. "You open your eyes and you can see me. No wall. There's light just flooding through, and there are flowers on a dining table between us. Pink oriental lilies that I got you, just because."

I can see it: The denim sagging at his butt and a white T-shirt stretching tight across his shoulders as he stoops over the countertop. The pollen-powder smell in my nostrils. Girls like me keep their favorite flowers as embarrassing secrets, but he knows.

"What else does this fantasy floor plan offer?"

"I look over and say, 'Hey, you're awake,' and you stretch and say, 'Tom, I'm so glad I agreed to let you take that wall down, it's improved the layout beyond my wildest dreams.'" He risks a grin.

"I'm pretty sure I'd say something different than that. 'Damn, those jeans. Get over here.'"

I'm imagining patting the couch next to me. He walks over with a half smile and a hand on his belt, vegetables forgotten. It's a beautiful fantasy, and it's just made me realize that I want it badly. A home. Being domesticated, caring about dinner. A dining table and flowers. Who would want that with me?

"Was this Jamie's idea? Drinks with the difficult client? Next time ask me questions about house stuff on-site. This was unprofessional." I twist away and signal to the bartender. "Your second-worst whiskey, please."

"Here's what just happened." He takes my hand in his. "I'm sitting next to Darcy Barrett, close enough to smell her perfume, and she's looking at me with a question in her eyes. And I know the question. I panic and I blow it. I'm not brave like you, Darce."

"I'm done with being the brave one, because it really doesn't feel great, hanging out on this ledge by myself. The next brave thing is coming from you. You're not the only one here with something to lose."

"That's why I'm working so hard on this."

"Not the house. I'm going to lose you. I'm going to fuck

things up with you." I put my elbows on the bar and my face in my hands. "Okay, actually that was the last brave thing I say to you."

"You can't fuck things up with me." He says it like we're family. Like he has to forgive me, no matter what I may do.

I look sideways at him. "Friends and family are the only ones I have a chance of keeping forever. And that's what I want. To keep you, forever."

He nods like I haven't said something too intense or strange. "That's what I want, too."

"We need to be eighty years old, hanging out on a cruise ship together, laughing our asses off about this one day. *Hey, Tom, remember that time when our young bodies tried to fuck up everything?* Your wife will be there, and she's someone I like, because otherwise I can't have you forever . . ." I trail off, and I feel it, right in my chest. That little old ticktock. "If I make it to eighty."

He's aghast. "Of course you will."

"I know you didn't mean it, but you telling me things that will never happen? Not in that house and never with you? It hurts. Well, fuck it, if it's so important to you, knock the goddamn fireplace down." I seize the glass of whiskey and absorb it into my very being.

I can't take the look in his eyes and walk to the bathroom, and spend a few minutes just staring at myself in the mirror. I wipe off my lipstick and jam my fingers into my remaining hair. I overlay Megan on top of me and my eyes fill with tears. I want to go to the second stall from the end and flush my heart. If this is what being brave feels like, color me yellow for the rest of my life.

When I'm composed, I push back out into the music and laughter and Vince takes me by the elbow. "Hey."

I shake him loose. "I'm here with Tom."

"I could see that," Vince says. He's not jealous, because the arrangement we have is a worthless waste of time. "What'd I tell you about him falling in love with you?"

"That won't happen." I can hear the flat desolation in my voice. "I can't have a guy like that."

"You could have one like me, though," Vince says with a smile. "The chick I'm here with keeps telling me about her rescue rabbits. Let's get out of here. Text him on the way out. Save me from getting my ass kicked."

"I'm not going to do that to him." Is this seriously the kind of person he thinks I am? "You think I'd just walk out of here and leave him?"

"You've done it to me. Darcy, you are hot, but you are a complete bitch." He's pretty matter-of-fact about it.

"Hey," Tom says, materializing beside us. He's regarding us both with an unreadable expression. "Fuck off."

"No need to be rude," Vince says, but he has no steel in his words. He's at risk of being stubbed out like a cigarette.

Tom steps behind me and wraps both arms around my body. I feel like I sink six inches into his rib cage. We're merging. Enveloping. Get in me.

"Don't come around, don't call her. Don't bother," Tom says above my head. It's that alpha voice. It turns heads from halfway across the room. "Got it? Or do you want to find out if I'm serious?"

"She's gonna leave, dude." Vince shrugs a shoulder. "She has left town on me like, six times now. At least."

"Yeah, she will leave," Tom says, and his words rumble right through me. "But I'm having her as long as I can before she does."

He turns both our bodies and we're walking, his arms still around me. We're a compass and we're pointing to a bed. Vince is flushed away behind us. The crowd parts for us; eyes flicker from me to Tom; women look jealous, the men avert their eyes.

When we halt to let a bachelorette party pass us in a succession of tiaras and feather boas, I tip my head back. How can I feel this powerful, wrapped in his muscle? Because it's mine now. "You never told me what you would do with me when you got me home."

"I can't tell you that," Tom replies, and when I miss a step in the crowd near the door, his body presses even tighter against my back. His hand finds the hem of my top and slides in, a flat palm across my stomach. "You know I can't tell you."

"All I need is a clue." Too soon, we're out on the sidewalk, the air so cold it burns. I turn in his arms but he's already stepping back, his warmth receding. The watch on his wrist from my father ticks.

"I'd say good night," he says with visible difficulty. He's reining himself back in, and it hurts to witness. It labors his lungs and the veins in his inner arms are cords. "And I'd make sure your door was locked."

"I don't think so." That bass hum in my bones is back. That trash-a-kitchen feeling. "I'd ask you really, really nicely to give me what I want. Everything," I remind him.

His white teeth bite into his bottom lip and he looks away down the street. There's so much conflict in his eyes. Finally, he concedes, "If I could, I probably would." It comes out of him, rough and soft, and his black pupils are ringed in violent color.

I've known him for most of my life, but this man is now someone I can't know.

Not until we're down to skin and sweat and kissing. That's all I'll ever want from him. I want those white perfect teeth. I want that narrow-eyed male possession, that *don't touch her,* that barrier his body created to block the world out. His vicious fist unfolded and his trailing fingertips gentle on my skin.

I want to provoke and tease until he gives himself to me, rough and tender.

There's no furniture left inside Maison de Destin, so I guess it's walls, sills, and benches for us. We wouldn't make it to my bed. I don't care if this ruins us, or the house. I need to feel him, deep. I never want to feel hungry again.

I want to kiss Tom Valeska until everything falls apart.

I may as well have said all of that aloud, because he closes his eyes briefly and when he opens them, they're like flames.

Chapter 18

I hurry down the broken front path because I'm chickening out in a major way.

The drive home was tense enough to break bones. Every red light, we looked at each other and had to grab on to the car. I'm aching from the effort. So now I'm possibly about to put my mouth on my childhood friend. The one person left that I can't mess up. And I'm the first woman he'll be with since his epic eight-year romance?

I'll be the second woman he'll sleep with, and meanwhile, my body has frequent-flier miles? I need a minute. I need to smell my armpits and brush my teeth. I only make it to the front door before I feel Tom's hand on my arm.

"Come down the side of the house." He squints up at the sky. "I think it's going to rain." He makes it sound like very bad news.

"I want to say goodbye to the fireplace." I'm not even

kidding. I want to sit against it, and think about Loretta, and ask her in my mind for her advice.

"It's not safe in there." He takes my forearms in his hands. "The power's off. Come on." It's weird and overly insistent. He begins to tug me, and my suspicion deepens.

"Why, what's in here?" I twist away and get my key in the lock, kick the door open with my toe, and finally see why he's holding me back.

My fireplace is gone.

Whoever took it down didn't do a particularly artful job. There's a pile of bricks remaining and a hole in the ceiling, covered over by a tarp. The worst part is, Tom was right. The house now looks huge, stretching all the way to the back door. I see now what all of this was.

"Did Jamie tell you to just do it and beg forgiveness later?" I don't turn my head. I know the answer. "Specialist demolition, huh?"

"I had to make a decision on the spot. I couldn't get those guys for another two weeks, so I . . ." He puts his hands on my waist and turns me to him. "I'm sorry. I was hoping you wouldn't see until the morning. I was going to get up early—"

"And you'd say that you had some guys in at the crack of dawn. I'd say, *Wow, how'd you do that so fast?* I click my fingers"—I snap them in his face—"and my wish is granted. You're the good guy just doing what I asked you to do."

"Yeah. That was my plan." His eyes get a little mean. "That's my role in your family, right? I've got to achieve whatever you guys need, instantly and perfectly. Or I'm out."

"What are you talking about?" What a bizarre thing to say. "I can't believe you took me out of the house while this happened." I try to shake him off. "You were counting on the fact that you can get me to say yes to anything." How fucking embarrassing.

"I was counting on you being reasonable and trusting me that this is the best way forward." He holds me back firmer as I push against him. "There's stuff all over the floor. It's a building site. Talk to me. Yell at me."

Outside, there's a rumble that for a split second I think is Vince's car. Light flashes, and I realize it's a storm, and it's rolling our way. We both look up at the new hole in the ceiling. The tarp puffs up in the wind.

"Oh fuck," Tom breathes. "This really was not in the forecast."

"Will it flood?" I step out of his hands.

"If they've done it right, it shouldn't be too bad," he says, but his eyes are doubtful as he looks down at the messy half-finished job, the bricks and the dust. He drops his grip on me. "I'll go up and check."

"Sure, like I'm letting you get on a roof at night when it's about to rain. You have to live with this now." I feel sick satisfaction when I see the look in his eyes. "You thought that you could get a little retroactive permission for something that had already been done. So, let's just stay here and see if it leaks. I hope it does."

"That makes no sense. This is your house."

"I'm very irrational. I can't believe you didn't even let me say goodbye to it." Another fresh wave of anger and disbelief strangles me.

"To a fireplace?"

"Yes, to a fireplace. You knew I loved it. You knew how much it meant to me. You said we'd light it again before the house sold."

"You lived here on and off for years. You could have lit it anytime." He leans a shoulder on the door frame and looks down at me in challenge. "That's you, though. You just think you can pick things up and put them down, and they'll always be there."

My insides jump and I scramble around for something to do. "Aside from being spineless, and bowing to Jamie like always, you were unprofessional." I bend down and pick up two bricks. "You know you were."

"I had one owner's agreement." He's distracted, watching me move back and forth across the room. "What are you doing?"

"Making a neat pile. There's nothing left for me to demolish, after all." I go back, pick up two more, but he takes my hands, turns them palm up, and dusts them off. Princess Mode activated.

The urge to slap his cheek shocks me.

"I expected better from you. If I'd opened the front door, and the fireplace was still there, it would have been proof that I'm your equal business partner. But it's obvious that I'm just another bit of red tape to get around. You are always going to choose Jamie. Always."

"I saw a way of getting more money in the sale. The budget is—" he clamps down on the rest of that sentence. "I know you don't care about money, but that's all I care about right now."

"You said earlier that we were a team. So let's wait here, as a team." A spatter of rain hits the porch, and a gust of wind blows through the house like it's just come straight off the ocean. "Let's see how bad this gets."

Tonight, at the bar, soaking in his attention and love? It was a glimpse of what I'll never get.

His jaw is getting that familiar stubborn edge to it. "I said I'm sorry. I wanted to stay ahead of schedule, and I knew this was the right thing for the renovation. If this happens, then the flooring can happen early. I'm not used to having emotions attached to a house I'm working on, or more than one person to ask."

"Sorry to inconvenience you with my feelings." I bend, pick up bricks, and add them to my pile. "Must be rough for you, having to work around me and my tiresome grandmother memories." I realize that the floorboards in front of where the fireplace stood are visibly worn. That's how often we stood there. And it's gone. "This wasn't yours to knock down, Tom."

"I can't understand being attached to a fireplace. I'm never going to inherit anything. Mom's broke. My dad, well." He half laughs, and it's bitter. "He lasted about three months after the pregnancy test. Consider yourself lucky to have had a fireplace in the first place." I try to interrupt but he won't let me. What he needs to say has been building inside him a long time. "I have all these emotions and memories floating around inside me, but I have no right to any of them." It's the closest Tom has ever come to complaining about his situation in life. "I'm hired to do this. Think about how that feels for me."

I pick up another brick. "As far as we're concerned, she was your grandmother, too."

"All I've got to prove that is an old Garfield key ring." It's a painfully true statement. He didn't get anything in her will. He realizes instantly what that sounded like, and adds, "But I didn't expect anything. I'm not a Barrett, after all."

He backs me all the way to the door, into the safe, clear zone striped by the streetlight. "Stop doing that."

I bump my fist on my heart.

"I've always been an inconvenience, my entire life. Remember how Jamie was so desperate to go to Disney, and I just couldn't get well enough for it?"

"Yeah," Tom says, sympathetic.

"I used to lie in bed, angry at my own heart. If it would just cooperate, everything would be easier. Jamie would be happy. We'd all go on a fabulous vacation. You are the only one who has never made me feel that way." My strong voice falters.

"Darcy, this wasn't about you. This was me, and my insane need to do everything perfectly, ahead of schedule, under budget."

"I don't expect perfection," I say, but he just laughs bitterly.

"What's the first thing you said to me when you got home and found me here? *What are you doing here, Tom Valeska, world's most perfect man?*" He points up at the ceiling. "Here's your answer. I'm not. You hold me to a standard I cannot possibly achieve. I've been trying for years, though. Believe me."

"You don't have to try anymore. Just be you. Do your best. Fuck up if you want." I can see the strain that he's been under. It's in the set of his jaw and the tightness of his fists. He's always the calm cornerstone holding everything together, since he was a kid, buying groceries and putting out the garbage. Every staff member left Aldo, except Tom.

He puts out every fire around him and he makes it look easy.

It's not easy.

He shakes his head. "You have a hole in your roof and you have tears in your eyes. I am permanently falling short."

"I think we're going to decide that doesn't apply anymore," I say and the wind blows through us, rattling the back door. "No more perfect."

"When you grow up dirt-poor, and adopted like a rescue dog, you will do anything to fit what you're needed for. And I'm fucking up. I am, Darcy. I've fucked up my numbers."

I feel a sense of dread when I look at his bleak face. "Fucked up how?"

"I told the crew I'd bring them over to my company on a better rate. And I had an error in my spreadsheet. The most basic error, right in my face. I have to pay them the rate I promised, plus their motel—so it's coming out of my margin. I'm doing this for free, basically." He sighs, resigned.

The overprotective part of me overrides everything. The anger and betrayal are now silver and bronze medalists. "I—"

"Don't say you're going to fix it. My problem, I am fixing it. If Jamie finds out about this, I'm done. He will never let me live it down."

"Why do you care what my brother thinks of you?"

His mouth gets a wry twist. "Your twin brother."

We're close enough that I look at his mouth. Just quickly, a glance. Another gust of wind blows through my clothes and his hands tighten on me.

"Why do you work so hard for us?"

"Because I don't want to know what it's like to be locked out. Ever again." His eyes are stark with honesty. "I will fit what I'm needed for. Don't forget, I was the wrong fit once."

"You've always been exactly right. I have measured every single man I've ever met against you. No one compares. That's been scaring me a long time now, because what do you do when you can't have your dream man?"

He says nothing, but inside he's on fire. I feel it.

"You are perfect, Tom Valeska. Perfect for me. Do you want me, even though I'm hardly worthy?"

Lightning flashes. "I've wanted you my whole life."

"Then have me. Choose me."

He takes one last stab at deterring me. "I've fucked up. I'm not the person you expect me to be."

"Don't care."

His unforgettable eyes are the last thing I see before he pulls me up onto my tiptoes and puts his mouth on mine. Thunder cracks above us and then, the world goes silent.

In a parallel dimension, we've always been right here in this doorway, since that night when I was an idiot eighteen-year-old and replied, *I know.* In this different timeline, he swallowed the hurt and decided to be patient one last time. He knocked on the house of destiny's front door, put his mouth on mine, and we've been kissing ever since.

We've survived in that alternate reality, backlit by thunderstorms and summer days. Holiday fireworks illuminate our faces. Years have passed for us there, in daylight and darkness. My hair grew down to the ground. Autumn leaves gathered at our ankles, and the seasons turned like a kaleidoscope behind us.

We've never endured another's touch, and we've never had to be apart. It's the place my true heart has always existed, beating unfaltering and perfect, and it's been safe, because it was with him.

Now we're leaning through the web-thin layer into this dimension and sinking into these older bodies. Every other kiss I've had in my life has been wrong. I've always known it.

It's why with other men, I never stay, I never sleep, and I never love.

Breaking from my mouth, he says in disbelief, "Is this how you kiss?"

Before I can think of how to answer, he puts a knee between my thighs and hitches me up a little higher. He returns to my lips with a groan caught in his throat. I have now found something I like better than sugar, and I'm an instant addict. Worse, a junkie. I've subsisted on his one-second glances my whole life, and now I've got his mouth on mine? I know what I'd do to keep him. He should feel afraid.

The first touch of his tongue loosens my knees and I'm grateful that he's holding me up. I shudder a breath out. He inhales it, changes our angle, exhales it back to me. Air is better from his lungs. Life is better with his kiss.

The word *mine* is now something I need to make him understand.

The second touch of his tongue is an inward slide, and it's not calculated to seduce me. I'm being licked for my flavor. I feel the point of his tooth, the scratch of his chin on mine. There's a pause of deliberation for a moment, and then I feel his pleasure shivering out of his body, absorbed into my skin. I've been tasted, and I am exactly right.

I think the good boy pipes up in the fogged logic section of his brain—*You're being too wet for a first kiss, too hungry, too animal, check she's okay*—and he tries to end the kiss with a gentle squeeze on my waist.

"Don't you dare," I warn him. "Do not go easy on me."

He obeys instantly, dropping back to me with a sense of relief. He presses his hips against me without shame, and how badly he wants me has me gasping. He's not going to go easy on me tonight.

"No one else is kissing you anymore," he tells me in a

conversational hush, not breaking our contact. "Your mouth is mine." The thought is more than he can bear; now we're twisting each other's clothes and the kiss is like a conversation with no words—louder and louder, talking over each other: *Listen to me. No, you listen to me.*

In unison: *I will kill anyone who touches you.*

We're changing the sky and affecting the air. When the cloud directly above us boils over and the rain pounds harder, I barely register it. A fine mist is settling on our clothes.

My breathing sounds like I have absolutely zero cardio fitness. I'm going to wear myself out here in this doorway, but it's okay—the person I'm kissing will look after me.

Don't fail me now, heart.

The thought knocks me out of my rhythm, and he trails fingertips up my neck and takes us back to soft. Sweet. Light enough to give me a chance to rebalance my body and my heartbeat. I become aware of sounds again; it's raining properly now, hammering on the tin roof of the porch.

The grumble of thunder above us is deafening, but it's a tiny wolf-howl that breaks us apart. We stare at each other and say at the same time: "Patty."

We don't care about the mess; it's the fastest way, so we stumble through the ruined house in the dark. Every time I trip, his hands pull me upright. Like bad, selfish humans we pause at the back door and kiss again to fortify ourselves for the run through the overflowing gutters. His tongue promises me more, if I can just make it to the studio. I'd swim the English Channel if I had to.

By the time we toe off our shoes and pull the glass door of the studio closed, we're soaked to the skin. The light switch won't work, my alarm clock display is black, and Patty is nowhere to be seen. On top of the wardrobe, Diana goggles down at us before ducking back down into her apple crate.

Tom is deeply apologetic. "Patty, come here." Her face peeks up at us from under the bed. "I feel so bad."

"You didn't know." We try for a minute more until she creeps out, tummy on the floor, until she's into her bed. I put a blanket over her and tuck her in tight. As we straighten up, lightning flashes and he gets a proper look at me. I see his wet shirt stuck to his body. We both make identical lustful eye flutters and heave simultaneous exhalations as the room goes black again. Then we laugh at each other.

"You've had a kiss like that inside you, all this time?" He begins on the buttons of his shirt, quick and thoughtless, like he's about to dive into a pool. He gets about halfway when he gives up and steps closer to me. Another few seconds without me against him is not something he can bear. "I think I need to update my life insurance policy."

"Better call them now." His laugh is in my mouth because we're kissing again. I feel flatness on my shoulder blades; I'm against the wall. Only my toes touch the ground. The gold bubble is skintight around us. When my head rolls to one side and his mouth moves to my neck, I can see the steam rising from his damp shoulders. The machine in his chest is working in overdrive.

For years as I've watched Tom's mouth as he talked, I've

known how he would kiss. Earnest and sexy and primal. Each lush press is to learn what I like—but he's realizing I like it any way he gives it. Soft, slow, teeth and tongue. Fast and rough. Bonus points for a hand on my throat. A squeezing handful of my butt has me shuddering and oversensitized; the seams on my clothes are like blades against me. He shows no sympathy and instead takes a tour of my body. When my breast is in his hand, he feels the stud in my nipple against his palm.

"Bed," he says in his alpha voice, and my Underswears lose their elastic. I've said the exact same thing to him. I wonder if I made him feel this way.

"You've finally caught up." I'm being transported backward with no effort on my part. I feel lighting cables under the soles of my feet but I'm not snagged or tripped. He's got me. "I tore a room apart and told you to get in my bed, and you just—"

He tips me down onto the bed.

"I'm going to make up for it, I promise," he says with a smile in his voice.

Chapter 19

His knees press on the mattress, one, two, either side of my calves. He's a huge shape in the dark above me. Hands either side of my head, one, two. I feel the downward dip of his body, and he's breathing against the side of my neck.

I say up to the ceiling, "Tell me I smell right."

He senses the uncertainty underlying my sharp order. "You smell like the only person."

I exhale. "Well thank fuck for that." I hold my arms above my head and he tugs my top off.

"Your obsession with lace has destroyed my sanity. Do you know that your bra is always visible, no matter what you wear? It's like your clothes don't really want to be clothes." He gives me a kiss on my neck that gives way to a suck and a bite. "You're like a self-peeling banana."

I start laughing. "That's how I feel around you."

"It fucks me up when guys look at the lace on your skin."

The thought has him returning to my lips, and jealousy is a spice in his mouth.

I know how he feels. I'm keeping my hands on this skin for the rest of his life, so there's never any doubt of who he belongs to.

He arranges me across a dim stripe of light from a gap in the drapes. My lace is admired, complimented, rubbed on his cheek, then it's slingshot-gone into the dark corner of the room. He slides his tough, hardworking palms all over me.

The nipple piercing is a blip that interests him intensely. He drops down from his elbow to investigate, and I finally realize the full potential of that metal, slid into such a sensitive tip. Other men have tried tuning me like a radio, but Tom knows what to do. I shiver and shake as he tests my reactions.

I wonder if he likes it. "So, pierced tough chicks are your thing?"

"God, yeah," he says with it in his mouth. "How is this metal so sweet?" His tongue touches it as he speaks and I'm levitating off the mattress. He laughs, pleased, and does it more.

"Every single time I've thought about this mystery piercing I've walked into a wall. Arch up," he adds with the right amount of bossy. His forearm slides under me, and I'm tipped up and he plays with me until I put my hand on the button of my jeans.

He releases me to speak. "Is this actually happening? Or did I walk into a wall too hard?"

"Yes, this is finally real." I break the remaining buttons

on his shirt. It falls open and I run my hands up his torso. His elbows lock and unlock. His hips bump forward. The involuntary reactions of his body are sublime.

His tight T-shirts have not been lying. Body, body, body. He's the most spectacular combination of flat and curved. Muscles for days. Lines and hips and so many hours of manual labor that I nearly hurt for him. Why does he have to toil this hard? His body loves my hands.

"This is really happening, unless I'm having another one of my vivid Tom Valeska sex dreams. In which case, I won't be able to look at you in the eye tomorrow."

He replies with amusement, "You probably won't anyway, after all I'm going to do with you." He feels the squeeze of my thighs and kisses me again. He loves my lips. "DB, I am going to get to know you tonight."

"You know me pretty well already," I shudder out, and he shakes his head.

"Not the way I want to." He feels me lift my hips in reply and his hands jerk my jeans to my knees. Everything pauses. When he speaks he's trying to compose himself. "But now's a good point to ask if you want to continue. And if you don't, that is completely fine."

My heart swells with love. He's the best possible guy. The perfect man. And I'm in a bed with him. I'm so lucky I could cry. I try to sit up but my body is saving its strength.

"Please, please. Enthusiastic yes. Pitiful begging, et cetera. I'm not even kidding. Put me out of my misery."

"Darcy Barrett, begging me in bed. I'm having one of my

fever dreams." He laughs softly and I feel his hand wrap my ankle. Then I'm rolled onto my stomach. When he pulls back on my hips I jolt inside with surprise. For a second, I expect the painful drag of elastic and a blunt breaching pressure, maybe tight hands marking my hips. It's a bad-sex flashback and I'm quaking.

He says, "Control freak." Then I understand. He's just reading what's printed on my Underswears. I love him so much all I can do is laugh and put my hands over my face.

Now he's rubbing the stubble of his jaw up my spine. I feel his brow bone press into my shoulder.

"Your skin has this silvery shine to it, and all I want to do is . . ." He shows me. It involves his tongue and teeth. My groans are muffled in the mattress. He uses his palm to turn me over. He spoils me, soothes me, and wants to know me. I feel him filing away every eyelash quiver and exhalation. He passes fingertips over me, chasing and creating goose bumps.

"You and your beautiful skin have been haunting me for years. One Christmas I kissed you on the cheek to say hi. It . . . overwhelmed me. I had to go sit in my car." He does it now, shaking his head like he can't believe it. "It was the best gift I got." Over and over, he presses on my cheekbone. "Thank you."

He's so sweet and open; how can I ever hope to match him? I have no experience being truthful or soft in bed, but I have to try.

"You're so lovely." I thread my fingers into his hair. "Well, I spent every Christmas waiting for the goodbye hug. Yeah,"

I sigh as he squeezes me to him. That deliberate pause that makes me feel like he's saying my name in his head. "Oh geez, that's even better now that we're horizontal."

"You spent every Christmas waiting to say goodbye to me?" He has heartbreak in his voice, even as he pulls down my underwear. "DB, I gotta make it up to you."

"Don't worry, I'll make sure you do." I feel his hesitation. He's gone shy. Biting my lip to hold back my smile, I take his hand and slide it up my leg. "Start now."

He feels me, he inhales how ready I am, and now we're back to vicious.

He bites my earlobe to hold me still while he tests and plays, his fingers easy and sure. He's very good at solving problems. My body shivers in the cage of his body, and his breath in my ear sounds inhuman. I tense; he tightens. I relax, he rewards me. He wants me compliant and soft. He wants me liquid and silky.

"Slow down or I'll come," I blurt, then I laugh in disbelief. "I've literally never said that before." I grab desperately at my nightstand drawer. "Lucky I'm in bed with the world's hardest worker."

"I'd better go easy on you."

"Why?" I've barely got enough light to see the glint in his eyes when he bites the foil square like it's a pack of candy. Then I access my memory vault and laugh. "Oh, that's right. I forgot about your dick."

"Oh, you forgot?" He laughs and gives me a little slap on the butt. "Thanks a lot, DB."

"How could I forget, really." His hand is between my legs again, giving me the sweep of his thumb, kind and tender. "Everything about you is sublime. I have been hurting from wanting you. Tom Valeska, get in me."

He always gives me what I ask for.

I can't shut my mouth to silence my moan. "Oh fuck. You feel like the world's most perfect man."

He's laughing even as his endless gentle push turns into an easy back and forth between us. He's bigger than anyone I've ever had. I hate the intrusive thought—how dare my brain even think of any of the others? But it's coupled with the realization that he's taking care of me, and it's the hottest thing.

"Thanks," he says with affection. "You feel like a dream come true."

My body is lit with pleasure. He has a reserved quality in his movements. If I can just get Tom Valeska to lose his mind over me, I can die happy. "No way. Don't go easy."

"Just . . . Just let me be careful."

"I don't want careful. I want honest." Finally, that first slip of his control. It's brain-meltingly good, feeling his body being so authentic. "I'm getting this every day. Deeper. Tom, I want you harder." Automatically, I put my hand down between us. My orgasm is my responsibility. Except, apparently it isn't.

"That's what I'm here for, dummy," he admonishes me in between freestyle-stroke breaths. He tickles his fingertips against me, even as he holds himself back. "Is your heart—okay?"

It's the first time a man has ever asked me that in bed, because no one's ever known. I bite back the automatic *sure* and assess myself. My heartbeat is a dim sloppy drum in my ears.

"I'm okay, but if I get too overheated or if you press me down, I'll start to feel all dizzy and claustrophobic. Then the palpitations happen and I won't be able to . . ." My private parts will shut up shop and I will not be able to release this agonizing lust.

He pulls away from me. Long and lush.

I scrabble with my legs. "Give it back. Have I just ruined the mood?"

"No, of course not. What about," he says with a thoughtful tone, "this."

"You don't have to change a thing," I beg, but he's rolling me onto my side and he's curling around me. It's comfortable enough for sleep, just a pair of platonic naked spoons. The blankets are lifted away and cool air is on my skin. For a dreadful moment I think he's given up on me.

Except I'm wrong. Like always, he's found a solution. He's kissing the back of my neck as he pushes into my body again. Now he rocks against me, a hand on my hip.

"Don't you worry about anything," he suggests, sliding his hand down. "Just relax and breathe."

I would never have thought that concern could be sexy. I speak into the dark. "Can I confess?" I feel him nod against my shoulder and the silky friction eases. "Coming sometimes triggers off my heart. And this is gonna be a doozy. So, if that happens, do not take it personally."

"I'll try to not completely blow your circuit boards." He groans when I squeeze him. "You want to try me out, see how I do?"

Have I ever had such a luscious offer? Tom's voice is sounding more like a growl.

"I want you to get in me." I press my cheek against his bicep to anchor myself as his touch gets me closer and closer to the edge. "Deeper. Harder. Not like you're sorry for me, or worrying about me. I want you to put yourself in me like we're doing this daily, from now on. For life."

Heated blood is prickling under my skin but I'm prepared to deal with what might happen. He does exactly what I tell him to do. He gives me everything he's got.

The orgasm hits me like I've just run face-first into a brick wall.

I contract and I hear my own inward inhale. Everything coils and I'm exhaling. Free-falling. And while I can barely hear over the noise inside my chest, I'm held safe in these arms, with someone who knows me, A to Z.

I don't have to worry about pretending to be normal. Just as I'm thinking how nice that was, he puts himself so hard into me that I'm now shaking with aftershocks, and I sound like I'm crying. But he's smart and doesn't let up. Now I'm wrung-out spasming, tears on my cheeks, contributing a nonsensical string of *more, yes, more.* His arms have to hold me against him or I'd be halfway across the bed.

"Now, now," I order, and he obeys me.

Tom is sharing this secret part of himself; I'm bitten,

spread, gripped, and I have never been wanted this intensely. He will kill and live and die for me. It's big, what he's feeling. All I know is, I'm his now. I put a hand on the back of his neck as he presses a kiss to my shoulder.

"Now, that's what I've waited for," he says after several minutes of trying to breathe. "Turns out Loretta's books didn't give me unrealistic expectations." He extricates himself from me with difficulty. In the dark, he says, "That's what it's like with you. Just . . . electric." I feel him lean away from the bed.

Hands smooth over me. I'm not remotely tired. I need another kiss. I need his skin against mine, so I'm never hungry again. I hear a cardboard sound in the dark, and a soft scraping sound. Is he putting away the box of condoms?

"I said to you at the bar that being the focus of Darcy Barrett is intense. I had no idea what I was talking about. *That* was intense. Okay, I count four more of these," Tom says about the condoms, and I thrill down to the marrow of my bones. "Shall we see how far we get?"

I can't resist. "Don't you have an early start?"

"Smart-ass. I'd better get to work." His mouth touches mine, we inhale, and we begin again.

* * *

I'M WOKEN BY a Chihuahua scratching at the door to the studio. Tom's gone, there's barely any light outside, and the sheets are cold. I wrap myself in a black silk robe and my reset alarm clock flashes midnight, over and over. All I know is, the power's on and it's incredibly early. "Yeah, yeah," I tell Patty. "Where's Daddy?"

I'm disappointed. I've never woken up with a man, and I was looking forward to another first. With each step I take toward the door, I feel echoes of what he gave me last night. I'm wrung out, gloriously so. Last night was a rough, soft playfight.

Let me spoil Darcy Barrett a little. Let me get a taste of that feeling.

It was the best night of my life. I wonder if he'd be weirded out if he knew that? I've finally got the one person I don't have to pretend to be cool with. If I told him, he'd smile. Then he'd use that boss voice that I like. *Get that robe off.*

I slide open the door. "Tom?" I call out. Instead of going to her usual patch of lawn, Patty sets off with determination in her stride. She's heading for the side of the house, with finding her owner the only thing in her mind. "Patty, come back."

The nearest shoes are a pair of heels I left against the wall. I jam them on. I inwardly shudder as the soles slip on mud and there's a repulsive snail crunch. My thigh muscles stretch and cramp until I yelp.

It turns out Chihuahuas can set an Olympic pace. She's now a tail disappearing around the corner of the house. She's hammering up the drive when a car pulls in. Patty has the survival instinct of a lemming. My heart leaps in fright. I blink and my eyes trick me; I think I see her go under the wheel. I blink again and she's fine, her tail waving like a flag in greeting.

"Watch out," I call with the last of my breath, and wave my arm to get attention, and when the truck brakes I see it's Tom. Where has he been this early? The sun's not even up.

I put my hands on my knees. If I could just catch my breath . . . Huff, huff, huff. I'm not this unfit, surely. My heart is pounding strangely, faster and faster, until I know what's happening. I feel like I could put my hand on my chest and take it out like a hamster. I press down on it, willing it to slow. The driver's door opens, I look up, and Tom's completely appalled.

The passenger door opens too, and there's a blond haircut the same as mine, and I close my eyes and will myself to get it together, because this is the worst possible moment for this to happen.

I'd know my brother's smell anywhere. Expensive cloth and a snooty Italian fragrance that smells like lemon peel mixed into window cleaner; it's supposed to be attractive to women, and it is to most. He's at my elbow and Tom's at the other, both talking at once. Tom's frantic. Fingers press on my wrist and when Tom leaves, I twist around to try to follow him.

"He's getting your medication," Jamie tells me, and I crumple against him. My heart? It still thinks it's a twin, because it sticks to my brother like a magnet until Tom is putting a dose in my hand, a bottle of water, and I'm swallowing.

Everything's gray. Everything's gone wrong.

"I'm fine," I manage, but I can't seem to unstick from Jamie. My hands are clutching and I'm pixelating into fainting when Jamie's steely voice brings me back up.

"Don't you dare, Darcy."

"Am I making the call?" Tom is holding up his phone. "Jamie, am I making it?" He's desperate. I shake my head vigorously. Jamie shakes his head, too. He's confident he's more qualified than a paramedic.

"You're too important," Jamie tells me in a hush, like it's our secret and not even Tom is supposed to hear it. "You're way too important to me. Come on, now, just breathe and let that heart settle down."

He's giving me a hug that only he can give. I missed him so badly I'm shaking. Fucking hell. I tried so hard, but I'm his twin sister now, more than ever. Until one of us dies, we're stuck with each other.

It's a minute or two more before the palpitations begin to slow. Tom's hands are on my shoulders, and I manage to cram my own personal whirlwind back into the lockbox in my chest. I try to push away from Jamie but fall backward into Tom.

"Congratulations on giving me a heart attack," Jamie says, and that's how I know I'm okay now. "We could have shared a cemetery plot to cut down costs."

"Any room for me in there?" Tom's voice says faintly above my head.

"Patty got out and ran away," I say, and Tom's arms hug tightly around my middle. I can feel the tension in his body, shivering out in palpable waves. "I thought she was gonna get squashed."

"And this is exactly why I'm here. I knew it." Jamie is furious. I'm certain we're busted—I'm lying against Tom in a robe and his arms are around me. But then he adds, "She can't chase a Chihuahua these days. Two weeks working here and she's nearly dead."

"I'm sorry." Tom is cringing behind me like it's his own personal doing. "She said she was okay—"

"She's been lying." Jamie takes my shoulders and pulls me away from Tom, setting us side by side like Barbie and Ken. "Look at her. I knew I had a bad feeling!" He walks a few paces to the car and then wheels back on us. "You are the only person I trust to take care of her. You've fucked up."

My brother, when he's angry? He's sort of spectacular, in a blood-thickening, terror-inducing kind of way. He makes me want to get my camera, just to show him what he looks like.

Tom sighs but doesn't deny it.

"He hasn't fucked anything up. He just got here! My health is my own business."

Jamie's beyond exasperated. "You know that isn't true. You're our business. Go get some clothes on. What time do the guys get here? A robe and heels." Another look at Tom, like that's also his fault.

"Let's all just relax," Tom says in this tone he uses, the

words and cadence always exactly the same. I don't know why, but it always works on the Barrett twins; it has for all these years. We blow out matching angry breaths and then Jamie begins to laugh.

"I was nearly full owner of this house," Jamie says with a grin. He's relieved—but he's also a jerk.

Tom gives him a dark look. "Are you really okay now, Darce?"

I pull at my shoe, which is sinking into the mud. "Yes, I just had a fright and it triggered me off. And yes, there's room for you in our cemetery plot. Open invitation."

"Gremlin, you're gonna kill my sister," Jamie tells Patty, and she stands on her hind legs and puts her muddy paws on his expensive trousers. He loves her secretly. He tickles behind her ear and her tongue lolls out. Then he remembers the pants. "Down."

"You came all the way here because you had a feeling?"

"Yes, my twin senses were tingling. You're right," Jamie adds, and I really don't think he's ever said that to me. "Watching this happen through a window is no fun."

I pull my robe tighter but wherever I tighten it, it loosens somewhere else. Thigh, neck, over and over. Tom's correct. My clothes don't want to be clothes. The memory of last night shocks through me, and we make proper eye contact for the first time.

Tom's got ruffled hair, pink lips, and dilating pupils, giving him away. He looks like he's been rolled around in bed by me. He looks like he's been licked and kissed and brought to the brink by me, over and over, minutes melting into hours, gasping and groaning, *please, please.* Who even knows what I look like. Probably pretty much the same.

Tom's attention is caught on my neck, then he stares up at the roofline with grim concentration.

"Come on, get dressed. I want to see the house." Jamie goes to the car and takes out an overnight bag. "Thanks for picking me up."

"You knew he was coming? What the hell, Tom."

Tom picks up Patty. "I did tell you." He's so impossibly cool, given the circumstances. "I was up pretty late, checking on the water damage, and saw the message from Mr. Impulsive. You always gotta get the red-eye flights, don't you?"

"Cheap" is all Jamie says.

"The title of your autobiography?" I grin when his gray eyes cut to me.

"Don't even start with me. What the fuck were you up to last night?" Jamie puts his hands into my hair and tousles it with expert fingers. He's doing my hair like his. I'm pathetic, because it feels wonderful. "I get the feeling my baby sister has been exerting herself horizontally, judging by that hickey. Are you sure you weren't chasing a guy up the side of the house?"

"Ha, ha," I respond.

Jamie looks at Tom. "That was one of your jobs. Get rid of the guys until I find her the husband option. I take it you weren't in your security post last night. I don't blame you." He means the tent and the rain. He's looking now at the mud on my shoes. "Seriously, go get changed. That robe is gross." Jamie takes his bag and walks to the front door, rummaging for his key.

I manage to make it halfway down the side of the house before my shoes completely sink in. "I'm beached."

Tom picks me up with an arm around my waist and carries me the last few yards to my private bathroom. When it was delivered he drew a lady stick figure on the door with a Sharpie. I love him for it. He puts me on the metal stairs, and Patty is still on his other forearm. It's honestly the only way to travel.

His skin smells different and lovely.

"Thanks," I say. The robe has sprung open indecently and he tries to pinch it together one-handed with not much success. The stair has me at eye level with him. Lip level. I lean in but he evades me.

He gives up. "Can I please buy you a new robe?"

"That would be a very romantic gesture. Make it something short and silky." I grin at his exasperated expression.

"Shorter and silkier than this? Please, don't walk around like this in case guys turn up early."

"This was an emergency and you know it. Don't be telling me what to wear, I don't like it." I lean on the door behind me and bite my lip. "Hey. We smell like each other."

He shushes me desperately. I cross my bare feet at the ankles and look at his body, my brain full of grateful thoughts and erotic memories, until he finds words.

"You really need to stop looking at me like that. I did

wake you up to tell you I was leaving for the airport. We had a complete conversation about it. You were comatose." He smiles despite his stress. "You said, *Okay, Valeska. Go fetch.*"

We hear Jamie's voice, echoing in the empty space. He could be on the phone, or just as easily talking aloud to himself.

"I swear, he even talked in the womb. Tom, I can barely walk. Every step, I can feel you. My body is just . . . squeezing. Now that you've been in me, all I can feel is hollow."

His eyelashes flutter and he swallows. "If he'd gotten a cab . . ."

"We'd be kissing on a cloud in heaven right about now. It's okay. We'll just talk to him."

"What, now?" Panic has him crazy-eyed.

I go into the bathroom and shut the door. "Yes, of course, now. You think I'm going to miss out on more of what I got last night, because of my brother? I'm surprised how calm I am, actually."

I wash my hands and dry them on one of Loretta's hand towels. My cosmetic bag is here, but I look in the filmy mirror and don't need it. I'm smoky eyed, with pink-marshmallow lips and a purple mark on my throat. Boy hair and girl body. I'm sexy as hell.

"This is a good look for me. Could you mess up my makeup for me every morning?"

He says nothing. I hope he's still there.

"This was a nice touch." I open the door and indicate my neck. I put my hand up to scrape his hair neater, but he steps away out of my reach.

"We can't say anything to him. We can't."

"You're a big boy," I tell him sharply, even though my confidence is starting to falter. "I'm a big girl. None of us are eight anymore. Let's just tell him and work through it." I look up at the house. "He might be glad. He hates my usual selections. You're like, the supreme option."

My brain mimics Jamie so loud I flinch. *The husband option.*

"Listen to me," Tom says, his voice like steel. "He is not going to be glad. He's going to cut my dick off."

"I'll protect you. I absolutely love your dick. Did I make that clear enough last night?"

His expression says yes. "If we tell him, the renovation is a guaranteed fail." He looks back up at the house. The first pink rays of sunrise mean that the crew will turn up soon. Tom's got even more on his plate, more roles to juggle. Employees and invoices to pay. Inheritances to secure.

"I'm helping you now, dummy. We're a team."

"If we tell Jamie he'll be angry and hurt. He thinks he knows everything, but he never saw this coming."

I'm remorseless. "He can deal."

"He's been working in the city awhile now and he suspects everyone of backstabbing. Except me. I'm one of the only people he trusts. The same way that you trust me. Completely and blindly." He softens a bit. "You don't know what that kind of responsibility feels like."

"Maybe he's a secret romantic," I try, but it's ridiculous to think that.

"He'll be so betrayed he'll fight us on everything, on principle. If we want to paint the house blue, he'll insist on pink. He'll want that wall put back up. I'll have to cancel every single thing I've ordered. This is the one person who will make my life a living hell."

"Maybe I'll be the second one." I give him an exasperated look. "I'd better get dressed so I can support you through this mental and professional crisis."

"Take this seriously. You're going to get forgiven, no matter what, Princess." Tom's eyes are angry now. "Me, I'm completely screwed."

Tom puts Patty down and hooks his arms under me. I'm easily hoisted, like a little dog being carried over the dirty ground. There's no exertion evident in him as we round the corner of the house, pass the fishpond, and take the path to my door.

"You know what he's like. Please, Darce, we have to keep this under wraps until the house is done. If we can't get a good sale . . ." He stops himself from saying more.

He puts me down over the threshold of the studio and looks at my robe, and I have never seen a more conflicted human being. He must rue the day he was found by the Barretts. My feet are princess-clean. Patty walks in behind us, muddy and miffed.

"You never did have to care about money. I have to care."

"I care. Why do you think I work at the bar?"

He huffs insultingly. "Surely that doesn't even cover your wine habit."

"It covers my health insurance," I fire back, angry. "You really think I'm a lazy little princess, leeching off my parents, don't you? I don't take a cent from them."

"But if you needed them, they'd give you anything you needed. That's not a bad thing," he says, softer. "It's what helps me sleep at night. You will always be taken care of."

It's true. Below me are multiple safety nets. If I lost everything here, I'd just go stay in one of the many empty bedrooms at my parents' place. Mom would probably bring me breakfast in bed and open the French doors so I could see the ocean.

"And you're about to inherit. Your financial situation is looking good. Meanwhile, I need cash." A ghost of a smile is on his mouth. "You think I break myself on a worksite for fifty weeks a year like this just for fun?" He blows out a long breath. "I don't think I can handle it if my business fails before it begins."

I wince in sympathy. There's no way I'd want him to live with the dreadful mix of failure and embarrassment I feel every time I look at the empty screw holes by my front door. Then I think about how the last three times I've been impulsive, it hasn't worked out. Tearing up the development offer, trying to buy Jamie's ring.

The *get in me* incident, barely a minute after learning Tom was single.

"Okay. Okay. I'm willing to wait and get a strategy together. You know I'll do anything to help you. Stupid Jamie." I look in the neck of the robe at my piercing. Tom's brought it alive.

The chafe of my silk robe against my skin is unbearable. "He literally never takes time off work."

"He's here, and here's your chance to be his best friend again."

"That's you," I point out, and Tom shakes his head.

"How do you always have it wrong? It's you. You're his best friend and he's been miserable without you. If you guys don't realize it now and get over this little meaningless fight you had, it might be too late for you both. Don't throw that away over me. You're twins. I'm the stray from across the street."

"You're not!" I can now see the full breadth of what he's trying to accomplish here. The renovation of the twins' relationship. "This is so you. Sacrificing and fixing and stepping aside. Fading into the background. Not on my fucking watch."

"Where are you guys?" Jamie is at the back door. "Tom, what the hell is wrong with the kitchen ceiling?"

"The kitchen?" Tom is dismayed. "I'll be right there. Please, Darce," he finishes in a hush. "Please help me keep it together."

"Give me your phone, then," I say, and he slides it into my robe's fun-sized pocket. "Where the hell is that guy Chris? He was supposed to be here by now. Should I call him and kick his ass?"

"I would be very grateful," Tom says, stepping a few paces away as the back door bangs open. It triggers off a sense of déjà vu. I think we've always stood a little too close.

"Quit wasting his time," Jamie barks at me as he clatters down the back stairs. "We've got stuff to do. I hope you're fixing these stairs, Tom."

We watch Jamie walk around to the Porta-Potties. He opens the door to the male one. "Oh fuck no." He goes into mine.

"That's my bathroom. Now I want to cry harder than ever." I exhale and put my hand over my eyes.

I will myself to trust Tom and see this from his perspective. I see everything he has to lose more clearly than my own potential losses. He'll always carry me. He'll never trip or drop me.

But I just can't help myself. I've felt this way before, so many times. My insecure, spiky self says: "So, last night was a one-off."

"Of course not. But as long as he's here, I can't touch you. You can't look at me. We're not . . . anything."

"Wow, so we're nothing," I marvel in a stage whisper as the hurt begins to shimmer. "Funny, it didn't feel like nothing. I feel like I had every glorious inch of Tom Valeska last night. Repeatedly. Just . . . over and over, making me come more than I ever have in my life."

My words cause a chain reaction; my body shifts, his shifts, and we look at the bed. It's a messed-up wreck. We want to be flat in it or bent over it. Any possible variation, we want to be moving, and deep.

I would have sex with him on a pencil sketch of this bed.

I stand up on tiptoe, grab him by the scruff, and bring

his mouth down to mine. It's instant. He's giving me everything in a blink, an intensity so strong I lose the ability to see color. I feel a surface under my butt; I'm on the edge of my workbench and he's between my legs. Ten seconds. I swear it would take another ten seconds for him to be back inside me. I yank at his leather belt and loosen the buckle.

"In, in, in," I order him when he changes the angle of our kiss. Against me, I feel a tremor run through him. Last night didn't ease anything between us. It's made it worse. So much worse.

Now he's facing away from me, shoulders heaving.

"Shit," he huffs. "You see what I mean? We can't do this all over the worksite."

"Shit, indeed." I put my hand on my throat where my heart is lodged like a frog. "If we're not careful I'll be three months pregnant with your giant triplets when the sold sticker goes up."

His shoulders shiver and roll. He turns on the ball of his foot and I'm sure he's going to step back and finish what we just started. Hard. Everything in him is straining. My God, his eyes. For one second, I'm terrified. I've provoked something I don't know if I can handle.

But he's got the willpower I do not, and I watch as he packs it all down again.

I cross my legs and try in vain to pull my robe tighter. "You think you can stop doing that to me for another three months? You think we can just pretend?"

His body says no. But he replies, "I've been pretending

around you since I hit puberty. I can do a few more months. Look, I thought we had time, and I didn't say much last night." He's rueful. "DB, you know you're special to me, right?"

"I know you love me," I reply without thought. He broke my world apart last night. His love is pressed into my skin and kissed into my cells. "How could you not?"

He bursts out laughing in response. "There's that Barrett confidence I like so much." He takes a risk and steps close, pressing a careful kiss to my cheek. "Yes. I do. But you don't know how much."

I put my palm on his jaw and kiss his cheek back. "Don't worry. I know it. You've always told me, one way or another."

Jamie's probably toweling his hands dry by now, or snooping through my cosmetics bag. Maybe dotting concealer under his eyes. I wouldn't put it past him.

"You don't really know. Princess, you're the one girl I never in a million years thought I'd get." He presses a kiss to my temple. "Hold on for me just a little longer. Please."

We hear Jamie's voice—*"TOM!"* The door slides closed behind him and he's gone.

I sit down heavily in his office chair. What is this beautiful complicated thing we unfurled last night? Maybe it's not a bubble that we have. A deflating silk hot-air balloon is filling this space. It's every color; it can float and take us places, but one single loose seam could end it all.

But still, I need to learn to be an optimist. After all, Tom didn't end things with me just now. He asked me to wait for

him. He loves me. I stretch luxuriously in the knowledge—
he's mine, he's going to be mine forever, until he dies.

As I turn over that last little part of the conversation in my
mind, I realize something that makes me feel sick.

I've made the same mistake as when I was eighteen. He
loves me? *I know.*

I do nothing but take, take, take. I never talk feelings with
a man I've had sex with. My brain just doesn't take that logical path, to reply in kind.

"Oh fuck," I say out loud. Patty tilts her head at me, hearing the desperation in my tone. "Patty, I didn't tell him I love
him back."

Chapter 20

I eavesdrop as I tread soundlessly into the back hallway, two steaming coffee mugs in hand and Patty jogging along ahead, oblivious to the trouble she caused me this morning.

"So, did she freak?" Jamie says. The room echoes, thanks to Tom's executive decision.

"Yes. I'm not doing that again," Tom replies, and there's the sound of bricks being moved. "She kicked my ass. Seriously, why did I listen to you?"

Jamie responds like it's a stupid question. "Because you give her anything she wants. If you asked her first, she would have made those big eyes at you, and you'd be rebuilding a fireplace that you know will cost us money in the sale. Come on, the place looks huge. She'll get over it."

"Yeah, I know the eyes you mean. She's good at those." Bricks, a grunt. "I do think the wall coming out was the best thing for the renovation. But she's not something for us to get around."

"She kind of is," Jamie says, wicked as usual.

Tom replies in a growl. "She's part owner. I'm never doing it again. Move, Patty."

"Okay," Jamie agrees after a beat. "Better tell her about the dining room now."

Exasperation. "I'm not telling her. I'm asking her."

"Asking me what?" I walk in like I've got impeccable timing. "Well? What? Chris will be here in fifteen minutes. How do I look, boss?" I smile widely at Tom. "I'm finally in uniform."

"A little big," Jamie says dismissively.

I give him a dark look. "Truly's going to alter it for me."

Tom stares at my Valeska Building Services shirt and I think he bursts a blood vessel. Or chokes himself. Something instant and painful. It's a huge fluorescent polo in a fabric blend I don't really care for. It's unbuttoned at the neck and the top of my bra is showing. This bra is a ten on the Richter scale. I am a bad person. As he watches, I gather the hem and knot it at my hip.

"Looks fine," Tom says robotically, but I'm honestly surprised he doesn't just walk over, pick me up over his shoulder, and carry me out.

"Who's Chris?" Jamie hates being out of the loop. "Why's he arriving in fifteen?"

I hand the second mug I'm holding to Tom. "He's reinforcing the foundation on the downhill-slope side. And he's late. I told him to bring us doughnuts to apologize for his poor time management."

"I need that so bad," Jamie tells Tom with a slight tremor in his voice. He holds out two fingers for the coffee mug. "Gimme."

Sugar is my blood type; caffeine is Jamie's. It's the crutch that keeps him upright and functioning. Tom just takes a sip in response. High five.

Jamie huffs. "Where'd you get that?"

"She has a coffeepot in her bedroom," Tom says, then freezes like he's busted.

"Okay, thirty seconds." Jamie makes a beeline to the back door. "There'd better be a third mug."

"Couldn't cover that with makeup?" Tom's looking at the hickey on my neck. "I'm going to have to deal with guys looking at that all day, thinking about you." A memory eclipses his eyes black. He presses his thumb against it and no doubt feels my pulse. "That's mine to look at."

I can't stop myself from tiptoeing up to press a kiss on his jaw. His stubble is like sugar crystals on my lips. He's forgotten my brother. He's forgotten anyone who isn't me.

"Let them look. I know who gave it to me."

"They'll know, too. They're not idiots." He looks at the back door and his next words are barely audible. "I can't believe Jamie's not picking up on it. Your clothes fall off around me." His fingernail drags across the corporate embroidery. "Am I a complete animal for loving my name on your chest?"

"You've always been a complete animal, Valeska. I'll

explain it to you sometime." I tiptoe up to his ear. "When I'm wearing this and nothing else."

I'm wasting time. I only have a minute. I've never told a man I love him, and this is the only one I'm ever going to tell. How do I do this right?

"Hey, what you were saying before . . ." How do I frame it? I'm scared I'm going to open my mouth and scream it in his face. I swallow and huff out a breath. "I wanted to tell you that—"

"I know." He cuts me off easily and I sink down from my tiptoes. He knows? Or he doesn't want to hear my cringe-worthy attempt at a declaration? He knows I'm emotionally stunted and is trying to spare me. How embarrassing to not be able to match his softness and depth.

He runs a hand down my collar to tidy it but ends up pulling me closer. He bends down to inhale at my neck. "Alex better have washed this shirt."

"He did. I think." This is what is easy between us. The lust.

The thought of another man's smell on me has him boiling down into his base self. It's palpable; the air snaps electric and I'm desperate for his hands on my skin. He's hard against me. If we were alone, he'd put me against a wall and himself in me.

We hear my brother grumbling and Tom puts a few feet between us.

"I don't know how you're physically capable of this." I look at the front of his pants. "What does it take to wear you out?"

He's still looking at his name on me. "Probably impossible."

One of my knees unlocks at the thought. "Anyway, what the hell? Not a drop from the massive hole in the ceiling, but the kitchen has a water zit?" I point up at the heavy brown bulge on the kitchen ceiling.

Tom shrugs, unfazed. "Welcome to my life."

"I counted four condom wrappers on the floor. I'm impressed, Darce." Jamie booms it so loud I hear the flap of pigeons on the roof, and Patty yaps.

Tom melts clean through the floorboards.

"It was nearly five," I whisper to Tom. "But . . . priorities." I remember his hand twisting my hair, tugging on my scalp, begging me. *Darce, Darce, no, okay, yes.*

I almost feel bad for tormenting him. His coffee is spilling in a thin stream on his boot. Footsteps clomp up the back stairs, heavier than mine but the same cadence. The screen door slaps and Jamie's back.

"Christ on a cracker, not even I'm that prolific. I'd give him a high five if I wasn't beating him up. No wonder you were nearing total heart failure." Jamie shambles in, coffee in hand. "Better let her recover this morning, Tom."

"Yeah, Tom. Maybe you should go easy on me." I sip from my highly appropriate mug.

I know this whole situation is high-stakes serious, but I'm hurting from holding the laugh in. "The virginity ship sailed many moons ago. I don't get why you're trying to be so macho and brotherly. It's not impressing Tom."

"Hey, I don't see this mystery guy here right now, do I?" Jamie gives me a look and miraculously I don't crack under it. "Any guy who just walks out on you after that kind of effort is a piece of shit. Can't you find someone who takes you out for waffles the next day?"

"He definitely would. He's just . . . busy. Wait, is that what you do?" I never once found a girl having breakfast in this kitchen. Maybe Jamie's gotten romantic since moving to the city.

Jamie puts a hand on his hip. "You're damn right I do. And I'm sure Tom would treat a woman better than that. What would you do if you saw some guy sneaking out of her room in the wee hours?"

Tom looks into his coffee mug, thinking. He can easily pass this test of Jamie's. His eyes meet mine, and they're brutal honesty. "I'd fuck him up."

I give him a withering look.

Jamie nods at Tom, satisfied. "Just get someone decent, Darce. Tom and I want to get wasted at your wedding and grind on your bridesmaids." He begins dancing, slow and sensual, with his mug held in front of him. He figured out when he was five years old that women love a guy who dances and it's served him well.

"Check out this body roll."

It's a good one. He doesn't even spill his coffee. Tom and I laugh, which only encourages him. This is what happens at parties. Jamie gets carried away, there's a ring of people clapping around him, and he ends up kissing a girl against a wall near the bathrooms.

I shake my head. "If you do a surprise choreographed dance at my wedding I'm gonna kill you, Jamie."

"He would," Tom agrees, his eyes fond. He loves my ridiculous brother.

Jamie's grinning. "I'll do one, with your hottest friend. Who is she?"

"You know who." I wait and wait, until I'm forced to supply it. "Truly Nicholson, from high school. She's such a goddamn peach. If I was gay, or the boy twin, I'd marry her."

Jamie coughs wetly. I think he prefers his women a little sparse. Now the fun is gone.

"So, we want to tell you . . . No, wait. Tom, you do it. You're good at asking her things." Jamie regards me thoughtfully. "I bet she'd say yes to anything you ask her."

"I'd say you're right," my mouth says without my permission. My toes are curling in my shoes.

Tom reboots his mainframe computer during a lengthy sip of coffee.

"Now that this is gone," he says, meaning the wall, "I think we should turn the dining room into a third bedroom. This is a two-bedroom cottage, which isn't as appealing for a family buyer. If we wanted, we could make it the master and add a small en suite. An extra room, an extra bathroom."

Jamie finishes the thought. "Extra bucks. A lot extra."

"Sure," I say, and finish my coffee in one hot swallow.

"Wait, what? You just agree?" Jamie tags along behind me as I go into the kitchen.

"What do you mean, do I just agree? I'm the reasonable one, when I'm asked correctly." I give Tom a look and he cringes in apology.

There are still tiles on the wall where the counter used to be in the kitchen. I get the crowbar and pop them off with neat little movements, because I'm a show-off.

I say to Tom, "It's a good idea. But if we're going to cut back all the shrubs, headlights will shine into that room at night. We'll need some good blinds. And I want the fireplace in there kept. Even just for decoration."

"Okay," Tom says. He's got a note of disbelief in his tone.

"Wait, wait, wait. We're all agreeing? This place will be done in no time." Jamie looks at the crowbar. "Give me a go."

"No." I try to hold on to it but it's no use. My brother is the much bigger, muscled version of me. He plucks it out of my fist with two fingers. I look up above us. "This water damage looks bad."

"Tom'll fix it," Jamie says without any thought. Every single time we say things like this with such confidence, the pressure on Tom just gets worse.

"We'll all fix it, together." I put my hand on his phone in my pocket. I wonder what else Jamie and I can do to help him breathe out a little more.

"You're not doing any more work," Jamie says to me. "You were a ghost barely half an hour ago and you've been up *allll* night long. You're fired."

"I took my medication. Tom, I'm fine now. Tell him."

Jamie taps the crowbar in his palm. "No, you tell him about how you got dizzy in the bathroom and practically collapsed after a day of no food. You were all white from low blood sugar. My mole gave me the update."

"I didn't." I look between them both. "Tom, it was barely anything." Tom's eyes change as my little heart-sized betrayal sinks in.

"Even when I'm not here, I know if something major's up." Jamie shoulders me aside and begins smashing tiles. He's leaving big shards intact instead of popping them off clean. "I'm protecting my investments." My brother is performing shoddy workmanship with a smile on his face. Why should he do anything carefully or perfectly? He was born male. "Connections, plus twin senses, equals Jamie knows everything. And I know you guys are getting pretty chummy."

I don't let myself bat an eyelash. "Let me keep trying."

"No." Tom's mad at me for lying. "No more physical work." Patty is looking at me even more gimlet-eyed than usual, balanced in the triangle of his arm.

"Great. Less than one hour since my brother arrived, and I'm kicked off my own project."

Tom looks at his watch. "In a minute or two, that phone is going to start ringing, and it's not going to stop, believe me. I've got a bunch of rental equipment to get and quotes I haven't finished chasing up. You know that's what I need you for."

"And hey, she has a coffeepot," Jamie says.

"You're not fired," Tom says with a vicious glare at Jamie's back. "You're reassigned. Focus on the sold sign, not a box of broken tiles. Get big-picture with me here, DB."

I need to pull back and reframe on the bigger, more beautiful picture of kissing Tom Valeska every minute of every day until we die of exhaustion. There's no point in scraping off the wallpaper if I'm too dead to have him after the sale check clears.

Tom is speaking like Jamie isn't here. "I've never run my own business, but you have. That's what I need help with. Valeska Building Services cannot function without you."

The protective beast inside me can't refuse. "Can I have a job title?"

"Deputy site manager of Valeska Building Services?" He has a spark in his eyes when they flick down to the polo top that's doing it for him better than a strappy set of lingerie. "Yeah, that suits you."

"Hear that, Jamie? I just got a promotion." I wonder if I slept my way to the top.

"He's got a soft spot for you about a million miles wide," Jamie grumbles. "And you take advantage of it, Deputy Darcy."

I guess my mouth is curling in a smile because Tom gives me a look like, *Don't*.

"What's your next flip?" Jamie doesn't wait for Tom to reply. "I'm buying that house the street back from my parents. It's not beach front but still a good location, and so cheap. What a dump. I need you to go get it inhabitable."

"Maybe," Tom hedges. I know he's thinking about his budget miscalculation.

"After this, Tom is not doing us any more favors." I try to take the crowbar back. "He's free and clear."

Jamie is making a brutish mess of the tiles. He decides in his mind that he'll convince Tom and moves on. Next topic. "I need to see whether I can get the time off for your heart appointment. Give me the date."

"How do you even remember these things? You don't need to."

"Christmas, Easter, Darcy's heart. I've come with you every single time since we were born," Jamie says, swinging the crowbar at his side like he's thinking about braining me with it. "You've skipped two years now. The damn thing is probably about to conk out. Even if we aren't technically talking to one another right now, I'm still coming."

He'd fly to my doctor's appointment? "Why?"

"I'm your walking talking organ donor. I'd better make myself available."

"You've got one heart, you idiot."

"I know," Jamie says. "I'm keeping it warm for you."

My idiot twin still loves me. I can't help it, I wrap my arms around him and squeeze until I feel his ribs creak. He does it back to me and now we're locked in a classic Barrett stranglehold. Tighter and tighter.

"Ow, ow," I cry as my boots leave the floor and Jamie begins shaking me around like a dog. "Too much, Jamie, down." Patty is jumping around beneath my toes, barking and nipping. I hear Tom laughing. Life is golden. I'm going to live forever.

"Send me the appointment details," Jamie repeats as he puts me down. He's flushed pink and smiling. I'm sure I'm the same.

"What if I've got someone else to come, too?" Maybe Tom's presence in the appointment will help the damn thing beat properly for once.

"Who? Mr. Hickey? Introduce him to me, and I'll consider it." Jamie grins over at Tom, willing him to join in on the messing-with-Darcy game. He pushes me back out of our hug, but not in a mean way. "I didn't know you finally disclosed your little cardio situation to a guy. Must be serious."

"Maybe I will introduce you. You'll like him."

"I doubt it. Have you seen this guy, Tom? Let me guess. He's forever seventeen, with a shank in his pocket."

Tom can't help himself; he laughs out loud. Jamie is gratified and begins hacking away at the remaining bits of tile on the wall.

"I'm going to introduce you to a guy I work with. A real adult human male. That'll be a novelty for you, Darce." Jamie grins at Tom to see if he laughs at that one. "His name is Tyler."

"Say no more. He sounds repulsive."

"It's not his fault that his parents named him that. He's tall, likes walking and animals and all that shit chicks love. He has a motorcycle and the looks." He turns to me to impress that very important selling point. "A motorcycle."

Behind him, Tom crosses his arms.

"He's down this way for a conference next week. I've given him the address. He's going to pick you up and you can go for a ride. On his motorcycle." To Tom, Jamie winks conspiratorially. "One of my foolproof plans."

I kick my brother's shin. "No. If he turns up, I'm going to turn the garden hose on him. Quit messing with my love life."

"Love life? Love?" Jamie chortles. "You've never said that word in your life. *Love* life? More like your vigorous sex life." He reaches toward my neck to pat at my hickey and doesn't notice how Tom's changing behind him. "Hope that fades before Tyler gets here."

"No plans. Forget it with that guy," Tom advises my brother, his voice dipping down into that tone that my ovaries like. "What did I just say? I'll fuck him up."

"Not required," I say, and maneuver the conversation swiftly back to my brother. "Still with that beautiful tall greyhound?"

"Rachel? I broke up with her. She kept dragging me past jewelry store windows. I've got my eye on someone else." Jamie realizes something and his mouth drops open. I hope that's what I look like when I smile. "I'd probably be the one dragging her past a jewelry store window."

For just one moment, he's filled with stained-glass color and his eyes brighten to cornflower blue. I wish I had my camera. Then he remembers something and resumes a half-hearted chipping at the wall.

I exhale. "Well, I'm glad she's not getting Loretta's sapphire. Thank fuck for that. I don't suppose—"

"No. She left it to me. It is for my bride." Jamie says *my bride* in a stupid falsetto voice. Heaven help whoever he eventually decides on.

"At least let me wear it. Or look at it."

According to Loretta, the sapphire turned black from being buried in a flowerpot during the war. Which war, I'm not sure. Is it the truth? Not sure. My favorite ring in the world is now living a fate worse than a flowerpot's: It's in Jamie's safe.

"Name your price." I just can't shut my mouth. "I'm guessing a cool billion?"

He'll never budge on this. "I'm gonna need that ring one day. The twins aren't getting any younger. Time for us to find a couple of unlucky victims to deal with our bullshit, for life."

"I'm sure *your bride* would prefer something from Tiffany. Let me have the ring, please. I might . . . I might not be around that long." I let my voice go feeble as I play the crappy-heart card and Jamie sees right through it. Even Tom half laughs, his possessive bristling easing off.

I sigh and give up. "Make sure she's someone I won't hate, sitting there wearing my ring when we all go on that cruise when we're eighty. She'll come drink whiskey Old Fashioneds with me before lunch and maybe let me try it on."

If Tom has a wife and it's not me, I'll lure her out of his cabin at night and hoist her old bones overboard.

"We're going on a cruise when we're eighty? Can't wait. I'm going to be so loaded." Jamie smiles, positively romantic about his future bank account. Then he remembers something. "Don't get your hopes up. She thinks I'm a nightmare. But yeah. She'd day-drink on a cruise ship with you."

It's a sore point and I really, really want to press it, because Jamie is actually having to do some chasing for once. I love her, whoever she is. "Well, sounds like she's got your number. What's her name?"

"Nope." His ears are red. Frustration gets me right by the throat. Judging by his body language and the crowbar in his hand I'd better leave it. Once, I knew every single thing about my brother. How can I get back to that place if he forever shuts me down?

I wonder if Tom knows. He shakes his head with a shrug.

"Can't wait to go on that cruise with you and your elderly husband, Tyler," Jamie tries, but I wave him off with a scowl.

"So, we're agreed, this is a bedroom?" Tom is in the entrance to the dining room, and also his own personal hell. I know what he'd whisper about Tyler—in the dark, rhythmically knocking the air out of me. That fucker cannot have me.

He's buckling something around his waist, slow, like it's revenge. It's an honest-to-goodness tool belt. There's a hammer on one side. It sits low on his hips and I can't take it.

Everything boils up inside of me, and the floor vibrates under my feet, my bones shake, my heart bumps. The stitches unravel out of the shirt I'm wearing, my heart unspools like cotton and I can't handle ten more seconds of not kissing him. I put my hand on my hickey and bite my lip. I clench everything so I don't make a sound.

He convinced me last night that I'm beautiful. From the look in his eye, I convinced him he's a sexual genius. The faintest smirk touches his lips. "Darce? You want a bedroom, right?"

I cough to clear my throat. "Make it a room fit for a princess. Wallpaper and a fireplace and a four-poster bed. Make someone fall in love with that room."

"Sure, like it's so easy," Jamie replies to me with some snark in his voice. "He's not your slave."

"Oh, 'cause he's your slave?" Tom's phone buzzes in my pocket. "Tom, it's your mom. Gosh, pretty early for her." I hand him the phone. Then I round on my brother. That familiar feeling is in the air. A Barrett Battle.

"So, you got Tom to knock down my fireplace." I know this is wrong. This won't lead to anything good. But I have to start getting Jamie used to the fact that Tom is going to choose me over him from now on.

"I told him I trust him. Isn't that what you do? Trust him? Why not now?" Jamie plants his feet right where the fireplace was and holds out his arms. "The room is huge. There's some chance of making it look modern now."

Tom is speaking in soothing tones on his phone and slips out the front door. "He's going to crack," I say as I watch him leave. "How much more can get piled on him? I'm trying to help him."

"You're never going to help him. Ever. You're a monkey on his back." Jamie hopes that hurt. When it doesn't, he tries again. "He's only here because I asked him to be."

"He's only here because I'm here." I've just blurted the wrong thing, and this time Jamie doesn't mistake what I mean. He laughs and looks me up and down like I'm nothing special.

"Who do you think you are?" He asks it sweetly. It's those same words he used in our big fight. The words that echo in my head every time I take out the trash at the bar or open a box of fifty novelty mugs.

"Who do I think I am? I'm Darcy fucking Barrett!"

Jamie laughs now. My short charade is over, clearly. "You think you have a chance with him?"

My temper is an erupting volcano. "I do have a chance!" I point at my neck. "That's his! He's mine now!" It's so satisfying, watching the air leave Jamie's body. It's luscious. I've won. "He's mine. He loves me. I'm keeping him."

"Keeping him," Jamie splutters. "Keeping him? You're sleeping with Tom? Darcy, what did we talk about?"

"You can't stand to see me happy."

"Oh, and Tom looks so fucking happy," Jamie counters. "Did you at least handle the morning after like a grown up?" He sees the minute hesitation in me and swoops on it. "You just did what you always do. You enjoyed yourself, did zero feelings, and you're going to be gone the next time a flight goes on sale."

"Not this time I won't." I even surprise myself with my intensity. Jamie blinks and backs up, but he quickly rallies.

"Only because you have no passport. Ever find that thing?"

"Give. It. Back."

"I don't have it," Jamie says, and he's telling the truth. He looks out the front window, distracted. "Seriously, Darce, why'd you have to pick Tom? He's way too good for you. You took advantage of him. He'd do whatever anyone asked him."

"Well I asked an awful lot of him last night."

"See? Compare yourself to him, would you? He's nothing but good and honest and deserving of a happily-ever-after. You're just . . ." Jamie racks his brain. "You're human flotsam, you know that?"

The phrase hangs in the air like a gong.

"What did you just call me?"

Jamie recovers seamlessly. "You're trash compared to him."

"No. Call me what you called me the first time." I feel like my veins are full of hot water. "You called me human flotsam. Human flotsam." I advance on him and he begins to back away. Images of Truly's phone flashing with repeated notifications begins to make sense. Her blush. Her averted eyes. The way she changes the subject from Jamie, every time without fail. "How? How did you get to her? Truly is your worksite mole?"

I pick up a brick and throw it at him. It hits the wall and takes a chunk out of it. Jamie bends down for a brick of his own. Now it's on. It's World War IV, with bricks instead of a dinner set.

"I can talk to whoever I want," he yells back at me, and

throws the brick past my hip. "I don't have to fucking answer to you."

"She's mine. My friend. My best friend."

"Well, he's mine." We circle around each other, furious. This is the fight that we never got to finish. A thin trickle of water runs between us but I barely register it. All I can see is my brother's furious face, red embarrassed ears, and the sheen on his brow.

I scream in frustration. "How? Tell me how you got her. Explain it to me." I pick up another brick and weigh it in my palm. I imagine throwing it at his face and it's vivid. "You couldn't just leave that one person alone. The one person I wanted all for myself."

"She's my friend!" Jamie roars.

"No, she's not!" I throw the brick and it takes a devastating chunk out of the floorboard. "Just because you think you're God's gift to women doesn't mean she'll fall for it."

That knocks some wind from his sails. I remember what he said—*She thinks I'm a nightmare.* "I'm telling the truth, Darcy. She's one of my best friends. We've been emailing each other." I laugh derisively at that, but Jamie silences me. "I needed a way to keep an eye on you after our fight. I emailed her from the Underswears website. She replied. I liked it."

I advance on him with my hands outstretched. I'm going to kill him. And her. And everyone. "Jamie, you little fuckwit."

"Stop it," Tom says from the open doorway. He's got his phone in his hand and a grimness in his expression. "Stop it, both of you." He looks up. The tarp covering the hole in the roof is leaking. "I leave the room for two minutes, and this." He sees the new damage we've caused and the brick in my hand. "What have you done, Darcy?"

"He knows everything. That we're together. You're mine, one hundred percent."

Tom just walks to me and takes the next brick from my hand. And he doesn't say anything.

"Well?" Jamie snaps. "Well?"

"I can't do this anymore," Tom says. He's cold and furious. Something inside me begins to slide.

"Just tell him that you love me, and we're together, and we'll go up and fix the tarp and stack the bricks. Tom, tell him."

"I asked you for one thing. Don't tell Jamie until the house is sold. Three months of waiting for me. But that was too much to ask."

"I've waited my whole life for you." I bite my lip. I put my hand out for him but he steps out of reach. "I'm sorry. You know what I'm like, I just—"

Tom glances at his watch. "Yeah, I know what you're like. I asked for three months. You lasted thirty minutes." He refuses to tell my brother that he loves me.

"Hello, I'm right here," Jamie says sarcastically. "You wanted to lie to me?"

There's more to this. "Shut up, Jamie. What was that phone call? What's happened?" I step into him again.

Tom exhales and closes his eyes. "My mom is being

evicted as we speak. Just . . . furniture and cats and she's hysterical."

I hate how my hands are not registering on him. "This early on a Sunday?"

"Her landlord is a jerk. I need to get there." The anger is dulling away into a frightening flatness.

"Look," Jamie says, flicking his eyes to mine with alarm. "We got out of hand, like we do, but we'll fix this—"

"We'll go now," I interrupt Jamie urgently. "We'll all go and—"

"Aldo was right." Tom is looking up at the hole in the ceiling. "I'm not cut out for this. I'm not the boss. I'm the muscle."

"You're doing great," Jamie and I say, practically in unison.

"I wouldn't have even made it this far without Darcy. I can't manage the phone and the site. That much is obvious. How unprofessional, right? Enlisting the client? I never saw Aldo do that."

"Aldo had you to delegate to. You can't delegate to yourself," Jamie argues.

Tom is unswayed. "So don't you think that's going to be a problem when I move to the next site, and when life gets hard again for you and you leave?" He looks at me.

"You've got everything wrong. I'm not going anywhere." I look at my brother and widen my eyes. "Help me."

"Let's just relax," Jamie says, attempting Tom's special tone and failing miserably.

Tom puts a hand on his hip. "Enough lies. Jamie, I fucked up the budget."

"Fucked it up, how?" Jamie's eyes sharpen. Money is his Achilles' heel, and it's pinching. "How much?"

"My entire five percent, probably. I used an old spreadsheet for the project. I didn't update it with the new rate I promised my crew to move over with me. Plus the motel costs for the core three. I just . . . fucked up." He lifts his arms and drops them. "A completely stupid simple error, and I was too distracted to notice it. So there you go. Some more ammunition for you to bring up over and over, for the rest of your life. Ha ha, remember how Tom couldn't swim? Remember how Tom screwed up his first solo job ever?"

"I want to see the spreadsheet," Jamie orders him. "Now. We have a contract—"

"I'm well aware." Tom turns his eyes to mine, and there's a starkness in them now. "And I've been lying to you about something."

"I don't care what it is." I will not break under this, whatever it is. "I don't care if she's still got her ring. If the wedding is back on. If you're already married. It won't stop me from loving you."

He silences me. "I've got your passport."

Everything drains out of me, and my Achilles is lanced clean through. "What?"

"I found it the night I arrived. It was on top of the fridge. Out of your eye line." The faintest tinge of a smile is on his face. "I put it in my pocket, and I kept it. I had a million little moments I could put it somewhere you could find it, but I didn't want to. I wanted to keep you here. So yeah," he says as he walks toward the back door with Patty at his heels. "I'm not the perfect person you both require me to be."

The screen door slaps. I go to chase him, but Jamie stops me.

"Let him cool down. Look what you've done." He passes a hand over his face, rattled. "What the hell?" He looks at the back door.

"I've never seen him look like that," I go again for the door but Jamie hooks his arm around my waist.

"Let me go."

"No, I won't." Jamie's holding me so hard it hurts. "If I let you walk out, that's it. It's going to be you and him, versus me. You're both going to completely forget about me."

I would reply with sarcasm but I hear the fear in his voice. "You're not going to be cut out. Nothing changes, except for me and Tom."

"If I find out that he's just been hanging around me all this time to get to you, I don't know if I can handle that. That guy is my only real friend." Jamie's body is defensive—arms crossed, looming over me, but his eyes are like he's a scared kid.

"Of course that's not true." I put a hand on Jamie's elbow. "Let's all just talk about it. You stay here and manage the site. I'll go with Tom and get his mom."

"Okay. Take her to Mom and Dad's." He thinks of something. "I'm settling soon on my investment property. I'll rent it to Tom's mom." Jamie notices something out the front window. "The foundation guy is here. With doughnuts." He opens the door for him. "Yeah, come in. Hi. We're just in the middle of a crisis, but . . ."

Jamie and I spend a minute or two trying to fake it that we've got it together. Chris marvels at the hole in the ceiling, and we pretend that it's no big deal. We don't have a gaping, terrible hole in the center of our universe, leaking rain like tears.

"I'll go get Tom," I tell them both. I walk down to my bedroom, but he's not there. I walk up the side of the house. I am stepping alongside the prints left by my heels this morning. How fucking typical. I keep walking the same impulsive, selfish path.

Tom's truck has reversed almost out of the drive. I'm running, but I'm not fast enough. I try. I've chased him as far as the corner of Simons Street when I lose all power, and in his rearview mirror if he looked he'd see me doubled over, cursing my heart, cursing myself.

But I feel like this time he doesn't look back for me.

* * *

AFTER TWO DAYS without Tom, I am a stone-cold wreck.

"He'll be back tomorrow," Jamie tells me, but his usual confident tone is slipping. He hands me a mug of tea. "Drink this."

"I can't." I twist around on the front steps and put it down with a slosh. "I can't." The sunset is soaking everything in obnoxiously pretty colors.

"You're gonna have to eat or drink something. And sleep

at some point. Your hair's gonna go gray at this rate." Jamie slaps my medication bottle in my hand. "Take them." He sits next to me with a groan. He's tired after living two days of Tom's life. "I can't believe how much shit he deals with."

Jamie went into recovery mode after he scooped me off the pavement and my heart regained the ability to pump. He half carried me inside, sat me on the closed toilet lid, and commandeered Colin the moment he walked in.

"I'll double your daily rate to be site manager. Tom's got an emergency."

"Done," Colin said. There's no *I told you so* glint in his eyes, only concern. "Okay, boys, set up, and I'll task Chris. Power's off from nine sharp." With Colin's experience, Jamie's bulldozer will, and my phone-answering skills, the renovation has continued to tick along.

"We need him back," I groan desperately, mashing my palms against my closed eyes. "We broke him." I hear a car engine. I sit up. It drives past, and I exhale and put my head in my hands. "Did you call Mom and Dad?"

Jamie has his arm around my shoulders now.

"Tom was there yesterday. He dropped off his mom around dinnertime. She's in their spare room, the nice one that opens to the ocean. She's okay. There are identical cats everywhere." Jamie takes out his phone and shows a picture that Mom sent. There are black and white cats on the bench. The couches. The windowsills and on top of the fridge. "Mom's kind of loving it. She calls them all Mr. Tuxedo."

There's another shot of Tom's mom, Fiona, waving at the

camera. The smile doesn't reach her eyes. It reminds me of when we gave her our welcome basket, all those years ago.

"I don't care about cats. Where did he go?"

"Mom doesn't know. She said he barely said anything while he was there, and said he had to get going. He didn't stay the night. She tried to make him stay, but he was just back in his truck. He apologized, but she didn't know what for." Jamie hesitates on something.

"Tell me."

"He left Patty with them." He wraps his arm tighter until we're hip to hip. Together, we shiver through all the scenarios.

"I don't care what he did." I found my passport on my pillow. I would put that thing in the toaster to get Tom back. "He really thinks we'll never forgive him. Over money and a passport!"

"It's not a hard leap to make," Jamie admits. "We're both psychopaths about—"

"Money and freedom. I know. I know. I hate us." I hang my head between my knees. "I can't bear this. He's just dropped completely off the grid."

"It sucks, doesn't it," Jamie says without any accusation in his tone. He's gentle. "This is why we get hurt when you do it."

"I won't anymore." I swallow a big lump in my throat. "If you can deal with me . . ."

"Yeah. You're staying." Jamie pats my hand and then takes Tom's phone from me. "You know we have to try Megan."

He says this with an apology in his voice that I've never heard before. "We gotta, Darce. I'm right here." He keeps his arm around me as he dials.

"Darcy?" Megan says when she answers.

"Darcy and Jamie," Jamie says when I have no voice. "Is Tom there?"

"Okay, so he told me what to say when you called. First thing: Don't panic. No, wait, that was advice for me. Second thing: Tell Darcy that we're not back together." Megan exhales nervously. "Hear that, Darcy? We're not."

"I heard it." My voice is croaky. "Is he okay?"

"He is. He said he needs time to think. He said he made two big mistakes, and he's made you both angry."

"He hasn't," Jamie and I answer in twin unison.

"That's what I told him," Megan responds. "Everyone knows how much you two love him. You know what he's like. So hard on himself if he isn't . . ."

"Perfect." The horrible word sounds like a curse out of my mouth. "Yeah, we know it."

"He's been under a lot of pressure and it's just gotten to be too much."

"Can I . . . Can I talk to him?" I am suddenly sick with nerves.

"He's not staying with me. He only came by to . . ." She pauses.

"Pick up the ring," Jamie supplies with no tact.

"Yeah," she replies, soft and sad. "He said he needed it for something important."

"Megan, I'm sorry I stared at you at Christmas." I blurt it out. "I'm sorry. I never wanted you guys to break up, and I think your skin is phenomenal."

She laughs. I hear the sounds of children in the background. Like she's outside. "You did stare at me, so much." She's not resentful. "But I stared at you, too."

It's laughable. She's a ten. I'm a solid six in the right light. "Me? Why would you?"

Megan covers the phone receiver. Says something like, *In a minute, sweetie.* Then she says, "Because I always knew how much he loves you."

"We grew up together," I say awkwardly. I look sideways at Jamie, but he's neutral as he listens. "Of course he loves me. We're like family. I'm like his sister."

"He came alive at Christmas," she tells me. "It took me years to admit it to myself, but if you were there, he was lit up. And if you were traveling, he was flat. It's okay," she rushes to assure me as I begin to object. "I know that technically, I was second in line to you."

"I'm sorry," Jamie interjects desperately. "I just thought if I introduced you guys, you'd help him get out of his depression. When you left he was pretty bad," Jamie adds apologetically to me. "Megan is technically perfect for him."

"No, I'm not," Megan says, and the happy squeal of a kid nearly deafens us. "I'm really not. But Darcy is. I'm sorry, guys, but I've got to go."

"How'd you get a kid so fast?" I'm glad she just laughs in response.

"I'm dating a guy who has a three-year-old. I'm just at the park watching them play around. It's been quite unexpected. Like falling in love, doubled." Megan pauses. "Can you guys let me know when he gets back? Please go easy on him."

"I realized something. Tom has never asked us for anything. Did you know that?" Jamie says, and looks to me. I rack my brains. It's true. "Nothing. Not a glass of water if it's hot. Not money, not help, nothing. He just doesn't know how to ask."

"That was something I had an issue with, too," Megan says.

"It's easy," I correct them both. "You just force it on him, and he sighs and says okay."

"I think that only works if you're you," Jamie points out. "And yes, Megan, we'll go easy on him. There's nothing he can do that will make us . . ." Jamie can't finish. His voice has choked up.

"Stop loving him," I supply, strong and steady. "He's made a few fuckups but they're no big deal. We love him. We just want him back. We'll make sure we earn him this time."

We hang up and stare at the street together. When the next car approaches, Jamie and I sit up straight together. Slump together. For the first time since we were kids, we lean together.

"You're right, Darce," Jamie says after an endless stretch of time has passed and we have goose bumps and mosquito bites. "The twins need to work out how we can possibly deserve someone like Tom Valeska. When he comes back, we have to be able to prove it."

I link my arm into my brother's. "How can we possibly do that? He's so . . ." The word *perfect* isn't allowed anymore. I look up at the sky, and a shooting star streaks overhead, trailing down.

Loretta's here. I feel her. I let the tears run down. "I miss him. I miss her."

Jamie knows exactly who I mean. "We haven't lost either of them, not really. They're both just . . . taking a holiday. It's okay. We'll make it right."

"But he left Patty." I have to marvel at how my heart can keep beating this slow and steady, even as I put my face into Jamie's shoulder and cry.

* * *

"I EMAILED HIM the appointment details," Jamie says to me as we take a seat in my cardiologist's waiting room. "I sent it to his old email address. I bet he still checks it. He's going to make it. I know it. Today is the day." Stronger, he assures me, "He promised you."

I don't respond. I'm not using my voice a lot lately. I'm just a faded half person, kept alive by Truly hand-feeding me candy and Jamie pouring water down my throat. It's bizarre seeing them in the same room. They bustle around together, arguing and pushing and cajoling. Jamie's right. She thinks he's a nightmare. A really handsome nightmare.

Luckily he hasn't noticed it yet.

"I'm sorry, I'm sorry," Truly had burst out with the moment she walked in to sit on the side of my bed, but I just shook my head wearily. Who cares. I know what my brother is like. Who could resist replying to one of his cheeky, funny emails? No one. Not a single person on earth who had met him could ignore him. I shouldn't keep holding my friends to a standard they can't achieve.

She hugged me until the sky went black, and Jamie ordered a pizza. If I wasn't so heartbroken, I'd dig around in their relationship a little, but I can't do anything except hold Tom's phone, and correct myself every time I falter.

He's going to come back to you. He will.

I watch as Jamie selects a magazine for me. "*Golf Digest,*" he says, trying to make me laugh, and unfolds it on my thighs to an article. "Come on, Darce. Gotta work on your backswing."

"Fine. But you need to improve yourself as well." I choose a magazine for him. "Learn how to bake a glazed ham." These days, we're all about self-improvement. We're determined to make ourselves better versions. We both focus on our assigned reading until Tom's phone buzzes. Like always, we jump and scrabble for it.

"It's a message from the real estate agent. Margie's coming at three. Will we be back in time?"

"Yes, and if not, Colin can take her through." It's been two months. It's hard to believe that we have a fairly well-formed house to show an agent. She wants to prepare a game plan. The demand for properties in our area has gone red-hot.

"Two months," I say to Jamie, and he knows what I mean. We sit and stare blankly at the receptionist's desk for a while. I turn my head with effort to look at my brother. My mirror. He looks as bad as I do.

"Yeah, we look shitty," he says as he rolls his face to mine. We're just two blond cadavers. "It's fucking ridiculous, isn't it?"

"What?"

"How we can't live without him."

"Yeah. That's what I'm worried they're going to tell me in this appointment. I'm a goner, Jamie." I groan tiredly and slip into a half snooze.

As the minutes tick along, I have to accept it. He's gone. He's not coming back for me and my stupid heart. I check the phone in my hand again. I want to squeeze a message out of it. Just one word that he's okay, and I can get myself hooked up and they'll find a heartbeat.

The name is called that turns both our heads. "Barrett?"

"We just need to wait a minute longer," Jamie argues politely with the cardiologist's assistant. "We're waiting for our friend to come to the appointment, too."

"I'll bring them in when they get here," the receptionist tells us. "We need to keep to the schedule." Defeated, the Barrett twins skulk down the long white hallway. I'm scared. My heart is a dead apricot kernel. They'll have to sew me to Jamie to borrow his, and we'll have to live as Siamese twins.

Jamie's hand closes on mine, and I've never been this scared for myself. "What am I going to do?" I whisper to him as we are seated. "What?"

"I don't know," he replies to me, hushed. "But you'll be okay. I'm here."

"Darcy Barrett," Dr. Galdon says to me with a flourish. He's known me for years. "I have not seen your face in a long, long time." His smile fades off when the witty rejoinder he's expecting doesn't happen. From either twin. "What's happening?"

"Just a little brokenhearted," I say listlessly. "It's not feeling good in there." I point at my chest.

"Hmm," Dr. Galdon says, and I try to not read too much into his expression as he checks my blood pressure. I know I look absolutely terrible. I've got blade cheekbones and my eyeballs are permanently pink. Tom thought my clothes were falling off before? I look like a mop slid into black fabric.

"Let's get you hooked up." I change into a gown behind a screen at the end of the room. Dr. Galdon helps me sit up onto the edge of the examination bench and wheels over the heart monitor. He sticks little pads all over me, connecting the wires to his machines. This used to scare me so much as a kid. I thought I was going to be shocked to life. Maybe that would be a good move for me now.

"She eats nothing, forgets her medication, it's expired," Jamie snitches on me in a dull automatic way. "Drinks too much. No exercise whatsoever. Cries all day. Sugar, good Lord, the sugar."

"Okay, okay," Dr. Galdon says, sticking the last of the pads to my chest. I swivel and lie down. "Don't get her all riled up." He's been in the vicinity of one of our snippy little jousts plenty of times. Again, he falls silent when I don't reply.

Little does he know, the Barrett twins have stopped fighting.

It takes too much effort, and besides, we need to cling to each other to stay afloat. Without our perfect-for-us buffer to level us out. I hear the upward inflection of a beep and we all watch as my heart begins to squiggle and bump along on the screen with all the energy of a dying tadpole. I hear a buzzing and for a split second I think it's the sound of me flatlining.

"Let me just get this," Dr. Galdon says. "I've got an emergency call. Just sit tight." He leaves the room, and I remain lying down, looking at the lines on the screen.

Bleep-bloop. Bleep-bloop.

"The solicitor sent the paperwork through," Jamie says to break the silence. "It came by courier. He's gonna kill us." He adds that last part on cheerfully, like he can't wait for the moment that Tom shakes his head at what we've done.

"Yeah." I sigh heavily. "I can hear him now. *I don't need your help—*"

Jamie cuts in, mimicking Tom. "*I don't need a third of the sale price.*"

"*I don't deserve it,*" I continue in Tom's tone. "*I'm not a Barrett. It's your inheritance, not mine.*" I rub my arms and try to not watch the monitor. "But he does. And he's getting it. Thank you, Jamie. It's the perfect way to show him that he's important, and equal, and that we love him forever."

"He didn't inherit a thing, and I didn't think twice about it." Jamie has been beating himself up over this. "All I thought about was my money. Not him. He was practically her third grandchild and he got nothing. This is just making things right."

"Can you get him to sign, though? He's so proud."

"When I find him," Jamie says with complete confidence, "I can get him to do anything. Even sign that document."

"When you find him." I exhale, Jamie exhales, and the room falls silent. It's impossible to find someone who's hurt and hiding. I should know. I've been doing it for years. Who knows where on earth Tom could be.

"Once I get the all-clear to travel, I'm going to go looking for him."

Jamie doesn't forbid it or say it's a stupid idea. All he says is, "Where will you look first?"

"Not sure. I'll take the Northern Hemisphere—"

"And I'll do the Southern Hemisphere." Jamie smiles at me. "We'll find him. We're very determined individuals. Two blond artillery tanks, rolling out. Covering every square inch." He's trying to make me smile, but I'm distracted by a feeling.

I've got a vibration in my bones. I've got a shiver on the soles of my feet and an upward trickle in my veins. On the screen, my heart rate is pipping upward. I'm starting to get warm.

"God, are you about to blow up?" Jamie stands and looks at the screen, making a face. "What the fuck is happening? I'll go get Dr.—"

The door opens.

"In here," the receptionist says, and Darcy and Jamie Barrett have twin heart attacks.

Tom Valeska always arrives, exactly when we need him most.

He's standing in the doorway, his brow creased and his T-shirt too loose on his body. One foot is slid back, like he's ready to make his escape. "Thank you," he says with his automatic politeness to the receptionist. His eyes dart between me and Jamie, fast and desperate. He's flushed and sweating. He's the most beautiful person I've ever seen.

"Hi," I say, tethered in place by my heart. "You came."

Jamie jolts out of his surprise and does what I can't. He walks to Tom and puts his arms around him and squeezes. "You came," Jamie echoes, and won't let the hug end. "You're here. You're okay."

"Of course I'm okay. Are you okay, Darce?" Tom's eyes are on the machine beside me and the wires feeding out of my chest. He's never seen this before, me lying here in a gown, hooked up to a machine. It's confronting. I try to pull them off, but they're stuck too well.

"I'm okay," I say with the last puff of air I have. I pull myself up to sit on the edge of the bench. The air is filled with beeping. "Come here. Please come here." My eyes are full of tears.

Jamie releases him and Tom steps between my knees. The entire world falls away. He puts his fingertips into my shaggy hair and tips my face up.

"What's happened here?" he says in a sympathetic husky voice. "You look terrible, beautiful Darcy Barrett."

I press my face into his solar plexus and I feel his warm hands on my nape. He threads his free arm through the wires and cups my back. I'm carrying the sensation of this squeeze around for the rest of my life.

"Tom, are you okay?"

"I'm okay," Tom says. "I'm sorry, guys," he tries, but we both shush him desperately. Jamie is feeling left out and squeezes onto the examination table beside me. We're just two little blond birds, looking up at Tom like we need him to survive. Oh wait. We do.

"But I completely—" he tries again, and we shake our heads. "I just totally—"

"We don't care," Jamie says, silencing him. "We don't care. You're back. That's everything. Please make my sister stay alive. By any means necessary."

"What does she need to stay alive?"

"You," Jamie says simply. It's one word, but it's a powerful one; Tom looks at him sharply, like he can't believe what he's heard.

"You," I echo. "Where the hell have you been?"

"I thought I'd fucked up beyond forgiveness. So I just drove. I guess I just left town. Maybe I am like my father." Tom sighs and rubs his face. "Maybe that's what I've been scared of my entire life. That I'm like him."

"You're not," I counter. I rub his forearm. "Is that why you've been trying harder than any living human being, your entire life?" He shrugs and I know I'm right.

"You left Patty," Jamie says with a little accusation. "We

thought you'd gone and driven your gorgeous ass into a canyon."

Tom laughs, even as his hands smooth over me, calming the terror that has the heart monitor squeaking. "Patty needed a beach vacation. Old girl looked all worn out."

"Ditto," I groan as his nails scratch in gentle circles on the side of my neck. "Tom, I nearly died without you. Dr. Galdon is about to confirm it."

"Yeah, where is he? I'll go get him." Jamie walks out with a frown on his brow, closing the door behind him. Holy crap. He just left a room so we could be alone. My heart is pipping so much that Tom looks sideways with concern.

"Settle down." His warm palms are on my jaw, and he's drinking in my face. A perfect kiss is pressed onto my mouth. It's soft and kind, like a friend. "I died without you, too."

"We've done so much work," I say, trying to bring him back again for a longer kiss. "Wait till you see." He evades my lips.

"I cannot tell you how sorry I am," he says with a wince. "I'll fix everything. I won't sleep until it's perfect."

"I don't mean the house. It's fine. Colin's been the site manager, and I've been his deputy. Jamie cut a bunch of costs and the budget is on track. Silly," I admonish him gently, rubbing him on the arm. "We can fix everything for you."

"That's all you guys ever try to do," he groans guiltily.

"What I meant was that Jamie and I have been working on ourselves. We've been renovating in here." I pick up his palm and press it against my heart, over the monitor pads.

"We are going to be working on ourselves for a long time. To make sure we never make you run away again. Where did you go?"

"I think I pretended you were sitting in the passenger seat beside me, and I just . . . drove. We've been a lot of places. We took the backroads, stayed in cheap motels, and one really expensive one. The beach. A really great diner that I'm taking you to for real—" His glow fades out, like he's remembering it's impossible.

"Take me there."

"But about your passport—"

"Don't care." I manage to get a hand behind his neck and pull him down. My heart is about to turn inside out when we kiss, our mouths open, and we taste each other again. He's sweeter than sugar, more delicious than anything I've ever experienced. My every birthday-candle wish.

"But it's unforgivable," he argues back as he lifts his mouth, and ends on a succulent bite of my lower lip. "It was the worst lie I've ever told you—"

"When you said you couldn't do this anymore? That was the worst lie. It was a lie, right?" I gasp when his hands cup my throat, warmer, tighter, and the next kiss is electric. I'm surprised I don't blow up the heart monitor. It's tongue and biting and exhaling and wanting. So much wanting.

"You still want me? Even though I'm a screwup?" he asks as he lifts his head, and there's that dark, dangerous glint that only I can recognize. Everyone else sees a mild-mannered sweetheart. But right here, in these moments between us, he's my Valeska. The one I've always needed beside me, every step that I take.

"One hundred percent mine."

He considers that, then maybe he remembers the desperate hug that my brother gave me. He tips his head toward the door. "Better let him have one percent of me." He smiles, and I laugh.

"Okay. Ninety-nine percent mine. That's got a nice ring to it. Never say that I'm not open to negotiation. Now. I'm going to tell you exactly how much I love you."

"I already know how much."

I shake my head. "You can't know. I haven't told you."

"You have always made me feel it. Always." His eyes burn with intensity. "It's how I can watch you smile at good-looking delivery drivers. No stranger is going to talk to you for two minutes and take you away from me. You wouldn't allow it."

He's not indulging himself in male arrogant bullshit. He's doing what he does best: He's telling the truth.

He keeps going. "It's why you've treated me all these years like protecting me is your job. And no one else has ever tried, by the way. Everyone else thinks I'm completely fine, but you've always known that I need you, in every way. You've felt it."

I nod, my breath stuck in my throat.

"You've never dated anyone you could love, because you didn't want anything to threaten how you feel for me. You were always alone at the Christmas table, looking at me and

Megan, with eyes like you were waiting for me to get it together and realize. Sitting outside alone on the back stairs, looking up at the stars, waiting on me."

He's touching me now, slow and easy, like I'm an animal he could startle. "You've avoided me for years and traveled, because it was too much for you. You're scared to death because a person like you only loves once. And it's me."

His words shock through me. His hands are on my waist and he squeezes to prompt an answer. "Am I right?"

"Of course you are. Now kiss me." This one is a sweet, gentle thing, until I ruin it with the slide of my tongue. He grumbles a warning in the back of his throat. Mmm, I missed that alpha bass.

He breaks us apart. "I never told you how much I love you. How do you think I feel? Tell me."

I have no experience with articulating feelings, let alone anything this alive and primal, but I have to try. This must be how Loretta felt when she turned over the first tarot card. *Use your intuition,* she'd instruct. *Feel the truth.* I press my palm against his heart and his fingers slide into my hair.

"You slept in a bunk bed in Jamie's room. That's one of the ways you've had to work hard for me. Putting up with my brother, just to sleep a wall away from me and put your toothbrush next to mine."

He nods with a smile and a memory in his eyes.

"You sleep on the grass outside my window just to be close to me."

"More."

"When we hug at Christmastime you breathe me in, and you hold it in. Whatever it is you like on my skin, it's deep in the caveman bit of your brain."

I have no idea where this weird truth is coming from, but I'm right. He drops his head down and on my shoulder I feel the pull of air into his nostrils.

"Even more." He says it as he exhales. Both of us are getting overheated. I don't even have to search myself to know what to say. These words have been on the tip of my tongue for a lifetime.

"Another man's diamond on my hand is your worst nightmare, and for years you've been jolting awake over it." I feel a tremor run through his body. Now I have to say the really hard thing.

"Putting a diamond on another woman made you sick to your stomach. But like a nice guy you couldn't admit it to yourself, let alone her, until the white lace started creeping in at the edges and you saw my insanely-in-love parents together."

"Even more than that."

"You'd kill for me. You'd dig a grave for me."

He laughs. "Yeah. Now you're getting close." We are kissing when the door opens again.

"Alrighty," Dr. Galdon says as he walks in, and then coughs when we break apart. "Let's take a look at you, Miss Barrett." He shakes hands with Tom and introduces himself. Tom takes a seat next to Jamie. I've never seen anything more lovely; my two favorite human beings side by side, and they love me.

"Look at her," Jamie remarks, jabbing an elbow at Tom. "Got your color back already, Darce."

"I was just about to remark on that," Dr. Galdon says with a laugh. He consults the monitor. "That's the fastest-healing broken heart I've ever seen. One hundred percent improvement on how it was five minutes ago." His smile fades as he writes something down on my chart. "But we do need to talk about your medication, and we need to do an ECG. There are irregularities here that I haven't seen before."

"It's okay, just relax," Tom tells me and Jamie when we both tighten up. It's in that tone we can never resist. "We'll get you fixed up, Darce. Good as new. We've got a cruise to go on when we're eighty," he explains to the doctor. "We need her there for it."

"I think that can be arranged," Dr. Galdon says with a laugh. "As long as she's got someone looking after her until then."

"She will," Jamie and Tom say in unison. Just like twins.

I'm so lucky that the room fills with it. Pip-pip-pip, my heart beats like I'm going to live forever. I need it to.

Chapter 21

I am in my own place of Zen: My passport is in my hand and I am leaving the country.

I love this moment—standing adrift in a sea of strangers, mocking them in my mind for their pashminas and full-sized pillows. Do they think there are no pillows where they're going? Some people travel like they honestly believe they're leaving planet Earth.

Mars doesn't sell socks or toothpaste.

I catch myself; I'm judging people and being nasty. That's not the person I want to be. I make myself lose the big gray glare and the forehead wrinkle.

I lean on the pillar beside the floor-to-ceiling windows and try to block out the noise. Everywhere, more and more groups are finding each other, crowing with excitement, taking photos together before departure. A group of young guys, dressed in board shorts, straggle over to the window to look outside. One of them looks over at me and raises his eyebrows in a *hey*.

I check my watch. Soon it'll be time to board.

"Hey," Tom says, and when I look up at him my heart unfurls. There's no better word for it. It's like a time-lapse photo of a rose opening whenever I think about how he is mine. So, all the time. He's got bottles of water for us. They're cold against the small of my back as he wraps his arms around me, a knee nudging between my thighs. He gives the group of boys nearby a dark look, then laughs at himself.

"I'm being Valeska again, aren't I." Getting a grip on himself, he puts the water bottles in his backpack.

"Every day of your life. Everything okay? You seem nervous." I tug his T-shirt straighter on his torso. An elderly woman nearby thinks to herself, *Lucky girl.* That's the effect this face and body have. It's something you can't argue with. I'm going to find him hot when I'm eighty years old.

"I'm fine," Tom says, but he's jittery. "I just had a surprise for you, but it might not work out." He checks his watch robotically.

"Hey, I don't need a surprise." I put my arm around his waist. "You're okay." I succumb to heady smugness as he drops his head and puts his brow to mine. Is there anything more obnoxious than blissed-out-in-love people? Don't care.

I put a kiss on his mouth and his hand tightens, low down on my back. Then, because we're against a pillar, he abandons his good-boy side and takes my butt in one hand and squeezes until I squeak up on tiptoes.

He's distracting me. I can't work out why he's flustered.

I try to keep my focus as he kisses under my ear. "The kitchen was delivered this morning." I am remotely supervising Tom's team as they renovate Jamie's beachside investment, just down the road from Mom and Dad. "Jamie's such a hard-ass, insisting on an outdoor cat run."

"Didn't I tell you? I got him to agree that one cat can be inside at a time." Tom laughs up at the ceiling and his hands tug me even tighter against his body.

We will always, always be like this. *Get in me.*

"Wow. That's a huge concession. Be proud." I run my hand up his back, admiring the muscle. "By the time we're home, you're going to be moving her into the last house you ever have to." Jamie gave Mrs. Valeska an open-ended lease. If Tom wanted to buy it, he could. "We're all organized. Nothing left to stress about."

"And you're organized." Tom returns to me. "You got your edits in. Any word?"

"My agent said that they're trying to decide which image will be on the cover." My unexpected book baby came kicking and screaming into my life a few months ago. Turns out, my photographs were good. Better than good. My first photographic art book, *Devil's End*, is due out in about six months. Plenty of time for me to start my next submission, *The House of Destiny*, chronicling the evolution of Loretta's cottage. All those little photos of mossy bricks and wallpaper cracks actually amounted to something beautiful, and it means my childhood memories can live on. I want to give this book to my parents on their wedding anniversary. Who knew having a goal could keep my heart beating so well? The new medication doesn't hurt either. I swore to Dr. Galdon that I'd care for my heart from now on.

Tom nudges me until the pillar chills the skin between my shoulder blades, and bends to kiss me. I feel people staring. I'm getting used to it by now. We're just so fucking hot, it makes me laugh. Take a look, everyone. Look what I have. Look what's all mine.

We break apart just as it's getting socially inappropriate. "All these people are so old," Tom says in between breaths. "We don't want to give any of them heart attacks."

Dozens of eyes avert from us as we face the waiting crowds. The older women, those with white hair and walking sticks, don't even bother looking away from us.

"They really are old," I agree. I wonder if Tom's checked his bank account yet. I'm getting the jitters, too. I hate having secrets from him, but this one was too much to resist, and my brother was far too clever.

"What'd you expect, choosing a trip like this?"

I remember something. "I got you a present. Something amazing to toast the house sale." I dig around in my backpack. "I can't even tell you how hard I fought for this. Some asshole was trying to outbid me, right down to the last second." I tug out the bottle and present it to him.

"You got me a bottle of Kwench." He laughs and studies the label.

"It's worth more than a bottle of Cristal champagne. If it's not fizzy, I'm going to be furious."

"You know I loved Kwench because it was the drink your parents gave me, the first night I had dinner at your place? I hope it wasn't too expensive."

"I'm rich now, remember?"

He laughs at the carelessness in my tone. "It's the settlement today, right? Your money should be through. Good timing." He means before our trip.

"Yeah." We're distracted for a second by an overhead announcement. Boarding will be soon. It makes him more nervous, his hands squeezing. What's tying him up in knots?

He refocuses on me. He's good at that, making me feel like the only one. "Sad about the sale?"

"No. It was perfect. I still can't believe the highest bidder was a family with twins. It was our last sign from Loretta. You did an amazing job on the final fitout. It turned out . . ." I don't use the word *perfect* anymore. "So well. I'm proud of you. I know it bothers you that you weren't there for the first bit. But you've got a lifetime of houses ahead of you." I thumb through my bank account app. My big, incredible gift of freedom from Loretta has cleared. So much money. More than I can ever possibly deserve.

"It's gone in." I hold it up to show him.

Tom looks at the amount in my account, and like I knew he would, his brow furrows. "That's not right."

"Yeah, it is. Has yours gone in?" I keep my face completely neutral as he takes out his own phone and logs in to his account. Then I see his face. He holds his phone next to mine; we have matching deposits. Down to the cent.

"What did you do?" he starts, but I just laugh and kiss him.

"You really gotta read the things you sign," I point out helpfully. "That's important as a business owner."

"No, Darce," he groans. "This isn't right."

"It isn't only right." I decide to make an exception to my rule and use that forbidden word. "It's *perfect*. It's a big slice of cake, cut into three portions. You deserve it. You're family. You're my family."

"You don't know what this means," he groans, putting a hand on his brow. I do know what it means. It means that Tom Valeska doesn't have to struggle and grind anymore; his mom taken care of and he can be selective on what he flips next. It means that Tom has a lifetime of possibilities, the kind that the Barrett twins have enjoyed so effortlessly.

He's just getting ready to scold me when he's distracted. "Oh wait, here's your surprise coming now. But seriously, Darce. I'm mad."

I follow his eye line as we see someone forcing their way through the crowd. For a second, my eyes play tricks. I look up at Tom with a frown.

He explains nervously. "I got you something. A surprise. Two surprises. I'm not sure if you're going to be happy about one of them."

I see what he means.

Through the crowd, Jamie is weaving his suitcase. "Excuse me," he says loudly to a chatting couple, and they jump apart in surprise. Plowing through to us, he screeches to a stop and looks at his watch. "Damn taxi driver had absolutely no idea." He looks at me like he's afraid. Then he looks back at Tom, down to the bottle of Kwench in his hand and booms, "Darcy, it was you bidding against me?"

"It was you? Christ, Jamie, I paid through the nose for that damn bottle of Kwench." I start to laugh. "What the hell are you doing here?"

"We just thought it would be fun to take the cruise together when we're under thirty, instead of eighty," Tom says. I can hear the note of uncertainty in his voice. In all of our naked bedtime whisperings and trip planning, it was always only us.

Us, kissing in the sun on lounge chairs, the ocean stretching around us to uninterrupted horizons. Us, face-first in the buffet. Alone.

"I will not get in your way. I've got my own cabin, obviously." Jamie grimaces at us both as the thought passes through his head. "If you guys want to lie around smooching, I'll sit by myself. Actually, I'll always sit by myself. You won't even see me—"

He stops talking when I put my arms around him and hug.

I feel the tension fall out of him. My brother? He's half of me. And I love Tom so much for inviting my twin to come with us. It's the only way to show him he's not cut out of our lives and that he will always be with us, floating in a pool like when we were kids.

"Thanks, Darce," Jamie says above my head, and I feel his emotion. Nothing has to change. No one has to lose anyone. Then he ruins the moment like only he can.

"You wouldn't believe how much my cleaner is charging to housesit my apartment and Diana. It's extortion. Did you know that cat is awake between two and four A.M every morning? She's killing me. Maybe my tenant can own seven cats. By the way, take a look at this." Jamie holds up his phone. Mom has sent a picture of Patty, sunbathing on a beach towel. It's nice she's getting her own vacation.

I won't let Jamie off the hook. "Nope. Diana is yours. Every evil genius needs a fluffy cat to stroke." I give him a final squeeze and release him. When I look up, my brother is looking at the crowd.

"Wait, isn't that—"

"My second surprise for Darcy." Tom tucks my hair behind my ear.

"Holy crap," Jamie laughs.

Through the crowd, I see my second gift. It's Truly, and she's got a suitcase big enough to stuff a dead body into. She has heart-shaped sunglasses on top of her head. She can't get through this throng of people. She stands on tiptoe, waves, and makes a frustrated face.

"Here's the girl who's gonna drink whiskey with you before lunch," Jamie says. His eyes are that bright cornflower blue that belies his excitement and pleasure. I think of him dragging Truly past a jewelry store. I can't believe I'm admitting it, but I think Jamie will get his way one day.

"Tom." I want to cry. "Too perfect."

Jamie transfers me into Tom's arms. "I'll help her." He walks through the crowd, like the blond artillery tank that he is, and extricates her suitcase handle from her grip. She takes it back. They argue and Jamie begins to try to charm her into a better mood. His fingertip touches her sunglasses. His hand cups her elbow and squeezes. She laughs out loud, unwilling, and when the music they're piping through the cruise ship terminal changes, Jamie begins to dance, silly and mock-sexy.

There's chemistry oozing out of them in pink clouds, and now Tom and I aren't the only hot couple that people can't take their eyes off.

Tom's gently amused. "I really am a smart guy."

Jamie and Truly assemble next to us, and again I feel a little bit of their vulnerability as they both stare at Tom's arms around me. They feel like they're intruding.

"My best girl is here." I lean into Truly. "How's Holly working out for you?" Our joint resignations to the bar was such a high-five moment. Holly and I walked out of that place side by side, bought a cake and ate it on the hood of my car.

"She's fabulous." Truly says with a kiss on my cheek. "I owe you big-time. Remind me to show you my garment tech packs later. I'm getting closer." Her dream of upscaling her business is so close we can taste it.

"When that happens for you, I'll be able to die happy." I smile at her.

"You can live happy," Tom corrects me. "Hey, did you bring that thing I asked you for, Jamie?"

My brother is taken aback. "You want to do that here?"

"No more secrets from this point forward." Tom takes out a velvet jewelry box and my heart drops out of my body. But before I can process it, Jamie does the same. They swap boxes. I recognize the one that is now in Tom's hand.

"Is that—" It's Loretta's sapphire. I know it. The patina on the old leather box is as familiar to me as the skin on my hands. "Tom, gimme it." I jump for it but he's holding it above his head, and he's six-six, stretched up forever.

"You swapped, for Megan's ring? Oh, pretty." Truly looks in the box Jamie has snapped open to show her. "But that's tacky of you," she amends.

"Tacky? How? I got a good deal on this," Jamie protests. "The clarity and cut on this are phenomenal. Tom's got good taste," he finishes with his usual lack of tact.

"But this belonged to someone else, and she loved it," Truly chides him softly. "Whoever you marry one day will have someone else's ring on her hand."

"That's not a practical way of looking at it," Jamie argues back. "Darce, stop jumping." He stuffs Megan's ring in his pocket. "Now you've made me think," he says to Truly, grouchy. "Tom, maybe I want to swap back."

"Sorry, a deal's a deal." Tom is completely unrepentant. He's crowded me against the pillar again. Behind my eyes, every time I blink, I see sapphires. Black sapphires. Refracting, dark and mysterious and brilliant. I want them. I need them.

I want the name *Valeska* on me so bad I could scream, and I think he knows it from the way he's looking at me.

"Oh, that's us," Jamie says as boarding is announced. "Let's go and get elderly." He gathers up Truly's bag and begins to herd her toward the gangway.

"I want it." I touch my fingers to the square lump in Tom's pocket.

"I know. That's why I did a deal with the devil." His eyes shine in amusement as people begin to stream past us. The sound of a thousand suitcase wheels is deafening. "Now, are you sure you want to live in a tent with me when we get back?"

"Very sure. I'm deputy site manager, after all. I need to be on hand."

He still can't conceive of it. To him, princesses don't sleep on the ground. "Because the moment we find a house that you want to keep, I'll make it your home. Everything you want it to be. It'll have a photography studio, and—"

"Come on, guys, you can make out on the boat!" Jamie turns and shouts at us. "We're going."

"I want it," I repeat. I mean the house, the ring, and him. The future. "I love you and I want it."

Tom leans down to kiss my pout. "Have you earned it?"

I falter. I shake my head automatically. "How can I possibly earn you?"

He removes my tremor of doubt as only he can. "You earn me daily. Come on. You know I give you everything you want. Just relax. Let me spoil Darcy Barrett a little, for the rest of her life. Let me get a taste of that feeling."

All I can say is, it tastes sweet.

Acknowledgments

Thank you to the following people for not bludgeoning me to death during the process of writing this book.

My husband, Roland, always responded *You can* when I wailed *I can't*. Thanks for being right and for supporting me when writing unexpectedly changed my life. My mother, Sue, is my number one fan. My pug, Delia, is my second biggest fan.

Taylor Haggerty from Root Literary is my agent and my lighthouse across the sea. She has cheered me on with unfailing positivity. HarperCollins has been so patient with me as I found my feet again after the unexpected success of my debut. Carrie Feron is my editor and her calm confidence in me has meant the world.

Thank you to my friends, but these two in particular: Tina Gephart messaged me every afternoon to see if I was having a good writing day. Spoiler: I usually wasn't, but Tina would still check in the next day. Thank you for being a friend and mentor. Thank you to Christina Hobbs for that long Skype call. I picked myself up off the floor one last time, and now I get to write this.

The Flamethrowers are a group of wonderful readers who found *The Hating Game* and loved the hell out of it. I wrote this book for all of you.

About the author

About the book

Read on

Insights,
Interviews
& More . . .

Meet Sally Thorne

Katie Saarikko

SALLY THORNE is the *USA Today*
bestselling author of *The Hating
Game*. She spends her days climbing
into fictional worlds of her own creation.
She lives in Canberra, Australia, with
her husband in a house filled with
vintage toys, too many cushions, a
haunted dollhouse, and the world's
sweetest pug. ∾

Behind the Book Essay

They say if you stare into the abyss too long, the abyss stares into you. Well, I'm here to tell you that the abyss they're talking about is a blank Microsoft Word document.

When I wrote my first book, *The Hating Game,* I didn't even know I was writing a book. *Ha ha,* I thought, grinning to myself as I tapped away whenever I felt like it. *How enjoyable, how droll!* How did I do it? Who knows, but it's printed with a cute cover! What was next?

I opened a new document and I stared.

Picture me, propped up in bed like Beth March from *Little Women,* slowly fading away from Second Book Syndrome. My expert nurses during this crisis spoon-fed me broth, and assured me it was a very common disorder for new authors and I would survive. I didn't believe them and honestly thought I was a goner. I doubted my creativity, talent, and skill so intensely that I nearly gave up roughly ninety-nine times.

But I loved my book title. It gave me goose bumps on my forearms. *99 Percent Mine.* I'd say it to myself until it became a mantra synonymous with *Don't give up.* The outside world faded away and I began to laugh at myself again, as I typed. *Ha ha, how droll.*

I learned a very hard lesson that I'm sharing with you now. That important, impossible thing that you have nearly given up on ninety-nine times? Finish it. Whether it's a success or a failure, ▶

3

no one can take your *The End* prize away from you. Finishing is the most important thing there is. It's proof of how hard you tried. This book is printed with environmentally friendly tear-based ink that I cried into a vat, but I wouldn't change it.

The first time around, I was astonished to realize that I'd written a book.

This second time around, I know I wrote a book. I was there for every single ugly gritty moment of it. Whether it's going to be a success or not is beside the point. I finished something that was impossibly hard for me.

I would now like to thank everyone who asked me how they could read more by me. Readers eagerly searched for my back catalog, and then were stumped to find out *The Hating Game* was all she wrote. To thank them for waiting for so long, I am so happy to include two additional pieces here.

The first is a glimpse into the happily-ever-after of Tom and Darcy. I've called this piece "1 Percent More." I really felt that after a lifetime of loving each other, they deserved this extra moment.

And the second—containing more spoilers than I can count— is the short epilogue I wrote for *The Hating Game*. This is the number one thing I'm asked for, over and over again: more. There has always been more. I wrote an epilogue in my original draft of the book and I've always known how things turned out. At the time of publication, we decided to end the book where we did so that the reader could imagine their own ending. I am happy to now share this extra little snippet with you.

It's one last peek into that world before I say goodbye to it. Lucy and Josh changed my life, and I am very grateful to everyone who loved them. ∾

99 Percent Mine
Epilogue: 1 Percent More

I get dressed alone in the dawn light.
My shorts from yesterday aren't too dirty,
so I tug them on, along with my Valeska
Building Services shirt. It's so splattered
with paint and grout that it's close to
retirement. In the tight confines of the
tent, I work my boots onto my feet, pull
my hair back into a short ponytail, and
walk through a puff of perfume.

These days, I sleep like the dead.
I wake like I want to live forever.

We're in a nice neighborhood at the
moment. As always, we have the worst
house on the best street. I go through
the empty master bedroom to my
favorite bathroom. It's got to be the
best one Tom's ever done. The lighting
he chose makes me love him more;
it's so flattering my skin looks almost
iridescent. I've got candy-pink cheeks
and my lips are kiss stained. A night with
Tom Valeska is the kind of cosmetic that
can't be bottled.

I'm more beautiful than I've ever
been in my life. I know it because Tom
tells me, and wherever I go, people fall
in love with me. I walk around in a cloud
of sex and happiness. I've got a grateful
squeeze-ache in my pelvis and a light
within. Even Colin has told me I glow.

Every second delivery guy asks me if
I'm free tonight. I laugh and say, *No way,
are you kidding? I'm busy tonight.* Tom ▶

5

overhears and smiles to himself. Then later he'll say in my ear something like, *DB, I'm planning on being extremely busy tonight.* Then he'll walk off, his phone will vibrate in my pocket, and I'll do battle with my active imagination. The guys are cheeky when they grin at Tom as they pack up in the afternoon.

Have a good night, boss.

We're potent to be around. Everyone can smell the pheromones mixing into the chlorine on Tom's skin—his testosterone, passion, and obsession. No matter where we are, what new crews are put together for our houses, Tom reclaims me as his in calm and subtle ways. In return, I'm shameless, pushing him against walls whenever I have a chance. We fog up building sites without even looking at each other.

Because of this cloud I'm enveloped in, I'm inspired. Everything's beautiful. My camera has earned me a nickname with the guys—the Paparazzi. Tom told them at one of our pizza Fridays that I haven't been like this since I was sixteen, and it's true. I'm in love with Tom, but I'm also back in love with my camera, and it's forever this time.

Tom submits to my obsession with his face and as the sun goes down we sit, knee to knee, in the garden of whatever house we live behind. I use my favorite lens and I take photos of his perfect face. His eyes change with every blink. These photos are my favorites, and I shoot him compulsively.

He wants me. He needs me. He breathes for me. I capture it all.

I look around the bathroom. It's honestly perfect. Whoever buys this place will love the fittings he chose. I think I admired this sink at a showroom in an offhand way—*How gorgeous is this?* Then the next thing I know, it's being installed. I buff my fingerprints off the faucet. I swear, with each house, Tom outdoes himself. I know what he's doing. He's trying to find my dream combination of paint, fittings, flooring, and address.

Ugh, the lighting in here is so damn good. I kind of hate whoever buys this house.

There's a mug that says *#1 ASSHOLE* on the marble kitchen counter, and it's steaming. Tom's laptop is beside the mug and I begin to go through our emails. There's one from a shipping company we use.

"They're claiming the front window panel on insurance," I say, not raising my voice. I can't see him, but he's got to be close by because Patty is here, asleep in a sunbeam. She's always within a few feet of him. "Apparently it was broken before it got out of the state."

"Mmm-hmm." He's not pleased, wherever he is. "Can you call the supplier and—"

"Make someone apologize profusely and give us a partial credit on our next order? Already did it." I sip my coffee.

"Damn, you're good. What's the deal with the floor sanding? I thought it was happening on Friday."

"It is, but unless I do it before I go to the studio, we'd be better off renting the sander on Monday. I don't think I can sand an entire house in one morning. Unless we get Alex to help."

"He's on—"

"Oh, yeah." We're increasingly using shorthand with each other. Alex is going to be up on the roof installing the solar panels on Friday. He's been promoted from general shitkicker. I try to rearrange the remaining team in my head, but nothing works.

I'd offer to reschedule my studio time, but I know Tom won't hear of it. Besides, I've got a really interesting elderly lady sitting for a portrait with me. She's a tarot reader that I tracked down with an old address book of my grandmother's. That's another series I'm working on: all portraits of fortune-tellers. This year, I'm going to enter the same portrait competition I won all those years ago. I want to see if I can re-peak my career.

"The floors aren't going anywhere," Tom says like he knows what I'm thinking. "They can wait to get sanded. You still want the original floors, right?"

"Yeah, I love them." I don't know what these floorboards are, but they feel just right when I walk with bare feet. Wood from a magic forest.

I open the kitchen cabinet nearest me a few times—silent, sturdy, and impossible to rip off in the heat of passion. The handle fits just right in my fingers. I'm having a weird sense of déjà vu; this house is more perfect than any other we've done.

"How are we going to top this? There's no way we can do ▶

7

better than this place." He doesn't reply but I feel his pleasure at this comment hum through the wall.

I sip my coffee and change a few prices from suppliers in our master spreadsheet. It's sad that I get a tiny adrenaline rush every time a price comes down. I must be my brother's sister after all. It's a further rush to know that I am good at this. So, so much better than my twin would be.

I hit save. "Can you believe that guy gave me such a good discount on the sandstone pavers?"

"Yes, I can, actually," Tom says, with an edge to it that makes me go in search of him. I walk into the living room and find him at the top of a ladder. He's got a screwdriver in one hand and the base of the ugly light fitting in the other, which he drops on the floor. It's destined for the trash. "You were very charming."

I take another mouthful of coffee. I know I shouldn't, but I love this game. "I'm a charming gal."

"He probably would have given them to you for free, if I'd given you another five minutes." He gives me a glance that is equal parts amusement and irritation before stretching up to press his thumb to the crumbling screw holes in the ceiling. He'll patch and sand them. You won't believe it now, but after some white paint it's going to be a perfect ceiling.

"I think you get off on flirting with guys in front of me," he adds offhand.

I let my eyes drift up his body. I know what I get off on. I've seen him stand on every rung of that ladder but it will always affect me the same way: a hot feeling in my throat and a watery weakness in my thighs. When he stretches up, I can see a sliver of the waistband of his Underswears. That sliver isn't enough.

A memory from last night drops through my body like a coin. Ripples spread through my stomach, shimmering down.

"I had a good time last night." We didn't do anything out of the ordinary. We ate dinner, wiped the marble countertops, unzipped our tent, and took each other's clothes off.

He bursts out laughing at the sincerity in my voice. "I know. I was there." He's going black eyed as he looks down at me. I wonder what memory is causing that. Is the soreness in my muscles from last night or the night before? It's all just an endless chain of nights, blurring together in the lushest way possible.

I shrug. "You were definitely there, under me. On me. Behind me. That's why you don't have to be jealous of guys who sell pavers."

"Jealous?" There's a deep timbre to his voice that something inside me always responds to. That ripple inside just gets deeper. I'm in trouble—or in luck. Let's see which. I check my watch. The crew is due soon.

He steps down to the floor, picks me up by my waist, and eases me back until my feet steady up on the bottom rung of the stepladder. It gets me closer to his mouth level. I feel the care he takes with me, even as his eyes turn a little dangerous. "You think I'm jealous? DB, they're all jealous of me."

He takes my hand, twists my sapphire engagement ring straight, and puts his lips on mine.

My world turns gold.

Throughout my life, Tom's been right there when I've needed him, his eyes narrowed in earnest thought as he assesses how to help me. Translate that to our sex life. I've never been able to test my physical limits with another man, but this one knows me, A to Z. Right now, there's a screwdriver in his fist and I feel it against my back. It makes me smile.

He's the hottest kind of capable.

Sometimes, when he's especially inventive, my heart cannot keep up. He'll ease off until our movements are languid, and he'll hold me together until my system reboots and we can resume. And we resume *plenty*. He nearly kills me and that's okay. I survive.

Sometimes I nearly kill him. That's my favorite thing to do.

He breaks our lips apart to ask, "When are we getting your bed out of storage?"

I shrug and in response he bites down on my bottom lip until he feels the shiver shake my bones. It's a little reprimand for dragging my heels on this decision.

We twist another screw into this lust. I feel a hand sliding up my back, tracing over the strap of my bra for a few shivering seconds. ▶

"Most girls would be sick of being in a tent by now. Not you."

"I wonder why." I balance better on the balls of my feet to tiptoe higher. I put my hand into the hair at his nape and encourage him to move closer. "Tent sex is just ruining me for any other kind."

"I'm serious, Darcy," he sighs when I allow him a breath. Then we're sinking back together, his tongue against mine. He tries to ease us into something slower. "Is this going to be our house? You just told me it was perfect."

I end the kiss and look around, pretending to consider it. "It'll shape up pretty nice," is all I'll say, covering the spike of fear inside. Tent life suits me. Am I the kind of person who can have a house forever? What would that feel like? When I inherited the cottage from Loretta, it had a built-in expiration date.

Ever since Tom put this ring on my finger, he's been challenging me to address my fear of forever. My heart condition has been so stable, I'm beginning to think I can.

"Do you think I can do it? Live in the one place?"

"I do." He leans me against him. "I think we both can learn together." I remember belatedly that he's got just as much to feel insecure about. He's moved around working on houses for years. I feel his hand put the screwdriver into the tight back pocket of my shorts. Then he squeezes hard. I like his grunt.

I try to explain myself. "It's my wanderlust. I think I was a circus worker in my previous life. I just love pitching that tent somewhere new."

"This can hardly count as travel." He gets that worried look in his eye. He's paranoid that he's stifling my international travel aspirations, but he just doesn't get it. I've already seen every corner, bar, and back alley. The novelty of these micro-journeys from house to house has been a delight.

One day I'll take Tom to all my favorite places. It's one of my daydreams, working out the short list. It's okay that we need a few more flips done first.

He kisses my cheekbone. "Every time we buy a place, I think: *This is it. She'll love this one. This is our house.* And then you sell it." He's melancholy now. "Two houses ago, you could have had a home studio. I saw your face when you stood on that Italian carpet. Then . . . sold." He sighs.

"We're house flippers." I smooth his hair down with my fingernails. "You got me addicted. I don't want it to end."

"Is that what you think will happen? That it will end?"

"You'll move to the next flip and be in the tent without me."

"You know I can't do this without you. We'll choose houses within travel distance and be home every night." Patiently, he hammers down every concern I have. "Choose a house."

"Why?" I'm just playing along. I know why by now.

"So I can make it your dream house."

"I think that tent is everything I ever wanted," I reply. We stare into each other's eyes and the edges of the room start to darken and fade off. "I once had an impossible thought. I decided that if you were mine—" I swallow my words when he tips my jaw to one side and begins to kiss my neck. It's not fair. He knows I short-circuit from that.

"If I was yours," he prompts with a smile in his voice.

"I decided, if you were mine," I try again, and my voice is a raw, husky outward breath that hardens his body and sharpens his teeth on my skin, "I'd sleep with you in a tent, all night, as the wind howled and the rain fell. To be with you, I'd sleep on the ground for the rest of my life."

"And I told myself that I'd build a castle for the princess." He moves closer still, and the stepladder wobbles under me. I don't even feel a moment of fear. He'll never let me fall. "That was what I promised myself."

"I don't need that," I argue, but he cuts me off.

"I promised myself that when I was just a kid. Back when all I knew how to use was a hammer, I decided that one day Darcy Barrett would walk into a house I'd made and she'd look at me like . . ." He trails off, and his expression turns wry and wistful. "Actually, how you're looking at me now."

"Like I've got everything I want, if I have you." I make sure he understands me. "I love you so much."

He's restless now, trying to work out how to convince me. "It's so hard to spoil someone who doesn't want to be spoiled."

"You spoil me every night."

I put my fingers on the buckle of his belt. His bottom lip drops open in surprise and I bite it. His hand tries to interfere, ▶

tightening on mine, but I just keep running my fingernail on the metal. It seems to be a conduit to some raw place of lust for him, because he can barely tolerate it.

"You really want me to choose a house."

"Yes, please." He sounds completely desperate. I look around the room. It's still waiting for a wall to be moved and the cornicing is hideous, but the light shines in so pleasingly and I like the hedge of lavender humming with bees.

I think how much I love him, and the next big way I can prove it.

"This house," I finally allow myself to say. They're words I've held in for weeks now. The decision feels like a key in a lock. "This is our house." I've got my hand on his jaw, tilting up his face just to look at his surprise. "Location, size, that lighting in the bathroom. Put me in that bedroom and never let me out."

"This is the one? You sure?" He pauses, a new thought giving him pleasure. "This is the threshold I'm gonna carry you over?" There's a flare in his eyes; that animal inside him wants nothing more than to add a second ring of gold on to my hand.

"Yeah," I assure him, bracing for the kiss that I know is coming. It's going to be something intense, with all of his heart and excitement in it. Finally, Tom Valeska can stop being that boy, locked out in the dark, waiting to be found. When he starts work again, it's going to be a new experience for him. It's going to be something he's never felt before, and I'm so glad I've given this to him now.

This house? It's Tom Valeska's house. It's Darcy Barrett's house.

Holy shit, I'm living my own dream come true.

He's gathering me up now in both hands, ignoring the sound of car doors slamming outside and boots approaching. They're going to catch us kissing, but that's happened a hundred times before, and besides, this is monumental. Professionalism be damned; Darcy Barrett and Tom Valeska now have a home. He tips my head back, ready to show me how happy he is.

"You know I'll love you even if you make me live in a tent for the rest of my life. Are you really sure?"

"So sure." I close my eyes, and his mouth is on mine, and we are happy. It's just as simple as that. ∿

The Hating Game Epilogue

It's a red dress kind of day.

It's Friday afternoon. I'm sitting in my office at Bexley & Gamin and I can see my reflection in my floor-to-ceiling window. Outwardly I look remarkably corporate, but on the inside I'm forever an immature little weirdo. I cross my legs and begin to play the Mirror Game with myself. The Staring Game. Even a whispered How You Doing Game. It's just not the same without my opponent.

It's been a shitty day. I spent the afternoon fighting a valiant battle against Mr. Bexley over electronic distribution royalties, and then I found out that there's a bug in our latest e-library app. I'm so tired I can feel my own skeleton. I need to be lying on my perfect couch but it's not going to happen tonight. It's so quiet I can hear the fluorescent tubes buzzing.

The elevator bings.

Whoever's just arrived on the tenth floor needs to be kept out of my office so I can get the hell out of here. Scott, our executive officer, is a pretty good gatekeeper. I can hear muffled conversation, and then there's a rap on the door. There's only one person in the world who can put so much short, sharp love into a single knock.

"Come in," I say. The door swings open and there he is.

Joshua Templeman is dressed in black. Everything, from his underwear to his cufflinks to his tie, is ink-black midnight. He enjoys the drama of it on a Friday, sliding into people's office doorways like Dracula just as they're loosening their ties and thinking about their weekends. All he needs is some devil horns and a pitchfork. I feel vaguely bad for whoever he's been terrorizing today.

He leans against the doorjamb and we're playing the Staring Game for a minute until his dark navy eyes spark. "Shortcake," he breathes like he can't believe I'm real. "I missed you so bad."

My. Heart. Bursts.

I stand up and go to him. He picks me up off the ground, kissing my jaw, my cheekbones, his fingers stroking my nape. He turns me in a circle and I cross my ankles prettily. The tiredness falls out through my feet and dissolves. ▶

He's here, and I'm lit up. It's the kind of light that never fades.

People in the opposite building might be able to see us. Motorists at the traffic lights below can probably make out the silhouette of a ridiculously large man twirling around a ridiculously small woman. During one slow revolution I catch sight of Helene and Mr. Bexley, standing near Scott's desk. They're all looking at us like we're the most gorgeously silly couple in the world. It's accurate. We are.

Helene glances at Mr. Bexley with a wry expression, and I swear I see a little moment of connection between them. I've been suspecting it more and more. I know love-hate when I see it.

I speak into Josh's neck. "I hate not being able to stare at your pretty face all day."

I breathe in his addictive, perfect scent. Deciduous trees in the sun. Evergreen trees in the snow. A pencil sharpened to a razor point, pressing into fresh white paper.

"It's against HR policy to stare at your corporate rival all day."

I hug him harder. "Whose HR policy?"

"One of them, I'm sure. I'll look it up." Josh sets me down and kisses my cheek again. Once he starts, he can't stop.

In the elevator I'll wipe off my Flamethrower lipstick so I can get my proper hello kiss. If I'm lucky he'll hit the emergency stop button, although we've been pissing off the security guards with that.

I treat myself to a nice squeeze of his torso before I remember the door is ajar. "Who have you made cry today, Overlord?" At the Sanderson Christmas party, I overheard his nickname and had to laugh. He earned it.

"Nobody," he tells me with adorable sincerity and a blink. "Not a single person. I'm a changed man."

I'm trying to teach him how to be more approachable. More understanding. More like me.

At the first Sanderson Christmas party, I stood alone and awkward for an excruciating two minutes, during which time I was the subject of speculation. I felt like the word *how* was said a lot. I could hear their drunk, high-pitched whispers. *She looks normal. Sweet. So small! How does she cope with that . . . monster? We should rescue her.*

Maybe he keeps her chained in his basement.

I waved like a dork to show that I was not shackled and was there of my own free will. They shrank back, then fell totally silent as their chief financial officer, aka the Overlord, approached me with a glass of wine. His eyes were soft with tenderness and my heart stopped beating until he restarted it with a kiss. The Overlord snuggled me into his side, fitting us together just right. Hard and soft. Darkness and light. Good cop, bad cop.

I registered the jaws dropping. *He's smiling!*

He's the Overlord, he calls them his Underlings, but I can see the little signs that he's getting better at this. At a lot of things, actually.

"Did you remember your dad's present?"

"Yep. We'd better get going if we're going to make the party. Mindy and Patrick have been texting me obsessively. *Don't be late, don't be late.*" He's sarcastic but I know how much this means to him.

I give his arm a stroke and a squeeze. "We won't be late."

I can't lie on the couch tonight because I'm needed in Port Worth. I'm Josh's little lucky charm. When I'm there, he and his dad don't fight. Luckily for them both, I'm always there.

"Got quite a collection by now, Shortcake," Josh says, looking at the rows of Matchbox cars on the shelf behind me. He forgets our hurry and takes a red Volkswagen beetle out of his pocket, sliding it into one of the gaps.

"My toys have given me a reputation for being quirky and approachable."

"No one would guess this strawberry-sweet exterior hides a complete hard-ass."

"I learned from the master. I'm known for being firm but fair."

"Mmm. Tell me more." He loves sitting at my desk to look at everything I surround myself with, and he lowers himself down into my chair like it's a milkmaid stool. His eyes are lit with a creepy kind of devotion as he looks at the castle of books against the wall, and the Smurf hidden in one of the battlements. He finds my bottle of perfume and smells the lid as he strokes my computer mouse.

"That's where you've been," he says in a scolding tone to the ▶

cardigan slung on the back of my chair. He folds it into a bread-slice square on his knee.

I've turned him into such a total freak.

I'm an even bigger freak when I visit his office. I once touched the speed dial button on his phone marked *SHORTCAKE* just to make my cell phone ring. Then I was jealous of myself. That's a sensation I feel a lot.

How am I living this life? How did I win so much?

Like he can read my mind, Josh picks up the framed photograph on my desk. It's us together in the strawberry fields. Our eyes are summer bright, and I am sitting between his legs leaning back against him. Around us is a carpet of green, studded with red. The picture is a tiny bit crooked because my dad was a little overexcited by the secret he was keeping.

Five minutes after this photo was taken, Josh said, "Hey, it's an old Smurf in the dirt."

He knew nothing would make me drop to the ground faster. I scratched frantically through the leaves. *Where? Where?* What I found in the vines at Sky Diamonds Strawberries was a Tiffany blue box. Then I realized he was kneeling down, too.

Lucy blue. True-love blue.

Even as he squeaked the box open and began to speak, I was dimly aware of cheering from the house. My parents were spying from the office window.

After I brushed the squashed berries from the back of his T-shirt, I learned that Josh had become an expert in diamonds. Carat, cut, color, clarity. He shivered with delight as he described staring at imperfections through a loupe. I could just imagine his laser eyes crumbling stones to ash. The way he tells it, he searched through a pile of worthless pebbles until he found something worthy of my tiny finger. I tell him it's too big, too much, too perfect. He just laughs and says, *I know,* then makes me forget whether we're still talking about the diamond.

I think my cheeks are going pink right now. When he looks me in the eye, he smirks. He's definitely a mind reader.

"We need a vacation," he decides, his finger straightening the terra-cotta tile I use as a coaster. I got that tile in Tuscany. "I'm taking you back. Cheese and wine and sleeping in the sun." His eyes follow the line of my dress down my body. "Red dresses and champagne and carbohydrates." A pause, and there's a little vulnerability in his expression now. "I didn't go crazy and dream it all, did I?"

"I have frequently assured you that I'm real." I take his hand in mine and use it to pinch my forearm. "I was there for every incredible second. I always will be. Now, quit talking about carbohydrates. You're turning me on."

He laughs. "We'd better get out of here." He grabs my coat and walks out to chat with Helene and Mr. Bexley.

I log off and lock away the stack of slush pile manuscripts I've been reading as my own little treat. I lock my door and just watch his reflection bounce around off the slick, glossy surfaces that make up level ten. The only thing better than having one Josh is having a hundred.

I look at the plaque on my office door as I lock it. It says, *Chief Operating Officer,* and usually it has me grinning like a dork. But right now, I'm smiling over something else.

The gold ring on Joshua Templeman's left hand has set off a shower of firework sparkles in this huge black prism. Each time I focus on one particular reflection, it fractures and doubles. It's a kaleidoscope of his love around me now. There are a hundred gold rings. A thousand. It's still not enough. I want to spin around while they circle me like fireflies. That's how he makes me feel, every day of our life.

It's wonderful. It's primal. It's nothing short of a miracle.

My name is Lucy Templeman. ෴